Dr. Ralph V. Wilson spent over 50 years healing people around the world. Along the way, he accumulated a treasure trove of incredible stories filled with wry humor, indelible characters, and hair-raising adventures. I learned much from each story and I suspect so will you.

Robert Dukelow

Author of nine books including
Four Strong Women and *Overkill on I-17*

I love the tone of Ralph Wilsons's book. It is a book of facts, that is written dramatically and insightfully to a broad audience. As an example in the chapter titled "*Pickle in a Pickle*," he talks of the advantages and disadvantages of having a penis. In "A Maize-Zing he talks about grains, corn (the British word for grain), and nutrition in general. And in "Pica" he talks about "Pica" the strange appetite abnormality where people add buttons, paste, and chalk to their list of edible food items. But humor is the strong threads that makes the book worth reading.

Don L. F. Nilsen

Assistant Dean, Division of the Humanities
ASU Emeritus College, Co-Founder of ISHS

Also by Ralph V. Wilson M.D.

Bony Baloney: Enlightening, outrageous, and humorous tales from an orthopedic surgeon

Write Side of the Grass (A book of memoirs including stories of Ralph's time in Vietnam as a doctor)

RALPH V. WILSON M.D.

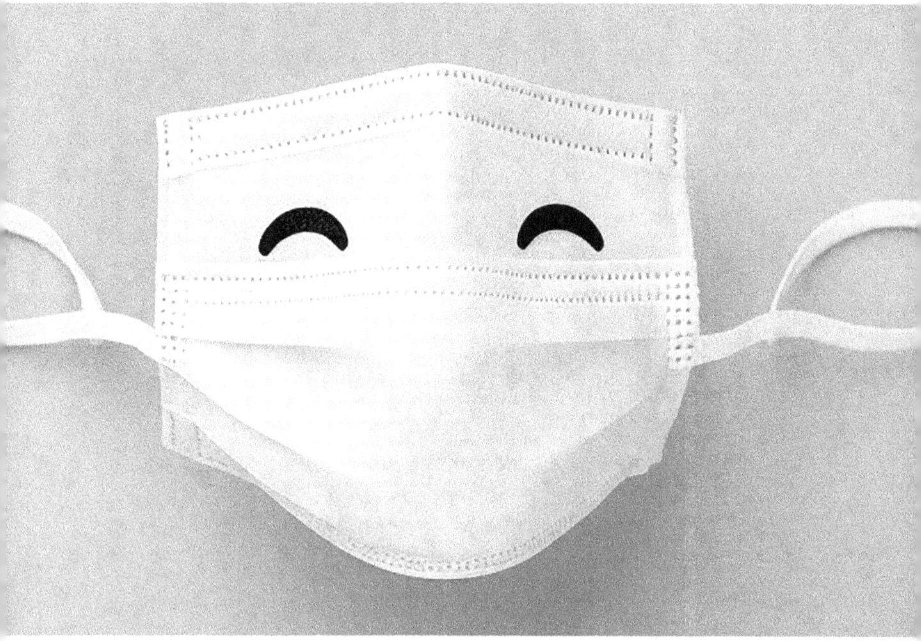

LAUGHING is **LEGAL!**

More enlightening, outrageous, and humorous tales from the orthopedic surgeon and author of Bony Baloney and Write Side of the Grass

MANYSEASONSPRESS

Mesa, Arizona • 2024

First Edition

Laughing is Legal!: More enlightening, outrageous, and humorous tales from the orthopedic surgeon and author of Bony Baloney and Write Side of the Grass

Copyright © 2024 Ralph V. Wilson M.D.

Published by Many Seasons Press
An Imprint of Multimedia Publishing Project
123 N. Centennial Way, Suite 105
Mesa, Arizona 85201
480-939-9689 | ManySeasonsPress.com

Paperback ISBN 13: 978-1-956203-47-9
E-book ISBN: 978-1-956203-48-6
LCCN: 2024907026

Printed in the United States of America.

Contents

CONTENTS

Preface

The primary purpose for writing this book was to create a fun read. I hope my stories will variously entertain you with insights from a physician's perspective, or explain unexpected and fascinating details behind prosaic topics like Money, Marbles, or Mosquitoes. Many vignettes are my firsthand accounts of dealing with puzzling personalities and unpredictable behavior of my patients. The non-medical, semi-serious subject matter also provides a scaffold for humor.

Robert Benchley, a humorist whose work I have appreciated from my high school days, has colored my writing style, as have Dave Barry and George Carlin. Russell Baker points out in his book about American Humor, too much levity can be boring. Thus, I have flavored the "meatier" manuscripts with humorous toppings be it frosting or gravy.

Historically funny authors such as Will Rogers lose poignancy with time. Mark Twain faced a cultural divide, which today is more of a political divide; either affects the reader's judgment or enjoyment of the piece. I, like Twain, feel no obligation to satisfy both ends of the political or cultural spectrum or all levels of medical understanding. Therefore, if a few readers feel skewered, no harm intended, humor is the objective.

I have included my everyday experiences, some unrelated to medicine, intended to be informative, thought-provoking and fun. The goal is to entertain and still provide exercise for your facial muscles crying for laughter.

May you be enlightened, surprised, delighted, and rewarded by spending your valuable time reading this collection.

No Rebuttal

"He was a mean dad. He wasn't nice to my mom**"** and I'm sorry that he died, but he was not a very good dad."

This was the voice of an eleven-year-old son at his father's funeral. The deceased had died at home probably from a cardiac condition. I watched the wife's reaction to the comments. They were measured, no burst of emotion, no "Don't say those things," just a pensive but involved look. Her comments later confirmed a troubled husband consumed with demons and mental problems, but a good husband. She didn't elaborate further on how he reached the "good" designation. The children left no doubt he didn't qualify for anything more than an obstreperous passenger on a challenging ride in their house.

I had heard similar comments at a funeral several years ago about a friend who was a generous, kind, and worthy husband/father, but the speaker/son had drifted into drugs and completely left the family. The son's appearance at the funeral was unwelcome and his thoughts were interpreted for what they were, the sentiments of an angry, vengeful son who brought himself down even further with unkind remarks.

In the equally unfiltered world of obituaries, I unearthed some classic comments not normally considered appropriate for the deceased to hear. The following are examples of iffy obituaries. I hope that reading one's own unflattering obituary after dying is not possible, but the survey suggests many folks think the dead will have that option. My in-office poll revealed 77 percent think the deceased have a vantage point allowing them to read and hear all earthly events.

LAUGHING IS LEGAL!

Kathleen Schunk, according to her obit, abandoned her children when she remarried. "The world will be a better place without her." Likely written by her abandonees.

"There will be no services of any kind except for her best friend, grandson, and great-granddaughter. No one cared to see her when she was alive and you sure as hell are not going to give her any artificial respect now that she has passed after 20 years of illness."

Bill was rewarded by expressing his fascination with farts. "Perhaps most important to Bill was educating people on the dangers of holding in your farts. Sadly, he was unable to attain his lifelong goal of catching his beloved wife Judy 'cutting the cheese' or 'playing the bum trumpet'—which he likened to a mythical rarity like spotting Bigfoot or a unicorn."

A one-line obituary read: "Stephen Merrill passed at 31 from an uppercut from Batman."

Stan Johnson's obituary read: "He respectfully requests six Cleveland Browns pall bearers so the Browns can let him down one last time."

The conclusion of a retired Colonel's obituary stated "A native of Northern Virginia for the last 30 years, he hated how all of you were incapable of driving competently."

It is not all bad. Jack's obituary read "In lieu of flowers, go see the last James Bond movie."

An unusual invite, the list of survivors was followed by: "So many of his childhood friends that weren't killed in Vietnam went on to become criminals, prostitutes and/or Democrats. He asks that you stop by and re-tell the stories he can no longer tell. As the celebration will contain adult material, we respectfully ask no children under 18 attend."

Too much information. "He was born in a log cabin to Ralph and Inez Holcombe and was circumcised with his dad's pocket knife. He loved to fish and caught a lot of crappies."

"Price Davis made his last inappropriate and probably sarcastic comment on October 25, 2017."

Apparently, someone was not always given plaudits by the deceased.

Nice pat on the back. "Dennis was survived by…. He was a wonderful brother, hell of a dad and a mediocre dancer."

Kudos: "Mr. Fuller died when he was travelling at a high rate of speed at one o'clock in the morning; he ran into a mailbox and was not wearing a seatbelt." Nice to have the blame squarely on your shoulders. At least it didn't say he was impaired which I guess is implied.

In the obit below his photo was a two-word caption on Doug's death notice, "Doug Died."

Mary Paul's obituary listed many of her personal possessions, which were now available for purchase. "If interested you should wait an appropriate amount of time to inquire. Tomorrow would be fine." It also listed her "Tell it like it is directness, including her love for four-letter words."

Favorite line. "Jack's cremation will take place at the family's convenience and his ashes will be kept around as long as they match the décor."

Odd consideration from auto-obituary: "I was preceded in death by my tonsils, adenoids, and appendix." His wife however, didn't honor all of his demands. There was no viewing since his wife refused his request to have him stand in the corner with a glass of Jack Daniels so he would appear more natural.

Ray Brownley's family composed a funny obituary, parts of which are included below. "Affectionately known as Big Al, he despised canned cranberry sauce, wearing shorts, and cigarette butts in his driveway. Famously opinionated and short-tempered—a quality he passed onto his daughter who is sharp tongued in her own right. He loved milkshakes, fried shrimp, the Steelers, the Playboy channel and taking afternoon naps in his recliner. He was world-renowned for his lack of patience, not holding back his opinion and a knack of telling it like it is. He liked four letter words and banana cream pie. He was generous to a fault and a pussy cat at heart. Big Al was strong in his beliefs in which he never wavered: dog shit makes the best garden fertilizer and ketchup does not belong on a hot dog. He had a stink eye toward organized religion but read the Bible every night." This was the most extensive portrait of a man's life I have ever seen in an obituary, the good the bad and the ugly.

Val Patterson wrote his own story before passing. "I am the guy who stole the safe from the Motor View Drive-In back in 1971. I also confess my PhD was the result of a clerical error and I still don't know what PhD stands for. Tell Disney World and Sea World to take me off the 'Banned for Life List' because I'm not a problem anymore."

A self-deprecating obituary by Richard Bacon reflected his graduating from high school without honors and experiencing one undistinguished year at college followed by two more failed attempts at two more colleges. However, he was a Rotarian for twenty-five years and spent 26 years publishing a newspaper.

Sybil Hicks last comment: "I finally have the hot body I always wanted—I was cremated."

An ending obit piece where a rebuttal is in order: "Leslie Ray Charping passed away January 30, 2017, 29 years longer than he deserved. He lost his battle with cancer due to the horse's ass he was known for. He leaves behind two relieved children and countless other victims including his ex-wife, relatives, friends, neighbors, doctors, nurses and random strangers. He was a model of bad parenting, combined with a commitment to drinking, drugs, and womanizing. Leslie's hobbies included being abusive to his family. With Leslie's passing he will be missed only for what he never did, being a loving husband, father, and good friend."

Fortunately, most obituaries and funerals do not require a rebuttal as these illustrated. If my poll is accurate, the deceased will be aware of what was written about them, but have no chance for rebuttal. Sad.

One way to beat the negative obit and funeral is to write your own obit, pay for it, submit it a minute before you die and skip the funeral.

Filter

I **have a friend who lacks what I call a social filter.**
She throws out questions that should not be asked,
especially in a group setting. "What did your breast
implants cost?" or "Do you still wear Depends?" may be
fair questions if the audience is deaf or in memory care,
not acceptable otherwise, not even for a good friend.
Twila is a lightweight in recognizing the embarrassment
factor. The First Amendment also gave her license to
reveal her personal information, facts which most of her
peers would keep under wraps.

Pointing out my fly is open is rarely addressed by
most women, primarily because it is extremely rare to
be unclosed, but I can count on Twila to say, "Looks like
Peter is going for a walk," if the occasion were to occur.

On more than one occasion she has reached around
my neck turned up my shirt collar and read the label, the
tag on the shirt identifying the brand. Then she'll comment on the cost or ask which store it came from. So far,
she has not checked the tag on my boxers but I know
that could happen so I keep a firm grip on my belt when
she is in striking range. She doesn't restrict her inquisi-
tiveness to me, but I seem to be a target more than
most. I counter this behavior by offering my tags early
in a group affair to avoid the mid-conversation hassle.

Twila has a strange belief that if she is speaking to
someone directly, she cannot be heard by others easily
in earshot. In a party environment, occasionally greater
decibels are required to be heard. Her voice can pierce
through metal, cement, and a white-noise-clouded
atmosphere. Coupling this vocal characteristic with
an inappropriate (negative) comment about another
attendee lends itself to classic adult bullying. "She

dresses like a whore," with name included. Although she is relatively unfiltered, her style has a certain appeal and we have seen how popular, to some, this approach has become.

I learned early in medical school that once you remove the skin, the insides of most people look remarkably similar. A liver is a liver, a heart is a heart, and most gallbladders contain bile. The bile related to comments about skin color makes no sense. I cringe when I hear a racial comment made outside the exam room door where I am interviewing a person of color. It is like passing wind and hoping no one heard the socially unacceptable release. My office staff may have no clue their remarks are passing through the exam room door and how offensive the remark may be, especially if it might relate to my patient's color. I address the issue after I finish seeing patients, but meantime I have to wonder if the slur was heard, thereby making me culpable.

Newscasters periodically have the open mike situation catching a bonehead announcer castigating a race or personal oddity that they thought worthy of a derisive comment. Often that comment results in the loss of a job. My employees receive a second chance for this behavior, but this lack of a filter makes them eligible for a career change.

Tom Brenneman—not a bonehead—whom I knew and respected as an excellent baseball announcer of national acclaim, was the last person I would expect to say a negative remark about anybody. His on-air comment was perceived as slanderous and, in spite of a clean history, his airtime ended immediately. Other announcers have been more obvious in their racial or sexual comments and have served time away from the mike and yet returned to duty with only a temporary setback.

Patients of every flavor visit my medical office. Is it appropriate to ask a technician to take an X-ray of the squatty fat lady in room six, or would a less descriptive comment suffice? The technician will not address the round lady of minimal height by that description: it is an internal method of identification. Consider for the sake of argument there were two women in room six, one tall and thin, the other short and very obese. To assist the technician, you could say X-ray the other one, not the tall and thin lady, or select the one with the historically enthusiastic appetite, or photo the corpulent one. After all, if I said, "Take the amputee, blind person, or cowboy in room six for an X-ray." would those terms be offensive if not heard by the patient?

Obese patients often refer to themselves as fat. There are also some patients, women particularly, who are not overweight yet consider themselves to be so. If I support the premise that they are absolutely within normal limits, they take offense. If the medical assistant is overheard using the terms fat, obese, or anything close, the likelihood of a patient feeling judged and disrespected is high. There are over 40 synonyms for obesity; all have the potential to be derogatory.

I had one receptionist who, unknown to me, acted the part of the modesty police. If she considered the patient was too exposed, halter top or short skirt, she would offer the patient a suggestion on more appropriate medical office visit attire. She was outed when the patients complained about this intrusion. It was an easy fix.

Saying something inappropriate is benign, inconsequential and totally harmless if not heard. My self-worth is unaffected if the comment never reaches my ears. If you say to a friend what a jerk Fred is and Fred is nowhere in sight, no harm no foul. If you say in a political rally that the governor is a slow-witted—and the governor is not there—is that offensive? If you say, face to face, that he is slow-witted and he soaks up the comment, clearly offensive.

If your elderly aunt with prefrontal dementia asks you, "Why are you wearing that trash?" are you offended? If a person is coming out of anesthesia says, "Why is it raining blood?" would anyone care? If he says, "Your sister is a whore," a slightly different emotion wells up. Even knowing the speaker might be compromised, a biting comment can be hurtful, particularly if it is true.

The filter story is more complicated than just hearing a comment judged to be racial. Society tends to tag deviant behavior to race, Boy Scouts, or some unrelated identifier that has nothing to do with behavior itself. When a discussion related to unfiltered speech occurs, the speaker, the listener, the time, the location, all effect how we interpret the comments. Today, race is overweighted when judging a person social behavior. Let the behavior speak for itself.

Look at all the words now considered derogatory that only a few years ago were used by many with much less socially demeaning effect. These include, chink, coon, apple, darkie, gringo, honkie, hymie, jerry, kike, monkey, n-word, gook, greaser, jap or pancake, oreo, peckerwood, slopehead, spick, and many others that relate to foreigners. Apparently there are unacceptable names for everybody. Next year will likely bring a new crop of unaccepables.

The Entomological Society of America is changing the name of the gypsy moth and ant to avoid the "slur" related to Romanian people. Monkey, orioles and pancakes may be taken away soon.

Consider: fruit, fairy, pansy, dyke, queer, and fag; all relatively new derogatory terms for "homosexual." The older terms Uranian, Sapphic, Achillean, and now LGBTQ+ seem to cover this group as more acceptable—politically correct—designations. I have never used any of these terms in a medical record, nor a racial reference, yet patients are asked to make a racial designation upon registration. The form also inquires about sex. I find that troubling as well, so I may fill in the space with a "once a week," or "once a year" response when I go to a new doctor. An unanswered box regarding sex is never followed by a doctor taking a peek to solve the mystery.

The trend is to ask, even on an application, how we wish to be addressed, i.e., by him, her or them. Should we also ask if a person wishes to be called fat, slim, tall, or short? How about smart or not, which might be splitting hairs?

Do you think we will evolve to a numerical system where each characteristic represents a number? A tall, thin, mentally challenged, bipolar, angry, bald cross-eyed, lesbian with webbed toes would be F5G34-R62-A87-99. That information would be on your chip and buried under your left breast. Oh, I forgot your political affiliation, easily added to the number above. I'm sure we could add a few more items, like ability to carry a tune, favorite drink, or horny factor. Maybe frugality, spiritual advisor, or type of firearms you prefer.

What a wonderful world; we have so many opportunities to insult our friends and ex-friends.

I have one other thought about words that become unfiltered. If someone is gay, Native American, black, white, or Irish, aren't they proud to be whatever they are? So why is calling them a name that reflects their identity considered offensive? Is a prostitute less proud of her job if she is labeled a whore? She is what she is. I am sure many people are not proud of their job title, but the job pays the bills. It is fulfilling a place in society. A Mexican, a Jew, a Gentile, a Black, these people refer to themselves by the so-called derogatory words which are continuing to evolve from year to year. Call a spade a spade, ouch, that is currently a bad example but haven't we gone a little wacky in our concern about offending people by calling them the names, which we often use when referring to ourselves?

If you have psoriasis or vitiligo, it doesn't make you a bad person any more than your race or gender. You can still be cheerful, happy, gay, funny, and have a feeling of self-worth. My older patients will usually give me their age as if they already had their next birthday. They are generally proud of being "old." I still haven't determined when the older folks start adding years rather than subtracting or hiding the true birthday.

So-called derogatory terms are overrated. We all should be racially blind, gender blind, and human kind. Filtering may be overrated.

Kids Really Do Say the Darndest Things

For the last ten years I have distributed dictionaries to third-grade students as part of a Rotary Club project. This city-wide project, which may disappear because of electronic media, has brought joy to many Mesa Public School children. The teachers have used this project to encourage/require the students to write thank-you notes. The notes, programmed in part by teacher suggestions, were directed to me as the presenter and the Rotary Club as the donating body.

About 100 students sat, squirmed, and chirped in front of me waving their newly acquired dictionaries. The teachers applied various, generally feeble quieting techniques to the three classes gathered in the media center. Apparently noise modulation is not a universally understood program like sign language. Because I carried out a dialogue with the students, often 100 children responded as one—loud answer. Therefore 30 minutes became 45. There was no lack of enthusiasm at the event, which had the characteristics of a rock concert.

First, I explained what information the unique dictionaries contained, then I tossed out questions to engage the group. I asked "Who can find the section on punctuation?" Eighty hands flew up. When I identified the student most likely to provide an accurate answer, they became mute or had forgotten what answer they were about to launch. The raised hands appeared usually before I completed the question, a classroom *Jeopardy* reaction. To avoid embarrassment if the responses were slow, I moved on quickly, pointing out page seven held the appropriate information.

When I asked what they liked best about the gift, many responded the section on sign language, but the most popular page was the world's longest word which, consumed an entire page. They all laughed when I requested a volunteer to pronounce the word that referenced a complex chemical.

The students' verbal responses reminded me of the book by Art Linkletter, *Kids Say the Darndest Things*, published in 1957. The book's stories originated from his popular TV program *People Are Funny* which ran from 1954 to 1960. The program morphed from a radio version that originated in 1942. In 1998, Bill Cosby MC'ed a program titled *Kids Say the Darndest Things* which lasted less than two years.

The kids' thank-you notes revealed sincere, unvetted, transparent comments with occasional awful spelling splashed on the pages. Some years the notes contained artwork of me, a hospital, school or building, which bore no resemblance to any architecture currently gracing our planet. Teacher influence varied greatly but usually the children shot from the hip and provided me and others who received these notes a huge reward for a relatively small investment. If teachers receive a similar satisfaction, no wonder they like to teach.

The joy of receiving the book, a dictionary to call their own, was a first for some. Those with older siblings who had shared a similar experience, were required to remind me I had previously given their siblings a dictionary.

Here are a few of the 500-plus thank-you notes:

"Thank you for the dictionaries. You sound sweet, I just can't stop saying thank you."

"My favorite letter is R. You guys are very Junrus and I thank you of crouse Kurchel."

"Is the Rotary Club hard work? I think it is. Dr. Wilson is a hard worker."

"Thank you for the dictionaries. I know you are a brave young man so I want to thank you for coming to Mesa Public Schools. I hope you really like my letter."

"Are you really in the rodowry club tell me if you can well thank you for the dictionaries, Bryce."

"Thank you for the dictionary. I wos it omost day. I appreciate what you don."

"Thanks you for the dictionarys. They are sow good for writer workshop. Now I don't have to get up and walk all the way to the over dictionary. Alice."

"I really like the dictionary. They are very cool. And you are. Very cool. Brent."

"The sign language page is asum. Can you come again? Max."

"I like the dictionary. I will use it for all the things you said. Your are the best doctor. Tyler."

"You are the best person do you have kids because I bet you would be the best dad to them. Larry." I am betting Larry doesn't have a dad.

"I love my dictionary. Most of all I will keep it safe."

"I like the dictionary. Do you have a fish? Alan."

"Thank you for coming in just tell us about a dictionary. I'm glad you were named after our school. Michelle."

Natalie wrote supercalifragilisticexpialidocious found on page 364 became her favorite word and she can pronounce it forward and backward. She sounded like a savant in the making.

"Thank you sooooooo much for the dictionary. I think I will keep it until I am 29 years old. Angel."

"The dictionary makes me think. I can make things right. My favorite game is Vampire Tag. Mya."

"Thank you for the dictionary. I am in the Nutcracker Dec. 10th it's in high school just go in the direction of cambles dance is from. Want to come?"

"Tank you for taking time to talk to us about the dictionary. Have you ever used a dictionary? Jose."

"Who invented the Rotary Club and why are these dictionaries so important? Why are these dictionaries for third graders and why did you join the rotary club. Noah" This inquisitive kid is headed toward engineering.

"You did a good job I loved it thanks for reading. You rock. Kyly."

"Thank you for the dictionarys. You are the best. I love it how you think of others. I think of you all the time and I can't get my mind off of you. The dictionarys are the best too. Mary."

How do you top that for a "feel good" note?

I couldn't help but reflect how much the one page "thank yous" reveal about those kids. Many struggled to spell and express their thoughts while others were clearly many grades ahead of their peers. On some the word order was jumbled and the next child wrote with a Spencerian script, advanced even for a high school senior. How does a teacher cope with these huge discrepancies? Many notes contained drawings, some with elaborate Van Gogh-like qualities; others, the Van *Noes*, drew stick figures. I am convinced these–one-page thank yous from third graders–would accurately reflect the future performance of these students. Some will write for the Atlantic, others will become social workers, teachers or homeless.

Kids do say the darndest things, and I hope with a little help from a third-grade dictionary project they can continue to be inspired as their notes suggest.

Following the presentations I always received five to ten third-grade hugs. The teachers deserve a thousand.

Rocky Point Plus

Rocky Point, a getaway town in northern Mexico, attracts many Americans, some drunk and others getting ready to be. In my clinic yesterday I saw several patients who had recently visited Rocky Point and a few other patients who filled in the day with non-Mexico stories.

Roland, an infrequent visitor to Mexico, was exploring the fringes of Rocky Point looking for a possible real estate acquisition. To gain entrance to a gated subdivision he relinquished his passport, his ticket to allow him to view the houses. His 88-year-old mind forgot about the passport when he left the development until several hours later. He quickly returned to the scene of his passport faux pas, happily stuffed the document into his pocket, and proceeded with friends to a local restaurant. While waiting at the restaurant he examined the passport and realized it was not his. He called the facility and they quickly invited him to come back and pick up the correct passport. Detecting no urgency, he deferred because he was eating. Several minutes later the real estate folks called again and requested that he come quickly. He again deferred only to get another call, eventually four. He finished his meal and departed with his friends but stumbled off a step as he left the restaurant, falling hard on his face and arm—the reason I saw him later in my office. As he lay bleeding, dazed, and crumpled on the street, a car drove up, and a man stepped out and handed him his correct passport. Roland didn't remember returning the wrong one, but he must have because he had only one when he reached his hotel. Following the exchange, he spent the next few hours in an urgent care facility.

The Mexican doctor claimed he removed three bone chips from Roland's elbow, although the before-surgery X-rays, which I reviewed, showed no bone chips, corn chips, or potato chips. I would say he was lucky to retrieve his passport, but his identity was likely no longer a secret.

To compound Roland's problems, he had an issue with another doctor's office. Several years ago, I had referred him to a neurosurgeon because I thought Roland had hydrocephalus—fluid buildup in the brain. Eventually he received a shunt, and within weeks he stopped falling and felt great. Recently Roland started falling again, therefore he tried to reach his neurosurgeon, but was never able to negotiate the frustrating challenge of making a medical appointment. So, while I evaluated his elbow, I called the neurosurgeon's office. The phone rang a mere 55 times before the line went dead. I called back again with a much better response time, but a receptionist answered with a "Hello" typical of someone anticipating a scam call. I introduced myself expecting the person to identify himself or the office name. I was sure I had called the wrong number especially since the call was fielded so quickly. No, I had the correct office but received a flat, annoyed, "Why are you calling us"? response. I felt I should apologize for interrupting a video gamer or a coffee break. Eventually I made an appointment for my patient. That call accomplished more than my treatment of his asymptomatic elbow.

Roland, whose wife passed away six months before coming to my office, offered me some sage advice. He had been married for 65 years. His bride-to-be was 16 at the time he tried to marry her and he was 20. She required no parental permission, but he, at 20, apparently did. His parents would not consent to the union until he turned 21. As soon as they married, his young wife placed a framed saying above the headboard of their bed that read, "Always kiss your partner before going to sleep." He felt those words were responsible for their successful 65-year marriage. Tears welled in his eyes as he proffered his comments.

• • •

Barry, the last of the Rocky Pointers, is a young man I saw regularly related to an ongoing arrangement with his employer. I filled out disability papers every six months allowing him to miss work and not require a doctor's visit to get clearance to return to work. A workaround, which saved him time and allowed flexibility for a "vacation experience" when he felt a need for one—without actually taking vacation time. His employer concurred with this program.

He took a weekend family trip—maybe with sick time or otherwise—to Rocky Point. Shortly after entering Mexico two policemen pulled him over and gave him a ticket. There were areas on the way to the family's destination notorious for this activity—detain without cause—and many travelers anticipated inappropriate police behavior. Consequently, he had his cruise control set at a non-arrestable speed. Not good enough. He reluctantly accepted a bill/ticket for a bargain price of only $46, much less than his previous ticket of $176 a year prior. He paid each of the two police/extortionists $23 to make it easier for them to split their earning.

Barry's mistrust of police carried over to U.S. cops and he described his method to avoid paying traffic tickets. For $35 he had a third party go to court for him. That tale sounded less believable than his Mexican story. Our traffic ticket talk led to 15 minutes of comparing the worst accidents we had witnessed. We released enough frustration in that session to give us six months of happiness.

• • •

Ida, barely 75, weak and wheelchair-bound in a Mexican purchased wheelchair, lived with her son, his wife and their 15-year-old daughter, a fully unmotivated teenager. My patient relied on a two liter-a-minute oxygen assist. Just for the record, the O_2 percentage in room air is 21%. Each additional liter from a tank adds about 3 ½ percent. So, two liters would bring her percentage up to 28. This was administered by nasal prongs, which are frequently in one or neither nostrils in older patients rather than two nostrils as desired. The fewer the nostrils the lower the additional O_2. Ida wore her prongs below her chin. This poor lady had only one lung, which is still plenty for a sit-in-a-chair-at-sea-level-hardly-lift-a-finger existence. Her weight would suggest she had actually lifted a fork or two at some time in her life.

Chronic back pain provided Ida's ticket to see me. I had exhausted many of my "feel-better tricks" in previous visits. If she experienced a modicum of happiness eating rather than losing weight, I would be happy for her. Certainly, carnal pleasures were not in her repertoire, which left TV, TV, and eating, actually maybe just eating. Regardless, she was super pleasant and I provided a non-cannabis medication to elevate her spirits. She confessed she refused to play video games with her granddaughter, which I thought might have been a good way for them to bond.

• • •

Sandra had just returned from Mexico when she managed to fall from a small stepladder to the hardest part of her kitchen—the ceramic tile of Mexican design. She arranged to land with well-distributed weight on her hands and knees. It would have been better had she landed on her feet, but gravity denied her that option. This unplanned event interfered with her altruistic passion for helping in the shower facility of a homeless shelter. In addition to the dirty-persons-reversal program, she walked homeless dogs that lived in a dog and kitten shelter. Significant pain coupled with guilt from missing her shift at the two facilities made Sandra profoundly unhappy. She had been appropriately icing her legs in the area that made contact with the tile and had even visited the urgent care to rule out a significant problem. The advice she received, wrapping the knee, proved problematic because it acted like a tourniquet, and her ankle ballooned to a worrisome, gigantic size, accompanied by an ominous darkness called bruising.

Once I restored calm and eliminated the threat of a terminal event, I presented treatment options such as, "Stop taking medication that causes bleeding and slows healing." The rainbow for recovery was in view. We selected an optimal day to venture back toward altruism, which I felt would be therapeutic. We were good.

The discussion branched off to prior orthopedic misadventures, which left her with a painful elbow and further appreciation for the destructive nature of gravity.

• • •

Arthur and I went back many years. He felt comfortable sharing the shortcomings of my office and, unfortunately, those of many other medical facilities. He reminded me about the time my office phone had not been answered for several minutes and then he was on hold for ten minutes before the line went dead. When he called back, he received misinformation from my clerk who mistakenly scheduled him to get a shot, which had not been approved by his insurance. That resulted in a wasted visit after a long drive and further embellished his frustration while unburnshing the glow on my unsuspecting halo. Order was partially restored when I allowed him to talk about more than one body part. Previously he had been told my office had a one-body part rule. That rule is not in our bylaws and is definitely not part of my DNA. He was delighted I rejected that theorem, one of the modern misconceptions my front office delivers.

Once I had agreed and supported his justifiable admonitions about my office, I moved on to address his physical complaints. He was happy with the resolution of his medical needs, but I still had to deal with the unresolvable office misadventures. These bunglings are not restricted to my office or just medical offices but have planted themselves like Covid in many businesses.

Fortunately, the majority of my patients have a good experience, which translates into a smaller allotment of apology time for me.

I don't think I did much from an orthopedic perspective that day, but at least this small group of patients will sleep better tonight, even without some going to Rocky Point.

Sleeping is a Challenge

I'm not a big fan of sleep because it diminishes my discretionary time. The average American is accustomed to about five hours of "free time" a day. That is the time left after working, grooming, eating, and sleeping. This free time is compromised by a cacophony of activities, (reviewing social media, answering scam calls, diffusing family squabbles, and other critical pursuits), which supposedly take three hours' worth. But who can truly identify what is necessary activity? Sleep falls into the personal choice category. Those who enjoy sleep seek more than is required. Required—approximately seven and a half hours per day—is just that, an average, and the bell-shaped curve covers all comers. I would choose zero, but five is more realistic. To "sleepin" is a total waste of time. I interpret the term to mean—I lead a boring life, and sleep is the best alternative. But what do I know? Some people spend 30 minutes or more in a shower, on the toilet, or fixing themselves—as in beautification war paint, braiding, and nail art.

Some events in our lives can deprive us of the optimum amount of sleep we desire/need. A tornado comes to mind. It is hard to sleep when one is flying around your neighborhood in an old T-shirt and dirty underwear. Trucks running into your house or the random home invasion fortunately are rare and have not yet interfered with my sleep.

My list of sleep interrupters starts with my neighbor's barking dog, a classic sleep impeder. My neighbor has a new rescue dog. When his wife leaves town he vacates the house at five a.m. He puts the dog outside during his absence, supposedly because she hasn't learned peeing is an outside activity. Did I mention his wife is out of town because she doesn't like dogs and might never return? There may be more to the story than the dog because I occasionally see his sister, or at least a lady, visiting regularly. The dog goes off as soon as my neighbor's tires scream out of the driveway. I swear the dog barks in my direction, requiring at least two noise-canceling pillows to give me the last hour of required rest. My only alternative besides alienating my neighbor again—since I have already asked him five times to sell the dog—is to turn in an hour earlier and miss the Late Show.

My list continues with my current nemesis: the fellow calling from Bombay asking if I wish to save money on Medicare insurance, or his brother telling me my car warranty is about to expire. These friendly callers must think I live in the East and have me on autodial well before completing my perfunctory rest period. My very sturdy phone has survived many cradle-crushing call terminations. Letting these calls go to voicemail serves no useful purpose because I am fully awake after the second ring. Ugh.

• • •

A Marriott sleep killer was "housekeeping," accompanied by the knocking request to clean my hotel room early in the morning typically after a very late night out. The later I returned to my room the earlier the housekeeper arrived. My room located near the elevator allowed me to hear the unrequested machinations of the midnight crowd discussing the half-naked lady sloshing around Murphy's Bar, and falling off her five-inch heels. Or worse yet, singing their version of a long-forgotten frat song. In either case my sleep was compromised. I hesitated to wear earplugs for fear of missing the guaranteed fire alarm.

• • •

Foreign travel brought into play an array of sleep compromisers. The rooster topped the list. Cock-a-doodle-doo resonated throughout South America. These birds were particularly problematic in Ecuador and Brazil where chickens surrounded my living quarters. They roamed the villages and farms, and in Tena, Ecuador—one of my mission stops—chickens were pecking everywhere. Each morning the roosters announced their wake-up message; the first bugler set the stage for the remaining choir members to crow along. The cacophony usually started before sunrise and faded later in the morning, although you could hear a few practicing their ritual throughout the day.

Roosters were not alone for the wake-up routine in third-world society. Spiders and an assortment of crawling bugs disrupted my sleep. If I knew the critters were not poisonous I could ignore them, but making that distinction in the dark without proper insect signage made the I.D. process uncertain. Therefore immediate murder was required. Mosquitoes posed a real problem. They didn't always give a warning before flying into my ear. With malaria as a threat, any buzzing had to be taken seriously. I have slapped myself silly more than once trying to eliminate a single mosquito. In Uganda I often spent 20 minutes before turning out the lights searching for insects resembling mosquitoes; somehow, they remained hidden until darkness prevailed. Not fair.

• • •

In Brazil my sleeping nemesis was a macaw. Even though only one macaw resided in the compound, it lived close to my cabin and screeched three times louder than any rooster. As the hospital's picturesque pet, it had protected status; consequently, the day calendar ran on macaw time. The bird made sure everyone started at the same time. Unfortunately, the bird could not control the shower temperature, which fluctuated from scalding to arctic freeze.

• • •

In Botswana our tent protected us from the savanna creatures, but a thin sheet of fabric didn't completely eliminate hyenas from consideration, making sleep more of a half sleep.

Tent sleeping always presented a sleep challenge. Air mattress deflation resulting in irregular rocky impressions on my backside is a guaranteed terminator of sleep. The last camping trip with my young children also involved a tent, which was less robust than the African tents. We pitched our Arizona tent near a lake at 10,000 feet. The weather was cool but dry until about one a.m. I heard thunder, followed by moisture in the form of water dripping from the inside of the tent. Tents are supposed to be waterproof, but I had an outlier. My sleeping bag, food, clothes: everything we had was soaked. Sleeping was no longer an option. The kids decided camping was a bad idea.

• • •

My last disturbed sleep story took place in a Breckenridge, Colorado, rented condo. Late in the evening, resting quietly on the bed after a full day of skiing, a drop of "fluid" splashed on my face. Odd for a nice resort to provide an unwelcomed shower in the bedroom. A few minutes passed before my family realized many chocolate droplets were dripping from the ceiling. Everyone had an idea of the source, but conjecture was not a solution. A call to maintenance at least got the ball rolling toward an explanation. Meanwhile we emptied the kitchen of every container available. The various high-flow dripper spots were identified and panned or bowled as quickly as possible. The bed looked like a party table filled with serving dishes. Maintenance responded quickly, but when they investigated the units directly above us, nothing, no leaks or overflow were located. After opening the doors of four units, none directly overhead, they found the problem. Worst case. A plugged toilet with abundant fecal material ran amuck all because of a diaper. For no good reason it flowed along the ceiling, finally spilling into our condo.

The odor was not overwhelming but highly sugges-tive of the described source. The bed remained rela-tively dry because of the bowls. The bowls then became tainted goods knowing what they contained. The drip-ping continued for several hours after the toilet was shut down. When the frenzied sleep-disturbing event concluded, we super scrubbed the dishes and remade the bed.

No other units had this unique experience.

Not desiring sleep in the first place, missing a few winks is acceptable, but I prefer to dictate my sleep terms, rather than have a mosquito, macaw, or descending stools mess with my melatonin.

ACL

The anterior cruciate ligament and I have a kinship, which I share with several monumental orthopedic events such as the development of artificial joint replacement and arthroscopy. Endoscopy and heart transplants are major advances, that have occurred since I became a doctor but fall outside the orthopedic arena. I feel like a proud parent watching his children grow, a farmer seeing his crop go from seed to grain or an author marshaling a book from an idea to fruition.

The ACL abbreviation is common enough that even Siri recognizes it as the anterior cruciate ligament—a strong but vulnerable ligament within the knee joint. A ligament is a band of strong fibrous tissue that holds joints together but allows the joints to move yet remain stable and connected.

I am not responsible for the amazing progression of the treatment for an injured ACL, but I have observed the modern evolution of treatment, almost the entire story from the beginning particularly after the arthroscope became a major contributor in the '70s

Claudius Galen in about 200 A.D. was the first to describe the ACL ligament, but he didn't identify its functional importance. Several authors in the 1800s described the findings of an injured ACL and how knee instability results. Several surgeons reported repairing the ligament in the early 1900s but met with limited success. Primary repair of the ACL means suturing the ends of the ligament together. This approach proved unpredictable and minimal progress in the treatment occurred until Willis Campbell, in 1935, performed a reconstruction operation of the ACL similar to what is done today, but the operation never caught on.

In 1963, I was beginning my medical career as an intern who had an interest in orthopedics. I read in a medical journal about a "new" operation called the Jones procedure to treat a torn ACL. A few years later when in the Army, I had an opportunity to apply this surgical innovation to several Army basic trainees who had torn ACLs during their first weeks in the Army. I worked in the orthopedic department although I had no orthopedic residency training. My boss was a fully trained orthopedic surgeon who gave me great latitude in the treatment of our troops.

The operation I proposed for one of the ACL injuries was the Jones procedure I had read about several years earlier. The torn ligament was replaced rather than repaired as had been done unsuccessfully in the past. Arthroscopy and more advanced options followed a few years later. The surgery was relatively simple: remove part of the kneecap with the patellar tendon and tuck the patellar bone into a hole in the femur where the torn ACL originated. I reviewed the operation technique before performing it. I'm sure my trained partner participated in the surgery, but I don't recall his level of enthusiasm. Of course, I had no long-term follow-up to evaluate the success of that surgery. When I went into practice six years later, I did a few more Jones procedures, but by then it had been around long enough for doctors to realize there were better options. By 1971, one year into practice, I stopped doing the Jones procedure and switched to the latest version of ACL reconstruction. Direct repair was still not an acceptable choice.

Several other surgical approaches became popular while the orthopedic world was on the cusp of a new and exciting trend—arthroscopy. Arthroscopy was a less invasive method of looking into a joint and performing surgery through a small opening rather than the traditional incision. I spent the next fifteen years learning and mastering arthroscopy and arthroscopic ACL reconstruction.

In 1986 Dr. Freddie Fu entered the scene at the University of Pittsburg. Rarely does one individual impact the advancement of medicine or any other discipline as has Dr. Fu. He put the ACL under the microscope. His staff dissected, imaged, and tested the ACL with FBI intensity.

This little ligament is just one of several ligaments within the knee joint. It happens to be a vulnerable ligament often injured in sports, particularly football, but also in soccer and other non-contact sports. In fact, the majority of the injuries are non-contact. Each year approximately 150,000 Americans have this injury which is 1 in 2,500 of the general population., but much higher in young male athletes. Unlike some ligaments the likelihood of primary healing is low. The ACL ligament loses strength throughout our lifetime and by age 80 is only 20% of its original strength.

Dr. Fu devoted his life to understanding the anatomy and function of the ACL and its reconstruction. He did research on gorillas and other animals in the local zoo. He traveled worldwide to teach and learn every possible detail about the ACL, and alerted us to the wide variations among our patients.

With the advent of arthroscopy and Dr. Fu's research, the results improved enough that now most athletes are treated with surgery for an ACL tear. Dr. Fu had a method of measuring by MRI what size and shape grafts should be used. If the graft is inappropriate in size the results could be compromised. Various types of graft materials have been used from a patient's own tendons to cadaver grafts and artificial material. The synthetic material had a brief following because it removed the need to take a graft from the patient, a time-consuming portion of the surgery. The problem, the body wasn't happy with the foreign material and often rejected the material with an inflammatory reaction. A similarly enthusiastic response was the use of allograft—tendons from a cadaver. Again, no donation by the patient was needed. This type of graft is still used and is popular, but adds to the cost because the patient is no longer providing the material. The retear rate is higher when a non-patient graft is used. Lately there has been a shift to the quadriceps tendon as a donor site, but bone-patellar-tendon-bone is back to being the most commonly used graft materi-al. Like many concepts in society, the source of the graft and variations of the procedure have cycled, failed, and reemerged.

The primary repair, which failed many years ago, had a brief rebirth a few years ago, but again fell out of favor. Even though some primary repairs have worked well, they have double the retear rate of an autograft. Recon-struction, which translates into replacement of the torn ligament, is the treatment of choice. Human tissue—graft material from the patient—is preferred because it can remodel and repair itself. A graft used to replace the torn ACL takes about 24 weeks to revascularize, which means the strength of the ACL is not normal for at least that time frame after reconstruction. It should be noted that some of the operations I did 45 years ago have resurfaced as augment procedures done in addition to a standard reconstruction. They didn't work well enough as a stand-alone operation but are back in new roles as augments—part of the cycle of medicine.

An evolution has occurred with the way a graft is held in place. Originally the tendon was sutured with heavy suture material. Then a metal screw was used which worked well as it made it easy to see with X-ray if it was properly positioned. Then a biodegradable (absorb-able) screw became popular, but at times caused reac-tions that could be seen on X-ray as a large hole in the bone. The endo button, a clever holding device, has also become popular.

The rehab time varies from doctor to doctor but the reality is there is an obligatory revascularization that limits the ultimate strength of the ligament. The time to return to sports varies from six months to two years. Deciding when the optimum time to resume normal sports activity is still debatable but depends on the patient's physical measurements, muscle size, speed, and agility. The patient knows better than the doctor in many cases. The return to football in the NFL is the outcome of almost two-thirds of the total ACL injuries while in high school and college only 43% play football again after reconstruction. A recent study revealed that the full recovery of a repaired ACL takes two years to be 100%. That number doesn't work for coaches and athletes.

There continues to be a progression of improvements, and I feel blessed to have witnessed modern evolution from start to present, although I missed the initial discovery by Galen in the very early chapters of the ACL story. In some ways it feels like observing the evolution of television from the small snowy black and white screen to the 350 channels, Netflix, Hulu, and Apple TV we now have available.

It is truly amazing that 150,000 people in this country can have a career-ending knee injury every year and now stand a very good chance of returning to preinjury activity. The Galens, Jones, and the Freddie Fus of the world are my heroes and because of them I performed this operation multiple times, many before the latest iterations of the procedure were developed. I hope all of those patients still enjoy the benefits of modern medicine.

The Ides of February

The day started with a "Get out of Covid funk" leisurely drive to McDowell Mountain Park. My GPS became flummoxed by my request to direct us—my wife and me—on a route in the general direction of our intended destination—a hiking trail. However, the deranged GPS led us several zip codes away. The winding, often dead-end roads north of Phoenix soon provided a technical challenge. The GPS guided me onto a road that morphed into gravel, narrowed, and became steep and dangerous on the edge of the mountain. It finally dead-ended at a house at the top of the precipice. From that vantage point I could see the desired destination about ten miles away as the crow flies. The GPS seemed satisfied it had done a good job, but we were far from our objective.

The verticality of the last half mile, coupled with cliff-hanging roads, produced significant anxiety in my wife. "What if the brakes fail? What if we meet another car? What if it starts to rain?" That was not happening. There was not a cloud in the sky.

Once back on the pavement and no longer interested in any regional parks, we headed to lunch in Cave Creek. Using the diner's guide wand for finding a good restaurant—go where there is a full parking lot—we stopped at the place with the most beer signs. There was no name on the building, just beer signs: Guinness, Pabst, and Millers. There were few empty seats, but plenty of maskless patrons shouting to be heard over the racket of a four-piece country band. We got our usual great seats; my wife had a nice view of the kitchen and I faced in the direction of the ladies' restroom. The meal was sufficient to feed Romania. Having lost our hearing and feeling full, we departed to the delight of those new arrivals looking for a parking spot.

Thirty minutes later when I tried to purchase gas, I discovered my Costco credit card was not in my billfold. I checked all the usual options but was convinced it had decided to stay at the restaurant 35 minutes away. A call to the beer haven was not answered. The place was so noisy they probably couldn't hear the phone. Back we drove rather than go home, which meant another 20 miles in the opposite direction. I located my waitress and she confirmed I was correct; I had left the elusive card on the table. Alleluia. She then proceeded to put in several orders and hand out a bill or two before resolving my dilemma. Eventually she retrieved my card from a tall stack of lost credit cards in the register, mine being on the top of the pile. Back to the Costco station we went. I then had three miles of gas left according to my gauges. The pump would not accept my card. "How could that be?" It worked at the restaurant but not at Costco. Not to worry, the attendant used his master card to activate the pump, which allowed me to use another non-Costco card and fill up.

A call to card-holder services clarified and confirmed my card was not renewed by my corporation. I was told this was a common occurrence, and a new card would be sent, but only after I paid the renewal fee. The good news: I did not have to change my card number and I had a full tank of gas plus a full stomach.

My company gave me no warning they had stopped paying for my card after 25 years. Ten days later my new card arrived in the mail.

• • •

The next day, more Ides of February stories. A former patient—Nina Parson— related her travel events. She and her husband had a bit of Lewis and Clark in their blood. They departed by car from their hotel near Rio de Janeiro, Brazil, and headed for a monastery located in eastern Brazil. Fortunately, the monastery sat in the middle of the maned wolf's natural habitat, the reason for the Parson's trip. These unique, crepuscular, omnivorous, 25-pound, thin-legged wolf-like animals sport prominent manes and are found only in central South America. This obscure mammal is a wolf in name only, having its own genus. No other animals fall under the same category including dogs, wolves, and coyotes.

The monastery took advantage of its ideal location to serve as lodging for the adventuresome folks interested in seeing the maned wolves, butterflies, birds, and a variety of exotic wildlife. The Parsons stumbled through Brazil with translation books in hand, arrived at the monastery the one week a year when the monks don't speak, and were rewarded with a mute priory of monks. This blanket of silence proved no worse than incomprehensible Portuguese; after all their main objective was the maned wolf. During their quiet phase the monks communicated with chalkboards. The guided tour to see the wolves was productive but quiet, other than for the unique bark of the maned beasts.

As a bonus the Parsons were treated to a rabble of Brazilian butterflies. More than one butterfly is also called a flutter, which seemed appropriate.

After a week of silent viewing, the couple returned to Rio to begin the second part of their journey. The road to the Pantanal swamp quickly turned into a challenging off-road experience negotiated with a standard two-wheel drive Volkswagen. Due to heavy rains, the narrow mud/gravel single-lane road presented multiple washed-out sections. They faced at least 30 such damaged areas where the locals had conveniently placed 2x10s boards. To cross the deep, muddy ravines the boards had to be aligned to match the car width and erosive pattern of the wash. These had to be positioned carefully and then crossed even more carefully because the tires were as wide as the boards. The bridge director adjusted the slats and coached his spouse, the driver, across each gulley. Occasionally running water filled the ditches, but mainly mud and the washed-out narrow road made each crossing an adventure. Crocodiles were seen near several crossings to add further flavor to the drive.

The birdwatching, jaguar sightings, and scenic beauty of the Pantanal swamp, the largest swamp in the world, made this stressful venture worthwhile.

During their five-day stay Joe Parson experienced many mosquito bites, two of which seemed uncharacteristically persistent and became bumps several days later. Mrs. Parson had no reaction to her mosquito bites, and the Parsons weren't concerned because the bumps were irritating but not severely painful.

They returned to the outskirts of Rio de Janeiro, Brazil, and to the hotel where their trip started. Early in the morning, before guests were up, Mr. Parson became short of breath primarily because of swelling of his tongue. The couple realized this new and frightening experience needed to be addressed.

They raced to the front desk for advice. The night clerk arranged for a taxi and directed them to a nearby hospital. He could not provide them with their wallet because the safe was on a timer and valuables would not be available for an hour. The deteriorating condition of Mr. Parson would not allow for any delays. The light traffic facilitated a quick trip to the hospital and he was seen within a few minutes.

Mr. Parson received several shots and some pills, but no explanation as to why his tongue was swollen nor any evaluation or mention of his bumps. He improved enough to be discharged. Total cost of the cab, $5. Total cost of the hospital visit: $15. Amount of money between the couple: $20. After reaching the hotel the return cab ride was covered when the safe was opened.

Three weeks later when back in Arizona, Mr. Parson noticed the two bumps were growing and becoming more uncomfortable. His medical internet search suggested a possible answer to his dilemma. Maybe he was the host to a bot fly infestation. He applied Vaseline to the bumps and placed meat on his arms near these tiny mountains. Just like the internet information stated, within an hour the bumps opened, and out crawled two, almost inch-long worms/larvae.

The bot fly, common to the Pantanal, had done its usual trick. These flies capture a mosquito and lay eggs on the now, vector mosquito, thereby allowing the fly to perpetuate the specie. Mr. Parsons had been kind enough to provide his body as a residence. Mrs. Parson kindly escorted the little worms out of their hiding place with a tweezer. Because they are covered with barbs that prevent easy extraction, the process took several minutes even when halfway out of the skin. Mrs. Parson was kind enough to show me the evidence, still kept in an alcohol preservative for demonstration purposes.

• • •

The last of my mid-February experiences was related to a longtime labile patient, Laura. Labile from an emotional standpoint, but with justification. Laura had frequent falls resulting in many bruises. She also had experienced the full gamut of hardships: spousal abuse, loss of loved ones, loss of job, and health problems including cancer. She claimed the title of my most transparent patient. Not that I could see through her, highly unlikely at 190 pounds, but transparent in the now political sense that everything she experienced was available for sharing. I encouraged her off-loading of voluminous concerns realizing that she had assigned me the role of listener.

Historically she received great benefit from having a pet. Her spouse provided less support than a cricket and he had no enthusiasm for a pet. He didn't want to share her attention with an animal. Laura persisted and purchased Shady, a cat, which adopted similar qualities to her husband related to spousal support.

Laura was anxious to talk about her acquisition, new since her last appointment two months previous. She saw me under the guise that she liked my cortisone shots.

"Your shots don't hurt like others I've received."

So, while I'm giving her the requested injection, I was treated to the new cat story.

Shady, a fluffy-black Maine Coon cat came from an ad on Craigslist. Laura liked the color, and apparently the inflated price. The cat cooperated with good litter box etiquette but provided little companionship. This feline remained independent, isolated, and aloof. She tolerated petting but had to be picked up from her hiding place behind an overstuffed chair to be stroked. Shady had a short timetable for receiving affection and leaped off Laura's lap after less than a minute of petting. She never voluntarily jumped up on Laura's lap even when called. Laura, the consummate optimist, was certain the cat would come around and fill her role as a support cat. Unfortunately, Shady had a way to go. The ineffective cat further increased my responsibilities as a listener of Laura's fables.

Shady's name was not changed upon purchase for fear of confusing her. I suggested trading up. Shady needed to be replaced by a Friendly or Happy or Deceased version of a cat.

Laura was a zodiac follower as well as being in tune with the Chinese calendar and this was the year of the ox in China. Maybe an ox was too much for Laura to handle, but she didn't shy away from a challenge. I did not see a happy ending to the cool cat relationship. I look forward to next month's guaranteed visit and more cat tales, maybe entrails because Laura is known for spilling her guts.

• • •

Missing credit cards, maniacal GPS devices, a mauve wallet, muted monks, maned wolves, a massive flutter of butterflies, and a mangy, Maine Coon, all made for an exciting month.

So much for the Ides of February.

Williams

In 1928, after graduating from high school, my father and two other 16-year-old buddies drove a 1926 Dodge from Boone, Iowa, to California. Much of that trip had to be on Route 66. Most of the drive involved dirt roads with the stretch from Grand Canyon to Williams, a muddy 60 miles, being the most challenging. The car and the boys somehow survived. The parents of the three boys gave them more latitude than most parents would today. The boys took off for the West Coast before starting jobs and college. My father married about a year after returning from his big adventure.

A yellow house, better known as the Historic Yellow House, is located a block south of the original Route 66, the highway from Chicago to Los Angeles commissioned in 1926 and fully paved by the late 1930s. The house, now a VRBO owned by my daughter and her husband, was the drawing card for a weekend in Williams, Arizona. Originally constructed as a bunkhouse, and eventually included in the National Registry in 2014, 125 years after it was built.

At 46 degrees in the morning the Yellow House proved to be an excellent retreat for my wife and me from 110-degree July valley heat, so I took a stroll around town. Tourist attractions within walking distance satisfied my urge for Grand Canyon lore and Native American art. Foreign travelers filled the gift shops and Mexican restaurants that lined Route 66. Once I completed the tourist sites, I walked to the medical facility, the high school and a covey of local churches: Born Again Baptist, Four Square and the Family Harvest. The church parking lots, empty on Saturday, were overflowing on Sunday. Being behind in my out-of-city church attendance, I encouraged my wife to attend a nearby house of God with me.

The original entry to the church had been modified. A narrow-tilted ramp had replaced the steps but was barely wide enough to accommodate a wheelchair. The ramp attempted to satisfy ADA compliance but was challenging and dangerous even for able-bodied parishioners. I called it a prayer ramp because negotiating it required more than skill.

We were slightly early, and as we entered several friendly hand-shakers greeted us and made us feel an instant sense of belonging. The welcoming committee enthusiastically directed us to the doughnuts and fruit. We passed on the doughnuts.

There were no printed bulletins to give us a road map or to help identify the players. The starting time apparently was not a hard number, but 15 minutes after the anticipated kick-off a preacher introduced the morning's worship order. He explained this was kids' day, which occurred once a quarter and today we would focus on children.

We had no expectations, having never set foot in this church, and without a program, the service unfolded with the mystique of a mystery. The first order of business included the weekly Meet and Greet. For the next at least 20 minutes, I shook hands and chatted with all 35 adults scattered throughout the sanctuary. I commented to those I encountered how much I liked the sayings on their shirts and queried another regarding the origin of his calf tattoo. One gentleman relieved his guilt about prior sins, "Drinking is a thing of my past. I really miss my ex-wife; we divorced two years before she died. I think she overdosed. I look forward to starting a job soon if I can find one." All this one-sided conversation stemmed from my comments about the information on his patriotic sweatshirt and body artwork.

Following the Meet and Greet a five-piece instrumental group plus two female vocalists led a sing-along with the words presented on two screens. The songs were what I call "camp" melodies. The verses were repeated up to ten times, often praising a quality of Jesus such as kindness. Occasionally the guitar player vocalized as if to keep awake but the cellist remained mute, I think. She was in an unlit corner and hard to see. This phase of the service lasted 40 minutes and I am pretty sure several songs were repeated.

Two twenty-year-old men paced back and forth to the music in front of the audience. Their random gyrations were unchoreographed. Both allowed personal impulses to direct their movements. Each periodically reached skyward when moved by the spirit. I wanted to join the pacers just to keep blood flowing.

My wife and I sat behind a mother with two young kids—probably two and five. The two-year-old was obviously on fruit loops or forgot to take her medication. She was all over the church, climbing her mother like a piece of playground equipment and breakdancing in the center aisle. Excessive parental restraint was rewarded with a loud, vocal retaliation. Overall, the child's physical activity was less distracting. Several church members made gentle efforts to hold her or at least slow her down. My daughter, also in attendance, left the service and returned to the Yellow House without telling us she was leaving. We thought she was ill or had an emergency. A few minutes later she reappeared with a handful of crayons and a coloring book. This temporarily pulled the acrobat back to her seat.

The little girl and her brother started to frantically color in the book at the same time, each decorating a page on their side of the book. Soon, competition forced them to cross over the centerline and embellish the sibling's page. The page-turning sped up, the coloring rate increased and a flurry typical of the last mile of a NASCAR race emerged. The mother remained engaged with the songfest.

As we were nearing the 60-minute mark and still had not experienced the anticipated "children's" program, I asked my wife if departing was a consideration. Her response was it would be disrespectful. I was okay staying because I wanted to see the much-hyped kids' program.

As I heard the fifth verse of the song with a refrain confirming that God will save us, I observed that half the members had a Big Gulp and doughnuts next to their seats. I also noticed one man wearing a tie but casual prevailed. However, no one was wearing a cowboy hat or spurs.

A sermon by the forest ranger/pastor filled the third segment of the service. He gave a talk theoretically directed at the kids. He knew everyone in the church except my family and he tried to engage many with questions. The concept had merit, but his portable mic was mostly not functioning. One adult near the front of the sanctuary wished to participate by responding to any of the preacher's open-ended questions. She was a loquacious special-needs person who spoke for several minutes when given the floor. The pastor was interested in engaging others, and things became awkward for him in his choosing. He also wanted different adults to join him on stage and sit in the rocker he provided to illustrate a point. Therefore, the rocker parade began with multiple participants running to sit in the "git off your butt" rocker. He explained Jesus wants us to be involved. Amen. He apparently didn't have a preaching role often because he wasn't the real preacher, but he seemed to enjoy his opportunity, and he used his full allotment of time.

So now we were nearing the 90-minute mark, and the children had not been on stage. The speaker gave the teachers a heads-up to get the kids ready for their "thing." Off the kids went to prepare, in this case to don their costumes designed to show God's love protected them.

They returned ready for battle. The main preacher was invited forward to be a target. Yep, he held a big red heart on his chest and watched ten children with water guns try to shoot his heart. They mostly drenched him. He then put on his Jesus protection shield and the kids took aim again. This time the heart stayed dry, but the preacher still soaked up a fair amount of holy water.

My family stayed dry.

The service eventually came to an end. Most parishioners had finished their doughnuts and drinks. I slipped to the front of the church, where the donation basket sat between the pumpkins, and dropped in the fee for two hours of entertainment before walking back to the Yellow House.

I'm sure there are other entertainment venues in Williams, but for me this was a great way to get a children's dose of religion. Next time we may not pass on the doughnuts.

Shoplifting

If shoplifting is your bag, you may prefer watching TV rather than wasting time on a subject you have mastered. If you are connected to organized crime involved in shoplifting, the following, depressing statistics, may surprise you. You have stolen only $700,000 out of every billion of sales. Seems you could do better. Only 3% of shoplifters are associated with organized crime but some studies suggest they account for a more significant percentage of the stolen goods pie.

"Boosters" are the thieves who sell stolen goods on the internet; "kleptomaniacs" are the sticky-fingered folks who steal for personal use.

As a shoplifter you have a choice of levels: petty theft is lifting merchandise valued under $1000, whereas grand theft is stealing goods worth over $1000. Maybe it doesn't count if you hit $1000 on the nose. Either one, even petty theft, can be rewarded with jail time.

Most shoplifters start as juveniles looking for a thrill. If not busted early, their success may encourage a lifetime of petty thievery. Many adults steal for the thrill rather than monetary gain. Lindsey Lohan, Winona Ryder, and other celebrities have stolen when money was clearly not the motive. But Covid and financial stress have increased the leakage rates, particularly in small stores like Circle K or Quik Stop.

For those of you who need something to do on a weekend, I am providing some useful tips on shoplifting. You may have your own tricks but here are some basic, generally successful methods.

Concealing items is a good starting point. It may be too obvious to stick a number ten can of tomato paste in your bra, but wearing an extra pair of jockey shorts out of the store is less detectable and if apprehended just say your boys get cold easily. Confidently strolling out of the store works for some. If the item is not protected by an alarm device walking out could be easy, especially if the store has several exits.

A slightly embarrassing twist to antitheft devices is actually having purchased an item and the alarm goes off because the clerk didn't remove the alarm sensor. You are forced to walk back to the clerk with multiple rubberneckers already convinced you are a felon honing your trade. I recently learned, the way to secure your walkout victory is to buy the item, leave the store, come back and quickly grab the same item and walk out with receipt in hand used for the first item. The next day you return one of your jackets, or hammers, or "whatevers", and pocket the return funds.

Amazon's new policy of refunding your purchase price and letting you keep the item is apparently to their advantage but appears to encourage abuse. I think Amazon negates their losses by giving credit rather than a cash refund. I learned the hard way when I returned an unwanted item, not realizing I could keep it. I never received a credit on my card. After several hours of calls and frustration I learned I was given credit on my Amazon account, not my credit card. You would think an e-mail explanation might have been appropriate.

Switching price tags works if the bar code is on the tag. This trick requires the switching be done out of the view of a camera. I inquired about the cameras at a local Target store, with 40 to 50 cameras I could count. Some may have been fake. Turns out the cameras are primarily for legal protection, recording slip and fall events rather than being used for security. If a suspicious customer is identified, the viewer can track them with the cameras, but there is definitely no one watching every camera all of the time. That job would induce sleep quicker than ipecac brings on vomiting.

Target shows an excellent proficiency to counteract shoplifting. They operate a top-rated forensic laboratory.

They will track down the perpetrators through a license plate or other clues.

Switching tags requires a bit of intelligence. It is bad form to switch a $25 shirt tag for a $100 video game.

Some stores have very generous return policies. I was treated to a true but unbelievable story of a store that didn't even require a receipt. A customer entered the store several minutes after it opened and presented the clerk with an item to return. The item she was returning had never been for sale until it was stocked that morning before the store opened. The new sales-clerk realized the item could not have been purchased because it had never been available. He gave the customer his explanation for refusing a refund. Another clerk heard the conversation and reported the new clerk to management for not following refund policies in spite of a blatant case of pathological prevarication by a pretty-pregnant-person. The poor-punctured clerk nearly lost his job but he did save the company $200.

Insider shoplifting can be an issue. The clerk may be a friend of the customer and an undercharge or no charge transaction occurs. Chances are good the customer works at a business where he can reciprocate for his friend's generosity.

Employees are a big factor in thefts, with 75% of employees admitting to stealing at least once from the employer. Employees account for large percent of significant theft and 30% of bankruptcies result from internal loss, mainly cash. A friend of mine opened a restaurant but within a few months had to close, primarily because of the theft of steaks, other expensive food items, and cash. He was shocked that the employees stole their way out of good-paying jobs.

Financial and insurance industries are the sectors subject to the most employee-related stealing. The larcenous consumer has to take a backseat to the employee because the consumer doesn't have access to the cash in these businesses. Seems like an unfair advantage to the employee when stealing is the goal.

Ernst and Young, a leader in fraud research, claims there is a 20% loss of profit from internal fraud. This includes removal of office supplies, inflating expense accounts, claiming extra hours and taking kickbacks from suppliers. I wonder if working from home changes those statistics. It is hard to steal cash if you never touch it, but the other aspects of fraud are still options for the employee.

Almost 50% of shoplifters fit the addictive-compulsive category. Once the lifters have tasted success, addiction follows. This group demonstrates other compulsive addictions such as alcoholism, gambling, and drug use. They usually can afford to pay for the item and likely gift what they have stolen. They often struggle with repressed anger, but so do most red-blooded Americans. Hey, this is America, I deserve to be angry. These folks are generally depressed, or at least their therapists think they are.

Last week a friend described how a fellow employee had taken advantage of a liberal expense account provision. The employees were given almost unsupervised ability to request computers, furniture, or anything that could remotely be associated with their job. It became obvious that oversite for this program was non-existent and he upped the requests to over two million dollars' worth of items over a twenty-month period. He hired a fencer who sold the loot on various internet sites. Naturally the program was destined to fail and did, but the employee never made the company whole for his thievery. He was asked to leave and never charged for his crime. He is looking for a job but has no record of malfeasance. Go figure.

Professional shoplifters, not counting organized criminals, account for 20% of the losses. Shoplifting supports their lifestyle. They are the group who has mastered the selling websites like Craigslist, eBay, and Etsy. This group often works as a team, cleverly picking the corporate pockets. One is the distractor, the other the thief.

Addict-shoplifters are the folks who steal to support a drug problem or at least another addiction. They don't like to be caught because having to go off drugs or alcohol when incarcerated is miserable. Besides it doesn't look good on their resumé.

The impoverished criminals are a sad group who steal food or other necessities. They often have no support system or income.

Mob shoplifting, as we saw related to Black Lives Matter demonstrations, is more acting out as opposed to pure shoplifting. Instead of burning businesses or turning over cars, retail stores became the focus of anger. The consumer still suffers the consequences. I can live without an expensive Rolex, but I hate to see my Timex double in price.

My favorite shoplifters are the kleptomaniacs who don't have control over their actions. They steal things they don't need or intend to sell on an impulse. Good decision-making takes a backseat to logic. Maybe they are closet politicians. This group leans toward obsessive-compulsive behavior.

• • •

Consequences of a shoplifting fail:

Misdemeanor: stolen items valued at less than $1000 could bring a $2500 fine and 6 months in jail.

Felony class 6: stolen amount between $1000 and $2000, fines up to $150,000 and 6-18 months in jail.

Felony class 5: stolen amount over $2000 or association with a syndicate gets you a fine of $150,000 and 9-24 months in jail.

Felony class 4: repeat offender or using a container to steal can bring a fine up to $150,000 and up to 3 years in jail.

The loss to shoplifting in the U.S in 2023 was $121 billion, with an additional loss of $85 billion resulting from fraudulent returns. In 2020, the average cost per event was $475. Roughly 35% of the loss is attributed to organized crime and a third to employee theft. The amount lost is likely accurate.

Security guards are not free and also not always effective. Many stores have realized that an aggressive guard could produce a lawsuit resulting in huge expenses. Walmart paid $17 million to a lady shopper who was knocked down and injured by a fleeing shoplifter being chased by a security guard. It is like being sued by your neighbor from an accident incurred as you drive her to the grocery store. Where is the logic?

Costco has a low rate of shoplifting—0.12%—for several reasons that don't apply to other retailers. Their products are wrapped in pallets and reach the floor still covered. They also inspect the purchases against the receipts at the exit. Employees caught stealing pay dearly for their misjudgment. The store has a card system that gives Costco a way to identify customers.

After careful consideration, I have decided the simple way to manage shoplifting is doing a strip search as the soon-to-be-ex-customer reaches the exit.

Loaded with shoplifting information last week, I asked a patient if she had ever shoplifted. She quickly replied as if it had happened yesterday. She had taken candy from a dime store many years ago. Her mother discovered the unpurchased candy and marched her back to the store. Lesson not learned. Several months later she lifted a silver dollar from her aunt's coin collection. That activity remained undetected until she entrusted me with her 80-year-old secret.

This led to her revelations regarding her 67-year-old son who has been out of jail for ten years. During the height of his drug use he blatantly shoplifted a big-ticket item primarily to get arrested and return to jail where he felt more comfortable. Which proves shoplifting can be a positive.

For most people incarceration discourages inappropriate behavior such as shoplifting.

I hope scientists are working on an antishoplifting vaccine for those who don't get the message from incarceration. So, stay tuned.

Haircuts

Not being a highly regimented person, I visit a barber at irregular intervals. The timing of each visit depends on my location, how short the last cut was, and whether I effectively provided an intermediate trimming by my own hand. A recent visit to a new "barber" made me focus on the random nature of my clippings. Since my regular barber retired I have been on an unsuccessful quest for the perfect fit.

Six weeks ago, I had a haircut at a beauty shop recommended by a friend. As I drove away I spotted a barber shop in the same shopping complex. Knowing, as a non-beauty shop person, I welcomed another choice. Last week on my way home from work I made a quick turn into the mall looking forward to my latest barber shop discovery—Hair by Us.

The shop sat neatly tucked away in the corner of the complex. The signage was bilingual, as are many local businesses; that dual-language information didn't deter me. When I entered the shop a loud-musical recording blared for about 15 seconds alerting all the occupants to look my way. The music, à la *Here Comes the Bride,* took away the anonymity I had hoped for. As I adjusted to the interior lighting, I noted two customers in barber chairs. I thought I would have a short wait to evaluate the ambiance when suddenly a young lady appeared from the back. She had heard the not-so-subtle door opening melody and greeted me almost before I had acclimated to the inside visuals.

Her hands directed me to the open chair in the front of the shop. The mute greeting made me ask her in jest, "Have you done this before?" and "Are you having a good day?"

Her dour expression suggested otherwise. She then said, "Short?" in an inquiring tone.

"Just shorten but not too short–regular," I replied.

Having never been in the place and greeted by such a welcoming gesture, I felt a little uneasy, but hair grows out so I accepted the possibility my $18 adventure could not fail. A few minutes of silence went by as she sheared the sides of my head. I asked, "How many barbers work here?"

Her response was, "Ye."

I followed up with an equally tricky question. "Where did you learn to cut hair?

"Uh."

I concluded she was not deaf but probably not adept at English. No reason to offer any more questions. She then began a dialogue in Spanish with another barber. They talked for the duration of my cut using none of the 12 words in my Spanish vocabulary. Meanwhile large chunks of my hair reached the floor as my head was cooling, as in being naked.

The lady had several techniques new to my haircutting experience. Rather than move around me, she gripped my head, similar to one unscrewing a tight jar lid. She turned my head from side to side and included an occasional tilt to create the easiest cutting angle and avoid any body movement on her part. She cranked me left and right, front and back, with the only warning, her vise grip on my cranium.

Her second annoying habit involved the dangling scissors, or at least some object attached to her fingers, which routinely banged into my face and eye when she worked on the left side of my head. I rebuffed the attacks by closing my eyes when she worked the left side over. I recognized this threat early and suffered no corneal abrasion. She seemed oblivious to my grimaced grunts of discomfort each time my face faced the scissor attack. Buyer beware.

Her third specialty was blowing with a powerful apparatus similar to the yard blower I use on my patio. She resorted to this machine throughout the haircut—probably 20 times—as if hair on the barber bib would somehow contaminate it. She maintained the Spanish conversation in spite of the blower. Several times she paused my cut to engage further in her lengthy discussion with her barber buddy. This dissing probably didn't change the outcome of her work, but it was frustrating not to be included in the conversation since I like to come away from a new barber with a deep understanding of their background.

This was a no-frills speed cut except for the conversational delays. No shampoo, no spray, no massage, no conversation, definitely no frills. Almost no eyebrows; she attacked and almost eliminated my previously bushy eyebrows. My Eugene Levy look was temporarily deleted.

She removed the drape and watched as I cautiously peeked toward the mirror. The stubble would hopefully recover. It should grow out in a month or two.

Her unenthusiastic response to my, what I thought to be generous tip, descended into glumness. I took her card, then asked for her autograph because the card did not contain her name. Also, no frills.

I am sure my neck will recover from the twist-a-drama, but I will not be back anytime soon unless Alzheimer's allows me to forget this haircut.

• • •

My previous non-English-speaking barber was in Brazil. I purposely let my hair grow before going to the Amazon River town of Santarem on a medical mission. After several weeks of additional growth, I was primed for a foreign haircut. The locals recommended a barber within walking distance from the hospital. Reservations were not required, and I didn't have to wait in line. There was no signage and nothing that looked like a barbershop. Using a crude map and a few hints, such as "The house across the street from the city dump," provided by a hospital employee, allowed me to find the right building.

I entered this gentleman's home/barbershop—probably 600 sq. feet in size. The barber chair sat squarely in the middle of the great room. He proceeded to do his best imitation of an American haircut. I had a bird's-eye view of the city dump across the street and a committee of redheaded vultures that ran the place. There were at least 20 hopping and jumping vultures, known as a wake, doing their part to keep the dump in order. When vultures are in flight, they become a kettle. How does one bird merit three multitude names: committee, wake, and kettle?

I had seen vultures at work in Africa cleaning up after the hyenas and jackals. The vultures could always find a few remains of a giraffe or zebra, but these were citified. Their Brazilian diet likely better seasoned and the threat of hyenas nonexistent. I hated to see my cut end because of the fascinating entertainment. No mirror review followed my haircut but it was the best and only cut I ever had in Brazil. The vulture show alone worth the price of admission.

• • •

A few comments related to vultures are worth noting since my non-English-speaking barber provided none. Vultures have no voice box and are nearly silent so a vulture analogy could refer to being silent rather than the more traditional "prey on the infirm" customarily used. Grunting and hissing are as close to singing as they are capable of. They also have powerful stomach acid making it possible to eat bacteria-laden edibles like a dead carcass, which other animals cannot tolerate.

Vultures urinate on their legs to cool their feet. I don't see that as a particularly effective coolant. It doesn't work for me, plus it brings disgusted looks.

They also regurgitate what they eat to feed their kids, as if eating carrion is not bad enough.

We can train parrots, pigeons, and falcons: why not vultures? They have a great sense of smell and would make good police animals. They could be called V-D, for vulture and death, just as good as K-9s. What else could locate a dead body from a mile away just by being the king of olfactory talent?

The next time I have a haircut across from a dump I will regale the barber with vulture facts such as, there are 23 varieties of these not-so-handsome birds.

There is nothing like an entertaining haircut.

Tears

Maragan's tears were already in cascade mode when I entered the exam room. Forty-year-old Maragan Vomix was a new patient to me, and she had not written down her chief complaint, which meant I was going in cold. I prefer the mystery patient rather than the person who knows the solution to their problem before I weigh in. She was nicely coiffured, wore a blue scooped-necked blouse with yellow slacks, and a tasteful amount of jewelry. Her expensive ensemble accentuated her auburn locks. Red hair should not make your eyes water or distort the face into a painful mask of terminal anguish. She appeared to be a normal patient, visiting without a support person or family member in the room. Maybe she just liked to cry. My immediate job was to discern what was seeding her cloud. Her eye-to-eye contact was diluted by eye rain, and she wasn't even Iranian, I mused. She did dry up long enough to give arid responses to hard queries like, "Is there something bothering you?"

What was her problem? She had to have something wrong besides excessive fluid in her lacrimal glands. Was she racked with pain, the most common reason patients visit an orthopedist; maybe a fear of needles, doctors, or questioning? Maybe she recently lost a loved one. I systematically eliminated each of those thoughts with a direct question: "Have you lost a friend or relative recently?" A vigorous search for the source of her distress met blind alleys and syntax errors, which stifled my interrogator's persistence. She gave me no leads.

I paused hoping for a refreshing wave of information.

"I have migraines sometimes."

"Are they disabling?"

"Not really, I don't have them anymore. I vomit all the time, but I've gotten used to that and just have to be careful where I am if I feel sick. That is happening more often."

She was dismissing what seemed a big deal to me, and we were completely off the orthopedic train. While talking about nausea, more tears flowed from an endless supply. She transformed herself into a red-topped, dripping baby boomer who was enjoying a furtive encounter. The tears came and went, randomly dispersed between slight smiles as I attempted to select the correct foil or at least a line of questions that might generate lacrimation with regularity. I am now in Freud mode, realizing arthritis and broken bones were not likely on her plate.

Further questions, however, did move a little closer to an orthopedic condition.

"I have had neck pain since my accident. The accident I had ten years ago when I hurt my shoulder." More tears.

"Tell me more."

"The accident wasn't my fault. A teenager pulled out of a driveway in front of me, and I hit him. He was driving on a permit without a parent. In fact his parents didn't even know he had taken the car. He said he was walking to the Circle K to get cigarettes. You know I don't smoke so I thought that was dumb."

I had to wonder if she was crying at the time of the accident. Maybe she didn't see him. She would need eye-windshield wipers just to see her own windshield.

Weirdly, the discussion of the accident and shoulder injury evoked few tears and even a jaded moment of glee, a moment of pride. I expected a different response. She seemed proud of her toughness, having survived an accident—a strong woman—crying was unnecessary at least when relating her trauma/drama.

She briefly referred to her worthless but loving spouse. A subject that seemed no more significant than a soggy French fry. *Ah, maybe a legitimate reason to be depressed and tearful.* He was adequate enough that a discussion about him failed to produce a teary flood. He had been banished to the waiting room during her visit. She painted him as an insignificant lightweight, more of a pet than a husband. I felt I could safely rule out her husband as a cause of anything.

I was still looking for an answer. What was the reason for her visit and repetitious crying? She mentioned her hammer toes and an occasional yeast infection.

"Have you ever seen a psychiatrist?"

"No."

At this point we were already into her fourth box of Kleenex. She used two at a time and barely dampened them enough to qualify as used. I would likely be sanctioned for exceeding my Kleenex budget.

"I know I should have asked you earlier, but why are you here?"

"My girlfriend Nancy saw you for burisitis," the patient's version of bursitis, "of her shoulder and she thought you could help me."

"I would be glad to. Do you have a problem with your shoulder or shoulders?"

"Not really, but you know about that accident when I hurt my shoulder. I don't remember which one I hurt, but it was bad."

More crying, but I noted a diminishing amount. The Kleenex was gone and I thought no Kleenex might be enough disincentive to cause her to dry up.

"I need an excuse from jury duty. I am afraid I will throw up on the judge or jury. And I know I will cry."

Whoa, I didn't see that coming.

"Are we done with your shoulder and neck?"

"Yeah, I just need a jury note."

"Might have been good to tell me that earlier."

I realized I had been consumed with trying to work a puzzle that was unnecessary to work. Suddenly I was in an awkward position of writing a jury excuse in an area that was not my expertise. I wrote a note stating Maragan Vomix should be excused from jury duty because of her medical condition associated with daily uncontrolled vomiting, truly something you don't want in your courtroom. I probably should have added she would likely cry throughout the trial, but I rationalized the vomiting was an adequate reason to dismiss her.

A note coming from an orthopedist without an orthopedic diagnosis felt extremely lame, but I had done my job, sort of. I considered the jury would not want a habitual crier or worse, a vomiting jury mate. Plus, the state could not afford the Kleenex bill.

Robots

Battling robots, old banana skins, and macramé flowerpot holders held equal appeal until my wife invited me to accompany her to a robotics competition. My grandson participated in a contest involving 37 robotic clubs from five states plus Taiwan. The clubs varied in size, with 20 high school students being average. Each team had to pay a $3,000 entrance fee. Fortunately, the robotic teams have booster clubs and fundraisers similar to other sports. But robotics doesn't have the school's financial backing for competitions like football or basketball.

I had no idea these brainiac competitors could generate such an enthusiastic following, eliciting more excitement than a normal sporting event. The local teams brought large crowds of noisy and colorful fans wearing identical shirts featuring the names of their sponsors. They performed "The Wave," complete with cell phone lights and popular rock songs. The palpable vibes spurred the robot drivers to perform at a higher competitive level.

It took me almost three hours to figure out the complicated format. Each robot had a team (a high school group). The club's members built the robot during after-class time at the cost of $7,000 to 8,000 each. They were designed for different types of competition. In the day's event the robot's task was to retrieve colorful cones and large balls from one side of the arena and bring them back to the "home" side where the vehicle had started.

Each individual team competed intermittently throughout the day to reach the playoffs. They competed as part of a three-team group—either red or blue—that faced another three-team group. The color of the team was not important. An individual club team was on a red group for one event and then might compete with two different individual teams as a blue group the next time. Approximately 60 different contests were held, each with a different combination of individual teams. Each race, therefore had six robot competitors, a red group vs. a blue group. The three teams making up the red or blue side had never worked together and now were supposed to help each other achieve a winning group.

The scoring was complicated in that points were given for an individual team performance in addition to the performance of the three-team group achievement. Bringing a cone or ball to your home side and stacking it on a shelf was worthy of points and mounting a tipsy platform before time expired also added to their score.

Several robots had no grasping arms and were considered defensive competitors. They generated points indirectly by interfering with the movements of the opponents.

The preliminary events produced the rating system which ranked the 24 individual teams allowed to continue in the playoffs. The day's competition would identify the best robot performers and make them eligible for the First Robotic Competition world event to be held later in the year in Houston, Texas. In 2022, there were 3,225 teams from 26 countries—2,646 teams from the U.S., a robust 105 from Turkey, and a single team from Vietnam, among others—all hoping to make it to the world championship.

Before the individual events took place, the team pulled or carried in their robots from the staging area, most weighing close to 100 pounds. They had to be strong enough to withstand damage to the mechanical or electrical components. Each robot had two persons at the controls, one to drive the vehicle and the other to control the robotic arms. My grandson manipulated the robot arm. The action took place indoors in an area slightly smaller than a basketball court. The computer drivers controlling each robot were stationed at the end of the arena behind the starting position for their robot.

They had to act in concert with each other to position the robot arm and basket to pick up the items. The drivers had to avoid interfering with other members of their team or being cornered while snatching an orange cone from the rack and attempting to make the appropriate deposit on the opposite side of the arena. Each race lasted slightly over two minutes.

The goal was to score points by quickly moving back and forth across the arena and dodging the competition. My grandson proved adept at gathering the cones but his robot occasionally encountered stiff contact from the opposition. During one high impact crash, his robot incurred the loss of a part. His disabled vehicle remained officially dead for the next two minutes. Robot failures factor into the results like losing a star player in basketball. Even a great team was vulnerable to losing if a robot tipped over or malfunctioned. Each team competed multiple times and could balance out a poor event with a stellar performance the next time. Inter-match repairs conducted in the staging area were ordinary and necessary to keep a team in the games.

Before each competition, the two announcers broadcasted the name of the school or club and town of origin of the contestants with the same enthusiasm as an MMA event, absent the semi-naked buxom bombshells strutting across the stage. Close competition generated vigorous and engaged crowd participation. The team members were the prime cheerleaders but the audience was completely involved when their team competed. The fun of trying to assess the strategies while cheering for your favorite team made for an exhilarating afternoon.

• • •

Before continuing with the "pride-in-grandson story," a little background about robots is in order. Homer, not the one on The *Simpsons* but the fellow who wrote the *Iliad,* has been credited for mentioning human mechanical devices. These were not functional or computer-operated; however Homer, with his prescient skills, described mechanical servants with human-like abilities. Throughout history a variety of mechanical devices have been built, such as water clocks, pneumatic organs, and mechanical birds that could fly. Many of these inventions originated BCE and involved the Greeks, Chinese, and later, the Muslims and Buddhists.

Robotic scholars officially gave Al-Jazari, a Muslim inventor, the "Father of Robotics" title for his programable humanoid robot made in 1206. This fellow also deserved the title of "Father of Modern Engineering" for his 50 mechanical inventions, including the crankshaft, considered the most important invention since the wheel. His contributions were many: a reciprocating piston engine, a suction pump, and a mechanical clock driven by water and weights.

Several types of remote-controlled torpedoes which were controlled by radio waves, were developed at the end of the 19th century,.

The word robot first appeared in a 1920 play called *Rossums's Universal Robots* written by Karel Čapek, a Czech playwright. The name came from the Czech word for slave.

Robotics appeared in a short story, *Liar,* in 1941, written by Isaac Asimov. He also came up with the Three Laws of Robotics: a robot may not injure a human being, or through inaction allow a human to come to harm, and a robot must obey orders given by a human being. Those laws may apply to science fiction but destroying other humans has become a major function for military robots, primarily drones, which have become popular in warfare.

George Devol invented the first modern programable robot in 1954. Joseph Engelberger acquired his robot patent and created his company, Unimation. In the 1960s, his early robots were used to lift hot metal pieces from the die-casting machines. Engelberger, although not the inventor, was known as the "Father of Robotics"—if you forget about Al-Jazari.

Charles Rosen led a research team at Stanford that developed a more advanced robot a few years before Engelberger came on the scene, but Engelberger received more credit and was a better promoter.

Before robotic clubs became common, the work-force-threatening robots that provided no social security, no life insurance, no complaining, and were union-free entered the assembly lines with automated production capability.

• • •

Robotic competition, titled Micromouse, began in Japan in 1979. Other events followed, including the international robotics competition under the name First Robotics Competition, founded by an inventor and entrepreneur Dean Kamen in 1989. He was determined to elevate the interest in technology, especially for women and minorities. He cleverly combined sports and science.

The culture of this program centers around two values, "Graciousness and Professionalism," also known as "Coopertition," which, as the word suggests, emphasizes cooperation and competition. The inherent civility of the program is an oxymoron for most team sports but seems to have enveloped the robot rivalries, bringing in considerable diversity as a side benefit.

The enthusiasm for robotics competition has grown yearly since the 1970s and includes multiple options age groups, indoor/outdoor, different materials and a variety of types of movement. The nature of the movements includes: wheeled, aerial, aquatic, and humanoid.

The high school student competition I observed was indoors. The robots were wheeled, had arms, and had arms that did multiple tasks, therefore requiring more than one operator.

I learned after attending this event that the teams are judged on one other factor: giving back to the community. As part of being in the robotic club, volunteer activities are a big component of the members' involvement, and a team can be chosen to go to the championship primarily based on its community service projects.

If you're looking for energy and signs that good things are occurring in the schools, visit a weekend of robotics excitement even if you don't have a grandson competing. My grandson's team did well but was not the top team. I was proud he competed as a controller and leader of his club. The experience will serve him well for next year's competition.

These budding engineers are the future designers of self-driving roller skates, invisible personalities, and perfume-scented flatus. I look forward to next year's competition.

Halloween

Halloween can be a time for psychic gyrations. On one particular Halloween the goblins were busy boiling a pot of misadventures. My friend Dan, an office manager in a medical office related the following scenario about his boss, Dr. Morgan, a super surgeon and an even better person.

Dr. Morgan's troubles began on the morning of October 31 with a routine operation—a shoulder replacement. For this skilled orthopedist a total shoulder surgery takes about 90 minutes with few anticipated complications, but when the witches are out, the "boos" prevail. Dr. Morgan's surgical assistant (not my friend) was strong and overly helpful. To provide maximum exposure for the surgeon, he twisted the patient's arm in two. Not literally into two arms, but his exuberance caused the arm to fracture. The responding cracking noise and angulation of the arm gave it away, and an X-ray confirmed the goblins had struck.

Worse, with a mid-bone fracture, the radial nerve is often injured, as was the case with Dr. Caldwell, a dentist and the victim on this fateful Halloween Friday. Dr. Morgan calmly completed the shoulder replacement and plated the humeral fracture. The nerve injury became apparent only after the patient awoke.

Dr. Morgan, confident the nerve was not trapped under the plate, which has been known to happen, gave an optimistic report to the dentist, at least related to the nerve injury. Because the nerve was likely intact, function may return. The use of a brace and additional physical therapy would be required while waiting for the numbness and paralysis to resolve. The post-op discussion was not well received by the athletic dentist who was anxious to return to golf and dentistry, in the usual recovery time. Early retirement was not part of his plan. Dr. Morgan could not throw the assistant under the bus although he had been responsible for the problem, and he could not blame it on Halloween. A highly awkward moment for any surgeon.

The surgeon would go to bed that night worrying about a lawsuit, and thinking about his unfortunate and angry patient struggling with life-changing decisions.

• • •

On the same day as the surgical misadventure, a call came to Dr. Morgan's office. My friend fielded a medication request from John Bugman. Dan immediately asked Dr. Morgan for advice because it was a repeat request from an unreasonable, unhappy and unreliable person. John was three months out from a simple operation on his right shoulder.

In John's initial interview with Dr. Morgan, John appeared to be distracted and anxious and responded with inconsistent answers, producing an ominous cloud over his sincerity, validity and capacity to be trusted. Dr. Morgan queried John about his HIV status and he volunteered he was negative, but his wife had died of AIDS; AIDS she contracted while he was living and sleeping with her. And her boyfriend was HIV positive. He didn't spell out the details of that triangle, which likely had more than three sides. John was not a choirboy, at least in any of the more recognized religions. He discussed these facts with the detachment and nonchalance typical to a reply on how tall he was. His descriptors relating to his pain were more graphic; stabbing, killing, burning, deep pain. "Pain no human should have to live with." Human should have been a clue.

John had insisted on having the surgery after many visits and Dr. Morgan finally acquiesced. John had calcifications and had not responded to all other treatments. There are relatively few occasions when removing calcification can be beneficial. Dr. Morgan warned John that the procedure might not work and there would be a cessation of narcotics at the end of two months post-op or sooner.

The request for additional medication was refused. A previous request was refused a month earlier after studies proved negative for any additional source of pain. Following the first rejection, John fired Dr. Morgan. He was good at firing doctors but was not always successful in finding a willing pain pill provider. So, he temporarily unfired Dr. Morgan to recharge his waning narcotics supply. When the request was refused, he unloaded his telephone rage vocabulary on Dan, expounding on his mood and desire to do some real damage to Dr. Morgan, his house and his family. This veiled threat disguised in a Saran wrap motif, left Dan more than a little concerned that this nut was just lucid enough and certainly ticked off enough to fulfill his vengeful plan.

When Dr Morgan received the information his reaction was one of justifiable panic because he and his wife had travel plans for the weekend. She would have trouble finding a travel partner if John succeeded in getting even with her husband.

Death threats are generally given top priority in the ranking of phone calls. Dr. Morgan called John back requesting clarification of his position. John was extremely cordial as far as assassins go, but admittedly Dr. Morgan had little prior experience dealing with blackmail situations. John said he wasn't mad, just upset no one would give him any narcotics. Dan had mentioned John was a chronic drug addict on probation. Dr. Morgan arbitrated a lifesaving deal with John that seemed agreeable to both parties. "I'll give you a few drugs, and you don't kill me." Not a bad deal when you think about it.

Dr. Morgan eventually made arrangements for a drug addiction therapist to treat John. Dr. Morgan could now sleep without the John threat over his head.

• • •

Several months later the dentist, Dr. Caldwell returned. The nerve had fully recovered. The total shoulder surgery eventually allowed the patient to resume a normal unencumbered life, but he remained resentful of the events. Dr. Caldwell claimed as a dentist, he had never had an unhappy patient. That would be like drinking seven Pepsis and never burping.

* * *

The final Halloween enlightenment was from candid Candy, a cheerful "bitch," to quote Dan. She brought her biological daughter in to see Dr. Morgan with the expressed request to obtain a letter of necessity requiring her two-year-old daughter to have chiropractic adjustments. The insurance company refused to pay for any more adjustments and wanted validation they were necessary.

Candy, a former patient of Dr. Morgan in her early 20s, appeared nervous, realizing she might be on shaky ground requesting this documentation from an orthopedist for chiropractic services. Candy indicated the whole premise for the treatment was because of her daughter's scoliosis. "My mother and grandmother both had scoliosis. And I have been adjusted since age 12 for a curvature of the spine. Grandma has been treated for years with adjustments and I started my daughter on adjustments at two days old."

To gain insight and establish rapport, Dr. Morgan examined the daughter. Then he took the opportunity to examine Candy who had a mild curvature. The toddler had no such problem. A deformity may present itself later, but no adjustment will influence the degree of scoliosis.

Unrelated to Candy's daughter, some chiropractors have even recommended adjustments to treat Downs Syndrome.

Candy was not surprised the baby was free of scoliosis because she had been treated so early. Dr. Morgan lost credibility when he proposed science doesn't support adjustments for scoliosis. None of the curved family members had required orthopedic care: no braces, nor surgery.

The economics of paying for all the adjustments was considerable and Candy did not have a high-paying job. Even paying for her daily pack of smokes had to be financially stressful. She interpreted Dr. Morgan's responses as biased, due to his perceived disdain for chiropractors.

She also sought another letter to give to a judge requiring the baby's father, but never Candy's husband, to pay for adjustments if insurance would not. She became less than sweet when that request was also rejected. She reached into her bag of profanities generally reserved for men who screw you and leave you pregnant with no support. As she departed, she shouted for all the elderly patients in the waiting room to hear what a bad f–king doctor Morgan was, and she was not coming back. The office personnel were heartbroken to hear that.

In all likelihood Candy will continue to take her daughter for adjustments. This is where AI could be beneficial, although Candy may be resistant to facts.

May next Halloween fall on a Sunday and spare Dr. Morgan another invidious, spooky day at the office.

Super Bloopers

The following are comments made by trained medical personnel who apparently were not connected to the real world. My comments follow each blooper.

Both breasts are equal and reactive to light and accommodation—*breasts are usually not examined with a flashlight, but every doctor has his own style.*

Remnants of a soldier can be seen in the vagina—*I am going to bet it was an* eyeball, but other parts may have wandered in there.

Patient has chest pain if she lies on her left side for over a year—*right side, no problem.*

She is numb from the toes down—*the author was numb between the ears.*

She has two teenage sons but no other abnormalities—*lucky.*

On the second day the knee was better, and on the third day it disappeared—*unfortunately, it happens all the time on the third day.*

Rectal exam revealed a normal thyroid—*again the prostate has to take a back seat.*

Patient was alert and unresponsive—*just tricking the nurse.*

By the time he was admitted his rapid heart had stopped, and he was feeling better—*slow or fast, a stopped heart leads to trouble.*

After she stopped smoking, the patient started smelling again—*not a good trade-off for her husband.*

The patient gets hives from strawberries, shrimp and also two of her children—*at least her other kids don't make her itch.*

The patient has no past history of suicide—*suicide is hard to repeat.*

Patient states she was constipated until her recent separation—*was her husband duct-taping her butt?*

The baby was delivered and the cord was clamped and handed to the pediatrician, who breathed and cried immediately—*another emotional pediatrician.*

The lab tests indicated abnormal lover function—*his horny levels were off the chart.*

Patient refuses an autopsy—*probably anti-vaxxer too.*

Patient is agitated but good in bed—*the doctor has a spy camera.*

Patient lost her heart the last time she was admitted—*she probably doesn't know where she parked either.*

Patient has done well without oxygen for the past year—*sign her up for the* Mars trip.

Written in the office notes: f/u ck up—*yes it was. How about follow-up check-up?*

Discharge instructions: return to ED for signs of infection...redness, fever, pu$$y drainage...—*weird instruction for a cat bite of the finger?*

Oxygen administered 2 liters per minute via Facebook—*a face mask would work better.*

The bleeding began in the rectal area and continued all the way to Vegas—*that is a messy trip on a bicycle.*

The patient left the hospital feeling better except for her original complaints—*like my last shopping trip, I needed a shirt and I still need a shirt.*

The patient is widowed and no longer lives with her husband—*hard to* believe.

The patient expired on the floor uneventfully—*he forgot to do his usual* breakdancing routine.

The patient's past history was remarkably insignificant with only a 40-pound weight gain in the last three days—*the average being 60 or 70 pounds?*

The patient was present when the suppository was inserted—*hard to insert if the patient flees.*

Vaginal packing out, Dr. Lee in—must be a small doctor on a mission.

The pelvic examination was done later on the floor—*is this Dr. Lee at work again?*

Large brown stool ambulating in the hall—*probably one of those four-legged ones.*

The patient was prepped and raped in the usual manner—*I know the doctor* who wrote that.

Social history reveals this 1-year-old patient does not drink or smoke and is presently unemployed—*sign him up for food stamps.*

Following the examination of her breasts we discussed her impending nasal surgery—*every office visit deserves at least one breast exam.*

Both her old and new noses were placed in our album—*I bet they have a few* breasts in there as well.

Office note: suppositories given with no results, will try again after Christmas—*but it's August.*

Admitting diagnosis gang green—*or black, white or rainbow?*

Patient previously hospitalized at Mt. Cyanide—*I hear they have a high* mortality rate.

The preoperative diagnosis is Stale Back Syndrome (Failed Back Syndrome)— *in case the surgical results are lousy.*

He went to see the chef of surgery—*he is handy with a knife but not so good* with condiments or desserts.

Heart rate of 40 beets per minute—*I prefer rutabaga.*

Able to tolerate gentile range of motion—*the therapist was obviously Jewish.*

Patient complained of an order coming from wound on buttock—*the order* was "Listen up doc, I stink."

Fatal care given—*Maybe should have selected a better care plan.*

Ambulated with a steady gate—*all part of his fencing and walking program.*

She was tossing and tuning—*naturally, she juggles radios for a living.*

She was probably identified and taken to the operation room—*where they* will remove her fingerprints, change her sex and do facial reconstruction, never to be recognized again.

Patient is currently undergoing message therapy—*to make her a better* listener, part of marriage counseling.

While she was in the ER she was examined, X-rated and sent home—*I have seen chimpanzees wear more clothes than some patients.*

Patient is to remain plastered for the next six weeks—*that recommendation* may not be covered by insurance.

I ask him to call and let me know who he is feeling this week—*too much* information.

Exam of the genitalia revealed he was circus sized—*he had the Barnum Baily* scrotum package with a hot dog

Patient had waffles for breakfast and anorexia for lunch—*what kind of syrup* goes with anorexia?

It should be noted there is no noticeable temperature difference between the legs—*who measures the temperature between the legs anyway?*

The patient had a left toe amputation last month and a left knee amputation last year—*it's impressive the toe survived the knee amputation.*

These bloopers have multiplied with the advent of electronic medical records.

I have read a signed X-ray report reflecting information about a goat and the weaving turknuckels. There were full two pages of complete nonsense. When I called the radiologist for clarification his response was maybe I need to read the voice recognition reports before they are sent—*a completely logical solution.*

The Cord

If you are like most people, you can't sleep at night because of the unanswered concern about your umbilical cord. What was it made of? What did it hook up with? How could I be so dependent on it and suddenly it was gone? Ever since I turned eighty, I have been giving thanks that I seemingly seamlessly succeeded in separating from my mother at birth to become an independent survivor. Like most of you, I shed the remnants of the life-giving cord. Adam and Eve didn't have to worry about the cord, but theoretically, since then, everybody has had to contend with this temporary inconvenience. Not to dwell on this situation too much, but they didn't have scissors or knives for cord cutting in those days.

As a staunch evolutionist, I suspect, like most animals, humans once ate the afterbirth. The chimpanzee is the exception. They ignore it and let things dry up and fall off, which only takes a day or two. Most animals gobble up the whole enchilada, including the amniotic fluid.

Neuroscientists have hypothesized amniotic fluid may stimulate the brain to produce natural painkillers. This is a scary thought with today's drug culture. Can you envision amnionic fluid on the shelf next to CBD at your local marijuana store? Hospitals would be forced to have armed guards in the delivery room. Social media would black out comments about "water breaking" to avoid pregnant women being stalked by amnio-addicts searching for a fix.

Research has not shown any culture to have participated in placentophagia, but in the 1950s placenta therapy—the consumption of freeze-dried afterbirth—was moderately successful in improving lactation in women with lactation difficulties. In response to those reports, some new mothers are now saving their placentas and ingesting them. Those following this path claim they have increased strength, less postpartum depression, and improved lactation. Neither Antifa nor the John Birch Society has taken a position on placentophagia.

A cookbook is available that describes 25 delicious placenta recipes. Placenta can be eaten raw or in a smoothie. You don't have to love menudo to enjoy a good placenta hors d'oeuvre. The Chinese have placenta pills, which for me would be a little easier to swallow.

The umbilical cord, whether eaten or tied off, is a fascinating, short-term throwaway. Like sloughed skin, once it has been used, it is discarded. An umbilical cord is about a centimeter in diameter and between 50 and 60 cm (20-22 inches) long. Most cords contain two arteries that carry deoxygenated blood from the fetus. We usually think of arteries carrying oxygenated blood, but not in this case. The umbilical vein delivers oxygenated blood to the fetus. That sounds simple, but where do they hook up, and what happens to the connections when the baby is born?

The urachus, the third pathway in the cord, is a drainage tube that hauls away the fetal urine. There is no passage for fecal material, but the embryo doesn't eat much and doesn't have bacteria in the intestine; therefore no fecal disposal problem.

To me. the clever part of these connections is the transition. The two arteries connect to the iliac arteries. The arteries remain in the baby, but the connection from the cord mystically closes off. Otherwise, the blood would pour from the umbilicus. The iliac arteries are the blood supply to the legs, and despite blood pumping into the iliacs, the junction to the cord always closes at the moment the umbilical cord is disconnected. This miracle seems as likely as a newborn singing the national anthem in Portuguese on the day she is born.

The umbilical vein enters the ductus venosus of the fetus and eventually feeds blood to the vena cava, the main vein in the abdomen. The ductus venosus sends most of the mother's blood to the fetal liver. Having served its purpose, the ductus disappears about a week after birth. Once the baby's lungs start functioning, which hopefully is immediately after delivery, the internal circulation changes. This process, although complicated, goes forth without any bells or whistles and is nearly 100% successful. The foremen ovále in the heart of a newborn occasionally remains open which is a problem that may need to be fixed, but usually the transition from fetus to baby is like driving a dirty car through a car wash and coming out with a shiny clean one.

The umbilical vein remains open for about a week after delivery. This lengthy opening was likely responsible for the survival of my daughter. Within an hour of her birth, she had a seizure, later discovered to be related to low blood sugar. The presumed diagnosis of a pancreatic tumor was made without the benefit of an MRI, which hadn't yet been invented. She required large amounts of IV glucose to prevent seizures from low blood sugar. The glucose solution irritated the smaller veins, but the umbilical vein was large enough to tolerate the treatment. The doctors catheterized the vein before it closed so it could be used long after it normally closes. This vein was her lifeline until surgery resolved the problem. I was told the plastic catheter broke and theoretically is still making its home in her vena cava, but gives her no problems. No one seemed interested in removing it.

Two umbilical veins are present until the seventh week of gestation when the left one spontaneously closes. How you can have a left and a right in a tubular, moving structure is beyond me, but for scientific purposes, that is the designation. If the left vein remains open, there is a high incidence of fetal abnormalities. An underlying problem is folic acid deficiency, which is associated with an extra vein. This suggests that folic acid is the problem, not two veins, but I would be vain to suggest the obvious.

I'm sure you want to know what happens if the cord is too short. Nothing good. The placenta can separate, thereby interrupting fetal circulation and leading to fetal death.

If too long, the cord may dangle from the cervix, causing the neighbors to talk smack about you or the cord can wrap around the neck of the fetus and contribute to fetal death. That stretches my imagination because the fetus isn't breathing, so airway obstruction seems improbable.

All the gyrations the newborn experiences after birth are amazing and critical to survival. Because we are still evolving, it would be exciting to look forward a million years to see if the umbilical cord is still needed. Maybe with social media and genetic manipulation, all babies will be free of malformations and hereditary conditions. Amazon will make deliveries and we will choose our children from a website. There will be no short or long cords. All babies will be smart, good-looking, and registered independent. All cords will be in harmony.

At least now you understand how the umbilical cord works. Stay tuned for the vas deferens story.

Fingerprints

Humans share fingerprints with gorillas, chimpan-zees, and koalas. The combination of ridges and furrows in different patterns creates a unique finger signature for each person. The patterns include arches, loops, and whorls. These same patterns also apply to primates with fingerprints.

Each finger possesses its own print, and even left and right exhibit differences. Identical twins with the same DNA have different patterns although they are close—closer than a random print—yet different. This phenomenon is based on "environmental differences in the womb." We will let the environmental enthusiast sort that out.

Fingerprints are altered by both genetic as well as physical events.

Adermatoglyphia is a genetic disorder of people born without a fingerprint. Genetic studies published in 2007 unveiled the association of family mutations with the absence of fingerprints. There have been other people who have no detectable prints but no genetic changes. Some with identifiable mutations have decreased sweat glands but no other anatomical abnormalities. People afflicted with other rare conditions such as dermato-pathia pigmentosa reticularis have no fingerprints and more severe health issues.

Fingerprint alterations occur from constant rough contact. Also, frequent washing, particularly by health-care workers, diminishes the ridges as do chemical or drying agents. Moisturizing creams can reverse this pro-cess. Powerful chemotherapy drugs pose new threats to fingerprints. They can remove the ridges that produce the print. With much pain and limited success, criminals have made concerted efforts to cut off the pads of their fingers.

The table presents an array of the various patterns and characteristics of fingerprints. These patterns show just how many combinations are available to make us all have personalized prints.

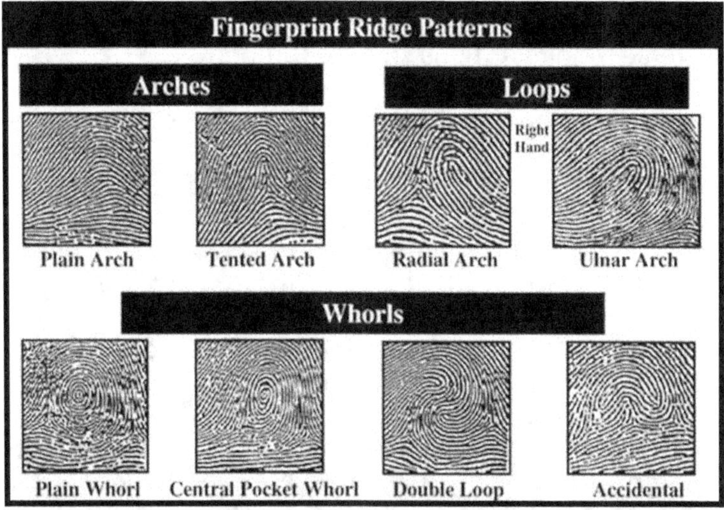

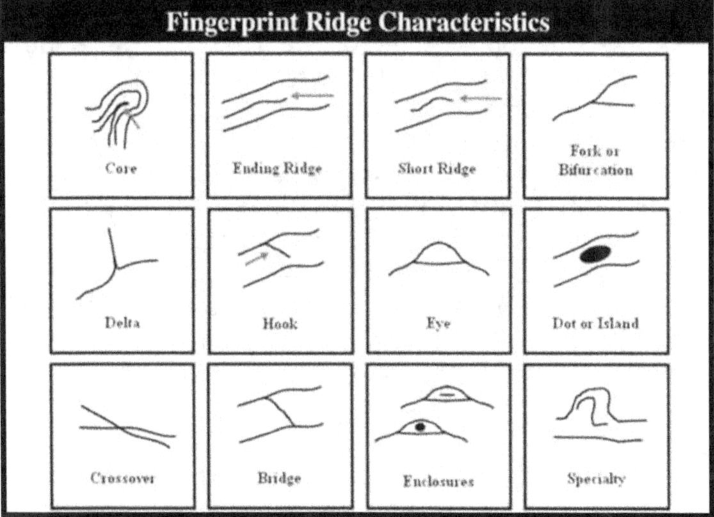

The fingerprint develops between the 11th and the 24th week of gestation. Many diseases can be anticipated by the finger print. One of the first print-disease connections revealed gynecological cancers were associated with a particular fingerprint pattern. There are fewer loops and more arches in patients who develop female organ cancer. The prints themselves are not the cause,, but they highlight genetic patterns that relate to adverse manifestations such as tumors.

High blood pressure is associated with a whorl spiral pattern and the more fingers that show the pattern the higher your pressure is likely to be.

A recent study demonstrated that men with coronary artery disease have a particular pattern of whorls. These patterns are not strong enough to screen and identify patients before they have heart attacks, but they often reveal the association after the fact. Because diet, activities, and medications come into play in coronary heart disease, there is no way, at least for now, that the print alone can serve as an adequate screening technique.

Breast cancer patients display a higher percentage of arches. Diabetic patients reveal bigger fingerprint differences between the left and right hand than the average nondiabetic person.

An association exists between pituitary cancers and a smaller number of ridges in a specific area of the finger. Poor dental health in children is associated with more whorls and fewer ridges. Similarly, multiple sclerosis patients have distinct patterns, especially on finger of the left hand. Asthma patients and infertility cases have their own print characteristics.

The diagnostic possibilities are just starting to blossom, but have made little medical impact other than to stimulate curiosity. However, a few years from now the fingerprint may become a meaningful diagnostic tool.

• • •

Forensic fingerprinting was used long before diseases were being tied to the various patterns most of us have.

In 1858, fingerprints were required on civil contracts in India. The concept was promoted by the British administrator. The first reported use in a trial was in Argentina in 1892 to convict a woman of murder. That same year Sir Francis Galton, a cousin of Charles Darwin, wrote a book describing the various fingerprint patterns.

In 1911, fingerprint forensics made its debut in U.S. Courts, and just 13 years later the fingerprinting division of the FBI was formed. The FBI database now has over 70 million prints.

Prior to the modern history of fingerprinting, Chinese records from the Qin Dynasty (221-206 BCE) revealed the use of handprints as evidence in burglary investigations. In 1400 AD, the Persians identified people by fingerprints. A 1685 book, *Anatomy of the Human Body*, describes finger ridges. Even Mark Twain wrote about fingerprints in *Life on the Mississippi,* which related to a dramatic court trial that included fingerprint identification.

You can have your Monet or your Van Gogh prints. But as for me, I'm sticking with my own unique fingerprints with their ridges and furrows; their arches and loops have served me well. I pray they will never be my downfall in a court of law. Hopefully my prints will continue to hold a pen or a scalpel and quietly perform their magic.

• • •

Fingerprints

Look at your fingers.

Extend and wiggle them.

Look closer.

Fingerprints.

Not another person on earth

Has the same ones as you.

You are alive.

—Berry

• • •

A print for me, a print for you.

How strange a koala has them too just like me and you.

They are so specific, that makes them more terrific.

They form so early on, and yet last till we are gone.

I'm glad I have these whorls and loops, their value I can't dispute.

They may foretell, someday we won't be well.

Their presence may from jail keep us, as a lawyer's rogue dispels the fuss.

I am happy with my prints that be, they alone belong to me.

—Anonymous

Lust for Dust

While resting on my daughter's generally unused bed (she moved out 30 years ago) I noticed the louvered register that provides the air for that room was blackened. I pride myself on being observant of my surroundings, what people wear, and how they act. The foreboding color of the register, possibly caused by toxic black mold, alarmed and disappointed me. I was certain it had been in that condition for years without being detected. Register inspection was not something I did on a regular basis. Rarely do I study the habits of any register in my home, particularly in a room seldom visited. Surely black was not the original color, and my scientific mind needed answers.

I arose like Santa from the rooftop to compare the black vent to those in the rest of the house. These vents are responsible for the flow of hot or cold air into the various rooms of my home. All were hidden near the ceiling of every room and basically had escaped, for the most part, my scrutiny for many years. I found none of the others had the distinctive, ominous veil of black, but some were thinking about moving in that direction.

My wife has an internal thermostat with an acceptable range between 77.5 and 78 degrees, requiring frequent temperature adjustments to maintain that ideal range. Realize the actual temperature and the perceived temperature are two completely unrelated numbers. With this focus on Fahrenheit, you would think I would have at least glanced at the registers occasionally. In reality the one very black register was in a sneaky, dark, seldom-used room. This justified, at least in my mind, a feeble excuse for it remaining undetected for who knows how long.

Once the pigmentation issue was recognized, categorized, and synthesized, I took immediate action, dedicating the Saturday to vent cleaning. This involved removing the vent, which involved a ladder, which involved the risk of falling, which involved the risk of failing. No problem. I spent six hours fastidiously cleaning, mostly with a toothbrush, four vents. Who would have guessed how hard it was to reach all the hidden places dirt can hide? The next time I will try the high pressure, outside hose method. Although I had intended to clean ten vents in one day, the process was labor intensive, and four proved to be my limit. The other reason I didn't clean more: most looked relatively clean.

Not being a specialist in the cleaning business, I worried about whether mold might account for the blackness. As I contemplated my next move to address the mold or no mold issue, I was coincidentally illuminated by a TV commercial explaining the necessity of air duct cleaning. I had always placed air duct cleaning in the same category as dental cleaning, nice but unnecessary: the clean is gone before you finish your next meal.

However, with the admonition from the TV ad combined with my mold concern prompted me to schedule a visit by an estimator guy from the company represented by the attractive-young TV lady. I suspect she didn't know an air duct from a Mallard, but I still chose Dandy's Vent and Carpet Cleaner as my mold expert.

Naturally they agreed that 50 years without a vent job exceeded the recommended timetable. After two random Dandy guys—one a trainee—handed me an estimate, I found out that my dirt was worth more than a square foot of real estate in Manhattan.

A week later another random crew from the Dandy company showed up to do the dirty work. I arranged to be home to prevent these unknown men from removing more than dirt. As part of my attempt to be of assistance and learn how to perform the duct cleaning task, I remained in contact with the crew throughout the house.

They arrived in a large truck that housed a vacuum capable of sucking up a large goat. Being goat-free, I didn't worry about animals disappearing but when the hose was left open-ended on the floor in the living room, I was sure I saw the furniture migrating toward the opening. My house feels a little smaller after all that negative pressure sucking on the vents for five hours.

They wished to see the air-conditioning units which were outside of the house. Unfortunately, I didn't anticipate that would be part of the game plan, and I had irrigated the yard including an un-grassed (muddy) area close to the air conditioning compressor unit. They managed to find the mud with their hiking boots. These boots had deep grooves designed to retain mud. The workers didn't seem to recognize how effective their boots were at mud distribution. As they stepped into the house, I tactfully reminded the two workers that muddy boots were not welcome. I also offered surgical booties but they downplayed my suggested solution and proceeded to decorate the carpet with mud. I recalled the commercial showing white shoe covers and white uniforms like you would wear in a chip manufacturing plant or a similar sterile environment. These guys missed the memo.

When I highlighted the footprints they'd left, they called the company and arranged for a carpet cleaner to come and remove the size 14 tracks. Seems like it would have been smoother to wear the booties I provided.

The outside temperature was only 100 degrees. To clean the vents required bringing a giant hose into the house. The motor for this vacuum apparatus sat in the truck parked in the street. The cleaner elected to use different doors for different parts of the house, which meant they had to leave the doors ajar to accommodate the hoses. Ajar is one thing, but two doors left wide open for five hours struck me as unnecessary because only one door at a time was needed to provide a path for the hose. This is where I became a doorman, closing the door, no longer hosting a hose. I'm sure the neighbors didn't mind my air conditioning keeping the neighborhood cooler than the rest of the city for a few hours. My electric bill may take notice.

In the vacuuming process a large metal cage—with a suction hose—is fitted to the vent. This vent-covering cage is cumbersome and prone to be wider than anticipated as my front door learned when the cage passed through the opening and left its autograph on the door.

The blower hoses were long and stiff. They, too, threatened the interior of my house; and on at least one occasion, tried to rearrange a painting. I took full blame for not removing any wall décor before the bunglers arrived.

To effectively vacuum the ductwork, the system had to be closed, and all vents had to be taped to allow maximum suction. On one occasion I reminded the team that at least one other vent remained unsealed. Telling someone how to do their job seldom meets, with approval. That rule applied in this scenario as well. Their gratitude for my helpful suggestions was met with a muted, "We'll take care of it." Their thank yous were left in the truck.

The curious aspect of the cleaning experience was the absence of any attention to the vents themselves. The black register that started this whole venture became an afterthought. When asked why the vents were not being cleaned, all I heard was a dismissive grunt. A response I took to suggest, "Not a big deal." That was a different take than the estimator person who seemed very concerned about the blackness and the health threat it posed.

So after five hours, including mud removal, I had closed doors, clean ducts, and safe artwork. This was a good thing because I could now pursue reestablishing the ideal temperature for my narrow-range wife. I promise to never worry about a black vent again, at least for 50 years. I never received a satisfactory answer regarding the true nature of the "blackness," but mold was no longer a concern. My lust for dust had been fully satisfied.

A Wedding

suspected I was invited to the wedding only to help fill the church, which would be minimally occupied. I knew the groom and had dated the bride, but glad the groom electee was the "lucky" one. Knowing the first names of both parties and attending high school classes with them merited an invite. Plus, I wasn't homeless and would likely pony up a gift. My presence still fell in the wedding crasher arena based on a weak invitation.

The couple had acquired a religious connection sufficient to become bowl-eligible, meaning they could use the church for weddings and funerals. This event was going to offer a little of both. The groom, a handsome stud, had chosen my ex-girlfriend to have and to hold. Blossom, a substitute for Beulah, a pass-me-down family name, had attracted my attention because she was flirtatious and acceptably attractive. Upon closer inspection I saw she had chosen to leave most of her body hair in place. Now, I admit there may have been some areas where the lawn had been mowed, but our six-month relationship as high school juniors did not include an investigation of the entire being. The overriding turnoff was the body odor, a combination of her own scent merged with a commercial concoction designed to compete with pepper spray or a comparable deterrent. I felt conveniently deterred. She was reasonably heady, gregarious, and loaded, but no amount of money could entice me to go through an olfactory eradication program.

I suspect Larry, the groom, had an olfactory deficiency or was convinced there was a massive pot of gold to be had. Blossom lacked a good scent; Larry lacked good sense, and I only spent a few cents on the wedding gift.

Larry was a conservative fellow as far as I knew, right to bear arms and the Bill of Rights kind of a guy. Blossom, leaning left and well versed in giving directions was a miss (stake) Larry should have avoided but didn't.

As I entered the huge, ring-shaped sanctuary an usher whispered "Bride or groom?" I recognized the fellow as a previous classmate and unfurled a bit of levity by responding, "No, I am a father of four girls and two boys and another who is undecided. Could I sit up front near the family?" He was a shy type and took me to a seat behind the bride's contingent. From that location, I'm sure I detected the faint odor of the bride, recalled from my previous exposure.

As I waited for the program to start, I could hear various nearby conversations of complete strangers.

"Larry is adopted, you know."

"I heard his uncle is in jail."

"He is out now, but he served five years for assault."

"Who did he assault?"

"I heard he hit a bartender when he was asked to pay for his drink. The man still can't walk."

"Who can't walk?"

"The uncle because the bartender delivered a full bottle of cognac to his head."

"It's too bad because he is such a nice kid."

"Larry doesn't drink, does he?"

"No, but he has seizures. Mary told me that."

They switched gears and began shopping chatter. "Millie bought a dozen eggs for a dollar with her coupons at Safeway last week. She always finds the bargains."

"I hate it when those coupon cutters are in my checkout line. Irene says she saves at least $500 a year by clipping coupons."

"That's too much work for me."

"You know the preacher at this church is, you know, gay."

"Really? He wasn't present at the last wedding I went to at this church. This is my third wedding here and none of the couples were members. They all wear white like they are 'pure.' What a joke."

"Shush. They're getting ready to start."

"It sure is a joke."

"We can talk later."

In a whisper, another guest talked about George Fellows and his broken hip. "George fell off a ladder while cleaning the seaweed out of his eaves because his wife had thrown his aquarium out the attic window. She had nothing against the fish but was mad at George for not putting the lid down."

"That's not what I would do, but Sal doesn't have an aquarium."

"Sal is too old to be climbing on a ladder anyway. You know George wears Depends."

"I didn't know, but they are on sale at Target."

"Why do you know that?"

"Oh... you know, I buy things for my neighbor, the one with, the one who had a stroke."

Blossom's mother looked tired, but I liked her dress. The head usher, who sported a black sling on his left arm, escorted her down the aisle. He had pulled in front of a garbage truck three days earlier. I had heard the head usher decided he didn't want to be in the wedding but didn't take advantage of his accident to pull out.

Blossom's father was a no-show and had been a no-show for fifteen years. When he came out of the closet, he went to Chicago with another fellow who came out of his own closet about the same time; must have been walk-in and walk-out closets. He was never discussed when Blossom and I dated, which was not surprising because we had a superficial relationship. We mostly talked about music, records, and artists, even though neither of us was "musical."

John, another usher whom I knew from Indian Guides, escorted Larry's mother to her seat. He was afraid of the dark, and on our campouts, had to have the cabin lights on. The farting stories which John thoroughly enjoyed were approved by his high-pitched, silly laugh. I tolerated his laugh, but keeping the light on all night was painful. I wondered whether he still had farting and fear of the dark problems. These issues should not affect his usher qualities. He was 23 and likely mature enough to sleep in the dark by now. He looked confident as he brought Larry's mother down the aisle, but she stumbled on the wrinkled runner as she turned into her seat. John caught her but grabbed her chest as she fell. Both brushed off this tiny mishap.

When the groom and his four groomsmen came in, I recognized two as former Indian Guides, so I am sure some farting stories surfaced at John's expense during the wedding party dinner.

The bride's grandfather, who looked 40, accompanied her down the aisle. He must have dressed himself because his white shirt sleeves extended two inches longer than the coat and his pants' legs touched the floor. Maybe he forgot his belt.

The soloist had an Ella Fitzgerald range but wasn't in synch with the organist. It sounded like their first practice session.

I especially liked the photographer who must have thought he was invisible. He walked in front of the audience, paparazzi style, and sometimes only a few feet from the wedding couple. The wedding video would at least be free of his distractions.

Vows were exchanged uneventfully until the time for the ring. The four-year-old ringbearer had a bathroom emergency at an inopportune time but eventually delivered the goods to the delight of those who like erratic children's behavior.

Departing the church to the traditional rice shower was a complete waste of good rice, but that is just me. I failed to see how rice would cement a union that has my guarantee to fail within six months.

After waiting two hours for the post wedding photos, a reception took place at a local "wedding reception center." The food was average and the talks/toasts were average and the parking was average. Almost five hours of my day was shot attending this average affair. As a dedicated wedding analyzer, I was happy to have spent my day with Larry, Blossom, and friends who provided a template, of sorts, in case I have a wedding of my own.

Blink and Winks

There is more to a blink than meets the eye. The word blink can be a transitive or intransitive verb and also a noun. I find that relatively useless information, but I get excited to know why you can turn your blinkers on but never say you will blink when you signal a turn. When your eyes blink, they don't use blinkers, just lids. Nowhere else do lids blink; they may slam, stick, or crash, but not blink.

Blinking is one of several things that is generally outside our control. Sneezing, coughing, and passing methane fall into these mostly involuntary activities. Sweating, salivating, and urinating should be included in the uncontrollables. A teenage boy mentioned he may have an erection when he is opposed to doing so, which adds another event to the list. It is starting to sound like our bodies are more independent than I originally envisioned.

Blinking is the rapid opening and closing of the eyes, generally an involuntary, spontaneous activity. A reflex blink, also involuntary, occurs in response to a noise, a bright light, or an object to be avoided, such as a fly, a fist, or a fortune cookie directed at your face. Actually, any foreign object perceived as a danger to your precious eyes will produce a head-ducking blink.

The purpose of the blink is to keep the eyes moist. One lachrymal gland in each eye produces the aqueous fluid of tears. Tears also contain meibum produced by multiple meibomian glands that produce meibum or fatty fluid. Aelius Galen in 200 AD. described the glands, but Dr. Heinrich Meibom, an observant German, more clearly described them in a 1666 paper. That piece of prose resulted in the gland acquiring his name. A blink would fail in its job to lubricate the eye without the grand glands providing the fluids. The blink, especially a tight, full-closure blink, is the best way to generate a moist eye. A sad movie also works.

Blinking merits little attention unless it is defective, excessive, or absent. We blink about as often as we breathe, at least when we are awake, about 10-20 times a minute. However, blinking decreases to three or four times a minute when we read or focus on an object. A man might read an entire *Playboy* magazine and not blink once. Reduced blinking occurs with Parkinson's disease for a slightly different reason. Tourette syndrome creates a rapid blinking rate, which explains why doctors might consider treating a male Tourette's with a subscription to *Playboy*. Babies blink only once a minute and produce no tears for the first few months. So, the term "cry like a baby" is an oxymoron. Watching a computer screen can dry your eyes unless you are viewing a sad episode of Mario Kart.

Blepharospasm, a blink on steroids, is a pathological and involuntary closure of the eyelids, treatable by Botox injections to weaken the spasming muscle.

Some studies suggest females blink more often than males, but that is not scientifically proven. If true, the blinking could be affected by the abundance of strange concoctions applied around female eyes. Look forward to a blink-speed adjustment cream. The weight of false eyelashes could produce eyelid fatigue, thereby leading to a product designed to strengthen the lids.

We already have a flutter effect associated with lengthy lashes. This coquettish mannerism, which, according to the movies, is a blink invitation to hook up, similar to a Tom turkey fanning its tail. The flutter thing is not dependent on the false lashes, but they accentuate the process.

Blinking is a good thing. It keeps our eyes lubricated and prevents the cornea from drying out. A dry cornea, unlike a dry martini, is not a good thing. You might have noticed women on birth control pills blink more. The reason being the volume of tears is decreased, therefore the blinking compensates for the decreased flow to keep the cornea moist. Coming soon to your local CVS will be a blink meter to count your blinks and assess your birth control level. A high blink rate translates into safer sex.

Blinking in humans is performed with both eyes in sync, but in turtles the eyes blink independently. Human blinking is primarily the upper lid coming down and a slight movement of the lower lid.

Lagophthalmos is a condition associated with the incomplete closure of the eyelids, which results in an incomplete blink, more of a blin or bink. There are many causes for this relatively rare condition, but the iatrogenic results of cosmetic surgery may be one of them. A disappointing result from an elective procedure. Even Covid has been associated with this condition on a few occasions.

Optophobia, a rare condition connoting the fear of opening one's eyes, is a real blink-buster. Referees are often accused of having this condition.

Blink has achieved a more significant place in the English language than just a quick closing of the eyes: "He was out like a light before he could blink." The "blink" refers to a finite period of time in the nanosecond range.

Blinking has been associated with unfazed behavior.

"He didn't blink even though the gun was pressed tight against his ribs."

"She didn't blink as the house crumbled at the start of a giant earthquake."

• • •

The wink, a voluntary one-eyed variation of the blink, involves the lower lid muscles more than a simple blink. I recall my first wink at age four. I had just burned my hand on one of the radiators that heated our house. The pain from the burn elicited a one-eye-closed response, which my mother noted and identified as a new skill—the wink.

Winking is affected by sidedness. Unlike right arm dominance, which usually means right footedness for most people, the dominant wink side is independent of the arm and foot. Most winkers wink with their non-dominant eye.

Winking with both eyes is difficult for some, and there is a select group of living folks who can't wink with either eye. This will be a problem if you wish to use a wink for communication—"right on" in agreement or a flirtatious wink.

I knew a doctor who winked profusely. When I first met him, I thought he was casting an "I approve of you" wink. Turned out his "romantic" wink was a tic, and everyone was the beneficiary of his "ticular" antics.

Culture plays a role in winking choices. In Nigeria, winking is a communication to children to leave the room. In China, a wink is a vulgar gesture and would be an invitation to a brawl. Whistling is also considered rude in China, but abuse of human rights is okay.

My personal favorite is the prolonged denial wink of "I don't think so." That is the one you implement when you have serious doubts about an event or comment. I find myself doing this wink when I hear what seem outrageous comments usually about political postures; what I call *two and two is five logic.*

• • •

I suspect you have no idea what your normal blink rate is and until now whether you can wink with both eyes. You probably don't care that a snapping turtle doesn't have the ability to blink. The point is blinking and winking are here to stay or at least until we evolve out of the need for them. By then we will all be bald and have heads the size of watermelons.

If this story didn't flow
you should know
you can always wink
if your humor button is on the blink

Día de los Muertos

The **2021 Day of the Dead event was anything but** dead. I and several others volunteered to host an exhibit table in space 53 for the Mesa Sister City organization at the Mesa Arts Center. We were participating in Día de los Muertos, a Latino-oriented festival celebrating the deceased, which attracted a large crowd.

I am a charter member dating back 40 years to the first Mesa Sister City exchange with Guaymas, Mexico in 1981. We hoped to inform the public of our group's existence and purpose and the share the benefits of membership in this unique organization. The public who visited our booth turned the event into more of a fireside chat/random vent-athon.

I knew we were unlikely to have large crowds visit our space because we had no handouts such as water, pens, candy, or firearms. Even the police booth next to us was giving away stickers and pens, plus their booth was partly manned by attractive young ladies wearing full gear—including mace, cuffs, and guns.

Our presentation was apolitical, but because of the nearby police booth, I think I'd have felt safe even if we had represented Planned Parenthood or an organization possibly threatened by protesters.

The theme of the event attracted primarily a Latino crowd. I saw no blonds but a few people with multi-colored hair: red, green, purple, and a rare orange. The majority of booths were selling hand-made Mexican crafts including a variety of skulls, large paper flowers and cultural memorabilia, which failed to make me reach for my wallet. Unlike my last foray into a festival crowd—a rock concert—there were no pornographic T-shirts, cage-fighting gear, or drug paraphernalia.

Most attendees dressed with a wholesome look, meaning a scarcity of cleavage and short shorts. A few muscle shirts and the usual number of tattoos, but no tuxes or bikinis were evident.

The first person to come to a full stop at our booth was a thirty-plus-year-old man who had been involved with Sister City activities in Mexico. The first ten minutes of our discourse centered around the physical description of his Mexican home: how many miles from Hermosillo, the border, and Rocky Point. He believed a pinpoint location was critical to establishing the merits of his experience and validating the time he was active in the organization. I concluded his involvement in the Sister City organization was legitimate.

The rest of his story was more intriguing. He owned a successful restaurant in Casa Grande, Mexico. This city is the home of a large archaeological site occupied by indigenous people from A.D. 1200. The ruins are remains of the Mogollon culture, which extended into Arizona, a culture that evaporated around A.D. 1370 for unknown reasons. He said something about this happening before Trump, so Trump couldn't take credit for the culture's demise.

He then expanded his discussion, explaining to me who is a Christian. I don't recall the segue, but he described the Trinity and how Mormons don't make the Christian cut. At no time did he ask me my religious preference. I could have been an LDS bishop, or a Jehovah's Witness—whom he also considered non-Christian—or an atheist. The religious analysis continued for about as long as the enlightening description of the Mogollon archeological site and history, roughly ten minutes.

Aside from one question about Mesa's Sister City activities, his final revelation was in response to my asking why he wasn't still in Mexico. He ran a restaurant until a representative of an unknown organization asked for protection money. The implication made by these mafia-like folks was clear. I suggested a drug-related organization was the primary force, but he deflected the question with a "probably" nod. He lived with his family above the restaurant, and rather than pay or die, the family left town in the middle of the night.

When I inquired about other eating places in their town, he said "They have all closed. The marvelous ruins, which could be Mexico's Machu Picchu, are rarely seen by tourists these days. The state of Chihuahua is still a dangerous and a very unwelcoming destination."

My next booth discussant was a 94-year-old author. She handed me four cards and two sheets of information promoting her most recent book. Naturally my focus was on her writing enthusiasm and youthful vigor. She was also proud, justifiably, of her independence and productivity. Her longevity led to her last book on coping with loss. She lost her 69-year-old son and promptly wrote a self-help book about how to deal with loss. I was impressed she had the ability to design her own book covers and do all the publishing details associated with writing a book. However, she gained no additional knowledge about the Sister City organization.

After finishing my absorbing discussion with Mary, the elderly author, I addressed a short, square-shaped middle-aged female. She seemed interested enough in our organization to stop, but it was a pretense. Although she was interested in travel, she quickly indicated she had never been out of the state and never would be. Naturally, I was sucked in and inquired why so. "I have colitis. I will never be able to go out of state because of my illness."

Colitis can be a big problem so I was obliged to pursue these "no travel" restrictions a bit further to ascertain what medical advice she had been given. Where and from whom did she receive information and was there another non-medical issue underlying her travel restrictions? My gentle probing to validate her sources was silently dismissed. She was unaware of my medical background and answered my questions with abundant verbiage, anxious to expand her answers far beyond the intended scope of my probing inquiries. She had a job and apparently missed very little work because of her disease, which seemed incongruous considering the severity of her complaints—bloating, humongous abdominal pain, and uncontrolled diarrhea, all beyond the scope of standard Sister City advice.

Urgency to use bathroom facilities is often a challenge, as is abdominal discomfort, but she didn't admit to those issues affecting her ability to work. She appeared to be a loyal employee with minimal absenteeism. In spite of invitations from her sister in Utah and others asking her to visit them in other states, she was certain those requests would go unfilled. That also meant that travel to Mesa Sister Cities would be out of the question.

As I sometimes do when I find souls lost in the continuum of medical voodoo, I try to right the ship. "What is your treatment program? Who is your doctor? How often do you have a flair? What foods are bad for you?" My questions were penetrating enough for her to lower her face mask and respond with a doctor's name, unfamiliar to me. She then reeled off 20 foods she was allergic to, "I am allergic to all foods."

It was clear she had assumed a new identity; she was now known as Ms. Colitis. She was no longer Carol or Jen or Sally. Aggressive treatment could be a problem. If she were cured or at least under good treatment, she could jeopardize her colitis, her persona. She would have no reason to be confined to Arizona and no longer warrant the sympathy of her coworkers and friends. As the Sister City's doctor in residence, I was not in a position to pull Miss Colitis from her namesake. She had converted, similar to a person undergoing a sex change. She will always be Miss Colitis and likely never find a Mr. Colitis.

Other than an hour's wait for a taco from the most popular food truck at the event, the rest of the morning was crammed with leisure, in keeping with the Día de los Muertos. The delay in food service primarily attributed to the cooks taking lunch breaks.

I can't wait until next year. I know there's at least one healthy soul eager for me to convince how important Sister Cities can be to their future.

Names

If you are known by a one-word name, chances are you are doing well: Beyoncé, Putin, Jesus, Brady, Siddhartha. Other than Vladimir and Tom, it is unlikely you know the real names: Beyoncé is Gisselle Knowles-Carter, and Jesus is Yeshua ben Yosef. Because the letter J was not present until 1600, Jesus is a more recent one-name guy. What about Buddha–Siddhartha Gautama?

The one-name-only thing falls into two categories: the ageless folks like Noah and Moses and the current newsmakers like Brady or Biden. If you grew up in a remote village in Brazil you wouldn't know a Churchill from an anthill or an Ali from an alley. Merkel in Germany is easily identified but a merkel in New Guinea might be a broken pipe or a burnt banana leaf. In the 1980s, Dahmer was a household name. He was a serial killer who dismembered 17 boys. Bobbitt was a popular one-namer in 1993 when wife Lorena Bobbitt cut off her husband's penis. Those single-name folks are unknown to the Gen-Z group.

Geography is a major player in the single-name game. Gandhi–Mahatma in India–was and likely is a favorite, but not so with the youth in Iceland. Gudjohnsen, a soccer player from Iceland, would not make the front page in India. An Australian rugby player and British cricket star may share a single-name identity but only within their country.

Within tribes, professions, sporting groups, and political organizations a leader may be known by a single name, but outside their group that familiarity dissipates. Meany, Reuther, Hoffa, and Capone were well-known to labor members, as were Mickey, Babe, DiMaggio, and Feller to the baseball crowd. Grant,

Crosby, Monroe, and Dietrich were single names that have long faded from the movie scene. Unitas, Brown, Patton, and Namath all well-known single names at one time; only Namath still holds forth among footballers because of TV ads. Tiger, the golfer, also has not faded from the well-known list.

To earn the single-name status, even in a limited geographic area, you have to do something unusual. You could be Baboni, the most fantastic balloon blower, or Simon, the winner of the Simon Says contest. If Chestnut—Joey—can be a stand-alone title for eating hot dogs, why can't your name be the standard bearer of Cheerio stacking or having the world's longest fingernails? Whoops, that record is taken by Shridhar Chillai with 358.1 inches of nails on one hand. It took him 66 years to nail that record. He is not a one-name superstar, but still unique.

How about naming a very deep hole? There is a hole in Siberia called the Kola superdeep borehole. A one-name hole, it is 7.6 miles deep, the deepest hole in the world, named after the Kola Peninsula in Russia. The name first appeared in 1565, but the origin is still a mystery. The Russians started drilling the hole in 1970 and eventually abandoned the project in 1992, primarily because they encountered temperatures of 350 degrees Fahrenheit.

A list of mononymous people represents many categories such as religious figures, singers, and actors. For performers, having one name is a popular direction to take. Cher, Selena, Prince, and Madonna have likely improved their careers through the single-name technique. Many on the list have not come to my attention, so having one name does not necessarily bring one to universal acceptance and fame.

For me a few on the list deserve credit for historical persistence. The writer Molière—Jean Poguelin—born in 1622, qualifies. Molière was his stage name, but he was considered a star of French writers. Curiously he died from TB. He had a severe coughing spell while playing Argan, a hypochondriac, in *An Imaginary Invalid*. He hemorrhaged and died a few hours after his last performance. He was only 51.

Voltaire, also a witty French writer, was born Francois Marie Arouet in 1694. Voltaire, a vigorous crusader against bigotry, tyranny, and cruelty, had a slightly bumpy life. Known as ZoZo by his family, he had at least 178 pen names associated with his 2000 books and pamphlets. He spent 11 months in the Bastille for accusing a regent of incest with Voltaire's daughter. *Candide*, published in 1759, was acclaimed as Voltaire's best writing among his plays, nonfiction, history, and novellas. It is considered a Western canon. The Bible and the works of James, Homer, Joyce, and Socrates also fall into this elite status. Suffice it to say, Voltaire deserves to be recognized by one name.

Mozart—Wolfgang Amadeus—born in 1756, Chopin in 1810, Beethoven in 1770, and Bach in 1685 all qualify as composers who obtained that mononymous status.

Artists who reached that lofty status include Michelangelo, the Italian painter. Michelangelo di Lodovico Buonarroti Simoni, born in 1475, was also a sculptor, architect, and poet. Monet, van Gogh, Picasso, Dali, and Matisse, among others, have reached that lofty place.

The one-name giants who contributed mightily to understanding our planet would include Newton (Isaac), a friend of Voltaire, who made a monumental number of mathematical and scientific contributions. Darwin (Charles) jump-started our understanding of genetics, as did Mendel (Johann Gregor). Galileo (Galilei), who was known by his first name, was an astronomer born in 1564. Copernicus (Nicolas)—1473-1543—helped us understand the orbiting planets. Da Vinci (Leonardo, born in 1452) was another multitalented, one-named, incredibly productive gentleman who contributed to many disciplines. Columbus (Christopher), made famous by his four voyages to the New World in 1492 was of historic importance to the world.

My review of mononymous contributors has to include the Greek philosophers. Socrates, born 469 B.C. He may be best known for his Socratic method—a refutation through questioning, which allowed him to dissect the arguments of others and disprove their validity. He may have been an excellent athlete or singer but gets no credit for those activities. His student Plato, born in 427 B.C., and Plato's student Aristotle, born in 382 B.C., had no other names than the singular for which they are known. Plato was an epigramist—one who makes comments with wit and sarcasm—the Greeks' Rodney Dangerfield. Aristotle was wise in poetry, physics, and ethics, among other interests.

Many others have obtained single-name recognition from Stalin to Mandela. This story touches on the many people in history who have impacted our world, usually in a good way.

If you happen to be a dwarf, you take solace in knowing there were seven famous mononymious folks honoring literary dwarfs: Sleepy, Grumpy, Dopey, Doc, Bashful, Sneezy, and Happy. These could apply to anyone in the world unrelated to physical characteristics. As a physician I have assumed the moniker of each of the seven titles at one time or another.

May you all have the talent to perform an activity that at least your family will recognize as worthy of a single name such as a good story, a delicious dessert, or an act of generosity. Even a kind word should count.

King Colon

As a general rule, most people are born with a colon. There are a few exceptions, but if something is missing related to the colon, it is usually the anus, granted a fairly important piece of equipment. So let's assume you have a colon and an anus. How did you learn to use it? The learning curve is about as flat as sweating and peeing, not a challenge. As we mature the colon may take on a different role than originally intended. Some find a number of options to use their colon in ways that would be considered off-label by others.

Certainly, you can't fault a prison visitor for using their colon to store drugs. Terribly convenient, although not so common since that location is no longer over-looked as a drug suitcase. A bag full of cocaine that ruptures inside your colon can be terminally fatal. Carrier beware.

I suppose you have heard of men who use the colon of others and probably their own for pleasure. To some that seems odd, like using your ear canal to taste food or your navel to land a boat. To put something in your colon with all that feces and bacteria—a billion per gram—not a concept taught in Sunday school. Here is a little five-foot-long piece of intestine designed to absorb fluid, to keep us all from a constant state of diarrhea and we try to make it into a playground.

That unique anatomical arena has also been visited by an eclectic group of male toys, if you consider light bulbs and bananas toys. Most are easily extracted but occasionally a misguided missile becomes incarcerated just out of reach of the inserting participant who then must visit the local ER for assistance in removal. Particularly embarrassing when the ER nurse is your next-door neighbor and loves Facebook. But we all know disseminating such information would never occur in today's ethically challenged society. Who would share the fact that your priest had a rubber pachyderm lodged just past his hemorrhoids? My favorite insertable being the cell phone, which kept answering, "We cannot take your call at this time. Leave a message and I will call you back once I am free of this gunk I seem to be covered with at the moment."

Doctors take editorial license to place tubes in the colon on the pretense of looking for malignant polyps or a launching point for prostate biopsies, but otherwise rarely invade the territory beyond the probing finger. A finger that seems larger than the largest zucchini at Kroger's.

The word "Colon" comes from the Greek word Kolon meaning intestine. If both o's were pronounced the same way, the word would sound like cologne which would give a distorted definition to a port far from fragrant. It is bad enough that colon also became a punctuation mark. And it takes an operation to anatomically achieve a semicolon.

While in the colon region, "What has two butts and kills people? An assassin."

The colon has taken the lead when it comes to a medical answer looking for a question. A papyrus from the 14th century B.C. tells of using enemas for 20 different complaints. Hippocrates, in the 5th century B.C., treated fevers with colonics. Celsus used enemas for disorders of the body but warned of avoiding a "too hot or too cold version." Just like Celsus to be concerned about temperature, but he was not the Andrus Celsius of temperature fame born 1800 years later. Religion played a role in the popularity. Internal uncleanliness was at times considered worse than external uncleanliness. What better way to purify yourself than a quick colonic?

Apoplexy, a vague catchall for a medieval illness, was treated by the equally catchall colonic. Louis XI of the 1400s was a profound believer and required his dogs to have regular enemas. Several hundred years later, Louis XIV was a bigger fan having received 2000 enemas. He was so busy with his enema obsession that he received court functionaries while having the procedure. Not a bad idea since that would prevent our leaders from having their heads in a dark place. Louis XIV should get the enema Emmy for the world's cleanest colon.

Dr. Kellogg, of Cornflakes fame, was responsible for a resurgence of colonics, reporting in the Journal of the American Medical Association in 1917 on 40,000 cases of gastrointestinal disease treated with great success by colonic therapy.

The high colonic (HC), very popular in the early 1900s and peaked in the 1970s, is not dead. At least five locations to receive a HC are available in the Phoenix area. All have glowing ratings. "I loved my treatment; my headaches are gone." "Stacy was so nice and I have more energy since I started my colonic therapy." "Georgena makes me so welcome. The place is spotless. Highly recommend colonics if you have trouble sleeping." Consumers love to have 25 gallons of water or water with coffee or vitamin supplements flowing ever so gently into their bowels. The water may flow in but the money flows out. What better way to spend an hour? You could even be watching the Three Stooges while experiencing your colonic. I suspect a colonic has a massage-like effect. King Colonic still reigns in many kingdoms.

Medicare doesn't cover colonic therapy. The current price for this treatment is $55 to $95, but I am sure you can find a family package or "buy-one-get-one-free" deal. You could do the standard colonoscopy prep for free by having your doctor set you up for a colonoscopy, do the prep, and cancel the procedure. Those preps leave your colon clean enough to eat off of.

The good news is there are relatively few bowel perforations, secondary infections, or electrolyte imbalance issues following a colonic. Be sure to have the therapist sift through your colon contents in case you accidentally swallowed a quarter or your dentures.

We still have phrenology, palm reading, astrology, and tarot cards, but it is hard to beat a good colonic for being involved in maintaining your health.

Why doesn't insurance cover a colonic? What do they know?

The next time a suppository is recommended be sure and remove the foil. A foiled pill is a failed pill. And don't be like my neighbor who gets mixed up occasionally and switches the correct location for his hearing aid and his suppository. That alone should disqualify him from driving.

King Colon wouldn't get much press if it just did its job and stayed away from odd folks.

Boat Floating

Most people would choose to be something other than the vomit cleanup manager for a Disney roller coaster. Dangerous, boring, repetitive, trashy, or socially demeaning jobs may not float your boat. Odor-offensive jobs are definitely out there, including jobs requiring armpit sniffing to judge a deodorant's effectiveness. Also, breath smellers determine how good various breath mints and gums do a job.

But for hidden reasons, like benefits, positive vibes from management or giant vacations can make a bad job good. Maybe applause gives you satisfaction, or you may require a title and big bucks. Cooking, clowning, conning, coding, collecting, or being a caregiver, chemist, or concierge, all offer employment opportunities.

I will focus on experiences with my patients who have supported their financial health with challenging jobs. The repo guys have one of the most dangerous and exciting jobs. Sam, a recent patient in this occupation, had a woman physically confront him by trying to take his truck keys and stand in front of his truck when he tried to connect it to her car. The fact she hadn't made a car payment in five months and kept her car hidden in a neighbor's shed didn't justify repossession in this woman's thinking.

Sam had been verbally abused with regularity and shot at several times. Naturally, he tried to load the repossessed cars when nobody was around, but that was not always possible. Usually repossession requires less than five minutes to load a car if he has access to the vehicle, but a man with a gun can show up in seconds. Sam resorts to Facebook posts to help find a car.

People tend to tell more than necessary about themselves online, which allows Sam to schedule his pickups at the safest time and location.

• • •

Bill, an undercover cop, worked alone for most of his jobs. He hung out in bars or wherever somebody might sell drugs. He had to assume the personality and appearance of the bad guys and remain anonymous. He was married with children so his real name had to be carefully protected. The stress of being somebody you aren't and being consistent had to be overwhelming. He admitted the felons were mostly less than valedictorian types, and they were all suspicious and knew the law was not their friend. More than once, Bill escaped detection and likely death by his guile. Somehow he survived for ten years before retiring from this double life. Each story he told was more mind-blowing than the last. He was a church-going, gentle man who spent many hours hanging out in sleazy bars late into the night.

Roger held one of my favorite jobs as a surveillance photographer. Unlike Bill, who was in daily contact with danger, Roger gathered evidence through a telephoto lens. I saw his videos when I testified in court regarding a patient's ability to work. Roger usually captured his subjects from an unsuspicious distance, while sitting in the safety of his van. He often sat for hours waiting for his subject to perform physical activity inconsistent with his professed disabilities.

Felix, a patient told me he had severe pain after a back injury and couldn't go back to work. I couldn't judge pain in his work context, so I requested surveillance videos to see the patient in his "unwatched" environment. The cost to the company for this service pales in comparison to the price of an employee missing work for months. Felix, my so-called disabled patient, lifted 30-pound blocks while building a fence. This side job was more strenuous than his real job and was cleverly captured by the surveillance cameras. He had plenty of time to do the side job because he could not work at his much easier real job and still get paid for it.

Another patient claiming similar disabilities appeared in a second video repeatedly lifting his camper shell as he prepared for his regular camping experiences.

As an expert witness I verified the subjects were my patients and appeared capable of heavier work than they indicated in their visits to see me. My testimony didn't typically encourage these fakers to be my lifetime patients. They probably told ten of their closest friends what a jerk I was, and likely didn't reveal the facts explaining why they felt that way.

On another occasion I treated a Mafia-connected patient who was scamming the system by claiming disability. I felt my livelihood was in jeopardy, so I pushed him down the road to a group disability team. This took the heat off me and resulted in the termination of his scam without pointing the finger at a single provider.

A doctor friend of mine who had removed a patient from the disability rolls was sleeping when his house was set on fire by his disappointed patient. Doctor Wanless smelled smoke and called the fire department in time to save most of his home. Luckily the family avoided injuries.

• • •

Fire towers and the people who staff them fascinate me. At one time there were 5,000 fire tower lookouts in the U.S., now less than 300 exist. One of my patients, a forest ranger, spent many months occupying a tower. This job presented a dual threat to sanity. Nearly one hundred percent of the time, nothing happened. No smoke, no flames, no one to talk to and generally a sleeper of a job, which included a minimal salary. Yet the job could be critical to life and land.

It took a very dedicated person to vigilantly scan the surrounding forest—360 degrees, twenty-four-seven—and remain awake. Akin to watching grass grow. I think the rangers would quickly tire of this stimulation-free occupation and resort to reading or its electronic equivalent. The job would have slightly more purpose than sitting in a jail cell, but equally boring. The smokey reward was so infrequent, buttock blisters would be a serious threat. The rangers needed a whack-a-mole-like device to remind them to occasionally take a quick gaze at the green smoke-free horizon.

Edward Abbey, author of *Monkey Wrench Gang*, spent much time as a forest ranger, but it allowed him to write about his passion for saving the environment.

• • •

Long-haul truck driving is another job that has always intrigued me. Before global positioning systems were available, and the drivers were not easily trackable, some truckers could have two families, one on each side of the country. I mean two families with kids and wives and a secret. The dangers of long-haul driving are bad enough without adding the domestic retribution of having two wives. None of my patients admitted to multiple family lifestyles. The cab on the new 18-wheeler provides Four Seasons accommodations: roomy, self-contained, and fully loaded, a turtle-like chariot, nice perk for a lonely job.

The stage play, *Run for Your Wife*, about a London cabbie who had two wives simultaneously, remains the funniest play I have ever seen. After an accident the cabbie was visited by both of his wives leaving him struggling to explain the problematic situation. He tried the two-family thing in two adjacent towns, even more challenging than truck drivers with hundreds of miles between families. Like the play, most dual-marriage relationships usually end up on the rocks.

• • •

Who can forget the CB radio? In the 70s the CB was used not only by truckers, but the general public also took up the craze. CBs are still used, especially by seasoned truckers, but their use has been diminished by the cell phones. Private calls on smart phones have replaced Smokey Bear and Breaker Breaker.

Driving an 18-wheeler, turning corners in tight traffic, and backing up to a loading dock, are tricky maneuvers that require a special talent and bravado. Can you imagine dumping a load of honey or pancake syrup on the freeway?

Load limits exist for safety reasons. A maximum weight of 80,000 pounds includes the truck and trailer, but an additional 34,000 pounds can be hauled if there is a tandem. That amounts to 4,444 pounds per tire, ouch. Try missing a dog at 70 mph with a 114,000-pound load chasing you. In Australia the load limit goes up to 140,000 pounds; look out kangaroos.

• • •

Recently one of my colleagues quit medicine to drive trucks. That may have been because he lost his medical license, but he said he liked to drive long-haul. I think I will stick to surgery.

I discovered a few jobs that might not be on the high school advisor's list. People get paid to stand in line, sleep in sleep studies, push passengers into crowded subways, and retrieve golf balls from ponds. You can even get paid for removing gum from the sidewalks in New Jersey.

Many job choices provide travel, challenge, and danger. Some guys kill flies, detect lies, act like spies, cook French fries, wear a disguise, make great pies, fall from the skies, check your eyes, catch walleyes, and say goodbyes. What's in your DNA? What floats your boat?

Hair

Alopecia areata universalis is a rare condition characterized by loss of hair, I mean all hair—no hair, no hair anyplace on the body. No hidden patches under one's armpits, or growing silently out of an ear canal or sprouting from a nostril. A human without hair would be like a planet without French Fries or ice cream. No option to wear a bow in your hair or stop at a barber or beauty salon. Hirsute embellishment would be dead.

Without hair there would be no more snarls or clogged sinks. No more curling iron burns or need for a mustache brush. No need to sculpt pubic hair. No more depilation, no more lip waxing, no more pulling your hair out when upset. Is this mutation a glimpse of the future?

Hair care is big business. Americans spend between 25 and 45 billion dollars on haircuts every year. Some men pay to have a haircut every week, and others either cut their own or never cut their hair making it hard to determine average yearly cost for the haircut experience.

The average American consumer spends about $80 a year on hair products (shampoo, gels, conditioners and sprays). A recent study revealed that women pay more than men for hair products with the same ingredients: keratin, sulfates, and extra virgin oils. This price survey for head/hair items included: razor blades, shaving equipment, things to stop bleeding, curlers, curling irons, rubber bands, and hair picks; the list is endless. We are talking about your basic home hair maintenance.

Americans spend 1.4 billion dollars a year just on shampoo. CBS did a blind study to see if a professional hair stylist could tell the difference in how hair felt exposed to three differently priced shampoos. The stylist picked the most expensive as the best but pondered for several minutes between the $4 and $20 products. The consensus of professional stylists, at least in 2023, suggests you should never pay more than $6 for a regular-sized bottle of shampoo.

Each bottle of the 75 shampoo choices available in Safeway were slightly different in shape and color. All of them, from $4.99 to $19.99, address various hair conditions like dry hair. According to the labels, hair deficiencies can be eliminated by choosing the correct shampoo containing the appropriate unique chemicals.

Keratin is touted as a hair thickener. You realize the quills on a porcupine are really thick hairs. I may be wrong, but wouldn't your curly locks quill up if one were to use these keratin-containing shampoos to the extreme? That would give your partner the proverbial quill thrill. Maybe colleges should promote a high keratin diet to the coeds hoping for quills, just a little added protection on a blind date.

Most of us don't have a hair keratin meter and don't know where we stand on the scale. You could probably find out about your keratin by committing murder and leaving a swatch of hair at the scene for a crime lab to work on. It might be easier to just buy the cheap keratin shampoo if you suspect your hair problem is related to inadequate keratin levels.

Even if hair care is expensive, for many, looks are important enough to make the expense worthwhile.

What is the best type of hair? The hair that everyone strives for, the consummate hair? Readers of Vogue would say, "I want natural, glossy, seductive hair: silky, vibrant, touchable, sexy, invigorating hair with body. I would even like a little bouncy, curly, replenished hair if I have a choice." What if you are stuck with frizzy, tangled, dry, unruly, dull, brassy, weak, or thinning hair? Now we are talking serious, presuicidal hairiness.

What about too curly? If that is an issue, it means your hair shaft is too short on one side, so it bends toward the short side. If your favorite shampoo has 30-plus chemicals it should be able to fix darn near anything in the hair department, but none of the shampoos have the ability to lengthen one side of a hair; that sounds more like the solution might be a hair chiropractor.

Oily hair may be one thing you can diagnose. If you wake up every morning with an Exon Valdez-size dark spot on your pillow—think oily hair—there are fifty choices on the shelf to address that problem. Curiously many have the same 20 ingredients that are used for dry hair. Oily hair can be a good thing; it could keep your pillow from rusting. Baseball pitchers would like the easy access to an illegal substance to junk the ball.

Dull hair is a definite curse. Just the other day I realized a friend had dull hair. I say that because I am not inclined to associate with dull-haired people. There are enough folks around with shiny hair that I don't need the dull-haired folks in my circle. I know they don't mean to have dull hair, but let's face it, they probably don't vote the way I do and they have cats. There are many products available to correct this anathema so my ex-friend will be okay. I couldn't tell whether kaolin clay was the right answer or whether he should use an antioxidant product.

What does the bottle say? If you have the time or desire to spend a day reading the shampoo information on all the shampoos in your local Safeway, you might be overwhelmed with terrible maladies that can befall your hair. Many hair issues problems can stem from your parents. You may have been saddled with weak or thin hair or, heaven forbid, split ends, so sad. Alas the shelves are replete with corrective action for almost any hair problem short of a fire.

The ingredients in shampoos read like a vegetarian diet. Sea salt, kelp, peanut extract, avocados, strawberries, coconuts, egg whites, purple figs, sweet honey, yogurt, plus other edibles are found in shampoos. No bottles recommend drinking the contents, especially the shampoo with gorilla snot. I have to believe the gorillas are unhappy about their snot being in bed with muru muru and rice cream. Muru muru was listed in only one shampoo for good reason: it is made from the seeds of a rare palm tree found in the Amazon rainforest. That clearly explains why the Brazilian tribal folks have such lovely hair. I am surprised sandalwood, bamboo, and quinine made the cut.

I see the appeal of keratin, argan, kaolin, lavender oil, and aloe; they seem therapeutic. Vitamins B, E, and F are dumped into shampoos to add alphabetical protection. Sardines are high in F so be careful you don't smell fishy if you select an F-fortified shampoo. It should be pointed out that Vitamin F is not a vitamin but refers to two important fatty acids.

One shampoo contained 80 ingredients, but only three were recognizable to the average non-chemist. This shampoo gave me itching fits, probably because I was scratching my head trying to figure out why there were so many components in something that only needed jojoba, a sulfate base, and a little olive oil to make it a winner.

The common denominator, the chemical responsible for the cleaning action of shampoos, is a surfactant, including sodium laureth sulfate or ammonium laureth sulfate. These chemicals break down the bonds between hair, dirt/oil, and dead skin. They can also be absorbed and make the skin produce more oil, which leads to more shampooing and eventually dry skin and loss of hair. The "good shampoo" can end up biting us. Over-shampooing can thin the very strands we are trying to enhance. Sort of like too much exercise damages our joints.

· · ·

Here is a hair fact not widely advertised: some dandruff is caused by a scalp fungus called Malassezia, which is different from toe fungus. The possibility of a fungus is the reason dandruff-fighting shampoos contain ketoconazole. Dandruff is surprisingly associated with HIV and Parkinson's Disease, neither of which respond to antifungals. Most dandruff is dead skin and is not a disease but a natural process.

My friend Flakey has bad dandruff. His shoulders look like he walked into a blizzard, but he doesn't have an answer to his problem. He has tried 20 dandruff-reducing shampoos without success. I think he has a congenital enthusiasm to shampoo too often. He finally solved his flakey problem by always wearing a white shirt.

• • •

I haven't touched on braiding, the cost and time involved, and the difficulty of washing your hair if you go the braiding route. A cultural thing that has no place in a scientific, sophisticated piece such as this.

Let us be glad most of us have hair—not alopecia areata—and can purchase shampoos with disparate elements. We can choose multiple ways to arrange those hairs and numerous potions to apply as we see fit. We can remove hair or try to replace it with plugs or rugs. We can comb it, brush it, sell it, and dye it. Many of us will eventually lose most of it, so treat it well before you go to...a wig maybe.

65 Years Later

"My husband died from his heart bypass last August."

"That's when my husband died with lung cancer."

Comments I overheard at a recent class reunion.

When 89 disparate persons, bonded by a three-year stint of learning in the same brick building fifty-plus years earlier, gathered at a reunion; their state of health, or lack thereof, was guaranteed to be a topic of conversation.

These creaky alums gathered through the force field of several passionate classmates who spent hours and days preparing, creating, anguishing, collecting, and searching. They successfully completed the task of inviting the now scattered student bodies from the Marshalltown High School class of '56. To create a viable attendance number, they also extended the invitation list to include the alums from all ten years in the '50s. This brilliant twist allowed slightly younger and more agile minds to help with formerly "vivid" memories of those yesteryears, now faded.

To achieve a larger group, the core organizers engaged alumnae and alumni enthusiasts from all ten years and met weekly on Zoom in the planning phrase. The discussions included locating the lost souls, planning the meeting sites, and solving the dietary requirements. As is customary with this aged population, many classmates failed to respond to repeated communications, some because of incorrect addresses and others because they had a non-beating heart—always an impediment to a warm invitation. Incarceration in healthcare and assisted living facilities, where Covid had isolated many, made the attendance lower than desired. The common, unexpressed regrets were the usual: obesity, five divorces, and abject poverty, which made even short travel undoable.

When queried most of those who attended responded: to see old friends or family, to see the town hard hit by a recent tornado, and to see an old lover or maybe a wished-for lover. Many needed a tiny post-Covid excuse to travel.

The planned events included two highlight dinners, one with a mayoral presentation. The more optional, but well-attended events included visits to the old and new high schools in a traditional school bus transporting the wrinkled and shortened bodies to the halls of learning.

At the first banquet the saving grace was the large print name tags. As attendees entered, they scanned the room looking for any familiar face, especially those who had traveled a long distance and had not been back for years. The gazes quickly dropped to the chest hoping for a familiar name to appear on the shirt of a long-lost friend. Some found many and others none, likely similar to prior experiences 65 years earlier.

"Where do you live now, Beverly?"

With her hand cupped behind a dysfunctional hearing device, Beverly responded, "Say again."

"Where do you live?"

"On a farm."

"What state?"

"Right here."

"Do you have kids?"

"Did I kiss what?"

"No children."

"Did I kiss my children?"

The next couple discussed the weather, a usually safe topic as an icebreaker. John had a tree fall on his barn and kill a cow. They lost power for three days, and the barn is still not restored. Larry, from Florida, had no problem matching John, because a hurricane had deposited a boat in his living room. The BS kept piling up like a wind-driven snowdrift. Both combatants proceeded enthusiastically detailing devastation, likely matched by others in the room.

• • •

"Didn't you raise dogs or some animals a long time ago?"

"We did, but Bill lost interest, and when our son came out, Bill had a hard time. He couldn't accept a gay son. It has been a real problem because Richard was supposed to take over the business, and Bill didn't think it would work if people knew Richard was gay. You would think selling insurance would be okay, especially now; that was 25 years ago. We think Richard lives in New York.

"Our former son-in-law replaced our daughter with his teenage employee. Out of the blue. They had three kids and a big house before the divorce. Now she lives in a trailer with my two young grandkids. I sit for her and take the kids to school. She works two and a half jobs, so she is trying. So sad, she is a good girl. Her ex had two more children. One of them goes to the same school as my granddaughter.

"Bill works from home mainly because he has a bad back. Too much football. Richard played football to make his dad happy. He wasn't very good so he never got into the game unless they were ahead by 40 points. He stayed with the team through his senior year. Once he missed the bus for an out-of-town game, but the coach was good about it and kept him on the team. It wasn't his fault, he had diarrhea and was not able to get there on time; you know how that goes sometimes.

I'm glad we don't have dogs anymore; they were a lot of work and expensive. I even showed them in St. Louis once. I wish we hadn't gone; we didn't place and the airline lost the dog on the way back. Freddy our dachshund, went to Denver for a day. Bill was not happy, but Bill isn't happy much anyway."

• • •

Janice bragged to Pat about their new house. She hadn't seen Pat for 50 years and didn't know 'Pat was down on her luck.' Pat lost her husband many years ago and never went to college, plus she had rheumatoid arthritis and could barely walk. Janice went into her back-patting dialogue with no filter, including the hand gestures to bring attention to her pretentious diamond ring. It had to be four carats.

"Pat, I'm so excited to tell you about our new house. We were not going to move after the kids left, but Ray did so well in real estate that he decided to spend the kids' inheritance on a new home. We found this lot in the country that had a great view and was only five miles from town. We see deer and birds and have a pond, really nice. The only problem is mowing all that grass on four acres. Seems like Ray is on the tractor, mowing 24 hours a day. We did it right. Ray likes nice things so we have gotten into collecting art. He has a giant nude in the bedroom that is a little too much but I am getting used to it, almost. The place is ginormous, 8,000 square feet, two fireplaces which we haven't used yet, and a full basement, plus a wine room. We don't even drink wine, but maybe we should. Maybe not though, because Ray is slipping a little. Yesterday he locked the house, but left the keys inside. That is the second time he has done that, so I'm a little worried. I had to remind him not to wear flip-flops to church. You know his father had bad Alzheimer's. Anyway, we finally moved in four months ago and the house is great. I especially like the sound system. Tell me about yourself, Pat.

• • •

The conversations above didn't reflect most of of those taking place among renewed friendships. Many talked about the undefeated state championship basketball team from the year we graduated. Everybody took pride in that glorious event and placed the five starters on a pedestal, although none were present to receive their appropriate accolades. Others talked about Jean Seberg, a classmate who became a movie star at 18. She was a good actress in high school, but no one could have predicted her meteoric rise to stardom, especially at such a young age. Her premature death in Paris somehow related to the FBI investigating her and pushing her to the limit for her support of the Black Panthers.

There was a strong Iowa, Midwestern flavor to the reunion. It was piggybacked—a term likely coined in Iowa—with the annual Octoberfest celebration. This included a classic carnival with multiple rides, games, and fried food opportunities. The evening entertainment featured high-decibel bands whose parents weren't even born 65 years ago. No hearing aids were required to hear the undecipherable lyrics being drowned out by an even more boisterous drum and electric guitar combination.

The mid-day parade featured two busloads of classmates. Over 100 floats, bands, old cars, local clubs, and businesses, and many in the parade threw handfuls of candy or packages of frozen meat to the spectators. The meat was provided by the city's largest employer, JBS, a packing plant. Spiffy small-town bands from central Iowa provided nostalgic marching sounds helping to recall homecoming events from 65 years earlier.

The classmates all tried to remember a favorite teacher, a first kiss, or first beer. Memories of sock hops, soda shops, and corn crops were bantered about. They covered 65 years in two days, not bad for old-timers. Our differences, muted by the passage of time, let us return to the core—the original Midwestern roots that shaped us.

Fifty percent of the alums returned home feeling good about the experience, fifty percent felt bad, and fifty percent felt a little of both. Who knows if this unique event will have a second life?

Invention

Ideas become art, buildings, stories, movies, projects, robberies, and inventions. As a kid, I wanted to create a new language, a secret language that only a few people would understand. Something like Chinese or Russian would be good, but Chinese was definitely too pictorial, too prone to mistakes related to bad penmanship. A blip in the wrong direction could be punishable by death or worse. I relied instead heavily on the forward slash (/) as a substitute for the intentional missing part of a word. I tried leaving out part of a common word if it were obvious what was left out. I probably should have spent more time using traditional shorthand already well thought out, but doing research would detract from the idea's idea. I decided to plow ahead with my own version.

The whole thing fizzled because I didn't write enough to make it worthwhile until entering college. I then resurrected bits and pieces, but never took the shorthand to a beneficial level. I still stick in a / or two, which represents because, and x represents anything related to exit, exhibit or exist. C is a c-word like could or can. You c s l have plenty of room to expand my shorthand. F words were originally find, fund, force, fish, fleece, flip, and flub. Fornication was not a part of that shortcut. A (-) was a conjunction, a, an, but I lacked abbreviations for nouns other than skipping the vowels. It helped a little but in medical school, bwl might be bowel, or bowl. Bld could be blood or bald. Warm/worm, cat/cut, tricky without vowels, but generally medical nouns were clear sans vowels. I hurt my little t or broke my rm, lost vision in my rt y. Who needs vowels? A plggd cln, for constipation can usually be understood. A hrt attack is an MI so no problem. The idea to have a shorthand system was not a complete wst bt cls to t. (waste but close to it)

• • •

My invention idea germinated in the early days of my orthopedic practice while trying to rehabilitate ankle sprains. I made a 2x4 into a piece of exercise equipment that could be nailed to the bottom of a shoe. The purpose was to strengthen the ankle muscles. For 35 years I demonstrated to many ankle-injured patients how to make and use the device. It worked reasonably well and was dirt cheap, but lacked pizzazz. Not to mention profitability.

The next step involved making a marketable, reproducible, and safe prototype. Stability was a significant concern because if the patients were to fall while using my fantastic device, I would likely be blamed and attract a kettle (referring here to a multitude of vultures) of attorneys. I spent many hours collecting scrap metal from junkyards and visiting metal-cutting businesses observing waterjet or laser cutters. I bought plastic bars and special screws. The businesses that sold rubber parts, such as heavy mats and roofing supplies, became weekend destinations.

I eventually abandoned the metal/aluminum foot plate for a lighter clear plastic design. Bending the plastic provided a challenge because the folded plastic proved fragile and broke after a five-minute test walk. New ideas evolved, and a sturdier heel holder emerged. Multiple CAD drawings made modifications easier and allowed for automated cutting of the plastic plates.

I visited at least 20 businesses to gather the parts: metal, plastic, rubber, Velcro straps, and abrasives. The experience opened a vast new world to me. I had to avoid large trucks, forklifts and people unloading sheets of scrap metal as I walked around these shops. The lady at the roofing company thought I was crazy, looking for abrasive roofing material for an ankle exercise device—the Ankleizer.

Building the prototype was essential in determining the proper dimensions and characteristics for the patent. The patent would only be valid if it reflected the finished design. Once I had arrived at the slightly tested prototype I went for the patent. I thought I would feed my drawing to an attorney and a patent would pop out the other end five days later.

To guarantee the rapid process, I embedded myself in the ASU Law Library for several weekends to research similar devices. Half the population of Eastern Europe had a patent with similar intentions. Elaborate drawings and detailed notations filled encyclopedic pages of information about objects designed to strengthen the human ankle. The good news was no descriptions were the same as my unique design. None were even close, but I was not an expert, and left this exhaustive investigation still concerned that I may have missed a comparable product.

When I explained to the patent attorney how much time I had spent, I received a, "You need to understand how to do a search," comment. This meant several thousands of dollars would be needed to "be sure" the search was done correctly. I felt that I would have a better understanding of the competition than a lawyer, but this was my first rodeo, and I didn't want to tell the legal minds they were wrong.

In part, based on the research from my library investigation, I understood the type of patent information required. I therefore completed the application with confidence; all the bases were covered. After our second meeting my attorney indicated he was handing me off to his competent associate. The new attorney was not my choice, and he was not as experienced as the man I had engaged. The new attorney was also unfamiliar with medical devices and made several "legal" suggestions for my application. The one that caused me to doubt his ability was his recurring reference to the body part called the "heal." His word, not mine. I had to correct his spelling several times. Those suggestions required a rewrite—not free—and often his suggestions were technically wrong.

I pointed out that I submitted the correct information, and he inappropriately changed the data, which meant another rewrite and another bill. I should have been charging him because I had to do the rewrite.

It took at least eight months of ping-pong correspondence to generate a sound document. I was starting to think going to law school would have been cheaper and quicker than the route I chose.

• • •

The patent process is not mentioned in the Bible. Appreciation for the protective nature of the patent began to emerge in the eleventh century relating to Chinese gunpowder. In 1421 the Italian government granted Filippo Brunelleschi, an Italian architect and engineer, protection on his boat design. After much fuss he launched his newly designed but flawed ship, which sank on its first voyage. A short time later the city of Venice offered a ten-year protection plan for inventions made in Venice.

Queen Elizabeth the First granted 50 patents during her reign. This approach was incorporated into the U.S. Constitution giving Congress the power to legislate on property rights. The first recorded English patent appeared in 1449 protecting a method of staining glass. The first recorded U.S. patent on July 31, 1790, addressed "The Making of Pot Ash and Pear Ashes." The patent law of 1790, failed to address slaves, and when a slave in 1857 submitted a patent application it was denied. He was not a citizen nor his owner an inventor—patent denied. That all changed after the Civil War.

The number of patents has increased rapidly with the biotech and electronic industries leading the way. By 1911 the one millionth patent was issued. Recently the majority of patents have come from computer companies. In May of 2021, U.S. patent number eleven million was issued. In the year 2020, 399,055 patents were registered in the U.S. That number dropped to 346,152 in 2023. In 2023, Samsung had 8513 U.S. patents with IBM a distant second at 4,744.

Gurtej Sandhu holds the most individual patents at 1,335. There is some debate, but IBM appears the overall leader because it owns over 140,000 patents.

The patent process is very protective. If my patent overlapped with a similar device, I would not have been given one. Fortunately, my design was unique and raised no red flags.

My problem now is distribution and salability. My device is currently not covered by insurance and the unit costs are too high for the average user. Plus, I still have concerns about potential injury from using the exercise device. Bikes and skateboards get by, so I should be okay. The Ankleizer, patent number 10065068, is for real but not in mass production. The few I have made are being field tested with handpicked patients. The Ankleizer is designed to strengthen the ankle muscles, particularly in those unfortunate folks who experience recurring sprains, but it can also assist neurologically impaired patients with balance issues.

The best part of the invention trip was the trip itself. Learning about various unknown-to-me-businesses hidden in metro Phoenix provided a good GPS test. I need another excuse to tour the inner workings of my surroundings.

Additionally, I have created several surgical instruments but elected not to go through the patent process. An instrument company that produces these tools gives me a few cents in royalties. Knowing a few surgeons worldwide are benefiting from my efforts gives me satisfaction.

The place to be in the invention world is the attorney who is driving the bus. At least the Ankleizer is "*un projet achevé*," unlike my shorthand.

Pickle in a Pickle

Please be seated. Select a seat in the orchestra section of life, and I will relate the true stories of the adventures of the penis. Virtual reality glasses are unnecessary. These tales are factual experiences unique to me, being a urologist. The penis just happens to be the main character, the hero and villain, the winner and the loser.

The phallus, our star, whether long or short, is loosely attached to the lower end of the urologic system, the end of urine production and toxic elimination. This usually flaccid appendage conveniently complements the amazing human body. As the body starts to fail in later years the penis has to work more at night in a non-sexual capacity. This is not entirely the fault of the penis. Diuretics, prostate enlargement and drinking habits all contribute to this disturbing nighttime activity—nocturia. The poor penis becomes overworked if the bladder becomes inflamed or the prostate, often called the prostrate, decides to dominate the scene. The prostate grows, which is odd because everything else shrinks including the urine stream. A blocked stream can result in an unfriendly catheter. This tubing frequently adorns the nursing home crowd leading to the conversation around the home as to who has the largest leg bag or who has worn a catheter the longest. How often do you change yours? An exciting conversation with a low level of one-upmanship. I am sure that no penis is happy having to be catheterized, especially if done by a rookie.

Perry, not a nursing home resident, suffered from priapism, an erection on occasion lasting more than six hours. Almost nightly, starting at age 12, Perry awakened with a boner. He iced it, jogged, did pushups, and usually had a relatively rapid resolution of his erection.

His tumefaction was generally a giant nuisance and not of his choosing. He had sickle cell disease; a condition commonly associated with priapism.

You can also acquire priapism from rabies, hanging [by the neck], and a Brazilian wandering spider, uncommon in these parts. It is slightly embarrassing for the average guy to walk around the workplace after appearing to have overdosed on Cialis. Even a full beard and a hardy laugh will not provide enough distraction to avoid notice. Therefore, most guys will share their concerns with a doctor reasonably early in the development of such a condition.

• • •

The second aspect of the dual-purpose penis is activated by the occasional sexual thoughts men have. Look out if you use Cialis or Viagra; you too can be blessed with the big hurt if misused, which is why you hear on TV, "Call your doctor if your erection lasts more than six hours."

• • •

In some circles it is fashionable to wear a metal ring on your penis. The benefits of this jewelry are unclear. The use of such a rustic ring led Bull to visit the ER with his purple penis, the color just before black on the penis-color-progression chart. As blood is trapped by said cock-ring, the penis chokes but is not amenable to a Heimlich maneuver.

My job as a board-certified urologist covering the ER for just such intriguing events was to remove the offending ring. A ring cutter was required because the situation had gone past the grease-and go-stage. The cutter had to slide under the edge of the already strangulatingly tight ring. The process could be as uncomfortable as catching your left testicle on a barbwire fence. Bull elected to experience this challenge without anesthesia, but only briefly. The harder I tried to extricate the purple appendage the more Bull bellowed. Bull's roar in concert with him screaming "uncle" exceeded my decibel limit. We exited stage left for the OR and a silent removal—except for the nurse's laughing—of the golden ring. Bull's member, although beaten up, survived, but the ring faced early retirement. He seemed a little miffed by the whole event. His guilt may have wiped out his ability to say thank you. My reimbursement was a slightly used, highly sliced ring. I intended to give it to him when he returned to the office, but that didn't happen.

• • •

As men age, the magic wand doesn't stand up well or maybe gets a little rusty. Brigham, a man of the cloth, visited the ER a week after Bull, but Brigham's organ was stuck in a vacuum sweeper hose. Brigham was not trying to clean it. Said penis rose to the occasion. Rose so much he could not remove his Johnson from his Hoover. You would think shutting the machine off would release its catch. Six hours later he and his vacuum dropped into the ER for help. He decided wearing a vacuum around for the rest of his life was not a good image.

After several medications, plus liberal use of jellies and not-so-gentle tugging, I was able to free Willy from the Hoover. His wife had no interest in attending the delivery but was glad his willy didn't end up in the bag. She was also glad she didn't have to replace the vacuum but wasn't so sure about retaining her elongated husband. When I found out he was a big Boy Scout guy I suggested with this newfound knowledge he might create a penile extraction merit badge. Probably won't happen. I also told his wife that it would be a good idea to lock up the vacuum or hide the hose.

• • •

Jake tended to drink. He was homeless, and one cool evening, while riding on a freight car, he lost his drunken grip and fell from the train. His luck ran cold like the weather, and he landed on his head. The details were sketchy due to alcohol and the blow to his cranium. He mentioned seeing a rattlesnake in the area. What was obvious when he arrived in the ER several days later was his huge penis. It was black, blacker than Jake, a sick true black with pus draining from every side. The odor wreaked enough to be a lethal weapon. The nurses stood a considerable distance away because of the stench. Jake was near death from the infection and complained very little in his obtunded state. Presumably the rattle-snake had bitten him creating more than a penile code violation.

To save his life, his penis was removed. It was about to fall off anyway, but surgery shorted the process. Jake survived after many weeks of antibiotics and detox. The loss of his friend and temporary abstinence from drink-ing at least gave him an opportunity to ride the trains again. He promised me he would never let another rat-tlesnake bite him on the penis. Duh. He did not promise he would stop drinking.

• • •

When I first met Wan, he calmly described the reason for his ER visit. "I have a snake in there," as he pointed to his lower abdomen. I was immediately drawn to Wan because I had not had a snake-in-the-bladder patient. I had treated patients with various foreign objects in their bladders—pencils, chopsticks, nails, string— but never a snake. Wan assured me it was not a rattlesnake, but he would have to ask the man who sold it to him to learn the breed. Hospitals require so much useless informa-tion they might wish to have the snake's bar code to satisfy the medical records department. Maybe garter snakes are reimbursed by insurance companies at a higher level than king snakes.

Wan had introduced other expensive objects to his penis, but this was his first snake, something about the Chinese calendar and the year of the snake. I was glad it was not the year of the monkey. In considering which snake to buy, he used the size factor. Too big, no good, but too small, it might get away as this chap did. The sales clerk didn't offer much advice, a smooth or rough snake, short or long. Wan didn't inform him as to why he wanted the snake, but Wan will be an expert for his next purchase. He might even become a snake-in-the-bladder consultant.

After a little head-scratching, it was clear the snake was not coming out. We considered placing snake food at the end of his penis, but no one knew this unknown breed's favorites, so we abandoned that tack. I went to my proven foreign body approach, a cystoscopy. There it was, a dead whatever snake. I think Wan was upset that the snake had died, but reusable penis snakes are not in vogue. Maybe he could trade it in for a frog.

As you can see there is more to urologic life than circumcisions and nocturia. My job is to bring order to chaos, to stop dripping and limpness, and make small things larger and large things smaller. As a thespian on the stage of life, I am immersed in questionable judgments demanding my humble assistance on a daily basis.

I could relate stories of penises cut off, bitten off, or caught in machinery and yanked off, but I respect your desire not to vomit in the theater, and therefore, I bring down the curtain on the "Pickle in a Pickle."

Favorite bumper sticker: Guys, just because you have one doesn't mean you need to be one.

I hope you have enjoyed the pickle presentation.

Money

The word for money, an item of which most people wish they had more, originated from the Latin word *moneta*. There is evidence of accounting, the recording of numbers, found on a tally stick that dates back 30,000 years. Later, 20,000 years ago, numbers were discovered written on a mummified baboon thigh bone in the Democratic Republic of Congo. More recently, a mere 7,000 years ago, a document found in Mesopotamia shows lists of expenditures.

As regions started to trade goods, accounting systems developed to keep track of commodity ownership. Cowrie shells, the shells of mollusks, were the oldest and most widely circulated form of money and were used in some parts of Africa as recently as 60 years ago.

Gradually, although solid evidence is lacking, society moved away from bartering with cattle and camels, replacing them with objects assigned a value. Initially, metal objects, shells, and assorted other objects were not given a specific value. Metal pieces were used as early as 5000 BCE. Around 700 BCE Lydians from the kingdom of Lydia, now western Turkey, were the first Western culture to make coins with specific value. China and India cast coins in the same time period as the Lydian culture. The term shekel, an early currency that originated in Mesopotamia, evolved from silver and was used for payments. One shekel might be worth a pound of barley. History is unclear, but shekels came into use at a similar time as the Lydian coins.

In the good old days you could barter with animals and even vegetable goods. I bet you could buy a dishwasher for 40 carrots and a manure spreader for a bushel of beans and a cow. Not really; coins and paper currency have largely replaced bartering, a system in which the money itself is expensive to produce and has no gold or precious metal backing, yet works nicely as an orderly way to exchange goods and services throughout the world.

On occasion, some of my uninsured patients who can't pay for my services have offered me eggs, house cleaning, or a variety of other services including landscaping. I passed on the massage therapy and duct cleaning.

As the monetary system matured, different countries used different forms of metal. Mesopotamia started with copper and moved on to silver coins. Measured gold coins became the standard in Egypt. Around 100 BCE, the Chinese used one-foot square pieces of inscribed leather, which became the banknote type of currency, tough to counterfeit. That was the age of the giant billfolds and purses.

As money evolved, metal replaced shells and livestock, and eventually weighted coins of silver and gold were created with specific value. Paper money, also a Chinese idea, began in 900 CE but it then disappeared in 1455 primarily because it was associated with rapid inflation. Several centuries later paper currency gained common usage in Europe.

In 1800, shortly after the emergence of the United States, the gold standard became the accepted underpinning of U.S. currency. This meant that money, the coins and paper (after 1861) used to buy things, was backed with gold. That system eliminated the need to carry heavy hunks of gold around just to buy a soda. The price of gold per ounce determined the value of your dollar. In 1971 the U.S. went off the gold standard and the dollar is no longer backed by gold.

When the Depression led to a run on the banks, Franklin Roosevelt closed the banks and took all the gold away from everyone except the government. We now use fiat money, money given value because of a government order. There is not enough gold in the government's possession to cover the fiat money in the U.S.

or any other country. Does monopoly money come to mind?

• • •

The U.S. dollar (USD) was adopted in 1785 and paper notes in 1861. Although the U.S. dollar is the most commonly used currency worldwide, 180 different forms of money exist. For example, in addition to the dollar there are: yen, yuan, pound sterling, euro, dinar, peso, and the lesser-known kwanza, cedi, and dalasi. In Iran, if you possessed 24 USD you could convert your money to rials and be a millionaire, at least in rials. A Vietnamese dong is worth less than one U.S. cent. A U.S. dong is overvalued. A Russian ruble currently is worth two cents, which is more than I would give for all of Vladimir's ideas.

The USD is strong, but seven countries including the Cayman Islands, Oman, and Kuwait, have a favorable exchange rate to the dollar. The exchange rate changes depending on the inflation and economic conditions of the times.

• • •

Minting money has a price. To make a quarter costs 9.63 cents and a dime costs 4.39 cents. The lowly penny costs 2.1 cents to produce. Do the math, pennies are a relatively poor return on investment for the government.

The cost of printing paper money escalates as the face value increases. A one-dollar bill costs 7.5 cents per note compared to a twenty, which costs 13.8 cents.

The $10,000 bill was pulled from circulation in 1969 leaving the $100 bill as the largest bill in circulation in the U.S. Around 400 of the bigger bills still exist. The average life of a dollar bill is 3.7 years while a $20 will survive 5.1 years and a $100 lasts 8.9 years. The U.S. Bureau of Engraving and Printing located in Washington D.C. and Fort Worth, Texas, destroys around 6 billion dollars of "ugly" notes each year, money that is worn or defaced. They also print a similar amount to maintain a constant money supply. Much of the shredded paper money goes into landfills as compost used in growing food, maybe shredded wheat.

• • •

In my visits to local banks to learn how they process distressed paper money, I was surprised by how little information the tellers and other bank employees knew about procedures. My questions about what I should I do with a dog-eaten, tattered $20 bill offended the bankers. Their response from the three banks I surveyed was, "Google it." It was strange they short-changed me on customer service. "It's your dog and your problem. Ask the government what you should do. That is on you, we can't help you." Even trying to talk with an upper-echelon person was discouraged. "Who makes the call to send it off? And where does it go?" You would think the process of destroying money required a top-secret clearance. I know it is more involved than the bankers' knowledge.

One employee intercepted me in the lobby and told me banks burn the old money, which flies in the face of the known information. Maybe her way of dismissing me and not referring me to a more knowledgeable source.

In my efforts to validate the banks' process of removing damaged money from circulation, I called a customer service number hoping to learn how the banks are made whole when sending off the bills no longer fit for circulation. My question proved too complicated because I was transferred to nine different people who then moved me to a phone message that claimed they would call me back. Never happened. I did learn that Loomis, the armored truck company, is responsible for the transportation of money coming and going to the local banks, but even their employees didn't know where the damaged money was taken. Almost everyone I spoke to recommended I Google my question, but I wanted to hear it from a bank. Maybe next year.

• • •

LAUGHING IS LEGAL!

In 1913, 4 cents would have the buying power of one dollar today (2023). The 1950 dollar had the value of $10.74 in 2020 dollars, an average inflation rate of 3.45% annually since 1950.

• • •

The government does not print all the money made in the U.S. Counterfeiters produce an estimated $45 million per year. Twenties and one-hundred-dollar bills are the focus of counterfeiters, many from Peru. In 2006, 30 million U.S. dollars were confiscated in a single Peruvian bust. The Feds keep improving the quality of the bills making them more difficult to copy but also easier to detect counterfeit money.

Seven steps to the detection of counterfeit money have evolved. The physical characteristic makes a good starting point for determining the validity of all seven denominations of U.S. currency. All seven are 6.14 by 2.61 inches and 0.0042 inches thick.

The material is a special blend of 75% cotton and 25% linen, creating a distinctive feel. A discerning finger can detect a fake bill just by the texture. Twenty-dollar bills are more popular to counterfeit than 100s.

In 2013 the $100 bill was redesigned creating the most advanced protection features ever. There is a watermark visible on the right side of the bill, relatively easily seen with bright light but not obvious in regular light. Seeing this verifies you have a legitimate bill. There is also a vertical line on the left side of the bill, again observed only with a bright light. A neat feature on an authentic bill is the color-shifting ink, which allows the 100 in the right lower corner to shift from copper to green by tilting the bill. The printing on Ben Franklin's right shoulder is raised and detectable by palpation. The final and best step in identifying a fake $100 is the security ribbon, a vertical blue stripe 6mm wide. This is a hologram, and the images move from side to side as the bill is tilted. Who would have thought your money contained a hologram?

Playing with a magnifying glass and a 100-dollar bill can give you hours of entertainment while waiting for your delayed flight to depart.

Printing counterfeit money seems more challenging than going to the beach and collecting seashells when that was the currency of the day, the original shell game. The beaches must have been inundated with homeless folks and druggies looking for loose change—shells. Beachcombing jobs must have required a master's degree to be among the lucky chosen few.

The profit from printing counterfeit $100 bills is about $15 because they are sold wholesale for $20 and cost approximately $5 to produce. That is still a 300% markup.

A final piece of trivia: The ruble fell to a low of 150 versus the USD in March of 2022 but rebounded to a 61 to one ratio USD in October of 2022. In October of 2023 the ruble fell to a 97-to-1-dollar position. Maybe U.S. sanctions on the ruble are not as tough as we are led to believe, because the exchange rate was 61 before the invasion of Ukraine.

• • •

So, you now know as much about money as the average chicken, and can use this information to put your friends to sleep or win a few bucks on Jeopardy. It took us a long time to get from bartering to credit cards and bitcoins; what will the next 1000 years bring? I hope we are not left in ruble rubble.

Reflexes

So, you think you have control of your body. Try to prevent your leg from moving when your doctor strikes your patellar tendon producing what is commonly known as the knee-jerk or reflex. Carl Westphal, a German neurologist, and Wilhelm Erb simultaneously recognized the reflex phenomenon in late 1875. Westphal noted a decreased knee reflex in one of his patients and therefore received credit and naming rights for the medical relevance of reflexes. Both doctors published articles about reflexes in the same journal with slightly different stories but still highly unusual for two to report a previously unpublished finding the same day. Time has eroded this modest event—the discovery of reflexes—and like forgotten once-eminent names of schools and streets, time almost completely erased Westphal's name from medical jargon. The Westphal reflex disappeared. I believe an electronic medical record's program would reject it entirely, like a statue of Robert E. Lee or bloodletting.

I have to reflect on why Westphal or anybody would randomly tap on the Achilles tendon. First, you would not have a reflex hammer, and what physical finding would suggest a knock on the knee would assist in making a diagnosis. Do you think he struck his patient in other places first? A smack on the schnoz, a kick in the keester, and maybe a bat to the back, who knows what preceded his reflex discovery. Erb mentioned he used the flick of his index finger to produce the reflex as one would do to remove an unwanted speck from your shirt. Doctors may be at risk for being charged with patient abuse in today's litigious environment.

Reflexes tested by current medical providers include the biceps, triceps, Achilles, and brachioradialis. Eliciting these reflexes allows me to gain subtle clues about a patient, and demonstrate my thoroughness. I place my thumb on the biceps tendon and then strike my thumb. By the end of the day my thumb is purple from beating it repeatedly with my 85-year-old stone-hard rubber hammer. I should discard it but I keep it for sentimental value. About five biceps reflexes a day is all my thumb will tolerate. The hardest tendon reflex to test in heavy patients is the triceps, because the striking point is often covered with reflex-defying fat blunting the contact and therefore stifling a valiant attempt to gather information.

A reflex results from a momentary stretch of the muscle tendon alerting the brain. This immediately causes the motor nerves to fire, thereby producing a muscle contraction, which brings the foot forward. I have been victimized on several occasions by a hyper reflex, one producing a giant, ball-busting response. I have now modified my knee reflex testing position to avoid a sudden painful kick to my privates. This happens so infrequently it is easy to become complacent, but an embarrassing jolt quickly reminds me to be on my toes or at least sit in a safe place.

An abnormal reflex test will identify pathology in the spinal canal. But like a lot of things in life, it can become much more complicated. A missing right knee-jerk suggests a ruptured L-4 disc on the right side, but it could be a L-3 or L-5 disc. Or it could represent a tumor, really anything that interrupts the normal nerve function. If all the reflexes are missing it suggests diabetes, hypothyroid, or maybe nothing. It also suggests the possibility of a spinal cord tumor higher than the L-3 level. The point being, an easy-to-perform test can generate much information and many more questions.

The nice thing about reflex testing: it is not a $500, preauthorized event. Medicare loves it until the procedure suggests the need to test for thyroid disease or perform an MRI looking for a ruptured disc. Discovering a parathyroid tumor for any orthopedist is like a paleontologist finding a new dinosaur specie. Evoking an abnormal reflex can be an adrenalin rush, akin to discovering a new melanoma, or a cold leg requiring vascular surgery.

We hear of reflexes related to sports. In medicine the reflexes are graded from zero to four (small to robust). In sports, a different reflex is present, the ability to respond with a motor activity such as returning a tennis ball, ducking an errant pitch, or reacting to a badminton birdie.

The connection of the knee-jerk to athleticism is not as one would expect. More elite athletes tend to have less active knee-jerks than non-athletes. It has been shown that exercise and stretching can diminish the magnitude of a response of a knee-jerk. Passive stretching of a muscle before reflex testing can decrease the response but doesn't change the athletic ability. The athletic ability and lower reflex responses may therefore be based on exercising more than the "ability" of a given athlete. Stay tuned because the jury is still out, but at least quick responding athletic individuals don't appear to have hyperactive knee jerks. Which means calling a jock a big jerk is inaccurate.

The response-to-danger reflex has the potential for magnifying a problem or benefiting us. If you touch a hot pan, your reflex will produce a quick withdrawal of your hand, a good thing. If you happen to be on a cliff and encounter a Gila monster, as I once did, retracting your hand is appropriate, but retracting your body has deadly potential. I withdrew my hand, but not my body, thereby avoiding a game changing fall from the cliff.

If a bug or bird flies in your face, jerking your head back is the usual response, but occasionally there is a hard object like a tree limb or brick wall to stop the natural reaction. Not good. If the offending object is completely unexpected, the response is equally unscripted, the results will be unpredictable. A friend lost his balance as he settled into a slightly unstable chair. To correct his landing, he quickly swung his hand and struck an expensive vase sending it on a terminal trip to ceramic tile. Later in the evening, after performing a bit of body hyperbole explaining a point in his otherwise boring story, his gesticulation nailed a full glass of red wine, which quickly decorated the white sofa. So, in the course of 15 minutes his bull-in-a-China-shop actions made future invitations to my home less likely.

Some of the worst cases of overreaction—reflex response— to a surprise event occur while driving. The dog in the road may be followed by the avoidance swerve and subsequent occasional fatal crash. The point being we are often victims of quick reflex actions that can cause more harm than good. I have encountered this response on the ski slopes when an out-of-control skier suddenly headed toward me and I have, without preparation, made a turn to avoid the crash. Meeting a ponderosa is less pleasant than meeting a 120-pound skier, but the period to analyze the option is usually brief or non-existent resulting in a bad choice. My most common choice when encountering a runaway skier is to simply fold my tent and hit the ground, often in the middle of several other skiers.

Twenty years ago my 92-year-old father stepped into my sister's van as his grandson slammed the sliding door, capturing my father's thumb against the frame. He jerked his hand back in response to the searing pain. By doing so he ripped off the tip of his thumb; a common occurrence to hands captured by car doors worldwide. We were on our way to a festive Christmas dinner with the entire family. My father felt sadness for delaying the meal, more than by the loss of his thumb tip. He likely would have experienced a lesser injury had he let his entrapped thumb remain entrapped, but who has the forethought to do other than jerk it out of harm's way? The body's reflex dictated he escape and not worry about the prime rib dinner he may miss.

Reflexes come in many shapes and sizes; my favorite is still the knee-reflex with my ancient hammer. Yours may be gagging when the dentist tries to water board you when cleaning your teeth. Just be careful that when driving you don't let a wayward kitty cause you to litter the shoulder by a reflex-driven sudden change in direction.

Hand Versus Foot Combat

As a physician I have witnessed the results of many apparent hand-foot battles. A fast-draw competitor shoots himself in the foot; a soldier on duty duplicates the mistake. The hand being the originator of these injuries with a gun, even a nail gun or hatchet-like device. The foot may be too small a target; the thigh or calf may also accept an unanticipated attack from say a case of beer. I witnessed a fellow Boy Scout carom an ax off a log he tried to split. The ax wound up buried in his tibia. He referred to the event as an *axident.* The ax remained embedded in his leg until I jerked it free, but not free from pain.

In recent years my own body has been victimized by an internal war between the extremities. I am unaware of any animosity these body parts may harbor, but there may have been words exchanged of which I am oblivious. Whatever the provoking incident, my legs have started to terrorize my arms—and particularly the hands.

The first attack came on a beautiful summer's day in Kauai. Clouds passed after a brief, air-cleansing thunderstorm earlier in the day. The afternoon sun warmed the three of us—my son-in-law, granddaughter, and me—as we began our hike. Not familiar with the area, we followed our map to the trailhead. No other vehicles were parked in the area, making me apprehensive about our selection.

The guidebook stated our hiking choice to be picturesque and moderately difficult. The trail was adequately identified giving me comfort that the book was not outdated. The flat open trail quickly morphed into a tropical forest with thick wet foliage obscuring the thin trail. Single file hiking, the only option, and roller coaster elevation changes were the rule. We dipped down to cross a stream and rose again on the side of a deep canyon. Our view was mostly of the immediate greenery, not the beautiful vista, because we needed to concentrate on the ground to secure solid footing. The rain left many parts of the trail muddy and slippery. We paused frequently to take in the canyon view, which opened when the trail turned along the mountain edge. The sloppy, slippery slope of the terrain seemed to invite us to go overboard—into the canyon below.

I spotted a glittering rain-enhanced spider web, but lamented the absence of wildlife: no birds, not even rodents.

When I led the troops on a relatively flat path, still hidden by the dense foliage, the trail became even narrower. I accidentally stepped where was no trail and tumbled over the edge. Falling into a tenacious, stickery bush was the only thing that saved me from descending several hundred feet down the side of the canyon. Fortunately, the unfriendly brambly bush extended my hiking career.

Because I fell just a few feet off the trail my son-in-law was able to pull me to safety. The bush/tree had autographed a generous part of my upper body. The two-inch long needles, although life-saving, produced more blood than the usual blood donation. We finished the hike with a detour back to the car, exercising caution to avoid another cliffhanger.

I blamed my legs for insubordination, particularly for attacking my arms and hands. My legs were not scratched in the least, despite wearing shorts.

Three days later a previously planned, well-traveled hike became my challenge. This time five family members accompanied me. A family shield, if you will, to protect me from cliffs and canyons. This time the trail parking lot was full, and some hikers had to walk almost a mile to get to the trailhead. Our driver let us out at the starting point to avoid the extra walk because we were going on a five or six-hour fairly steep climb. I hiked about twenty minutes when I realized my water bottles were still in the car. My athletic young grandson volunteered to bail me out and he returned to join us after collecting my water. The rest of us kept walking to avoid nightfall, but the fleetfooted lad caught up in less than 40 minutes, covering the steep trail in record time. Because we started later in the day than planned and wanted to see the prize—a waterfall at the end of the trail—we had to maintain a brisk pace.

We came to a helipad about a third of the way up the trail. The number of hikers who try to do the hike and have no business on the trail led to the installation of a rescue pad. A double-sized hiker waited for just such a lift back to the base.

We sped by this area but then encountered a series of water crossings. If I had been 50 years younger, I probably could have crossed each spot by stepping across the fast-moving water on dry boulders and partially submerged rocks, but I wasn't comfortable with that approach. I didn't particularly like my choice either because I waded across each stream, stepping on the slippery hidden rocks in the almost waist-deep water. I passed each test with colors; I wasn't flying, however.

Once again on dry land we sped along to avoid a night hike when out of the ground a rigid root suddenly arose in my path. The toes of my boot caught under the inconsiderate root, and I crashed to the earth in a nanosecond. I landed face first on my left long finger splitting it open and leaving me peering at my flexor tendon. We rinsed the wound with a little drinking water and I pulled out some tape to close the opening on the palm side of my finger.

With one hand wrapped over a towel balled in my palm to stop the bleeding and provide comfort, we continued hiking with renewed enthusiasm. At times the trail required two hands to grasp rocks or branches, but my daughter provided the essential help to traverse tricky spots because I was one-handed.

We reached the end, the pool and stunning waterfall, but the lateness of the hour allowed us only a brief swim before returning. As we descended, we encountered no other hikers, which meant we were late in the day to be so far from our car. After completing the last stream crossing, I noticed one of my hiking boots had a floppy sole. Within a few minutes the bottom of the left hiking boot fell off. The remaining sole of the boot consisted of a thin fabric liner, equivalent to a thick sock. This would have been a tolerable arrangement if the trail were soft and flat, but the trail was generally rocky and rough. Within 15 minutes the scenario repeated itself when the sole of my right boot experienced a similar departure. Now I was left with two vulnerable feet.

My feet had punished my hand with the clumsy fall hours earlier. Was this sole departure revenge from my injured finger? I will never know. The next hour of hiking was miserable. I'm sure it would have been no challenge for a caveman, but a Cro-Magnon, I was not. We passed the helipad a few minutes after I lost my second sole, but I declined to wait for an airlift.

We reached the start of the trail just as the sun slipped into the ocean. Thirty minutes later I gave my dirty, injured finger a more thorough rinsing at the McDonald's while waiting for my food order. I wasn't happy with the foot/hand war going on, but I had an exciting hike with my family and enjoyed an iconic waterfall.

• • •

My most recent fall—again, the responsible and guilty party being my own incapable legs—occurred at Papago Park, 15 minutes from my home. I was trekking, actually more correctly stumbling, up a steep incline trying to keep up with my teenage grandsons. The trail was unclear, unfriendly, and unfortunate, at least for me. Rather than selecting a safer, indirect route, I charged up a steeper path, the one with the loose rocks and unstable footing. My legs failed to cooperate. I teetered momentarily on my lead leg before realizing *up* was not happening. My trailing leg was ill-positioned on loose gravel to give the required support.

Blindly falling back, I dropped like a fallen oak. In the half second before landing, my thoughts covered an encyclopedia of possibilities: starting with an ensuing concussion, multiple fractures, need for dental repairs, time lost from work, unsigned will on the kitchen table, and who would drive home if that was an option. This was no cliff, just a 40-degree incline, which did not include a soft-landing zone. I would have preferred the Hudson River, Sullenberger style, to the jagged rocks I was about to encounter. I tried to protect my head but really had no choice but to land where God was casting me. *If I died at least I beat Covid.*

The last bounce resulted in a rock firmly impacting my temple. *I am still conscious.* I pulled my right arm out from beneath my chest to see a mud-covered bleeding area of exposed tendons on the back of my right wrist—also my dominant hand. *At least the injury would not affect wearing a watch.* My grandkids, farther up the trail, returned to help when they heard my profane assessment of my landing. A concerned family hiking behind me quickly rendered assistance. They helped me to my feet and washed the mud and gravel from my bloody arm. Their little girl asked why I wasn't crying. I responded with a, "Thank you for caring." I was busy with other emotions: anger for going too fast, for not bringing gloves, but elation for not breaking my neck or splitting my head open. As the saying goes, "I was happier than a two-peckered goat."

The couple helping me held my good arm while I elevated my bloody one. They treated me as if I were an intoxicated mental midget. After all I didn't have enough sense to walk uphill without falling. They offered more medical advice than the Mayo Clinic website. "We will call 911. You will need tetanus. Are you on a blood thinner?" Mentioning I was a doctor and had war experience never occurred to me. They were very friendly and handed me off to the rest of my family.

I spent the next six hours in the hospital ER as my injuries were addressed. A plastic surgeon tried to patch up the large wound on my arm, but I left too much skin on the rocks. At least he covered most of the exposed tendons. I would not know the conclusion of this story for many months.

· · ·

It appears my feet won this war against my hands. I hope for a truce soon.

I hate it when there is conflict.

Addendum: Everything healed up. My scars have stretched and my hands and mind function as if nothing had happened. However, my hikes are now less risky.

Cats Plus

My patients provide me with hard-to-believe stories like the hummingbird-catching cat. You say no way a cat can catch a hummingbird. Maude's cat Chance would regularly catch hummingbirds and bring them into the house alive. Maude opened a window and darkened the house to encourage their egress—not to be confused with egrets. The cat had the Golden Retriever gene; he also captured ground squirrels, bunnies, and lizards, all equally alive when delivered to his not-so-grateful owner. She painted the tails of the captured ground squirrels with different colors for easy identification and then took them for a ride to distant locations. If a pink-tailed squirrel reappeared, Maude knew where it had been taken. Its next ride was to a more remote port. She had painted the tails of a dozen such captives, many of whom returned for their second capture and more distant release. The other critters were not decorated as were the colorful ground squirrels.

The cat deposited a lizard on the sofa, but it quickly sought a hiding place. Chance stood nearby with a slowly swishing tail to alert Maude that something was worth her attention. Maude cautiously played the "Find an Animal Game" until locating a nine-inch-long, black, nonlethal lizard buried under the cushion.

Chance the clever, capturing, pertinacious cat was clearly no ordinary feline. She was in Maude's will, which contradicts the adage "Don't leave anything to chance."

• • •

While visiting a friend north of Toronto, I was awakened in the night by what sounded like a dish meeting its demise.

My host and I gathered in the kitchen at midnight to investigate. He suspected the noise came from a broken plate that had been knocked from the shelf by a determined raccoon trying to remove a stick of butter. The raccoon was clever enough to open the unlocked but closed kitchen door and the cupboard and then snatch the large butter stick, usually without the broken plate as a giveaway. He always made a hasty exit with butter in tow.

• • •

My vegetarian friend's TV suddenly stopped working without explanation. The problem was not the TV set, but a cable difficulty not shared by his neighbors. The cable company's troubleshooter correctly identified the two ends of the TV cable. A cable that had been neatly gnawed in two by roof rats. Some cables have soy insulation which is tasty. But rats will also chew on wires to keep their teeth from overgrowing. The rats' motives for the disruption were never revealed.

My friend's wife and daughter were very strong animal rights advocates and didn't allow any resolution of the chewing issue by injury or death of the rats. No poison, no death traps—only a high-pitched sound wave that could deter the rats was acceptable, but barely. Initially the high-frequency noise didn't seem to work; eventually the rats left but only after several more cable outages. The animal versus television conflict sounded as challenging as a neighbor's barking dog, a problem not easily resolved.

Following the resolution of my friend's rat problem, a rattlesnake visited his laundry room. It was discovered one morning by the family's barking dog. Again, animal rights prevailed and the hoe was set aside while the family waited for the animal rescue team to arrive. The snake was a friendly, non-aggressive rattler, happy to rest under the washing machine. If she had not been wearing a tail rattle, she may have become a permanent house guest. But she was and therefore wasn't staying. The snake was around long enough to be named—No—Biz. Amana Mama was their second choice. Because she departed fairly quickly, the name thing was of little consequence.

. . .

My sister had raised her pet hamster, Harry, for almost a year. In her attempt to show the talented rodent off during my family's visit, she released Harry from his cage into the hands of my son, Brad. Harry's freedom had never been a concern before, but he became spooked, jumped from Brad's grasp, and raced toward a crack at the corner of the cupboard. My son barely grabbed a hind leg, but Harry wriggled loose and slid into Hamster Kingdom. My sister, who loved Harry and spoke a little hamstereez, was unable to coax him out of his kingdom. He scratched around in the kitchen area for a day or two and then was heard in the back of the house. After the fourth day the scratching stopped, suggesting the end of Harry. We tried food and water near the departure hole, which obviously was futile. We hope he escaped the kingdom through an undetected hamster-size opening in the back of the house and is now living a happy dog-free lifestyle somewhere in California. My sister's dog will miss Harry's presence.

. . .

I was lucky to have a monkey invasion of my tent while on an African photo safari. The monkeys were unhappy to see me return to my quarters since they had not finished eating my snack stash. Because I inappropriately entered my tent without knocking, the monkeys became flagimagusosed, which loosely means they pissed and shit all over my bed and clothes. They covered the tent like motorcycles in the globe of death, bouncing off the walls and ceiling and chair and beds with high-octane screaming in monkey talk. Both of the visitors finally left, but only after creating a monkey mess. Monkey pee, monkey doo-doo, all over every exposed item.

. . .

While attending my parents' 50th wedding anniversary party at a lake resort in Minnesota, a bat visited our cabin. Bats to me mean rabies in the air. I respect animals but I had no desire to have anyone in my family hallucinate or have a cardiac arrest from rabies. So, after making everyone leave the cabin and inviting the bat to do likewise, it came down to the bat and me. My most scientific bat-defeating tool was a tennis racket. Bats have an incredible radar system and can change direction with warp speed. I didn't wish to upset the bat and encourage a direct attack on me. I'd left my bat-proof body armor at home, along with the directions on bat combat. I was on my own. I tried my forehand and backhand with equally anemic success. I almost took out the overhead light but could not connect with the elusive bat. I studied the erratic flight pattern and eventually nailed him with a top-spin forehand, ending the celebratory evening with a stunned bat. No doubt he survived because he picked his plucky self up after being dispensed to the outdoors and flew away.

• • •

When serving as a doctor in the Army at Fort Polk, Louisiana, I moonlighted in Converse, a town about 50 miles north of Fort Polk. The town consisted of 300 people, mostly poor, black, and unemployed The Converse hospital was very small, only 10 beds and one OR. Moonlighting involves trying to make a few bucks outside of your military job. For doctors at Fort Polk there were only a few moonlighting opportunities close to the base. I had no staff and couldn't process insurance claims, meaning cash only. My advertising budget was small, zero. The positive feature was a free building situated near the hospital, which anybody could use. This building had at one time housed a viable medical clinic but persisted as an abandoned unlocked wooden structure with four rooms and only one chair. I don't think there was electricity, which didn't matter because I only visited in the daytime and had no electrical equipment. A fan would have been nice, but I didn't work there long enough to bring in any improvements.

An uninvited visitor—a roadrunner—complicated my second moonlighting trip. A small broken window pane may have allowed the intrusion but was not likely to be her exit route. A broom, my best and only weapon, proved ineffective as an extraction device. The bird seemed obsessed with her domain and a broom-wielding doctor was not about to evict her. She flew in roadrunner fashion at me and around me and simply had no inclination to leave through the building's only door, which I had propped open for her benefit. I tried screaming in an agitated voice, singing roadrunner love songs, and ignoring her. All worked equally poorly.

I was concerned the patients would be frightened if they encountered the unhappy bird. Finally, I left the building and went across the street to the hospital for coffee. In my absence the roadrunner departed. Turned out the bird was the only visitor I saw that beautiful cool spring day—also my last trip to Converse.

• • •

I haven't mentioned cows, pythons, bears and even elephants that have entered homes around the world.

I will add a note about a do-it-yourself friend who tried to do all the work himself in building a swimming pool. To bring in equipment he had to tear down a fence or hoist a Caterpillar backhoe over his house. He chose the latter and rented the crane and backhoe.

Now I admit this is a stretch to call this crane an animal invasion, but as he slowly maneuvered the heavy equipment over the house the crane tipped. He dropped the "Cat" (Caterpillar) through the roof and into his kitchen. The house repairs were far greater than the savings he anticipated by building his own pool. This was particularly embarrassing because the neighbors had all gathered in the street to watch what they anticipated—another mishap by their mishap-prone neighbor.

These personal experiences highlight my exposure to uninvited animals entering homes where they don't belong, though I avoided the "Cat" invasion.

Cruising

efore my flight left Phoenix for an Adriatic cruise starting in Venice, I wandered over to the water bottle-filling fountain. The traditional yellow sign indicating maintenance blocked the side-by-side drinking fountain and bottle filler. A cleaning lady was methodically spraying and polishing the fountain and chatting with someone on her cell phone. I started toward the bottle filler dispenser and was brusquely told I would have to wait until she finished. Being in no rush I stepped back a few feet and waited for her to complete her job. She maintained "back-to-me" control. She continued polishing and repolishing the same area on the fountain and persisted with her conversation. I waited over 15 minutes and saw no evidence she would be done by the next day. She knew I stood waiting, but did not allow me to fill my bottle. Granted I could have been more aggressive and filled it, especially since the drinking fountain held her attention. She was a nondiscriminatory rejector, denying fountain access to all races, sizes, ages, and sexes equally. I suspect the chrome has been completely removed from the fountain. Maybe she was responsible for only one fountain. Her stout construction made me reluctant to challenge her authoritarian commands. Strange. Her behavior starkly contrasted to the cruise ship crew I met a few days later, who were super friendly and helpful.

Cruising is an expensive way to acquire Covid, get mugged, or miss the bus back to the ship. Having recently completed a ten-day cruise with my family, the sounds and smells of the trip are still fresh.

We had planned an extra day in Venice before the cruise began. However, our connecting flight from

Atlanta was delayed for mechanical reasons, but it still looked hopeful for a later departure the same day as scheduled. No luck; someone had jacked open an overhead bin and pulled it off the track. Three maintenance men labored for 40 minutes and finally repaired the bin. This added delay meant the crew could not fly because of time constraints for the pilots. Two hundred disappointed flyers deplaned. The mile-long walk to the international terminal at midnight took forever, then another 25-minute Uber ride to the designated hotel. Fortunately, we didn't have to pick up our luggage. When we reboarded the following day, we waited another 30 minutes for the bags to be reloaded. You would think a Big Boy Airlines that had all day to load could have figured out how to avoid what was now the third delay.

I shouldn't complain; another couple on our cruise experienced a three-day delay and arrived in Venice to board the ship ten minutes before the final call. A second couple also had a flight cancellation but made it to Venice on the anticipated day. However, they have yet to receive their luggage and still don't know where it is. They went shopping in Venice, hopefully at the expense of the airlines. The airlines are understaffed like many businesses, but if you have saved up your whole life for a dream vacation it is hard to laugh it off when defugalties occur. Such is the travel and cruise business.

Every time I visit Europe, I realize how young America is. America has never had an abundance of castles or ancient churches. We have never been affected by the Crusades or invaded by the Ottoman Empire. America even skipped walled cities. Unlike in Santorini, pirates have not threatened our citizens. Learning the ups and downs of ancient civilizations and seeing Russia act today in a way typical of the old bully empires makes me wonder if anything has changed.

Cruises are big business. Before Covid, 24 million people were cruising each year. Ocean cruise ships range from 147 passengers for a National Geographic vessel to the Royal Caribbean's Symphony of the Seas with 6,988 possible passengers. My family sailed on a

Viking ship with 1,000 other passengers and 474 crew members. Carnival Line has 24 ships, but is surpassed by Royal Caribbean with 25. However, under Carnival's ownership are 10 brands of cruise ships, such as Holland America and Princess. The total number of ships owned by Carnival corporate is over 100. Carnival is a British-American enterprise. Viking Cruise Line is independent and includes river and ocean ships. China also has a cruise ship line operated by Viking Line. Viking Cruise's primary owner is Torstein Hagen, a Norwegian billionaire.

Although the U.S. is involved in the cruise industry, none of the ships have been constructed in the ship-yards of the United States. Italy, Germany or South Korea build most cruise ships.

The Adriatic cruise we took offered port stops and adventure tours in eight different cities No one under 18 was allowed on this trip, unlike a Disney cruise, which is designed primarily for families with kids.

Slovenia, our first stop after departing from Venice, provided several good tour options. I had selected a walking tour of Ljubljana, which turned out to be a scorching day. We walked across a bridge over the Ljubljana River that held hundreds of locked padlocks placed there by newlyweds who threw the keys into the river to create symbolic permanency to their union. The bridge became so overloaded with locks they had to be removed for fear of the bridge collapsing.

Our tour group took a glass-covered boat trip down the river. Unfortunately, one unshaded-Canadian lady experienced heat stroke, but the rest of us were also close to being fried.

Debi and John—our daughter and son-in-law—were smart; they chose a hike into the world-famous Postoj-na cave, which claimed to be one of the longest caves in the world—15 miles. The temperature in the cave was 46 degrees, which meant they were under-dressed. They were freezing while I was melting just 20 miles away.

This cave is home to the olm, a unique blind sala-mander. These critters are extremely rare, and not found in a zoo or any place outside of the cave. They live to be 100 years old and can go years without eating. Part of the cave is lighted, which creates a threat to the olms.

The next port, Zadar, Croatia, offered a hike in the Paklenica National Park. The hiking trail in this popular canyon was steep and slippery. The mules and hiking traffic had polished the trail of large rocks to create unpredictable footing. On several occasions my 21-year-old grandson kept me vertical as I tried to negotiate the ice-like slipperiness. As I struggled to stay upright, we observed a couple of rock climbers hanging from the side of the canyon, El Capitanesque, several thousand feet above us.

The narrow canyon would not accommodate a "washroom," so the park service had carved a hole into the side of the mountain and created one.

When I return to Croatia, I will pick a less strenuous hike that provides a view of the many waterfalls. Months later two sore toes remind me of the steep trail.

When we docked in Dubrovnik, it was imperative to explore the old walled city and walk around the top of the city wall. I was amazed how many tourists paid $38 to walk up many narrow steps in 95-degree heat. The view from the top made it almost worthwhile. The city's high walls prevented the Ottoman Empire from ever conquering Dubrovnik.

Part of my group—not including me—went for a more leisurely and cooler venue at a vineyard. Near the vineyard they observed the harvesting of oysters and mussels, consumed as part of their fine wine dinner. I would suggest the unique old town trip as a better option even though the dense crowds made it more of a Covid risk.

The port of Montenegro provided a nail-biting bus ride up the mountain next to the coast. If the bus had slipped over the edge there would be no story. The museum visit and information provided the common theme of nobility staying with nobility. A princess from one country would marry nobility from another. Even with the transportation challenges of the 16th century nobles found a way to continue mating with other nobles.

The cruise ship sailed farther south bringing us to Corfu, a Greek island. My side trip choice was a bike ride, advertised as difficult. Considering I hadn't ridden a bicycle in 50 years and was not informed as to the challenges the route might bring, I hoped having my family involved would help if I had a problem. After all, the ship was mostly older tourists who were not likely to choose a challenging ride. I mastered the brakes early on, but had trouble with the shifting levers, which required the use of both hands or at least I thought it did. The guides insisted I raise my seat to the point that I could not reach the ground without getting off the seat. The first mile of the ride was on a busy street. I never knew when a parked car's doors would pop open and force me to quickly swerve into fast-flowing traffic. Blaring horns were not therapeutic when I was trying to shift, brake, avoid parked cars, and stay on the bike. Once the bikers reached the corner—and waited for me to catchup—we were escorted across the busy street. I realized why it was advertised as difficult. I had made a tactical error.

The foreboding road went directly up a mountain with what seemed at least a 20-degree grade. I was already exhausted and hadn't anticipated the challenging climb. I also noticed that the next oldest rider was probably my daughter at 57, who rides 50 miles a day. The trail car mercifully picked me up for the remainder of the trip. I enjoyed the ride and the scenery. I would get my exercise with a sit-up or two, but there was no way I could have pedaled up that incline.

After a snack break one of the slower riders lost contact with the pack. The lead guide eventually realized someone was missing and notified my driver, now tasked with finding the lost lady and directing her to the correct route. Eventually we went back to the road most likely to have a lost rider, and found the poor lady blissfully pumping away, unaware she was off course. The biker now had an additional mile to ride before catching up with the group but she was no longer lost. The slower rider initially made a wrong turn but no one was behind her to correct the situation At least she kept up better than I did.

The second Greek stop we visited was Olympia, the home of the original Olympics in 776 BCE. Walking in the spot where ancient Greek athletes competed brought back memories of my high school track experiences and my visit to the Los Angeles Olympics in 1984. Old columns from the original structures remain or have been restored. Stones making up the tall pillars were attached with a connecting plug that provided a shock absorber mechanism to guard against earthquakes, a common event on the Greek islands. The site is vulnerable and continues to experience the effects of Teutonic plate activity.

Skiing, synchronized swimming and skateboarding were not included in those early venues. Future Olympics will likely add computer hacking and space shuttling as signature events.

Santorini, our next stop, was an island formed from a massive volcanic eruption. The original land disappeared at the eruption and continues to subside below the water surface but left Santorini high, and for the moment, dry.

The early Santorini inhabitants were cave dwellers, and the original caves persist. Supposedly a farmer gave his son rights to many caves, which at the time were not considered valuable. His 60 plus caves recently became highly desirable even though they are small and often without water. Many cave homes with a total space of 600 square feet now sell for several million each. The views are lovely but is it worth it when you have to walk through your neighbor's property to get to your house?

Santorini has no fresh water from wells, rivers, or lakes. The water is produced by desalination.

In 1976 electricity came to the island. If you owned a church, as many did as a status symbol, you were given the first option to have electricity. The private churches were next to the owners' homes and pirating the electricity from the churches was easy. Now everyone has access to electricity. Sounds like a political decision originally. The many blue-domed churches give Santorini its unique personality. The mules scattered about the city add their own flavor to the landscape.

Cruise passengers generally depart the city and narrow streets by cable cars rather than walking down 800 steps and competing with donkey piss and other deposits. Those who took the walk regretted their decision because the donkeys blocked the walled path, making it a challenge to pass when on the piss-poop pathway. Plus, it was 95 degrees. I reluctantly rode the cable car to keep my family happy, even though we stood in an unshaded line for 40 minutes waiting for a ride.

Santorini is one of the islands where the pirate threats were significant and consequently the citizens moved to the top of the cliffs to live in the caves and avoid the pirate invasions. The narrow streets and crowded walkways caused our guide to offer advice about modern-day pirates—the pickpockets. I heard of no incidences of pickpocket success on this trip, but I have talked with my friends who were victims. They related bump-and-run team tactics and how quickly theft unfolds with no chance to recover your purse or valuables. Tourist beware. The cruise line does not supply a Taser, although a few rentable models should be available.

We concluded our adventure in Athens. Part of our group, my wife Marilyn, John, and I, took the standard tour, including visiting the archeological museum. We learned the nude statues of men could be dated by which foot was in front of the other and if they had long hair or short. Women statues were generally clothed except for Aphrodite, who retained modest coverage. But not Zeus; he was in Jaybird mode.

My recollection of the Mycenaean culture was awakened by the museum's displays of the old city replicating a culture lasting from 1620 to 1200 BCE. The artifacts in the museum provided evidence of an advanced society. There really was no awakening because I don't remember ever reading about Mycenaeans. Now I have a second word to go with paean—a rare word containing an "aea" sequence. I hope to research this advanced culture after completing my study of the olm.

Those travelers who took other tours focused on the Acropolis or other historic sites may have received more information, but my muddled brain can retain only a small amount of trivia. I will not apply for Jeopardy.

My grandchildren, Kathryn and Jeff, enjoyed being gastronomes by going on the excursions, which included collecting oysters and mussels, then truffle hunting, and being forced to have wine with a truffle pasta meal. Another meal on board included escargot. The grandchildren probably drank more wine in one week than their entire earthly consumption. Jeff also came down with Covid with two days left on the trip. A two-day quarantine resulted. Room service continued to provide gastrointestinal rewards.

The final meal of the cruise was *prix fixe*. That brought in the palate cleaners, which might have been the favorite offering. The first course consisted of a tiny potato chip and several creamy drops of an unknown unique flavor. My taste buds had so little to work from they missed the whole chip experience.

The flight home, a 24-hour odyssey, included a mile walk in Chicago to collect and recheck our luggage with only an insufficient 70-minute time interval. Fortunately, the connecting flight was delayed, so we made it home almost as scheduled.

If the cruise brochure states the ship tour is an easy hike, it will be uphill, into the wind, and twice as long as stated. The closest W.C. is a buck; the free ones are a mile away. Any seat you occupy when you board a tour bus is yours for the rest of the day. There will be no scales in your room. By the end of a ten-day cruise, you will have lost your room key at least twice but will likely know aft from forward and stern from bow. A knot is 1.15 mph. Port is left and starboard is right. Finding the dining room will always be challenging.

My sore throat developed on the plane and was the precursor to full-blown Covid with a positive test 24 hours after we returned. My timing was perfect, but my body didn't enjoy the Covid as much as the wonderful family cruise.

Improv 101

A casual stroll through the emergency room, now known as the ED, provides pure, free entertainment. While waiting for the OR to open my surgical case, I lingered in the ED, glancing at the open bays and chatting with the consumers of the best health care in the world. Some bled, others vomited. Moaning and groaning added to the cacophony of unhappiness.

I paused when I saw Jack, a physician friend whose right shoeless foot was pointing in a north-by-northeast direction, far beyond the normal range. He had been riding his wife's horse, at least until it reared and fell backward, landing on Jack's foot. All was well until the horse rolled over to establish verticality, pinning his leg beneath the Appaloosa and the rocks. His fancy alligator boots were insufficient protection to prevent the fatal twist that cranked his foot into a previously unattainable shape. His wife, a nurse, somehow removed the tight-fitting boot off a painful, unstable foot: a procedure that posed more than a cobbler's challenge. Forget the fact that he and the horse had to get back to civilization before he could come to the hospital to share his sorry tale.

After a brief hello and why are you here, a slightly redundant question after seeing his deformity, I said something like, "Do you mind?" My compassion leaped ahead of political and medical correctness as I grasped his foot in a diagnostic ruse and quickly reduced the subtalar dislocation. From a medical standpoint this was the right thing to do because the foot was blue and the circulation compromised. Jack had been x-rayed prior to my arrival; so I was not treating an unknown diagnosis, although I admit I hadn't yet seen the films.

Once the reduction was accomplished, the color reappeared, and the pain abated, followed by a smile of relief. The brief moment of discomfort associated with the reduction produced a slight "ah" from my appreciative friend.

Technically he never asked for my help and he wasn't really my responsibility. Plus, no permit was signed and for all I know he didn't desire my assistance. No billing took place. Because I knew him well, I presumed my unofficial treatment would go down as a positive move.

If I had not been wandering about the area and the curtain had not been ajar, he would have likely waited for several hours for help. Then an orthopedist would have been called and who knows what might have occurred; he may have lost his foot. In those days the ED doctor would not have treated him until the radiologist read the x-rays and his insurance checked to see who was eligible to treat the patient. Somewhere during the stay the lucky patient would receive an IV. Don't forget the necessary family history to make sure the patient didn't have a genetic tendency for a subtalar dislocation and that his flu shots were up to date.

The results justified my impromptu action and all parties were happy. If we had not been friends and comfortable with our knowledge of such issues, I would have had to follow the "protocol," counterproductive on several levels. I checked on Jack later; his care reverted back to the emergency room doctor who saw him after his problem was resolved. Jack did well in the follow-up but never rode his wife's horse again.

I continued through the department primed for more instant resolution opportunities. A bed or two away from Jack was a one-armed man with an infection in his remaining arm. Rocky, an IV drug user, previously lost his left arm from the elbow down when it became infected from using contaminated needles. Obviously, lesson not learned, because he now had an infection in his right arm. The area surrounding the injection site was swollen and draining pus. I asked how he could inject the drugs without a second hand.

"I draw the heroin into the syringe with my good arm and transfer the syringe to my mouth and easily inject into the veins near my elbow."

His only remaining target veins were on the right arm. The veins on the left arm were scarred and closed from future business.

Considering the problems some blood-draw personnel have obtaining blood, his adaptive ingenuity was remarkable, but his arm was still infected, and the loss of his right arm definitely possible. He seemed very matter-of-fact about his situation. Remorse and redirection for his life appeared remote.

The depth of his commitment to drugs despite his limb loss shows how powerful drugs can be. No wonder the overdose rate is so high if losing a limb is not sufficient to discourage drug use.

Farther down the room I saw a nearly famous patient I had heard about but never treated. She was a Munchausen, a person who achieves attention by creating their own illness. Her shtick—knee infections. Candy would inject her knee with urine or some non-sterile fluid and shortly produce a knee infection. A "frequent flier" to the ED, she enjoyed stumping the new doctor unaware of her history. He might spend hours trying to figure out the story. That's when the ED nurses would bridge the gap and recognize the patient. This type of patient can be a problem because they get pigeonholed with the repeating diagnosis but occasionally have a new unrelated issue that is missed.

Candy obviously had psychological needs that remained unmet. The ED personnel focused on the knee infections but rarely had time to resolve the primary issue. I'm sure attempts had been directed toward resolving her mental issues, but her support team—friends and relatives—were not sufficient to deter her from what was a rewarding charade. The attention derived from ED visits and hospital stays apparently fulfilled her addiction. She, like Rocky, had learned how to use a needle to her advantage. She didn't appreciate permanent damage to her knee would result from recurring infections. This twenty-year-old didn't get it.

The EDs are full of needy people who consume so many resources it doesn't seem fair to the patients with true emergencies who must wait their turn to receive care. But we know the world is not fair. At least my friend Jack had only a short wait to have his problem addressed.

In my early days of practicing orthopedics in Mesa there were only a handful of us bone folks around. Emergency room doctors had not been invented, at least not in Mesa, and it was standard practice for the on-call orthopedist to "live" in the ER. On my call nights I remained at the hospital rather than go home because I knew any orthopedic problem was going to be my responsibility.

The operating situation was also user-friendly. Based on information from the emergency room nurse, I often scheduled a patient for surgery before I arrived at the hospital. This preemptive approach put me in line for surgery, which markedly expedited the care. This atavistic approach has been replaced with convenience: the convenience of the ED doctor. Orthopedists no longer live in the ED.

Other changes have occurred in ED care. Propofol, a safe sedative, was not available until 1989. This wonder drug changed the treatment of fractures and dislocations. It was no longer necessary to give local injections or enlist the services of an anesthesiologist. During that same time period ED doctors were appearing as a specialty.

Pre-Propofol I had a secret technique for reducing a dislocated shoulder, which didn't require anesthesia. If done slowly, the patient tolerated the reduction without complaining. I used a light dose of hypnosis—vocal anesthesia—to encourage cooperation.

Many wrist fractures in the elderly were also treated with a "gentle" reduction and no anesthesia. For the difficult fractures, including older people, I used a Bier block. August Bier first wrote about this intravenous anesthetic in 1908 but it gained popularity when it was reintroduced in the 1960s. I became a big fan because I could start my own IVs, do the reduction, and didn't have to rely on or wait for assistance. Waiting could be a problem in a busy ED.

There has been a Teutonic shift in the treatment of fractures and dislocations since my first years of living in the ED nearly every other night. Most fractures now "require" surgery. However, if a reduction is necessary the ED doctor provides the initial treatment aided by Propofol. Orthopedists now need a GPS to find the ED because they visit so infrequently. The patient is given directions for a follow-up with the specialist. Today, to see a Bier block, you need to go to Ethiopia or some other third-world country because the procedure is rarely done in the U.S. any longer.

I suspect it would be more difficult for the average orthopedist to start an IV than to perform a difficult revision hip surgery. The Trauma One hospitals have well-trained traumatologists who usually resort to surgical fracture management. Small hospitals don't have ER doctors or traumatologists, so the "old" style orthopedics still exist and a Bier block may occasionally show up.

A stroll through the ED brings back the distant memories of enjoyable times, of high-speed, efficient, no-frills treatments of standard orthopedic problems. Many newer orthopedic doctors will miss the excitement and challenges of the ED. I liked Improv 101 better.

Marbles

Iconsidered writing about the meaning of life or whether we should replace Libor. Instead, I settled on an equally meaty subject—marbles. Not so much marbles, like have you lost yours, but the round, usually glass variety. Granted they have taken a back seat to electronic games and social media, but from 1900 to about 1970 these little balls played a large roll/role in the socialization and entertainment of American youth.

Clay marbles have been found in American Indian burial grounds, the ruins of Pompei, Egyptian tombs, and Aztec pyramids as long ago as 2500 BCE.

The word marble originated from the German word for rock. In 1503 a marble-like game was played in Germany, but I can't find a date for the actual use of the term marble. In the 1600s, stone mills in Germany were polishing marbles from alabaster and marble found in the surrounding quarries. The glass marbles we know today were likely first produced in Venice or Germany; history is still being researched.

A British book printed in 1815 describes the history of the game of marbles. In the 1800s China apparently had a corner on the marble market, making marbles out of glass, clay, and even marble. The marble craze took off in 1884 thanks to Sam Dyke from Akron, Ohio, who started mass producing clay marbles in unbelievable numbers, five train cars a day, a million marbles. His factory employed 350 people.

Akron stepped up the marble game in 1910 when M.F. Christianson invented the automated glass marble-making machine process, which is still state-of-the-art for producing marbles. The Christianson company closed at the beginning of World War I because of rationing. Marble King, the last remaining American marble producer in the U.S., located in Akron, Ohio, still makes a million marbles a day. Only 20% are used in toys or marble games; the rest are for decor or commercial use. In the early 1900s, Akron had 32 marble manufacturing plants and is still the U.S. marble capital. Akron was to marbles what Wichita was to the small plane manufacturing. A factory in Guadalajara, Mexico, presently manufactures 12 million marbles daily, shipped to 35 different countries. Most marble manufacturing companies have diversified and make toys or other glass products like windshields.

Modern marbles are glass, a combination of silica, soda lime, feldspar, and coloring agents, heated to 2300F. The molten glass flows into a tube where a cutting device snips off chunks of glass, which fall into a series of rollers, automatically shaping the chunks into perfectly round balls.

The traditional game of marbles is played in a circle three to ten feet in diameter with two to six people, 13 marbles or mibs—1/2 inch in diameter and a shooter marble, a taw, ¾ inch in diameter.

The game known as Ringer begins by lagging to see who shoots first. Then a random number of marbles is placed inside the circle. The circle can be in the dirt or a carpeted area outlined by a string. After lagging, the player with the marble closest to the line plays first. The shooter tries to knock a mib out of the circle, also known as shooting off the marbles. The proper shooting style to release the taw requires a knuckle-down position. Knuckle down means just that; the shooter holds the marble on the curled index finger with the knuckles touching the shooting surface and then propels it by a flick of the thumb. Watching YouTube videos reveals that young players may modify the shooting technique slightly. Shooting rules strictly apply if you are in a tournament setting.

The shooter marble is shot from its landing position after a successful shot. If an opponent shoots your marble out of the circle, your next shot is taken from a knuckle-down position outside of the circle. You lose your turn when you fail to knock a marble out of the circle.

There are many regional variations of playing the game. Sometimes the players alternate shots even when a marble is successfully knocked off, and other times continue to shoot if a scoring shot is made. The loser of a game of marbles may lose all of his marbles, or not, depending on the rules made before the game started. Keepsies is the game my father played, meaning you kept all you won. You could also lose all your marbles. Sounds like the stock market.

Archboard is a variation of marbles. Instead of shooting at a marble, the object is to shoot into a shoebox that has holes of different size on one side. You score points by passing through an opening. Each opening has a different assigned value.

The game of marbles encompasses at least nine variations where marbles are shot or physically directed. I am not including Chinese checkers or other games using a board. Bungums or Bun-hole is one variation. For these games a one-foot-wide hole is dug in the center of the circle. Marbles are shot toward the hole. The winner is the marble that is closest to the hole. If the marble goes into the hole it is a loser. This game is seldom played indoors for fear of parental reprisal.

Cherry Pit is similar to Bun-hole, but the object is to knock the mibs in the hole without the shooter going in.

Amazingly, there are still people in the world who play marbles. For some of us, the game of marbles creates an excitement equivalent to hunting for truffles, but a few have attached themselves to this sport with the penchants seen for darts in England or soccer in Brazil. The number of marbles for sale on the internet and the presence of marble tournaments suggest marble enthusiasm still exists.

Every year since 1922 the four-day national marble tournament has been held in Wildwood, New Jersey. The competition is for boys and girls ages between 8-14. Over 1200 games take place in a four-day event. The tournament crowns a King and Queen and gives out prizes or scholarships. To be eligible to participate, one has to have won a local tournament. The list of rules related to this tournament is longer than the U.S. Constitution. Still there appear to be no articles referring to breaking a marble or hiccupping during competition.

The annual British and World Marble tournament occurs in Tinsley Green, West Suffix, Great Britain. The event dates back to 1588, but the modern event has been ongoing since 1932. The game is Ring Taw, known as Ringer in the U.S.. Two teams of six players compete and the winner must knock out 25 of the 49 marbles.

There are even people who have in-depth discussions about the various characteristics of marbles: the colors, the seams, the opacity, the swirl pattern, the company where they were made. The same kind of discussion fashion folks have about high-end clothing. I am not talking about the volume collectors; several collectors have over a million marbles. Marble collectors speak a language as rare as code talkers. Dogs may take on the personality of their owner, and marble collectors take on the personality of a marble. These glass balls become their children or at least their prized possessions. Their homes overflow with marble displays, carefully organized to promote marbles in the best light. A problem occurs when several outstanding characteristics are present in the same marble—which shelf should command their presence, a swirl or color pattern? I could never understand how dogs are judged. How does one dog match the AKC standard better than another? Marble grading seems even more arbitrary.

Bragging rights to the best marble collection, the most exotic assortment of marbles in the world, seems personal rather than scientific. The collector's life savings are definitely concentrated in marbles. Only one person out of two million of the general public would have a remote clue why these collectors are so gaga about marbles. A Lutz marble sold for $25,000 a few years ago. It is common for marbles to bring $100 for special types like agates and even radium—radioactive, glowing marbles.

A similar cohort collects porcelain rabbits or thimbles. Chances are, there is no item in the world that is not collected by somebody. I have a small toenail collection plus a few human bones, but I don't save fossilized feces or barf bags as some people do.

The largest marble collection is supposedly in the Marble Museum in York, Nebraska. There is also an Akco Marble and Glass collection in Akron, Ohio. Both of these collections feature over one million marbles each.

My father, a fierce competitor, spoke about his experiences of almost daily marble competitions as a young teenager. I do not plan on competing or collecting marbles even though I have a drawer of 80-year-old mibs.

Now, Tiddlywinks—those I could get into.

Haiti

Disney parks have yet to choose Haiti for their home, and Four Seasons has similarly avoided this island paradise. Hurricanes, earthquakes, floods, and landslides generate more attention than entrepreneurial investors or concert venue seekers. Haiti sports miles of lovely beaches, unfortunately buried under mounds of plastic trash. The roads with potholes large enough to swallow a VW bus represent the worst of highway maintenance. The gross national income ranks 200 out of 216 countries. Literacy rates barely reach 50%. Most people walk to work or take a tap tap, a cab. The term "tap tap" stems from tapping on the side of the vehicle to indicate you wish to terminate your journey before it terminates you. Five passengers on a cycle is common occurrence. Trucks and motorcycles function as tap taps as well. Poverty, filth, and low educational opportunities all represent the sad state of Haiti.

Ninety-five percent of the current eleven million population descended from African slaves brought to Haiti by the French in the seventeenth century to work in the sugar cane plantations. In the 1800s former American slaves migrated to Haiti, further swelling the population.

The Haitian president's job carries inherent risks, as demonstrated by a recent assassination in 2021. Since 1804, only four of the fifty presidents served out their full term. Most were overthrown, a few were assassinated, and a number died in office, which sounds a lot like assassination. Whatever the case, post-presidential-office retirement money remains a tiny budgetary item.

. . .

When I traveled to Haiti in 2011 our mission group of twelve consisted of two surgeons, three nurses, my assistant, several non-medical volunteers, and a prosthetic team with a well-established limb fabricating facility in Haiti. We arrived at the Port-au-Prince airport eagerly anticipating serving the Northwest Haitian Mission. Instead, we encountered a non-reception. After an hour of waiting and wondering if we were in the wrong country, a driver casually strolled toward our group gathered outside the airport and assuaged our concerns. We loaded our gear and climbed into a military truck with bench seating along the sides of the truck bed.

The travel time to the destination remained an unknown. I was intermittently seated on the hard, unpadded seat as we bounced over and around the potholed road in the capital of potholed roads. My bony anatomy reluctantly absorbed every irregularity. Many times I descended as the truck ascended, an uncomfortable mismatch. Eventually, my buttocks told me standing suited me better, especially when I learned this was a four-hour journey. Standing made holding on a challenge, but received kudos from my derrière.

Before leaving for Haiti, I knew about their poverty, post-earthquake destruction and the relatively high number of AIDs patients. The Northwest Haiti Christian Mission provided senior care, an orphanage, a birthing center, and a well-stocked surgery suite. Most mission trips worldwide, including American Indian reservations, lack room service unless the wakeup call by the loudest rooster or macaw qualifies. Haiti would likely be the same.

Several of the twelve volunteers were repeat visitors, some for the fourth time, but it was my first trip. I sponsored my regular medical assistant, Francisco, a young man fluent in Spanish. His proficiency in the language would come in handy. With Haiti nestled in the Caribbean Sea fifty miles away from Cuba, I mistakenly assumed Spanish constituted the primary language in Haiti. No. Creole dominated their language. Haiti has the largest Creole speaking population in the world; my assistant had no proficiency in Creole. Francisco could speak Spanish to others on our team, but of was no help with the patient translations.

The day we arrived Easter celebration began. Street noises and drums banging alerted us to the festivities. An eight-foot wall and guarded gate protected the Mission hospital and the other facilities within the compound. Our group and the other 30 volunteers from several countries were told to remain in the compound during the wild demonstration. One problem, several volunteers were wandering through nearby neighborhood shops unaware of any danger, and they never heard the warning. Noise alone posed no threat, but the noise-makers were high on Easter mood elevators, and they also wielded machetes. I heeded the warning and remained inside the wall, although tempted to investigate as one might, wanting to observe a building fire or street riot. The tourists returned without damage, but in a short time the hospital where I stayed began accepting many wounded by the drunken machete enthusiasts. My friends later described the random, lawless, slashing behavior of the Easter celebrants. Americans were targeted due to a pigment issue, but the volunteers were quick enough to outrun the whacky wielders of weirdness. They scrambled through the guard gate barely in time. The regularly scheduled evening prayer service extended longer than usual.

A sudden flood of lacerations entered through the same singular gate. We were unknowingly locked into a compound with no alternative exit and one rifled defender. Under normal circumstances that would be more than enough, but as the noise increased, I envisioned a throng of thousands coming after the white guys. Welcome to Haiti.

Voodoo exists in New Orleans, at least in the shops of the French Quarter, but I had no idea Voodoo enthusiasm had a violent side. The religion represents a syncretism of a West African Vodun religion and Roman Catholicism.

Throughout the Easter evening the wounded locals were bedded and limited attention was given to their injuries until the next day. The doctors were unaware of the injured until the morning following the celebration when we visited the hospital ward full of manchette injuries. We abandoned our anticipated surgical schedule and preceded on the new Easter list. The hospital was not a designated trauma one center, and trauma was addressed Haitian style: deal with it tomorrow.

The American staff immediately began repairing the victims. Badly damaged thumbs were removed, facial lacerations closed, and chest and abdominal injuries were addressed by the orthopedic team the best we could. Fortunately, we could handle the majority of the patients with confidence. However, we had no access to blood replacement and several victims were severely anemic. One mother of five had lost more than was compatible with life; we sadly had nothing to correct her blood loss. In Vietnam a soldier might receive 20 units of blood and survive terrible injuries, but in Haiti that option didn't exist. We spent the next few days mainly closing lacerations and amputating limbs we could not repair.

The church-based volunteers greatly supported the injured, their families and the medical providers by praying and singing each evening after consuming the nightly, acceptable dinner. The Voodoo shenanigans were a one-and-done event, with no more demonstrations and no more noise.

Our team had a full schedule of anticipated surgical procedures. The club feet and other elective surgeries were delayed for several days by the machete victims. We worked in the regular schedule as soon as the emergencies were addressed. Even in the U.S. surgery schedules are affected by Murphy's Law. In Haiti there are additional factors that disrupt a smooth day; no transportation, no money, fear, confusion as to the surgical day, and relatives that switch with the scheduled patient even when not seen by a doctor as a possible surgical patient.

We held clinics to evaluate the prospects for future surgery and treat minor problems. The X-ray unit at this hospital was broken as were many parts of the hospital. To overcome this problem, we sent clinic patients to the nearest X-ray facility located twenty to thirty miles away. They charged a minimum of twenty dollars, but our patients could not afford the tap-tap fare, let alone the fee.

I learned from my fellow traveling doctor, who had been to Haiti many times, the solution was to give the patient twenty dollars and hope they returned in a day or two with a readable X-ray. Some returned but I think a few took the twenty and healed themselves. We had no choice if we expected to help them; we needed the X-rays. I felt terrible because I had not been alerted to the twenty dollars per patient requirement. I had some money, but not the ideal wad of twenties. After the initial flood of unexpected surgeries, we settled into correcting club feet and revising injuries incurred from the previous year's earthquake.

Once the Easter celebration concluded, I felt safe outside the compound and walked to town and nearby beaches. As I ventured through the narrow streets, I encountered a street soccer game, allowing me to demonstrate my bumbling, old-white-guy soccer moves to the ten-year-olds while trying to avoid the dogs and their droppings. The size and beauty of the many churches amazed me.

This beauty didn't show up on the pathetic beaches. A never-ending expanse of sandy beaches buried with thick plastic debris brought home the sad condition of our world, not just Haiti. At the edges of the beach dried fish stands displayed five to ten of the most unappetizing fish, all blanketed by layers of flies. Who would buy these delicacies? I saw no sales.

Our sleeping quarters deserved mention. I had two options for sleeping: one outside under the stars, or in a dorm. After arriving I made the difficult decision to bed down in the dorm. My concern about bugs, bats, and bursts of rain convinced me that in, trumped out. The dorm contained ten bunk beds and only nine volunteers were signed up. This gave me a reasonable chance to select the ideal bed and location. None of the beds came with an ocean view, even though located less than two blocks from the ocean.

The wall of the compound and the absence of dorm windows canceled the view. The vintage beds came with wire mesh springs barely capable of supporting a mattress slightly thicker than the sheet. The beds were no more than a foot apart. That meant if a person lying in the next bed had halitosis and turned my way, I would be the recipient of bad positioning. I could go head to foot but that brought foul-smelling feet into play.

My first night was uneventful until about two a.m. when an oversized photographer settled in. His size placed him clearly in my space. He snored with enthusiasm and I prayed the decibels would miraculously diminish, but my optimism was built on quicksand, and I quickly gave up. A sharp elbow to a close overhanging body part produced immediate quiet—but only for a few seconds. He remained unresponsive so I persisted with repeated blows to achieve those momentary spots of silence. At times, quiet lingered, but I remained awake, waiting for the next round.

The photographer was African American, and I worried about being labeled a racist by becoming too aggressive. The pattern continued, but I realized he didn't come to bed until two or three in the morning, so I turned in at nine, hoping to get my usual five or six hours before Snore Man hit the sack. I continued to poke him, but he never woke up or said anything about his sleep experience. When I returned home, I couldn't sleep. I had become addicted to the evening roar.

The shower became another source of frustration. The amount of water, especially hot water, was random. A full and acceptable flow, or more likely an enlarged prostate dribble, might occur any morning. I often stood fully soaped hoping for that brief burst or even enough water to brush my teeth. Some mornings the would-be shower lovers were denied more than a thimble of water.

Showers became an anytime-of-the-day event. If dryness prevailed in the morning, we would pop in during the day to steal a shower. Even that tactic didn't succeed every time.

. . .

Throughout the week I kept trying to figure out a way to avoid standing up for the four-hour ride back to the airport. With my seniority and sensitive bottom, I felt an entitlement to a real seat in the truck. Turns out we returned in a van with many seats. That small blessing seemed like a reward for a somewhat emotionally draining experience, but I would do it again with no hesitation.

Our team performed more surgery than anticipated thanks to the Easter excitement. More was good. Everyone in the group came away from Haiti proud to have helped this poverty ridden, gang-run country in our small way. We realized just how lucky we are to be living in America.

Stellar Cellar

Ihave enjoyed my lowly position since the day the footings were poured. I knew I would be special, not just a basement like others but a place offering a unique atmosphere. I remained humble, but I knew I shone over the rooms mounted above me, rooms that claimed a higher purpose, and offered loftier status—sleeping, feeding, and entertaining the family. I was proud of my domain and how it supported the clan—the distinct homo sapiens genus. I strove to make them happy and fulfilled with my exceptional style and offerings.

Mrs. Wilson, the mom, was a delight: calm, detailed, pretty, and appreciative of my gifts and talents. She valued a clever clothes chute that started on the second floor with a straight passage to a quiet corner in the cellar near the wringer washing machine. The clothes chute was serendipitous. I didn't design it, but I was given credit or at least praise for its presence. It was highly acclaimed. The clothes rushed down the chute, not having to be carried down the long stairway, a definite safety and ergonomic benefit. I never figured out a way to push the clothes up the chute, a task I will delay until after the digital age. The dirties eventually found their way into the wringer washing machine. I always felt a little nervous about that machine because it was capable of catching a tit in its wringer, creating a black mark on my rating as the best cellar in Iowa. The machine provided a rhythmical, sloshing, musical experience, my early attempt at surround sound. To provide the ultimate convenience, I supplied four clotheslines, which stretched across the low ceiling above the Ping-Pong table. The table caused a slight challenge to hanging clothes, but more than redeemed itself by being a table, especially a Ping-Pong table, which provided many hours of competition. The son Butch and father Ralph played a spirited game at least weekly.

"How do you hit the edge so often?" Butch complained to his father.

"Practice, practice, practice."

"That's crap, and you know it."

"I heard you broke the snow shovel."

"I bent it a little, but it still works. I hit that big crack on the front walk where the roots have pushed up the sidewalk. I know it is there, but I hit it every time I shovel."

About that time, the overhanging clothesline redirected a shot, and Butch groaned as the ball hit the edge of the table again, producing a winning shot for his father.

• • •

My concrete block walls housed two small windows below ground level. The window wells provided a light source but acted like little lakes when it rained, allowing dampness to form on the wall of my domain on those stormy days. On occasion the lakes produced a freely flowing stream, which added to the musty atmosphere. The chewy odor of moisture was classic for a Midwest basement, but I enjoyed the distinctive aroma. A shiny, smooth concrete floor and a few bare light bulbs complemented the austere ambiance. A storage closet hid at the far end of the room, home to jams and jellies, especially rhubarb, compliments of Mrs. Wilson's canning talents.

My furnace room was adjacent to the Ping-Pong room and contained a coal-burning furnace. The coal room was a separate room holding several tons of large, shiny chunks of unburned coal. Clinkers, craggily, volcanic-appearing shapes, also rested there for a few weeks until their accumulation interfered with the transfer of coal into the hungry furnace. The job of clinker removal and the input of coal fell to Butch from the time he was strong enough to lift the pieces of coal.

At the far end of the furnace room I provided a short workbench and pile of tools: a hammer, saw, an assortment of screwdrivers, and a can full of assorted nails.

This meager collection proved sufficient for the Wilson family since none were adept with carpentry equipment. The bench eventually became home to hundreds of hospital pillow radios—soft green radios with an umbilical cord attached to a round speaker, which slid under a pillow.

Butch and his friend Richard purchased a flock of pillow radios that ate dimes and were placed in every room of the local hospital. The radios frequently had indigestion if a bent dime or other coins were introduced into their delicate coin slots. The infirmity rate usually exceeded the healthy, money-producing machines on any given day. Butch and friend, both who had the electrical knowledge of a beetle, worked long hours nearly every weekend trying to restore the wounded flock, but they never seemed to shrink the stack of disabled radios. I felt like I provided a rehabilitation home for these unfortunate, raspy-noise boxes, which guaranteed a source of frustration for the pillow-radio doctors.

"Someone put a slug in this machine," groaned Butch.

"This one is plugged with gum. Did patients think it took gum instead of dimes? At least it's not covered with vomit," replied Richard, Butch's skinny, not mechanically inclined associate who later became an electrical engineer.

"This radio is cracked; looks like it was hit with a wooden leg or at least a cane. They probably got mad when it didn't work."

"Someone pulled the speaker cord off this one. That's a problem a hearing aid can't solve, and neither can we, but we need to save the parts just in case we can actually fix one of these things."

"I'll try to replace the damaged coin box that has been pried open, with a coin box from the speaker-free machine."

"What should we do with number 27? It plays without putting any money in it?"

"We could put it in the kids' ward because they might not have any money to work these stupid machines, and since we can't fix it, we may as well let somebody use it."

"You know about the only thing that was good about these radios, I didn't have to practice the piano when I worked on them," cracked Richard.

• • •

Beneath and behind the stairs rested a cache of storm windows or screens, depending on the season. The storm windows returned in April and the screens in October. These window coverings were the old variety, heavy, with multiple coats of paint and big hooks to hold them in place. They seemed content to rest quietly beneath the stairs when they were retired for the season.

I appreciated the opportunity to sit under a warm and friendly home. A home that appreciated me for what I provided: a resting place, a clean place and a place for fruit, Ping-Pong, and clinkers.

Then there was no more canning and no more rhubarb. A new modern washer and dryer replaced the wringer washing machine. The radios disappeared, and an oil-burning furnace replaced the coal and clinkers. Even the Ping-Pong table left its musty room. Only a few clothes made their way down the chute.

Butch and his sister moved away. College took them both to distant towns leaving me void of the weekly excitement of Ping-Pong and shop activities. The new, quiet, Amana washing machine was seldom used, and foot traffic slowed to a trickle. The seasonal changing of the storm windows ceased. The rooms above me received new décor, paint, wallpaper, and furniture. I got nothing.

I became misty when I realized I was no longer important. In just twenty years I slipped from the most important room to a dank, dark memory. I still treasured the times when I carried myself high—as the cellar.

Then something happened: noise and trucks and crazy activity. A new family moved in. The three new kids think I am the greatest. I am the center of games and dogs and roller skating. I am alive, just like the old days. It is great to hear laughter and excitement. I wonder how long it will last this time.

Do People Still Do That?

During my years in medical practice my "willing-to-share-everything" patients have divulged behavior, often their own, which falls outside the norm. I have added a few episodes where I proffered activities of my own making.

Ned pulled a chair from beneath his pastor as the unsuspecting man of the cloth plummeted to the floor. To me it seemed dangerous and not funny, but to both him and his victim, his pastor, this childish stunt apparently qualified as hilarious. He respected the preacher and worked with him weekly to distribute food for the homeless. Ned, a humble and caring man, used the sophomoric-disappearing chair trick as a mainstay of his "gotcha" repertoire. Although the preacher never suffered a major injury by his "funny maneuver" it seemed Ned hadn't considered the injury possibility.

Cindy visited the ER, a victim of boyfriend Larry's vertical, number two pencil placed purposely under her descending butt. This resulted in a vaginal laceration requiring several stitches. That *lead* led to a breakup. He messed up his own playground.

Dr. White, a racially neutral retired doctor, told the story of his venture while working in the ER at Fort Bliss. While eating lunch, Arlene, a frequent, well-known hypochondriacal patient demanded immediate attention. This pulled Dr. White from his lunch even though he knew no emergency situation existed. He politely listened to Arlene's story and informed her she needed to see the obstetrician immediately.

He swiftly moved to the office next door, assumed a new identity, and reinterviewed the patient. She looked uncertain but accepted the new advice, which included criticism of recommendations she received from the first doctor.

Arlene was then referred to the general surgeon. Dr. White finished his lunch before he appeared in his new role as the general surgeon in an office 50 feet down the hall. Dr. White had donned a new coat and rumpled his hair to lend an additional but minimal disguise to his latest role as a general surgeon. Arlene paused only briefly before telling her complaints a third time. She presented with renewed intent, not dissuaded by the obvious ruse. Dr. White, now a general surgeon, gave a lengthy resolution to her problem and suggested both doctors she had seen that day were highly trained and factual. Yet no one could solve her obtuse condition and he determined she again may need to seek help from a higher authority. Arlene shouted "I demand to see the Colonel in charge of the medical facility."

Dr. White, realizing the Colonel was out of town, jumped on the opportunity to grant her wish. She was quickly shuttled across the street to the Colonel's office. Dr. White, however, reached the Colonel's office before Arlene arrived. He dropped his voice an octave plus, added a New England accent, and again heard the thrice-told tale. He quickly agreed with her sad circumstances and disappointment. He also blasted the incompetent doctoring she had received and saw the need to remove the three previous doctors from the military.

"We have had a hard time finding good doctors of late." He promised to address their incompetence as soon as possible and gave her a "Thank you, ma'am." Arlene, being supremely self-absorbed, didn't tumble to the "made-for-TV charade.

Arlene made no ER visits for the next six months.

• • •

The following two stories lack a medical connection but deserve reporting for insensitivity.

My father often related his favorite practical joke. At age 15 he and his best friend tied a small rope to an old suitcase. In the evening they placed the suitcase in the road that passed their farmhouse. When a car came by, the occupants spotted the suitcase, and most would stop to examine the strange object in the road. This took place in 1926 and cars traveled at a 1926 pace. As the driver approached the suitcase, my father would jerk the rope, which usually surprised the curious driver.

The victim's shriek delighted the boys and confirmed their little trick worked. This levity encouraged them to continue their prank. The entertainment lasted for several hours until one of the victims returned, and rather than avoid the suitcase or slow to investigate, ran full speed over the suitcase, thereby ending the evening's fun.

• • •

My good high school buddy's girlfriend was selected to perform in a singing competition at a radio station. I accompanied them to a nearby city and my buddy and I waited while she sang. I hatched a post-audition plan and he tacitly agreed it sounded worthy of delivering. We both were stupid, insensitive youth and didn't anticipate the collateral damage that resulted from the event that followed her audition.

When she finished singing, I called the station and asked for her. The competition director quickly located her, and she answered the phone a minute later. I, in my most professional voice, expressed my enthusiasm for her talent and, as an agent for Universal Studios, offered her a job and movie contract. Unfortunately she didn't recognize my voice and believed the offer legitimate. We talked for several minutes as I outlined the timetable and possible movie roles. Finally, I ran out of BS and confessed I made the whole story up. I realized immediately I had been far too convincing. Devastation covered both of our emotions. As the three of us drove home, levity was absent. She blamed my friend for setting her up. Not true. He barely supported the ruse. He and I remained friends, but the girlfriend terminated their relationship even though I accepted full responsibility, including an apology for the misadventure. I had that same feeling one has after running over a dog or breaking someone's personal treasure—not good. She was an excellent singer and I hoped she signed a big contract later.

• • •

My ventures into the medical world of practical jokes helped relieve tension, yet was not at all dangerous. I had occasion to fix the broken elbows of children in the five to twelve-year-old range. I placed several smooth wires/pins across the broken area but left the pin tips out of the skin for easy removal. Most patients lived in fear of the time when the pins were to come out. The parents could minimize the fear but often remained unconvinced the extraction process was painless. When the dreaded, tension-filled day arrived, I plied my magic. As I lifted the dressing from one anxious child, I explained I would remove the pins by standing ten feet away from the hallowed elbow. As the dressing came off, I slipped the pins out undetected, but left them hidden in the dressing. I gradually backed up, using a variety of moaning and swishing sounds as I raised the dressing with pins included above my head. With the David Copperfield flair, I revealed the pins and exclaimed they were no longer in the elbow. The child quickly looked toward his elbow to confirm there was no hoax, followed by a sigh.

Pins occasionally fell out of the elbow, and no one recognized their absence. This created a whole new illusion allowing me to toss the open dressing into the air as I declared the pins had vanished. No pain involved in removing pins in this fashion.

• • •

My response to my alleged surprise office birthday party fell loosely under the practical joke category. When I was tipped off about the party, I prepared a pair of boxer shorts. After the cake and birthday song, I stepped onto a steady chair, turned my back to the gathering and slowly dropped my drawers. The saying I had glued to my boxers was "Thanks 4 coming." The economic 4 gave me more room 4 the message. There were some groans of disbelief as I lowered my pants but those utterances turned to smiles upon reading my prose.

When I went to my car after work, the inside was filled with millions of tiny little heart-shaped confetti. It took months before I eliminated the last of those cardiac wonders.

Sometime in my travels, I acquired a toy chainsaw. I pulled the cord to activate it then pressed the saw against a firm object such as my finger to create a realistic saw sound. This noisy saw plus a realistic plastic finger created a perfect opportunity to entertain the kids visiting the cast room. Before removing a cast, I demonstrated with the toy saw and accidentally cut off my finger. The finger fell to the floor as I gave a cry of anguish in front of the child about to have their cast removed. The surprise and smiles that followed my silly trick made removing the cast much less problematic—a good thing.

• • •

Removing the kneecap was a common operation for severe fractures of the patella/kneecap, also employed when the patella was arthritic or damaged. I did a patellectomy (removal of the kneecap) on a tennis-playing friend for such a condition. Convinced she would need the patella back at some point, I kept it in my bone collection to be resurrected at some future time. Several years went by before I remembered my intentions. I drilled a hole through the bone and looped a leather strap into the hole, long enough to be worn as a necklace and reach to my friend's knee. A birthday party provided the perfect venue to return her kneecap to its original—almost—location. Turned out a long necklace with a kneecap as the jewel was not stylish and she refused to wear it to any fashionable events.

Life is more interesting when we cavort on the edges of normality. So, go out and do what others might not do. Just don't hurt anybody.

Jesse and James

Being self-assured, confident, and all-knowing works if you are the Pope or the President, but it doesn't work if you are a first-time patient pursuing the cause of your knee pain. Don't get me wrong, as a doctor, I am usually okay with a confident patient but irritated when a patient attempts to sell me on their diagnosis. There are exceptions to every rule and I have patients who have researched their symptoms and have recognized their problem. Those patients may have a familial disease, which likely would not be on my radar. I will accept any help I receive, including newspaper articles, escorted by my patients to help me resolve their ailments. Many have Googled their way to an accurate diagnosis and I simply validate their assessment.

Jesse, a new patient, raced ahead of my assistant as she attempted to room him. He opened the door of an occupied exam room before she could stop him. "Sorry, I think I am in the wrong room," Jesse apologized. An elderly lady barely registered any surprise and remained silent as Jesse backed out. I entered Jessie's room once he and his female companion were seated. Without notes, but with the voice and demeanor of a TV anchor he began. "I know what is wrong with my knee. It is nothing serious, but my wife insisted I see you. You know women. Probably a *cartridge*, and I just need a little therapy to fix it." So far, I hadn't said a word.

The point of this story is not to criticize Jesse, who might be a wonderful person, but to show how well-meaning patients can do themselves a disservice by their eagerness to help.

Other examples come to mind: the guard in football who is frequently offside in his enthusiasm to contribute;

the third-grader whose hand is up before the teacher finishes the question and then keeps it up to guarantee an opportunity to pounce on the next query without a clue what the next question will be. And If called upon the eager beaver states he/she forgot the answer; and finally, the lady at the bridge table who has an incredible amount of bridge knowledge and an even greater enthusiasm to share her considerable insight with her less informed partner who has, by the way, not requested any assistance.

This patient type, like a pot boiling over, or a geyser erupting, deserve names such as George Carlin or Roseanne Barr.

When Jesse-like patients present their case, they will cite references and history, which clearly give validity to the oration. Jesse continued, "The reason I know I have a torn *cartridge* is it's just like my friend Larry had when he wrecked his Harley. He ran over a dog about two months ago and ended up against a palm tree with a bad knee injury. They found a torn *cartridge* and he had to have surgery. He had to go to three doctors before they found it. You know, the torn *cartridge*. The first guy at urgent care blew him off and didn't even give him crutches. The next day he was hurting so bad he went to the E.R. and had more X-rays but they didn't find it either. They sent him to Dr. Clum. Clum is the guy who ordered the MRI and found the tear. Clum did his surgery but Larry still hurts. Anyway, that's how I know I have a *cartridge*."

Jesse continued on his roll; I sat back and listened. His dissertation would likely cover the answers to questions I would ask.

"I've never had this before, but my brother had one. But he is heavy and out of shape. Like an idiot he rode an ostrich in one of those carnival things. The bird was probably pissed because he weighed so much. Anyway, he fell off and Beulah finished the race without him. First place. He never got his *cartridge* fixed because he is so lazy; he never does any sports other than drinking contests. His fridge is mostly a beer cooler."

You could see Jesse was building a strong case for

a cartilage problem even though he indicated it was nothing and his wife made him make the appointment. So far, he has yet to refer to Dr. Oz or TVs Grey's Anatomy for solid medical backing. He did throw in an aside about his visits to his *choirpractor*. That experience didn't change the trajectory of his "no big problem."

We were now at the point in the interview where I introduced myself to Jesse and his female companion. I guessed wife, but whiffed. She was a coworker at the pawn shop where he worked part-time. *Who is watching the pawns? HIPAA would probably require him to sign a release for her to hear his story, but he wasn't whispering his comments, so I figured he was cool with her presence.* His wife, a hairdresser, couldn't get off work, hence Patsy the pawn person.

He answered all my questions, and other than for a bad burn on his back when he fell into a campfire at age two, he had experienced no significant medical problems.

I conducted the hands-on physical exam. Because he was obviously interested in medical stuff, with each maneuver, I explained what I was doing. "This is a Lachman's test to rule out an ACL and this is a McMurray's test to check for cartilage injuries." He remained totally locked into the tutorial. He nodded approvingly and was poised with open lips to interject a question. I raced along with medical clobberation, so fast he never interrupted until I concluded the exam.

"Okay."

Jesse added no more self-diagnosis info suggesting he was pleased with his efforts to convince me of his extensive knowledge regarding the knee, allowing me to start the wrap-up phase.

"You are a lucky man. For a man of your girth, I mean weight, and as active as you have been, your knee is in good shape. There is no need for an MRI at this time. I suggest you buy a bike. Start riding a few miles a day and work up to 50 over the next two months. This may cost you 20 pounds or more, but that is a good thing. Jesse, you have it in you."

"Damn, you are a winner Doc. Thanks"

• • •

James Pojans, a plural-sounding name with a singular purpose. That purpose was to demonstrate an above average knowledge of his body, which the average doctor should find useful for the future of his practice. His or her practice, of course, since political correctness must be considered at every turn on the information highway. The average doctor should be grateful to have the opportunity to talk with James because James is so full of it (wisdom and knowledge), particularly related to the internal workings of James's unique homo-sapi-en-like structure.

James appeared to be a regular guy on the outside. He wore a short-sleeved, bright-red shirt that exposed an abundance of red-hair, even on his knuckles. He began the interview by stating his problem, "It is on the right side." That's where John Birch came from, but I felt there is more than just some political leanings involved here. "My right side is hurting and hard to use comfortably." An acute onset situation that developed twenty years ago but was becoming progressively worse, leading up to his E.R. visit a few days ago. The emergency room personnel were clueless as to the cause of his festering problem. People don't wander around with right-side pain without some serious reason.

"According to my chiropractor I have a tilted pelvis, tilted by several inches. It causes my back to lean to the right. The worst part is the *scolosis*'." (He was referring to scoliosis which is a curvature of the spine, usually not associated with any disease or condition unless it is severe.) The James-to-doctor lecture was just beginning.) "*Scolosis* is caused by muscles that are out of alignment. These muscles (*a generic unnamed group*) are deficient in vitamins, which leads to the 'trouble.'" *Also, a generic commodity.* "This whole thing has affected my joints so they don't work right."

I remained in a cosmic fog since I missed the chief complaint. Where did he hurt? I decided a full dose of causation made sense. His right shoulder was exceptionally touchy. To my surprise, James suddenly grasped my hand and placed it firmly on his right shoulder. At least for the moment it was good no testicular problem existed, but we were early in the interview and I anticipated other body parts might surface.

The laying on of hands did not result in an exorcism of his condition. An early resolution was a negative because James had lots to teach me. He moved on to his now assumed lotus position, leaving me still attached to his shoulder. This position was not accompanied by a cobra or pungi musical, but became a backdrop for a dialogue regarding the muscles that control the hips and how they are so, not right. After multiple subtle movements to produce the position that was particularly not right, James bolted from the table to a vertical posture, turning to show me his back and the "terrible *scolosis*." I was again invited to lay my hands on his spine to better understand the distress first hand. Apparently only the Palmer application (Palmer Chiropractic School) could bring real understanding of the scientific truth on a cellular level. I complied with his request, but can honestly say I learned nothing from this act of cooperation.

I assured James he had mild scoliosis, but received no reply. He was on a mission to reveal the whole truth about his body and his complicated ailment. He had no time for meaningless/diversionary questions.

He did mention he had moisture in his watch and he tried to remove it via a short time in the microwave, which resulted in his timepiece being correct twice a day.

He then resumed his right-sided discussion, first regarding his right knee and then the foot. Both have muscle disorders leading to his problems. Both had a unique "loose stiffness" that was omnipotent. My questions relating to aggravating factors such as weather, time of day, or activities were largely ignored.

After letting James express most of his medical perceptions and convincing myself, following an exam, that he was free of any major ailments, I carefully showed concern about his future. I asked him to return in one-month to see if there were any new symptoms to worry about. I discussed his right-sided connection as purely random, but worthy of follow-up.

"At this time your findings fail to reveal any serious problem but you have enough going on that a one month follow-up would be important. During the next 30 days I want you to watch my YouTube about exercises."

Jesse and James, neither are true cowboys. Both were on a mission to provide me with their version of medical reality. I appreciated their enthusiasm, but deprogramming this type of patient can be a tough rodeo.

Mania

The word mania, coined in the 14th century, suggests mental derangement, excitement, and delusions. Mania has been tagged onto borderline activities, such as nymphomania, kleptomania and megalomania. The male version of a nymphomaniac is a satyriasis, void of mania but is still stuck with a mania-like gene.

Mania, as it relates to the behavior of sports fans, manifests and becomes the mood of choice when a national championship is a possibility as was the case in 2021. The Phoenix versus Milwaukee NBA seven-game basketball series created an emotional outpouring that fortunately fell short of the destructive behavior of political activists attacking the Capital and federal facilities throughout the country.

In sports mania the fan may be sucked into a mindset that his entire or at least 90% of his success in life depends on his team winning. A beer or two helps secure this belief, as does the camaraderie of like-minded friends, at least friends of the cause. The fans don the wardrobe of the maniacal group, including the team shirts and hats—generally worn backward. Unlike the political manifestations of mania, sports mania usually doesn't focus on attacking cops, destroying buildings, or stealing merchandise. Fans mostly yell and chant slogans and raise their libations, saluting any positive performance from their beloved warriors.

In their own way, maniacal fans may suddenly go nuts protesting their team's prior underperformance or maybe their own failures by celebrating when success arrives. It's great to see the fans' reaction when an 84-inch-tall person pushes a rubberized sphere through a metal hoop, and suddenly the crowd goes bonkers. Or when a fan slaps his buddy on the back, spills his beer, and yells at the top of his lungs to declare how great the world is. However, he is obligated to remain silent when the other team accomplishes the same amazing feat.

The mania may affect family members. The participant leaves home four hours before game time to secure a parking space and relish his $500 seat. This early departure gives him time to enjoy the warm-ups and knock down a few $12 beers in preparation for the big game. He is not alone: three of his buddies have also spent most of their current assets, not including the interest they will owe on their now overloaded credit cards, to be a part of the collective mania embedded in the arena.

The media takes advantage of the local enthusiasm and builds the case for shaping rabid fans. The personal stories of the players' roads to success, the growing up in a small town or foreign land, the rejection by other teams, and the family hardships all make for a more personal attachment and greater connection to the fan base. If the team members consistently lose, the stories fall flat.

Most fans root for the underdog and the Phoenix Suns qualify more times than not. Coupling this with the absence of a championship trophy propels the average fan to reverse their frustration by increasing their team support.

Enthusiasm crosses into mania the more the team achieves. When Suns fans remain at the arena for hours after a game—maybe to sober up— mania has a foothold. When stickers cover their car windows, making driving a challenge, or when fans spend an hour painting their body with Suns' colors, you have mania. If you kick the TV screen when the Suns lose, you may have to rethink the rebarbative behavior and the repercussions of your unwavering support. Bar fights with people from Wisconsin may be justified when supporting your political position or gender choice, but fist fighting to demonstrate your Suns' shine pushes the limits. Granted,

Coors decreases your choices of rebuttal when told the Suns suck.

Who gets caught up in their enthusiasm for the team? All walks of life in the Arizona nation immerse themselves in supporting the Suns. Economic status is not a barrier to filling the arena seats. What personality type characterizes someone who goes from an enthusiastic fan to a higher level of support—mania? Does mania translate to personal success or greater self-worth in someone looking for their missing positive identity?

Studies show that fans are fans, and among the many people who support a team, some are dysfunctional followers. This cohort stands out for their aggressive, confrontational behavior. Their sports mania for a winning team may be further accentuated by alcohol. Most fans are functional and not aggressive. These people can demonstrate great enthusiasm and still have acceptable behavior. They may appear out of character but behave within social guidelines. They buy the team paraphernalia to demonstrate their love and benefit from the euphoria of being a loyal fan. When winning, they experience a feeling of belonging, have an increase in testosterone, eat a better diet, and experience a sense of well-being.

Sports mania has another curious element, the illogical defense of the sport's hero or program. An article criticizing the cost of a winning football program at North Dakota State caused the reporter to be severely scolded for giving the facts. A similar reaction occurred following an article written after Kobe Bryant died. The story recalled his involvement in a rape case. Was he being held on a higher pedestal than he deserved? Many defended Kobe suggesting he didn't merit this posthumous criticism. O.J. had similar support. Sometimes our loyalties cloud clear thinking.

• • •

Sports enthusiasm has been around at least since the events at the Coliseum in Rome. Although it has been rumored that many Christians were killed in the Colise-um, a perfect venue for mania, the facts suggest other-wise. Apparently, Christians initiated the myth. Chariot races, a much less emotional experience, took place instead, and neither Christians nor mania were involved, even though movies would suggest otherwise.

Frenzied fan behavior is certainly fodder for Freudian fascination. The upper end of enthusiasm is especially obvious when the end of any sport's season arrives. We saw it in year 2021 in Phoenix and Milwaukee with the professional basketball finals. We fans are free to drink the Kool-Aid. This success-laden opportunity rarely presents itself to most regular fans, so grab your seats for a fun ride. Mania be damned, but civility is encouraged.

Marketing 101

Medical education, at least for me, failed to contain any meaningful financial information. No marketing class, no investment class, no money-related classes of any type. I don't fault the schools for this deficiency; as far as I know, financial education remains absent from current day curriculum. During medical training there was no need for financial advice other than how to obtain a student loan.

I still remained virginal regarding money management during my four years of residency. A familiar story: the spouse provided the bulk of the income.

Fast forward to my first job after residency. When I started practice in 1970, I had no experience with marketing and hadn't given it any consideration. In those days there were almost no ads promoting medical practices. Lawyers and chiropractors took the lead, and doctors remained reluctant to commercialize their businesses.

My four-man office didn't talk about marketing at our monthly meetings. We focused on medical challenges and matters related to moving the practice forward, like hiring a manager or an X-ray tech. When Christmas rolled around, I learned the office holiday tradition included providing a gift to the referring physicians and hospital staff. That gift, a 40-pound box of oranges, historically chosen by my senior partner, remained in place for several years after I started practice. The rule was to give one box to each referring group, maybe two boxes for a large group of over four doctors. These were soft guidelines and subject to the discretion of the delivering doctor. As the rookie in a new town and new practice, delivering gifts to meet the mostly family doctor recipients presented a perfect holiday opportunity. I took a day off from seeing patients to become the *DoorDash* guy for this festive event.

I didn't consider it a marketing tool so much as a means to get to know people and thank those who sent me referrals. The same applied to the oranges I delivered to the hospital, which accounted for half of the total delivered.

I modified the original hospital stops and included the housekeeping crew, medical records, security, in addition to the nurses, O.R., E.R., and administration. I used a wheelchair to assist me in moving the oranges around the hospital without breaking my back. My first year distributing to the hospital personnel proved challenging because I had no idea where the housekeepers hid out or the location of the maintenance office. I felt like Santa Claus giving away oranges to employees who generally didn't see gifts from anybody and had never received them from my group before. They gushed with gratitude and happily chatted in their dank offices hidden in the bowels of the hospital. Naturally their grateful responses guaranteed them an early stop the following years.

The visits to the referring physicians were equally positive, particularly during the first few years, because those stops gave me a chance to meet the faces behind the names of doctors to whom I sent medical notes on a daily basis. Visiting the offices during business hours proved to be a little awkward because the doctors often persisted with patient care rather than taking a break to receive my citrus treats. Some schedules prevented even a brief contact, but most doctors seemed friendly and interested in establishing a relationship. On several occasions I provided a "curbside" consult regarding an orthopedic problem one of their patients demonstrated. I would have enjoyed visiting those offices daily or working at their offices once a week, but that has yet to happen.

The biggest problems with the orange drop-off were locating an office that had moved from the previous year's address or finding the office closed on my delivery day or locked for "lunch." Who takes a three-hour lunch break? I always wondered if the office staff received a fair share of the gifts. They probably did better if the doctors were absent when the oranges arrived, which happened frequently.

This pseudo-marketing tool soon outgrew itself. The population of physicians exploded several years after I started practice. The oranges seemed to weigh more each year, and the number of deliveries, cost, and delivery time exceeded my group's collective enthusiasm.

We abandoned the oranges as a Christmas project and switched to large cans of almonds. This greatly decreased the physical challenges of the deliveries. We also became more selective and reduced the number of office visits by gifting the physicians who provided the most referrals—target marketing. The hospital employees still received a full allotment of almonds, but no more oranges.

An additional piece of connecting with the medical universe was an appreciation party. My office hosted several large parties; complete with games, a band, swimming, a nice dinner and more. These events, orchestrated by amateur party planners, began with an open-ended invitation to hospital medical staff and nurses. We sent a singular invitation to doctors' offices, which included staff. This approach was "safeguarded" by a call-in RSVP, which may work for some events but not for our parties. We never knew how many people to expect. Behavior is predictable enough to know that ten percent of yeses don't show and, in our case, double that number showed but didn't reply yes. It seemed to work out okay, but alcohol modulated statistical errors better than careful planning.

Alcohol provided a major point of discussion. So, did we risk unlimited drinking and "benefit" from free marketing by being named in a lawsuit involving drunken driving? Fortunately, the goers proved to be reasonable people, and we pulled in security to enforce the non-existent rule against overindulging. We debated about charging for alcohol as a deterrent to overdrinking but decided that would appear cheap. The brakes on drinking for the larger-than-predicted crowd occurred when guests exhausted the liquor supply before any drinker could get completely soused.

Due to the expanding number of medical providers and two additional hospitals in our area, our "nut and party" approach fell into antiquity. This was about the time when doctors began to advertise in the newspaper and on T.V.

In talking with my patients, it became apparent that advertising attracted many folks. It also became obvious many patients underwent unnecessary surgery. People were persuaded by advertising terms like laser, no stitches, pain-free, and end your worries. These claims enticed many patients and appeared to be too good to be true, yet the resulting visits generally qualified for insurance coverage. Many unhappy patients were surprised by hidden charges or out-of-network services. The insurance often didn't cover the treatment as promoted. And when I saw patients drawn in by the misleading advertising, many also had not benefitted from the prescribed surgery. Sadly, some did not seek another opinion before undergoing the knife, although they were advised to do so.

Today the average doctor is heavily booked. If one resorts to advertising that usually means the practice is on life support and needs an injection of patients. As you might expect, the advertising doctors are frequently cited for inappropriate practices and are shuttered for their misadventures.

Currently my group's advertising budget is mainly for sponsoring youth sports and supporting worthwhile charities. I miss the oranges, nuts, and parties, but fall back on word of mouth as the marketing gold standard.

P.S. Just saw a full-page ad in the local rag promoting my medical group's practice. Explanation from administration: Everyone else is advertising so we need to stay in the game. Sad to see us go down that rabbit hole.

Witch Doctors

In 2019 I joined a mission trip to Uganda with Pipeline Worldwide. The six-person team intended to assess the medical needs of this often unstable and economically challenged country. We focused on Gulu, a city of over 200,000 in North Central Uganda with a large hospital and orphanage. Dr. Sylvester, the only orthopedist in the area, serviced two million potential patients, not including the Sudanese refugees. He worked at St. Mary's Hospital Lacor in Gulu and provided our primary contact for the mission endeavor that planned to bring medical equipment to two hospitals, one in Gulu and another in Moya.

The Gulu hospital had well-trained doctors, but most patients in Uganda were treated, at least initially, by witch doctors. The witch doctors had no formal training but tradition and availability were significant factors in the medical community. They functioned like family doctors for most Ugandans.

The traditional witch doctor performs exorcism—to cast out evil spirits— improve fertility, and are expected to provide medical advice and financial security. The medical functions are often related to mental conditions requiring herbs and incantations as treatment. The treatment for injuries, including fractures, is similar to that given for schizophrenia.

Witch doctors impact the medical system in two ways. Their patients are expected to follow nonscientific advice. The delay of appropriate care often results in irreversible situations or death. Secondly, many witch doctors engage in child mutilation and sacrifice. If you haven't sliced off a penis or cut out the tongue of a child, you probably are not a Ugandan witch doctor.

It is common practice for even a severely injured person to have their initial and sometimes long-term care provided by the local witch doctor. Eventually the futility of the treatments leads the patients to the emergency department at the local hospitals, but sometimes it is months after the injury. The delay in treatment, particularly with hip fractures, creates unhealed fractures and deformities that make walking impossible. Arm and hand injuries suffer the same fate: deformity, malunions, and markedly compromised function. A fresh fracture, if treated by modern methods, requires less than a third of the time to treat versus a delayed deformity and malunion.

The poor Gulu orthopedist is overwhelmed with work. The additional time to correct the complicated patients is an unwelcome intrusion into a hectic schedule. The ratio of patients to orthopedic surgeons is one to 20,000 in the U.S., compared to one to two million in Uganda—a hundred times greater. In addition, the stress of treating complicated cases often without the assistance of X-rays further compromises the treatment. Because many injured patients are never initially seen by a real doctor, the ratio of challenging fractures the Ugandan specialist sees is higher than it would be in the U.S. In Uganda many believers in witchcraft often suffer irreversible damage or death by their choice to first see the omnipresent witch doctors. Witch doctors are not helping by delaying appropriate care.

In addition to delaying proper care, the witch doctors demonstrate a more egregious action, the frequent dismembering and sacrifice of children, to satisfy the witch doctor's clientele. At times adults also become victims.

The history of the local healers started before the British came to Uganda in approximately 1894. The bizarre bloodletting practices have become more archaic over the last ten years, a transition from sacrificing animals to sacrificing children to improve the safety, wealth, and general well-being of the witch doctor's patients. Children's blood and body parts are given to patients with the belief this will bring them good luck.

Some patients visit the witch doctor with medical problems, like AIDS, anxiety or malaria, and are willing to pay up to $100,000 to be cured. The charge is dependent on the ability to pay. The more affluent the patient, the more likely the source of the cure is human blood and human body parts.

Witch doctors may pay money to the victim's parents to sacrifice their child. If the parents are poor even $200 sounds fair and they give up their child. If the doctor can't secure a volunteer, the witch doctor enters a village, usually at night, and finds a victim. A common pattern is the removal of an ear or tongue, but beheading and removal of feet and hands are also favorite body parts. Often a boy's or girl's genitals will be removed and the child is left to bleed to death. These body parts are given to the "patients" of the witch doctor. The witch doctors charge their patients far more than the payments given to the parents who sell their children.

Girls can be "immunized"—protected from sacrifice—by having their ears pierced, and boys are protected if they are circumcised. These minor alterations somehow destroy the mystical benefits of their body parts. It seems uniquely odd that a deranged doctor would be dissuaded from removing a foot or other mutilations based on the absence of foreskin.

Several years ago, a mutilation event was brought to the attention of Bob Goff, a U.S. lawyer visiting Uganda to establish schools for the underserved. He was introduced to the case of a ten-year-old who had survived the loss of his manhood. In the past, the local lawyers, authorities, and judges were reticent to interfere with the spiritually powerful witch doctors. Bob, however, was not intimidated. He pushed the case to the highest court in Uganda and prevailed with a guilty verdict that sent the witch doctor to prison. This landmark decision encouraged a change in direction but did not end the bizarre actions of the witch doctors who still perform the ritual of human sacrifice. They even kill their own children.

The number of Ugandan victimized children is likely

underreported but probably less than a 100 per year. When witch doctors kill or mutilate children people lack the courage to finger the perpetrator, even if they witnessed the atrocities. Recently there has been an uptick of arrests and convictions in spite of fear and reverence of the spiritual power held by the witch doctors.

In the early 70s, a friend working in Uganda witnessed the circumcision of an 18-year-old performed by a witch doctor without using anesthesia. That too seems unbelievable, but shows how strong a belief some folks have and in what most Americans would consider a terrible idea.

One out of every 290 Ugandans is a witch doctor. The number varies from source to source, but regardless there are many, and they are sustained by the general support for the spiritualism they espouse, even though the public is slowly moving away from those beliefs.

When the country was under attack in the 2010s by the Resistance Army, the number of mental illness cases was estimated to be 20% of the population; that group likely increased the barbarous activities. The Rebel Army killed 650,000 people in what became a civil war. The witch doctors, whose number may be as high as 3 million of the total population of 46 million, were responsible for treating those injured in the conflict.

Canada, recognizing this mental problem, sent a million dollars to train the witch doctors. That program educated the witch doctors on how to recognize mental illness and taught blood sacrifices and other holistic nonsense was inappropriate.

Referral to a psychiatrist was the correct treatment, and suddenly, many referrals were made to real doctors. The problem was there were only 32 Western-trained psychiatrists in the country.

In one small town 44 people were "sacrificed" to provide blood and body parts to "help" the patients. These victims were mostly adults who experienced mutilation and dismemberment, loss of eyes, limbs, tongue, and genitalia, followed by death on the premise this practice restored safety and wealth to witch doctors' clients.

As the country has stabilized and the number of witch doctors going to prison has increased, the bizarre sacrificing and murders have diminished. Other countries, such as Australia, have intervened with medical teams and have treated maimed patients with reconstruction and rehabilitation.

Uganda is surrounded by countries affected by similar witch doctor behavior. Progress is being made, but spiritual beliefs are hard to alter, and a dead child's blood pays well.

I never saw any victims of mutilation, but I saw many cases of injured patients whose treatment was compromised by the sad ministrations of witch doctors. Ugandan medical care will continue to be adversely affected until the public is educated regarding the evils of witch doctors. They are still mainstream. No reason to go underground as long as they are accepted.

The most unbelievable piece of this story for me is that people "sacrifice" their own children, truly believing this is the right thing to do.

My advice: If you are ever injured in Africa, be cautious about whom you select for care; definitely not a witch doctor.

Drugs

I **took a Percocet once when I had a kidney stone.** Barfing followed within 20 minutes. I had been on the floor writhing in pain before I took the pill, but I felt better before the narcotics. Apparently, most people have a more enjoyable reaction to opioids.

When people have their personalities replaced by drugs, I always wonder if the drugs washed out the personality or if the personality leaked out and was slowly replaced by drugs.

Kory, a 33-year-old motorcycle mechanic, ran out of methadone. His drug treatment program allowed him to receive a three-day dose for the weekend, but he came up short, possibly because he took two pills one day. Kory had been on vacation for ten years, receiving cheap drugs and Social Security. His application to the Horatio Alger Association, which honors perseverance, excellence, and integrity, will likely require an extra reference or two if he is going to get in.

The need for methadone called for a solution—namely, more methadone. The Circle K didn't stock it, so Kory called a cab and headed to the closest psych hospital, hoping that would serve as a quick solution—his Salvation Army of drugs. The hospital folks felt compelled to offer Kory a room in the lock-up area. They wanted to accommodate what they interpreted as a cry for help. He rejected their lock-up suggestion and exited the property even though the staff attempted to help him.

The sudden departure was not well thought out; he had to scale a 16-foot-high fence. He did well on the ascent piece and then got entangled with gravity, resulting in a nasty injury to his left ankle. His sudden tactless departure incensed his host, the hospital, and they called the local authorities. That was timely because Kory was severely hobbled by his soon-to-be-verified broken ankle. He was quickly apprehended and transported across the street to a general hospital where I first met him. He rejected the lock-up suggestion, having been down that route before.

I surgically repaired his fractured left ankle. Kory was concerned there would be pain and the need for narcotics. He thought they might not be prescribed because of his history. I was aware of the drug issue and used methadone plus standard narcotics to deal with his pain. Kory, being a nervous type not inclined to trust anyone, departed from his second hospital in two days. He had not been locked up. The hospital provided free night wear, nice cuisine, a thirty-inch flat screen TV, and methadone. Not a bad reward for a 16-foot fall. I think he was concerned he would not make it to the methadone clinic on Monday to receive his weekly prescription.

Drug addicts create a dilemma: how much narcotics does one prescribe if any, in addition to methadone. I gave him more narcotics than I preferred, but also opened his cast to make sure it was not too tight and creating a source of pain. The saying goes, "Even a crock (patient who prevaricates and complains about minor ailments) can experience real pain." I was extremely careful to eliminate any other source of pain: infection, blistering, or cast pressure. I realized that due to his being on narcotics, his pain-med requirements were going to be above the norm. I also wanted to avoid reintroducing his addiction.

When Kory departed the hospital I prescribed a generous six-week supply of narcotics. His daily requests were accompanied by the usual explanations about why he needed more pills: the dog ate them, his pills fell in the toilet, or they were in his pants that were washed. The drug litany went on: they fell in the sink, he was robbed outside the drug store, and his wife threw them out—bad choice because he was not married. I literally saw him almost every other day to check his temp and circulation. This type of patient, an almost always unsatisfiable person, is also a legal risk.

Six weeks post-op and at the end of casting, his narcotic adventure ended. He was back on methadone and no longer a candidate for any more *happy pills* from me. On his final visit, 12 weeks after his injury, his ankle had fully recovered, although he claimed it still hurt—no surprise.

• • •

Narcotic use can also be an office issue. Barbara, a trusted employee, was overheard by another employee ordering medication as if it were a prescription call for a patient, but the name was allegedly her husband's name. Initially my antenna went up to determine the facts. Was the employee's tip real? I needed proof of inappropriate behavior and didn't want to accuse her of wrongdoing until I was certain of the facts. I searched her purse (probably illegally) on several occasions without finding any drugs. Just by luck, an alert pharmacist called our office to validate the prescriptions because of the frequency. Also, the number of pills was uncharacteristic of my usual number. The prescriptions were under my name, and I clearly had not authorized them because he wasn't my patient. Problem, she called in meds for her husband without my directions to do so. It was subtle, not a large order for narcotics, but an under-the-radar amount of a commonly used drug.

There was another twist to this employee. She was also in charge of ordering small amounts of narcotics for office use. One day I asked for a few pills to give as a sample to a patient. A few days earlier a box of narcotics had arrived, so I knew we had some in stock. To my surprise there were none left. I immediately investigated how many we ordered and who was dispensing besides me. Barbara was the person ordering as well as the dispenser. Not only was she borrowing narcotics from the office supply, but writing prescriptions for her husband. I never felt certain who was the user, probably Barbara.

Once it was clear Barbara was behind the schemes, she was terminated. I learned a few weeks later she was hired by another orthopedic surgeon who never asked me why she left her previous job in my office—one she'd held for 13 years.

The process for writing narcotic prescriptions has improved and now the prescribing doctor retrieves a revolving number from his phone app, which changes every minute. Only the doctor has access to the number, making it very difficult to steal.

• • •

A longtime upstanding community member who traveled to France yearly for the French Open Tennis Tournament requested a refill of her narcotic. I wrote her a prescription about twice a year for chronic pain. Apparently, I was not providing enough for her needs. When she came in requesting pain pills, she discussed the tournament and her annual attendance. She was always concerned she might need pills when she was in Europe and would be stuck if she didn't have enough.

When I received a call from the police a few weeks later, they asked if I had written a prescription for her. I confirmed I had but for a small amount. The pharmacist correctly suspected my prescription had been altered and called the police. Mrs. Fancy Pants had written over the amount I ordered and made it for 340 rather than 34 pills. The pharmacy knew I never wrote for such a quantity and that ended her trip to Roland Garros for that year. She spent a year or two behind bars. Seems she had performed this trick before and the combination of offenses from previous years and multiple doctors' prescriptions were enough to limit her tasting of French cuisine to french fries at the local prison.

• • •

Johnny, a clever patient who'd received small doses of narcotics over the years, and I were on good terms. He gifted me a unique cane from his collection. The cane was made from a shark's spine—at least that is what he told me. It was quite flimsy, and not sturdy enough for his use but it enlarged my cane collection. Johnny had a war injury and needed a good cane for balance.

I received a call from a pharmacist inquiring about one of Johnny's prescriptions for 100 Percocet, an amount I never order, so I was sure I had not written it. Turns out Johnny had stolen a prescription pad from my office. This took place before the new and more secure system was in place. I never heard how Johnny was punished and I never saw him again.

I write narcotic prescriptions for odd quantities like 33 or 34 instead of 30 or 50, so when the pharmacy sees a more conventional amount, I will get a call asking about the prescription. Patients have been known to disappear from the pharmacy waiting line before the police arrive. Some were using stolen pads similar to Johnny's approach for obtaining drugs.

It is no wonder that some physicians will not write prescriptions for any narcotics. The new rules with electronic prescribing have taken the consumer out of the equation. Physicians can still provide addicted patients large quantities of drugs and the doctors who do so can still go to jail, but the patients can't steal prescription pads or alter a written script as was done in the old days. The office shenanigans should also be a thing of the past.

Dimples

Iwant to share the events of my last several weeks, which in the life of a golf ball is equivalent to seven dog years. I was resting in a dark pocket of the golf bag of my new owner Ted, when I decided to tell this story. I had many new friends in there, guys I met just after being pulled from the pond on the seventeenth hole. I go by Dimples—I have 350 of them— which are about par for my brand. I am a lady's ball, but most of my life I have been in the custody of men.

My journey started March 4th at 8 a.m. when John Hacker pulled me out of a box. I had no experience with John, but you should know golf balls are reincarnated and, therefore, have a keen insight regarding the game of golf. Plus, we quickly learn about our owners. We have an uncanny sense of hearing and feel no pain other than the pain of those trying to play this silly game.

John teed me up—one of the benefits; I momentarily sat on a little pedestal, king-like. Not for long, but I would be so honored many times a day if I didn't become a lost soul or take a swim. Wham, off I went. I went farther than the other balls belonging to John's friends. Next, I found myself on the green; two more pokes and I was in the hole. My first hole and I was part of a birdie. John jumped with excitement and I couldn't be happier. On the next hole, I almost became another birdie. John was good. I mean really good. On number four I rolled into the sand but John lofted me out near the pin, and bingo, an easy par. What a great start!

As John waited to hit, he mentioned that he wasn't paying any taxes because he only accepted cash for his work as a painter. Worse, the other players were also cheating. One on his wife and another had some deal with switching license plates and buying cars out of state, but not paying sales tax. The whole group was a bunch of hot-shot no-goods. What was weird was they were extremely ethical about golf; they followed golf etiquette and rules one hundred percent. I was never moved from a divot or pushed from a bad lie. It was a classic case of honor among thieves. John finished four under. I should have been happy but felt deflated to be a part of this group who should be wearing prison garb not golf shorts.

John was so good; I might never get lost. The following weekend I was out there again, but he pulled me into the bushes and was in a big hurry; he left me, so I became available for a new owner. The next day I was discovered by a nice lady Margaret, who immediately put me back into action. No more birdies; she was awful, at least at golf.

She whiffed me several times, and four putts were her average. She did not look handicapped, but she had to have some issues. She left me in the cup on 12 and had to walk back a few minutes later to find me.

She and her friends were very chatty, discussing recipes and shopping tips. I never knew there were so many senior discounts. Almost every national chain restaurant has a discount option. What Margaret needed was a 50 percent discount on her golf score. She was what I call a practical golfer. If she didn't like her lie, she kicked me to a happier place. There was no betting in her group so a little gentle cheating was harmless. She compensated for her lack of talent with her "I love America" stylish outfit, a red and white patriotic get-up complete with a Brink's load of jewelry. Her diamond ring was so big she had to cut the ring finger on her golf glove to fit over the massive rock. If she messed up a shot she chirped "maga posa," which means absolutely nothing but sounded like a nice Yugoslavian swear word. Because of her talent she repeated her admonition at least five times per hole. The rest of her group used more traditional words of disappointment and self-flagellation like "shit" and "you idiot." She made one putt of five feet and almost came out of her shorts. She was so happy. That made up for the seven shots it took for her to extract herself from a sand trap. She played almost every day after her husband died—better therapy than a psychiatrist. My pedagogical self wanted so much to give her a tip, but that wasn't happening so I just rolled with the punches. Finally, I was hit into a pond on 17, and I had to wait a day for Ted to scoop me out and continue with more adventures.

Ted was a preacher from a megachurch. He apparently played a lot of golf—three or four times a week. Not a shy guy, he related his background to the other two players who joined him that day. He had several associate pastors who did not play golf and it was Ted's responsibility to interact with God on the links. The huge donation pipeline he had created sounded like the Crystal Cathedral megachurch with unlimited funding. Ted was willing to bet a little of God's money on a golf game. He dressed like a dandy with fancy-polished, high-end golf shoes and played with top-quality clubs. He boasted that God wanted him to be a worthy representative of his flock. That's why he would bet, I thought, to be a worthy fleecer of other flocks.

Some golfers can justify anything.

I think God was in on the deal. Ted played poorly the first few holes until a substantial bet was established. He was good but his "luck" even more extra-terrestrial. He would hit a ball out of bounds and it would hit a tree or whatever God put in place to reflect the shot back onto the course. He could skip me over a water hole with the spirit of walking on water. On two occasions a rake stopped me from entering a trap. On one shot I was headed for a pond when I hit a tree and ricocheted onto the green. When he putted, the hole seemed to expand and swallow me up. I felt sorry for the poor and eventually poorer fellows betting with Ted. They lost their collective shirts.

Ted quoted scripture as he played, which in itself can be a bit unsettling for even a low handicap golfer; a little

Luke and John can be troublesome when you are playing with God and haven't been to church in years.

Ted's first love was probably himself, with golf second and the church a distant third. The church provided the foundation for his other loves to flourish. He never mentioned his family but think about it, you don't hear much about Jesus's family or those of Moses and Noah—they also had families.

I would have enjoyed hearing Ted preach at his megachurch, but the closest I came was being buried in his golf bag in the back of his red Porsche convertible. Several weeks went by before Ted chose to tee me up again. We were at a new place for me, a public course with high rough and terrible greens. Ted pulled me into the rough next to a shiny, cleaner, and easier-to-find ball. He never really looked for me once he found my replacement. Within an hour I was discovered by Barney, who also had deposited his ball in the same tall grass. I was off again with a new friend.

Barney was intense. If I didn't go where Barney wanted me to go, he threw his clubs and ventured into traditional golf talk with a slew of expletives. Unlike the lady I spoke of earlier, Barney was using the more traditional swear words. He was good with his limited vocabulary, using the same words for disappointment as he used for elation. A good putt would become a "fucking good putt," and a surprise good shot was, "I'll be shit." A lucky sand shot was followed with "I'll be fucked." And so his round continued with a steady stream of invectives in keeping with a bar scene.

My luck ran out when I was skipped across a cart path and was badly cut. That released another flood of sour golf comments but also placed me on permanent retirement after only three weeks of fun in the sun. My dimples were abraded and sliced. I was sad to no longer be relevant, but it was fun while it lasted.

Dimple's funeral is pending "Fore" a while.

Progress

Modern medicine would be unrecognizable to a consumer 100 years ago. William Osler was anointed the Father of Modern Medicine before he died in 1919. For my story I will focus primarily on the last 100 years, or post the modern medicine designation, as a convenient period to illuminate the prodigious progress made in medicine, especially in orthopedics. I have been fortunate to experience 60 of those years of progress first-hand.

The first medical school was established at the University of Bologna in Italy in 1200 A.D. Like many early medical schools, the curriculum evolved from teaching anatomy and a few other medical courses until a true medical school emerged, which contained the broad range of medical subjects taught today. That was true of the first medical school in the U.S., the University of Pennsylvania, established in 1765. In 1892 A.T. Still, an M.D., started the first osteopathic school in Kirksville, Missouri.

William Osler, an M.D. by way of the McGill Medical School in Montreal, was heavily involved with medical progress, and in 1893 he helped start the Johns Hopkins Medical School in Baltimore, Maryland. He founded the first specialty residency training program. Osler was a keen observer and established teaching techniques encouraging student-to-patient contact and book learning as keys to medical education. This approach continues as a major element of teaching today. Osler was highly respected and wrote *The Principles and Practice of Medicine.* Despite his excellent training he believed in bloodletting, and his writings helped perpetuate this now antiquated treatment.

His bibliophile upbringing was out of step with his view on race. He often said Canada should be "White Man's Country" and "I hate Latin Americans." He expressed a disdain for indigenous people more than once. These comments seem incongruous for a man dedicated to helping society through better medical training.

• • •

In 1891 Professor Gluck, a German, implanted ivory in the hip of a patient with T.B., an isolated event but probably the first person to perform an orthopedic implant.

Sir Robert Jones, a contemporary of Osler was a general surgeon in Liverpool, England, and was the driving force to make orthopedics into a specialty. The general surgeons had taken care of crippled children and fractures, but Dr. Jones recognized the need for specialty care and established an orthopedic hospital in the early 1900s. He, like Osler, benefitted from the discovery of X-rays in 1896.

Sir Reginald Watson-Jones was the next significant player in the progress toward treating orthopedic patients, particularly those who had hip arthritis. His surgical approach was used by Marius Smith-Peterson in 1925 for the first American hip joint replacement using a glass implant. Over the next 40 years he tried several other materials and settled on vitallium, an alloy of chromium and cobalt, which was in vogue in 1960.

Progress in orthopedics has been jerky at times. The total hip replacement evolved from cup arthroplasty, which used a cup sitting on the top of the femur. In 1940 Dr. Austin Moore developed a stemmed femoral head replacement; the stem was placed into the femoral canal. In 1953, Dr. George McKee implanted a metal-on-metal replacement—both cup and stem were metal.

• • •

As a medical student in 1960 I received my first taste of orthopedics. The University of Iowa Medical School housed a cutting-edge department of orthopedics. I learned about the cup arthroplasty, the state-of-the-art method of managing hip arthritis, which was in vogue in Iowa and continued to slowly evolve even though it had been around for 35 years. But ten years later the procedure became irrelevant.

In 1960s surgeons were experimenting with various options for hip arthritis. Regional enthusiasm developed for the femoral osteotomy, which altered the position of the worn-out hip joint without the need for an implant. This choice also gave inconsistent pain relief. The Girdlestone procedure—the removal of the hip ball, leaving the patient with several inches of shortening on the operative side—offered another option. A few surgeons performed hip fusions, as a rarely used choice to treat the arthritic hip.

In 1964 I attended a meeting in Los Angeles where the leading hip surgeons from the best U.S. medical schools argued vigorously for their preferred way to treat hip arthritis. Egos were in full view as the eminent orthopedic surgeons of the day took direct hits from each other as they tried to support their personal biases. This epic conference revealed to me, an untrained observer, how science can be clouded by emotion. That meeting became the terminal presentation for the soon-to-be-deceased litany of outdated hip operations.

• • •

The surgical results of the early procedures proved inconsistent and even the main proponents of those surgeries switched to joint replacement later in the 60s as new procedures primarily from the work of Sir John Charnley were recognized. He was responsible for the next giant step to manage hip arthritis. His contribution was based on ceramic fixation—a bone glue borrowed from dentistry and used to hold the joint replacement in the bone. When I was an orthopedic resident, we could use only a cementless prothesis called a Ring because the cement was not authorized outside of the U.K. other than at a few university hospitals.

The Ring prosthesis was metal-on-metal and required a long screw-in socket filling cup. The placement of the cup had to be very exact and I still don't know how anyone could routinely orient it correctly. Because the Ring was the only prosthesis I was familiar with, that is what I started using in practice. To my knowledge my first joint replacement in practice was also the first joint replacement performed in Arizona. It was almost my last. The hard part of the operation, the positioning and insertion of the screw-in cup, went well. Unfortunately, the patient was tiny and the stemmed femoral component that came with the set was way too big to fit in my patient.

I was showing the local world how to do this new operation and I had trouble finishing it. After three hours of surgery and ten pounds of sweat and frustration, I was able to use a small Austin Moore prosthesis to fill the femur with a ball that fit in the cup. These metals were not intended to be used together, but it was my only choice. Fortunately, the hospital had a small size that would fit, otherwise I would have had to close the incision and come back when I obtained a matching set.

That problem never happened again, and within a few months I was able to train on the Charnley-style operation because the cement became available in the U.S. It was the end of the Ring for me.

• • •

Since 1970 multiple companies have competed for the best-of-show prosthesis. Initially there was no clear winner, and during my 50 years of performing joint replacements I used at least six brands, always seeking the product that had the best features. Some were easier to implant, others were backed with good service, and others were less expensive. The competition was fierce and still is. Subtle design changes, better wear characteristics, instrumentation, and product service, all were considered in choosing the ideal prosthesis.

Some faulty designs were identified early and eliminated. Others died a slow death, requiring years before the deficiencies of design became obvious.

Metal-on-metal parts reappeared and were considered to be the newest and apparent winner for the best prosthesis until a few years passed when big problems surfaced that were not discovered in the pre-release period. That was odd because less than 20 years earlier metal-on-metal had failed due to the excess metal particles reacting with the body. It is not just politicians who have a short memory.

Some doctors are quick to try new designs or follow a salesperson's enthusiasm, only to learn years later they have been implanting a bad product. Even in the car industry, a recall may occur five years into the life of the vehicle for a brake or airbag problem. That has happened more than once with hip components. It is problematic and frustrating to have a research trial of 5000 patients who have operations with products A, B, and C, then wait ten years to see which company had the best design.

While surgeons tried to figure out the best products, the instruments used to implant the parts steadily improved, making the operations easier, quicker, and more successful. The number of hip revision surgeries because of a faulty prothesis have decreased. The training and specialization also helped diminish revisions. However, the surgical revision rates among aggressive, financially enthusiastic surgeons have remained the same. Hospital rules and oversight have lessened surgical misadventures, so the future looks bright for better outcomes.

$$\bullet \ \bullet \ \bullet$$

Hip pain has multiple causes, and before X-rays in 1895, understanding the source of the pain was markedly limited. Identifying bacterial causes was nonexistent before Robert Koch identified tubercle bacillus. Eventually CAT scans and MRI further enabled doctors to more accurately identify why hips hurt. Laboratory assistance helped classify conditions related to rheumatoid arthritis and gout.

As the diagnostic progress improved, it became apparent the treatment would not be a singular approach. The majority of patients with hip pain have some form of arthritis, especially degenerative arthritis (D.A.). With D.A. there is a familial variety for which there is no blood test, but a strong hereditary pattern. The D.A. associated with trauma can be a separate category if it follows a severe event, but often repetitive trauma overlaps with familial arthritis.

The principal reason for surgical intervention is pain, but limited motion can occasionally be the more important cause for surgery. On only one occasion I took apart a painless, fused hip and implanted a total hip. That procedure was a major challenge. I anticipated as much, but it was even more challenging than I expected. There were none of the usual landmarks and pure carpentry was required. Like several other procedures I have done, one was enough.

In the modern era the non-operative treatment for hip pain has remained consistent, including shots, auto-inflammatory meds and physical therapy. There have also been complementary medicine approaches such as rub-ons, TENs units, cold lasers, and antioxidants. Magnets, ultrasound, herbal wraps, pomegranate juice or like products continue to be touted. Removal of silver dental fillings and treatment with electronic waves are part of the exhaustive alternative programs still used to diminish inflammation.

Initially, particularly in the early 70s, the Charnley style hip replacement was the gold standard, but his surgical approach was modified to a simpler and quicker version of hip replacement. It is interesting to note the first hip surgeries were done through an anterior approach. This approach was abandoned, but 80 years later, the anterior approach was "discovered" and became the new normal, the Super Mario of the surgical approach world.

The improvement in the component design and the more durable plastics used for the hip cup gradually produced longer-lasting results. As companies vied for market share there were missteps in design that were generally short-lived. Various surgical approaches, smaller incisions, and computer-generated parts were introduced to improve outcomes. Better instruments, new coating on the components and more secure cup fixation led to longer-lasting results. And now robotics are creeping into the operating room.

The differences between the components of the many companies in the race are relatively minor. The results now are more dependent on surgical technique. A skilled surgeon who uses the acceptable methods to prevent infection, appropriate hemostasis, and proper use of pain management will likely produce an excellent outcome.

Having ridden the treatment of hip arthritis wave from the rejection of multiple inadequate procedures to what now seems a marvelous, reproducible solution gives me satisfaction. I have performed a few total hip replacements with designs that are no longer available. I much prefer the current joint components to solve a once dicey problem. That is real progress.

More Progress

Learning from my personal history was an idea that excited me. Having a hoarder mentality allowed me to save many paper records and photographs from the past. My filing cabinet contains operation reports from my two years in the military, my three years of orthopedic residency at Vanderbilt University Medical School, and random reports throughout my time in private practice. Like looking at old pictures, reading these onionskin reports elevated memories long buried. Some were painful to recall while others brought a smile. Most were stale and devoid of any emotion, revealing routine procedures involving patients long erased from my memory.

I also have a three-feet-tall stack of "interesting X-rays" retained for training purposes. These films further cement the evidence of how far orthopedics has progressed during my medical era.

During my residency training years I dictated over half of the reports of the surgeries I participated in as the surgeon or assistant. Dictating places the spoken word into the official typed report of the events related to the procedure. In many surgeries I was not the surgeon but the assistant to a senior resident or staff doctor. When I became the surgeon, my assistant dictated my surgeries. Strangely the dictating party was not identified on some of the reports.

Many features of the reports surprised me. The "voice" of the surgeon didn't resonate in the reports, meaning a reader would not be certain as to who did what. In a teaching hospital this vagueness of not revealing the identity of the surgeon prevailed—a co-surgical approach. This apparent lack of transparency arose because Dr. A would suggest a surgical step and Dr. B would actually do it. Really not meant to deceive; it would be impractical to state all of the intraoperative discussion. The senior surgeon received credit for the case, no matter who did the majority of the work. He may not have been present for the majority of the procedure. If the patient knew who actually performed the surgery they may not have approved.

This sounds like a charade, but supervising professors or experienced surgeons rarely put themselves in a vulnerable legal situation. They evaluated each trainee and made sure the "student" was capable before moving on to another room or instructional opportunity. I did the same thing as a senior resident when I supervised the less experienced doctors being sure they were not over their heads in any given situation.

Basic surgical information often needed to be included in the reports: which shoulder was operated on, how much blood was lost, length of tourniquet times, and the size of the implants. Granted, when I was in training my reports reflected the earliest days of learning. I also worked with many surgeons with a wide range of teaching aptitudes. I gained knowledge from the good teachers as well as the bad. Some of the reports were done by experienced staff doctors who should have provided a better example of how to dictate an excellent operative report. I know that the surgeries I reviewed were much different from the reports I dictated when I started in private practice, suggesting I learned something.

Each training program may emphasize a different style. I have overheard dictations by private practitioners that reflect information overload. "I incised this and looked at that, and I tied off that vessel and I cauterized a bleeder here and a bleeder there." The reports read like a Michener novel; key elements of the story were lost—buried in minutiae.

Most of the old reports contained all the necessary information. Removing a superficial foreign body requires very little detail, although "foreign body removed" is still considered inadequate documentation. Some reports failed to mention an adequate description of the anatomy. "A rock was removed from the leg" needs to state a muddy, jagged, four-by-six-inch rock was removed from behind the left knee revealing no evidence of nerve or vascular injury. Simple modification but unlikely the report of a rookie.

My second observation related to the lack of justification for the surgery. The information should have been available, otherwise the surgery would not have been performed. Yet many notes, including mine, were lacking in those details. Easy to say, "The surgery was performed because a large disc herniation was seen on a myelogram on the left side at the L4-5 level."

Before MRI's, CAT scans and bone scans were invented, shoulder, knee, and back surgeries were often performed as diagnostic procedures. State of the art meant relying on one's clinical judgment. The myelogram was the best tool available to confirm a ruptured disc diagnosis, but it missed several conditions that an MRI would have detected. The back was particularly vulnerable to "exploration." The surgeon made his incision at L4-L5 level anticipating finding a disc bulge based on whatever sketchy information he had. If he found no disc bulge at that level, he then extended the incision (explored) to the next level. The exploration part started when pathology—disc rupture—was absent at the suspected level. The MRI has greatly decreased the surgical "exploration" of many surgeries, especially of the shoulder, knee and back; although an occasional surprise is encountered in spite of the MRI assist.

MRIs obviate the importance of a physical exam in many cases. A current problem is finding pathology on an MRI that isn't necessarily the cause of the pain. This information can lead to expensive and unnecessary studies such as a biopsy of an old valley fever spot in the lung. Most of these biopsies are negative for cancer, but if the radiologist states that he cannot rule out cancer, the biopsy is performed in response to the legal threat of ignoring the radiologist's advice. MRIs sometimes suck the doctor into an awkward situation.

Following X-rays of most complex fractures, a CAT scan further clarifies fracture pattern by giving a three-dimensional picture. This allows the surgeon to have the proper equipment and plan in place before starting the surgery. These diagnostic tools are akin to the surgeon taking a giant tranquilizer before surgery. The surgeon knows what to expect rather than guessing. Taking a real tranquilizer is not considered appropriate, although the alcoholic version appear from time to time.

The MRI obtained prior to shoulder surgery allows a more accurate assessment of the pathology in addition to clarifying alternative procedures, prognosis, and scope of surgery. The MRI information may change the anticipated procedure from a rotator cuff repair or a shoulder replacement to something as simple as an injection.

The last revelation I gained from reviewing the old reports: over half of the surgical cases performed during my training and military service are no longer done in the same way or with the same equipment today. Exceptions being: carpal tunnel, Dupuytrens contracture, and trigger finger surgical procedures, which are generally performed the same way now as they were 50 years ago.

Currently, almost every fracture is managed with modern equipment including newer intramedullary rods, external fixators, and better designed plates. The wonderful C-arm, a potable X-ray used in the operating room allows the surgeon to see the location of the surgically implanted hardware immediately. We also have wound vacs, hyperbaric O_2 chambers, robotics, and other equipment advances making treatment much more predictable.

Arthroscopy, not available in my residency, is now used in all major joints to minimize discomfort, shorten the hospital stay, and address problems more effectively in most cases.

My op notes reveal that the use of X-rays in operating room is more frequent now than in my training days. Fifty years ago, the surgeon decided, by his experience, if the screws were the correct length or the bone was aligned properly. The extra time waiting for X-rays to be developed or even waiting for the X-ray department to show up and take the films was aggravating. In the 70s polaroid X-ray bridged the gap in the OR before the C-arm replaced it.

My prepractice reports mention three methods of managing hip arthritis; cup arthroplasty, femoral prosthesis, and a Girdlestone—removal of the femoral head. No artificial joint surgeries were done in my program until the last year of my residency. The original iteration of a total hip replacement had a short existence in the U.S., probably less than five years, but it was the type I used when I first performed hip replacements in practice, before a new kid on the block showed up, the Charnley hip.

Knee replacements became popular after I completed my residency. Osteotomies—division of the tibial bone below the knee to change the knee forces—were used in the 60s but were still not wildly popular because they didn't produce great results.

A few orthopedists have adopted navigational capability. This is a computer-programmed surgical tool that assists the surgeon in total joint surgery by making most of surgical bone cuts based on the presurgical information. The surgeon still needs to be prepared to override the system if the computer information is inaccurate, but many of the younger surgeons have been trained to use these advances. Older surgeons still trust their experience and use more economical approaches to joint replacement.

Overlooked but real is the greater concentration of procedures in the subspecialty hands—such as a doctor who performs only knee replacements. If a doctor, does 300 hip replacements a year for example, his results are statistically better than those of the five-a-year doc. I can cite situations where that is not true, but this "concentration" statistic is usually a valid metric. Fifty years ago, most orthopedic procedures were done by every orthopedist, as was my case.

My old op notes clearly demonstrate how far orthopedic care has progressed in all areas from trauma to management of arthritic joints. Hospital stays are shorter as are surgery times.

Medical care is in a much better place than it was 60 years ago. The training in all specialties has improved, the same with diagnostic and mechanical options. Information regarding genetics advanced as well. If medical providers pay attention to and use the available information, life quality and life expectancy will continue to benefit from the great strides being made.

The consumer doesn't need to see my op reports to know that medical care is in a better place today compared to 60 years ago. Medical missteps occurred but were necessary for the learning process. Many prostheses made the first cut but failed in the long term. That has been true of medications that held great promise for arthritis but were toxic and deadly. What sounded like wise medical choices occasionally proved to be folly.

At least the quality of my operative reports has made progress.

The Salesman

Selling was the last thing I wanted to do, just another thing that made me uncomfortable. Selling requires enthusiasm, sex appeal, a persuasive personality, and a reasonable product. I lacked all of the above. I was short, prematurely grey, and in early the stages of thinking about whether I should continue wearing a coat and tie or switch to skirts. This gender confusion probably didn't affect my sales ability. I was generally confused, confused about why I couldn't get good grades; five years of high school was too long, confused why I kept wrecking cars, so far three red Camaros, and confused about why women ran the other way. Life seemed to be uphill.

At twenty-nine I lived in a small, dank, one-room apartment that looked out over a lot full of used tires. I thought of it more as a rubber plantation. I had bills to pay while trying to stay in trade school. My busboy or girl job, depending on the day, didn't work out. I couldn't blame the loss of the busing job on my B.O., as stated by the jerk manager, but that was his story.

My parents gave me lukewarm support, but at least I could visit them, despite our thread-like relationship. They did not brag about me to their friends. My father had been a salesman when he was younger. He never sold big stuff like cars or houses. I think he sold shoes before going to work at the post office.

Mom was a buyer, not a seller. This led to domestic confrontations. She took her credit card for a wild ride every week or two, with no restraints. She had inherited money from her parents, which fueled her habit and accounted for the hundreds of shoes and unworn clothes in her closet. My father returned many of the items if he could find the sales slips. Most of the time she didn't know the difference because she had a big closet stuffed with far too many new items for her to keep track of. She claimed she had to have new clothes because her size constantly changed. She felt compelled to keep up with the Joneses, but since she was a Jones, no winner emerged. She once bought two mink stoles the same day from a consignment store. I guess she thought one would be lonely without the other. Two happy mink stoles remain warm and content in her Arizona closet.

Luckily, or so I thought, I fell into this deal where I could sell burial plots bundled with a prepaid funeral. My company offered different plans depending on how elaborate the box was. If you bought the expensive box, there were more amenities, music, and flowers. The hole was the same—8 by 2½ feet and 6 feet deep. The boxes ranged from the pauper's package—cheap pine—or the moderate package—mahogany with music in the casket, and the luxury package—oak trimmed in gold with music and flowers. Locating prospects who were willing to die or at least accept the fact that death might be a possibility was my challenge. I received a one-hour-long training video and a stack of brochures outlining seventeen options, including cremation and a family plan. The options had options: including ash scattering or a can designed for backyard burial.

A health club close to my home allowed me to do my first demo. The owner happened to be a family friend. The demo coincided with the coldest day of the year. My assigned location for the demonstration was in the lobby near the front door. Each time the door swung open an icy blast chilled me and scattered my brochures onto the floor. People in need of exercise who fought each other for the closest parking place were generally blind to my impressive presentation. I needed a picture of a hunky dead person holding barbells.

"What's that, Bud?"

"I'm selling burial plots and funeral packages. You can get a great deal if you buy before you need them. There is only so much land, and you will die. So, I have this smoking deal that is cheaper now than it will ever be."

"Look at me. Do I look like I am going to die?"

"Odds are you will, and you can save your loved ones time and grief if you are farsighted and invest now. Buy now at a discount and get the hole reserved where you want it, near that special tree or by the brook. We also have the cremation package."

"Get real, by the time I die, Obamacare will pay for dying too."

That was the longest conversation I had with anyone the entire three hours I stood at the display. Only two people took a flyer.

I did learn one thing: people who exercise all smelled the same when they left the building. I thanked the management for allowing me to show my stuff but decided no more health clubs even though I did see some lovely-looking men.

• • •

On a home visit, a thin, elderly lady and her rat-like dog answered my knock on the door. Without hesitation, she let me in. The dog was a nervous sort with a pathetic yippy bark, which he offered as he retreated behind the tiny lady. She wore a cross on her necklace as did the dog. The room behind her was covered with pictures of Jesus-like folks. Most of the pictures were portraits but some showed action: Jesus appearing to be playing soccer or Jesus sipping wine. The lady had a quiet demeanor and sported a nasal cannula connected to her oxygen tank. This was a good thing for me; the reaper couldn't be too far away.

With no mention of a husband, we chatted about the next step and how being ready for the big one was important.

"My husband should hear what you're saying. He makes all the decisions about our business. He is not home because he is getting a new hearing aid and a haircut. He gets a haircut twice a year. Really could get by with once a year."

"You look like you are in good health."

"I feel good if I remember to take my pills, but I get up four times a night, and I've lost twenty-five pounds since May. I wonder where my husband is? He gets lost sometimes. What are you selling?"

"Just introducing you to a great funeral package and how vulnerable we all are. The flu could take a person any time. I have a package for two that includes pets. If you died first, I would keep the dog until his passing, a special service of our company. If the dog went first, he could move in with you on your passing."

I told her about the glow-in-the-dark feature of the casket under plan K. for those afraid of the dark. She was taken with plan K's lighting feature which would also allow at least two pictures of Jesus to be in the box with her. She had to feed the dog, so I said I would return tomorrow. I had not perfected the closing pitch yet; really hadn't perfected any pitch.

My spiel to the silver-haired dog lover was a step in the right direction, but I still had not moved any product (as it was referred to in the video).

I needed to find someone like my mother who would buy things just for the sake of buying things. She recently got onto Craigslist and bought a naked picture of Obama's mother when she was a baby and a tongue blade used to examine John Wayne. She bought enough moon rocks to start her own galaxy. That was the kind of person I needed to find.

So, I tried Craigslist looking for funeral packages, which strangely were listed under adult toys, subcate-gory funeral packages. I found no category for deceased white females. I listed my funeral/burial combo under *Happy Ending.* A day later Barker David contacted me. Barker seemed very interested in the dead or things loosely related to death. He came to my apartment that same day, which was a good thing for me unless he had turned out to be a mass murderer. I didn't consider that possibility until after we started talking.

Barker showed up wearing white short-shorts, black, well-worn tennis shoes, and a purple t-shirt that said, "Just Finished." I was afraid to ask what that meant but hoped he was through with life and was looking for a nice deal on a funeral ceremony with plot included. I pulled out the brochures and went into the seventeen available options. He immediately showed interest in D, which included a plastic palm tree next to the hole and a recording device that played two of his favorite songs for as long as the batteries lasted. I told him that if he bought the D package, I would put in new batteries monthly for at least a year. He had a pet who liked dark places, so for no charge the snake could join him in the casket. Barker preferred a pine casket covered with an Arkansas flag. He had no interest in flowers, so I suggested a fruit basket every month as his graveside decoration. He quipped "I prefer salads."

Things rolled along great, especially when he told me he would pay cash for the funeral package with money he could borrow from a sick uncle. He appreciated his uncle's generosity so much he wanted to buy a funeral package for the uncle and the uncle's family. He indicated Uncle Oren might be dying soon. Barker should know about his uncle's health because he was in charge of Oren's medications. I noticed Barker had on rainbow socks; maybe that was why we connected. Because of the cash discount, Barker signed the contracts for five people and paid me in ten-dollar bills.

Three days later I read a shocking story in the paper: a tragic automobile accident occurred the day before; five members of the Barker David family plunged off the Reaper bridge. No one survived.

Surprisingly, those plots were the only ones I ever sold. I returned to the fitness club to see if they had a custodial job. I crossed sales off my list.

Ps: Information was more or less provided by a gracious, loquacious patient while receiving a knee injection. No fact checking was performed but I am confident that the story is true— I think.

Fake Fake Fake

For me, the dynamics of lying is a chicken or egg thing. Do people lie to improve their self-esteem or just lie as a stand-alone behavior? George Santos, a New York congressman elected in 2022, presumably lied to gain a seat in the House. His illuminated behavior revealed the majority of the stories of his education, family history, previous jobs, financial successes, and athletic prowess were pure fabrication. His whole life is rife with rip-offs, Ponzi schemes, and other ways to scam the public—Madoff-like movie material. Mr. Santos demonstrated behavior more consistent with a psychopath, a person who lies for personal gain and power. Psychopaths also reflect no guilt when taking a lie detector test. Lying is a part of their personality. By telling falsehood after falsehood, Santos hoodwinked enough voters to be elected. When outed, he demonstrated the depth of his ethical disdain by refusing to resign from his elected position. He continued to fabricate the facts of his degrees, birthplace, or almost anything about his past. Mr. Santos is the glowing star of this year's crop of policymakers and is creating difficult decisions for those in his party who believe lying is inappropriate.

Studies suggest that about 13% of people are pathological liars who tell at least ten lies a day. Pathological lying is a symptom of narcissism, antisocial behavior, or histrionic personality disorder. For some politicians, strike me down if I am wrong, the percentage might be higher.

People qualifying as pathological liars—not psychopaths—respond to a lie detector with stress and arousal. They often lie without an obvious reason for their behavior. The examples I describe in this story, including Mr.

Santos, were motivated clearly to gain from their lies, moving them into the psychopathic category.

On occasion physicians have sullied the profession by slipping through the conventional screening processes to practice without appropriate credentials. As was the case with Mr. Santos, the bigger the lie, the more likely it is to be accepted. Physicians have been known to forge letters of reference. Resumés may refer to a mentorship as a six-month experience when it was only a half-day visit with a well-known doctor. The committee of doctors on a hospital staff who review applicants are usually busy, trusting physicians with little time or enthusiasm to pursue the details of an application. The possibility of false information slipping by a reviewer is high. Often a call to the department where the doctor was trained or a hospital where the doctor worked will give a superficial or neutral response for legal purposes. Would the head of a department say they let an incompetent doctor graduate from their program? Not likely. Passing along a bad apple is also a common problem in law enforcement and education. In medicine the required reference letters are usually straightforward enough to give the reviewer a clue, a heads up. "He graduated from our program" should alert the committee to dive deeper. A letter referring to high moral character, outstanding performance, and impeccable ethics is more in keeping with a solid candidate.

Adam Litwin, now Adam Litwin M.D., had an intriguing journey. As a nine-year-old he watched his grandfather, a podiatrist, treat broken feet. In high school he wore a beeper and pretended the hospital would call him for a consultation. He attended St. Louis University as a premed student. Depression caused him to drop out of college and move back to California. His interest in medicine persisted so he started reading medical textbooks at the UCLA library. At this point his enthusiasm to be a doctor was typical of others I have known who initially failed to be admitted to medical school, yet persisted and eventually became physicians.

While spending time at UCLA someone mistook Adam for a resident and he did not correct the misimpression. He fabricated a story saying he was a resident who transferred from another hospital. He was invited to watch complicated surgeries, stole a doctor's parking pass, pilfered a key to enter the doctors' lounge, and slept in the on-call room. Like other doctors he wore a white coat, but strangely silk-screened his name and picture on it. He never treated a patient, but hung out with the doctors for nine months. He could enter restricted areas because the name on his badge was covered by a meal ticket obscuring his credentials. He also forged prescriptions for medication until the pharmacy became suspicious, which led to his arrest.

Jail time and psychiatric counseling were his reward for faking his identity. Seven years after being released from incarceration, he married. His wife was under the impression he was a cardiologist. The marriage lasted several years, and it appears she still thought he was a doctor at the time of the divorce.

At 38, several years after his divorce, the St. James School of Medicine on the Caribbean island of Bonaire accepted him. Obviously, their entrance criteria were lower than most U.S. medical schools. After spending two years on Bonaire, he completed his third and fourth years of medical school in Chicago. That medical school was no more discerning than the Caribbean school.

This is a heartwarming story of a pathological liar who even after going to jail for his fake life convinced a woman to marry him. Plus, she bought the cardiology tale. That's the kind of man I want to take care of my family. Really, a leopard who lost his spots.

Malachi Love-Robinson also demonstrated that it's hard to change your spots. He opened a practice called New Birth Life Medical Center pretending, to be a doctor. He was arrested at age 18 for prescribing medication to an undercover cop. Before the arrest he had used his patients' checking accounts to make his own car payments. Even after being arrested for taking money from an elderly client, he was arrested again for using a stolen credit card to buy a Jaguar. He did not rebound and never became a doctor.

Another beacon of fakery, Charles Akoda, passed himself off as an OB doctor. His downfall followed the death of a newborn, which resulted from him not recognizing the mother was in labor when she presented to him with vaginal leakage. The delay in discovering her real condition led to the fetal death.

Akoda, his real name, Oluwafemi Charles Igberase, had 11 pseudonyms. He was born in Nigeria and entered the U.S. on a nonimmigrant visa. He obtained multiple Social Security numbers with multiple names and addresses. He then applied many times to the Educational Commission for Foreign Medical Graduates using a variety of identities and was given two certifications with different names. These certifications were revoked when the board discovered he used different names and addresses on the applications. However, five years later Akoda passed the exam again and was recertified even though applicants were not allowed to take the exam multiple times. He skirted this requirement by applying with the plethora-of-names approach. Anyone who had taken the test ten times could figure out how to pass it. It seems implausible that he could be certified after having been discovered earlier to be a fraud, but his persistence beat the system.

Then he was considered a medical school graduate despite not attending medical school. He applied for residency and Howard University accepted him into the OB program at Prince George Hospital Center. Akoda obtained the residency position by writing fraudulent letters of recommendation in addition to a fraudulent document he obtained showing he had completed medical school. Thirteen years after starting his residency the Maryland Medical Board licensed him. The thirteen-year interval was never explained.

After being in practice for five years his subpar performances and failed personality caught up with him. He lasted as long as he did because he was working with low-income clientele who were accepting of his ability.

His medical partners lacked awareness or they were complicit with his unacceptable performance.

In spite of having completed a residency he proved to be an F-level practitioner He spent only six months in jail for fraud but deserved at least ten years.

Another fake procedure that deviant physicians have been known to use is expanding their care outside of the training typical for their specialty. Liposuction comes to mind. A specialist in OB or ENT starts offering liposuction, which is customarily performed by a plastic or general surgeon. The non-plastic surgeon decides, "Why not me?" and starts performing liposuction. Liposuction is easy and financially rewarding. So easy that a surgeon's office staff performed the procedure after hours, presumably without his knowledge. Unfortunately, the patient died in the office.

The good news is the vast majority of doctors follow the traditional pathways of training and practice according to their specialty guidelines

The fact remains that 13% of the population tell ten lies a day including a range of ages, ethnicities, educational levels, and incomes.

We all have been guilty of expressing facts that later turn out to be false. Who knows what will be considered factual regarding Covid, vaccinations, mask-wearing, global warming, and multiple other politically charged data? For now l hope that the George Santoses and shady doctors of the world don't breed.

Whine and Vinegar

You are now a mouse in the corner of an operating room. Usually, you would not be allowed to stay, but for literary reasons, you are accepted unless you create a distraction. You are allowed to record the sounds, photograph the action, and remember the odors, flavor, and tension of the hallowed environment. If bored, you should be able to move about from room to room to experience the full spectrum of your O.R. visit.

The typical cast includes a surgeon, an assistant in most cases, a circulating nurse, an anesthesiologist, a scrub tech, and the patient. Instrument reps, orderlies, and cleaning personnel play bit parts. The participants come in every flavor, including Muslims, Mormons, gays, blacks, browns, whites, and many nationalities. Sizes range from ultrasmall to XXX. A few belong to A.A., and a few more should. Some players can afford a ticket to outer space, while others will never pay off their student loans—which could include the doctors.

Room one features a quiet, shy ophthalmologist, Dr. Marvin, and his equally quiet longtime assistant. The scrub tech is a seasoned (old) gal who is unlikely to speak and the circulator also is experienced enough to be quiet. Hank, the anesthesiologist at the head of the table, has been with the surgeon before and is also known as a nonverbal guy. After the required opening validation of which eye is to have surgery, there is no dialogue, no music. If one were to break wind, it would be easily noticed. The case lasts 15 minutes and never once were the 69-mile-an-hour gales of the previous night discussed, nor Covid, nor Biden, nor Trump.

The scene in the next room has the same number of players but slightly different personalities. The surgery is an abdominal exploration. This implies an adventure into the unknown. Surgeon Fred begins with, "This could be a F-ing hard case. What did you think about the Dodgers getting a walk-off after trailing by four runs? They are so F-ing lucky. I don't think Frank should be playing until he gets vaccinated."

Dr. Barnes, the anesthesiologist, pipes up with, "The Diamondback's skipper has more goddamn bad luck. He needs a long vacation. Why did he leave that shitty pitcher in as long as he did?"

Just before a pus fountain erupts from the patient's abdomen an overhead page blares for Dr. Parson to call extension 2702. Fred's response, "Is that SOB still on the staff?"

"Holy Shit, we may have a problem. He must have a ruptured viscus," the assistant ventures, "It smells like brown stuff."

The circulating nurse, her first time in a case with Fred, is in the corner snickering about the belly laughing events when Fred rips her for not having the lights in the correct location. She is immediately reduced to full-blown embarrassment with a weak "I'm sorry" response.

The lights are adjusted, the pus is collected, and sports talk quickly resumes. The surgical challenge, to find the leak in the gut, continues with twenty feet of intestine pulled out of the abdomen and sprawled like a fat snake on top of the patient. A small but significant perforation is eventually located. Once the gut is stretched across the belly it always seems to grow and looks impossible to replace inside the patient. The surgeon manages to tuck it all back in with the assist of additional expletives.

The patient doesn't realize he has been the recipient of a Home Run; his life has been saved by removing a gallon of pus and closing the bowel leak. It seems little attention has been given to the task, but the job is well done and the results are going to be comparable to a miraculous surgery done by the Pope or maybe having the Pope in the room. The patient is a Baptist so the Pope reference is worth the price of a smoked cigar.

LAUGHING IS LEGAL!

The chatter in the next room is mainly from the scrub tech, Brick, who has a confrontational flair. His longevity at the hospital is legendary because most surgeons have complained about his lack of "respect" for surgeons in particular, and yet he remains employed. He is flip, arrogant, and, at times, uninterested in the surgery. He'd participate in any discussion between the doctors, usually with a contrarian opinion. That is not a bad thing, but his inflections and loudness are like alcohol to raw skin, irritating. He was never assigned to work with the ophthalmologist for fear the doctor would never return.

Once the patient is asleep the conversation turns to politics. Normally the surgeon initiates a conversation and not the supporting staff, out of respect for his need to concentrate on the task at hand. Brick has no filter; he begins with a slam about the Governor. Brick feels the Governor acts like a high school dropout citing at least five examples of mangled decisions he made in the last ten days.

John, the insensitive, braggadocio anesthesiologist, pontificates about his long summer trip in his new Cadillac, then adds his support of the Governor. John routinely describes an expensive item he has purchased and usually details how much each cost. Even a mouse in the corner would realize how completely insensitive it is to those in the room who are not as financially secure. His mother must not have watered his "Think what you are saying," gene.

Hans, the vascular surgeon, has no interest in the Governor or politics but has an anti-Alzheimer's strategy. He calls all females "sweety." The males are tagged with "boss," or "captain," and an occasional "chief." This eliminates the need to remember any names and gives a subtle compliment. His generic greetings are accompanied by a sincere, infectious smile providing a bit more warmth to the salutation.

Sharon, the circulating nurse, claims the Governor is a third cousin and he is kind of a black sheep in her family. Seems he has stepped on a few toes pursuing his ascent to the top. She doesn't like his politics but feels sorry for him for all the criticism he is catching. "His ego had been battered like a birthday party piñata."

Brick agrees, "The Governor should be the piñata."

Hans continues the surgery with persistent ambivalence to the discussion by intense silence. However, the surgery is delayed occasionally because Brick talks when he should be passing instruments, a typical Brick-like performance.

The scene in the last room orbits around Warren, the whiner. This bone doctor was built for speed. If anything increases the surgical time, someone must be held accountable. This brings into play the bagatelles, the bit player like the cleaning crew or an instrument picker, possibly the prosthesis rep. If Warren could identify the laggard, he would swiftly hang him in effigy or lay open his scrotum. His style creates a moderate blood pressure issue for some. Only hard-shelled employees are assigned to his room, those who consider hazardous duty part of their reward for a low-paying job. In a way Warren is rewarded for his crass behavior because the assigning nurse doesn't want to risk losing a young nurse or tech to a caustic blast from the king of pillage. The anesthesiologists are spared because they too enjoy the benefit of rapid surgery, and they have no need to be vocal with Warren holding the Dangerfield megaphone.

His Machiavellian approach is effective in eliminating delays and probably improves the overall OR efficiency, but the mouse can decide whether whining is a winning approach.

The vinegar, the unsavory events, shows the mouse the crazy spectrum of the operating theaters from pus to politics—often hard to separate.

Day Trip

On a warm, sunny day in March, I decided to experience the local transportation system in Phoenix known as the Phoenix Metro or Light Rail. To avoid being a possible target for mugging and blend in I selected a workman wardrobe with a worn baseball cap and old shoes. I thought about hiding cash in my shoes, other than for a buck or two in case I was robbed, but finally decided I didn't look wealthy enough to be accosted. A recent rash of random bus stabbings remained a concern.

I walked six blocks from my Mesa home to the bus stop and plopped down on the bench with four other would-be riders. The man next to me tried unsuccessfully to roll a cigarette. His slight tremor countered his repeat licking and it was obvious a smokable cigarette was not in his immediate future. Without thinking, I spontaneously offered to help. He rebuffed my offer, which, when I think about it, was inappropriate. Was I going to lick the paper for him, or hold his unsteady hands? "No," was his correct response. A few minutes before the bus arrived he and his toothless lady friend departed without saying goodbye, never to return. That left me with a nervous, pacing, middle-aged man, and a young fellow asleep on the bench. The sleeper woke enough to see the bus but made no move to join the ride. My encouragement didn't change his mind.

I bought an all-day pass and learned where to depart to catch the Light Rail. Several bus passengers overheard my conversation with the driver and recognized my naiveté in bus ridership. They made sure I departed at the correct place. Sitting in the back of the bus gave me a broad view of all the busomania. We stopped every two blocks and picked up another rider. The majority of the passengers soon departed at the Mesa Light Rail transfer stop. The first leg of my trip produced no drama: no seizures, robberies, or confrontations, and I followed the crowd to the train station.

While I waited at the terminal a young man asked for a cigarette. I had none and he moved on down the platform encountering similar rejections. I boarded an almost-empty Light Rail car, not surprising because the westbound train starts in Mesa. By the time I reached Tempe the cars were half-full of riders—many appeared to be students. The common feature of the under-thirty crowd was the earbuds or earphones, with at least 80% compliance. Most everyone carried a phone, but one rider read a book, the only one on the entire three-hour trip. Tattoos were popular, and the more a person was decorated the less skin covering they wore—muscle shirts and spaghetti straps. Riders complied with the "Wear-a-mask" policy in force at the time.

On the way to Tempe I saw the site of my first bust 20 years earlier. When my parents were in their late eighties and living in a mobile home park, they answered an air-conditioning commercial offering a $39 special to clean your AC unit. A few days after the service was completed my daughter noticed a receipt on their kitchen table relating to an AC cleaning charge of $150. A discussion followed regarding the apparent overcharge. It was quickly apparent my father was the one who got cleaned. He claimed what he signed was different than the receipt he received. I think what happened was my father signed the paper and the worker then added additional charges before giving him the final document. He never agreed to anything more than a cleaning. After I researched the company and the ratings, the company qualified as a sleazy scam machine deserving more scrutiny.

I notified the Tempe police and the Better Business Bureau. Their information confirmed this AC business likely preyed on the elderly. They needed more information before any action could be taken. Where was Clark Kent when I needed him?

A visit to the address listed on the bill made sense at the time and the scam event resurfaced as my train passed the site of my house call.

A week after my brief research I visited the address on the billing receipt, a seedy area a block down a dead-end gravel road. Two unlabeled buildings sat at the end of the street, either of which could have been my destination. I stepped out of my way-too-high-end car, leaving me isolated in an alley with no police backup. Sinister ideas, suspicious behavior and "why-am-I-here?" thoughts surfaced, especially when I talked with two shady-looking smokers standing outside the larger building. They invited me inside the dilapidated building behind them, revealing at least 15 people in small cubicles chattering about the very subject that led me to this awkward situation. When my concerns were voiced to the callers, they directed me to the smaller, less-than-palatial building next door.

After walking the thirty feet, I opened the door rather than running back to my car I was coolly greeted by a, "What do you want?"

"I come on behalf of my father." I'm pretty sure I did not introduce myself, almost like I wished to remain anonymous, although the police could probably identify my body by the dental records. I unfolded the receipt and handed it to a middle aged, slightly disheveled man, sitting behind a large desk in the center of a dingy, disorganized 20-by-20 room. I sat back while he digested the document. "Your organization has taken advantage of my elderly father using illegal tactics."

Surprisingly, he disagreed.

We went back and forth, each having a slightly different perspective. I pointed out his company had been reported to the Better Business Bureau on several occasions. He was dismissive and threatening with, "You need to leave now."

I thought he implied, "Or else." I agreed with him, particularly when he offered no immediate reimbursement. After about eight minutes of escalating conversation, I started to back out of the office, "You will be reported to the Better Business folks and the Attorney General unless I hear from you in three days." He was going to be reported in any case, and three days was dumb if he had henchmen. He still didn't know my name, which was a good thing.

Naturally I didn't hear from him but decided not to call him even though I needed a fourth for golf.

My daughter, who discovered the transgression in the first place, also successfully removed the bogus charge from the credit card bill.

The following month an article in the newspaper described in detail what I had seen up close. The place was shut down but the article didn't detail the charges or if anyone was in jail. I felt sorry for the call center guys; they needed money for cigarettes.

I continued my Light Rail trip through Phoenix and eventually to the northwest as far as Dunlap and 19th Avenue, the end of the line. Nobody ever asked for my ticket on the train, but this is standard. A security person boarded the train and handed out masks. He arrived just after a student type, who sat inappropriately in the handicapped area, finished his taco and departed, leaving food and trash on the three handicapped seats. He even left the bag, which could have contained his mess. I felt sympathy for his wife.

I anticipated taking a bus even farther west but real-ized I might not make it home for an important "wife" event. Rather than retrace my route I boarded the first bus and headed back toward Mesa but had no idea what direction it might take me.

While I waited to enter the bus, three passengers boarded: one with an outdated pass, and two had no pass and no money. The driver motioned all three to take a seat but suggested they follow the rules like everyone else. We had traveled only a few blocks when a new young driver took over the reins.

The new driver was determined to catch up the time lost by the previous driver who interrogated and admonished the three ticketless folks. He sped along at a surprisingly fast pace not slowing at any unoccupied stops. He ripped by a second stop until at the last minute he spotted a customer waiting in the shelter. By then he was beyond the designated bus stop. He finally parked fifty feet past his target. The bus entrance was now adjacent to a gravel area past the sidewalk. The passenger was a slow walking, disabled elderly male with a severe limp typical for a stroke victim. It took at least a minute for the poor man and his walker to cover the extra distance imposed by the delayed stop, plus dealing with the loose gravel. Backing up must not have been an option. Neither the passengers nor the driver commented on this modified stop and the driver sped off, still in catch-up mode.

When the trip started I tried to download the Metro app but was denied several times and gave up. It would have helped when I needed help finding the correct bus on bus connections back to the Light Rail. Finally I asked the new, high speed driver for help. He stated, "You already passed it." I changed the question to, "Where do I get off so I can find a bus going toward Mesa.?" "Right now," he replied.

"Okay," and I stepped toward the door.

"You have to wait till we come to a bus stop," he quickly and incredulously replied.

"That makes sense." I got off thirty seconds later after the bus passed the intersection. After a twenty-minute wait, I caught a connecting bus that took me to the Light Rail. While waiting for that bus, I watched a middle-aged woman curled up on a bench talking to herself and not willing to engage me on any subject. She was trying to smoke a cigarette but kept burning her fingers and dropping it. I thought she was going to board the bus, but she preferred to wiggle and smoke and remained isolated from her surroundings. Sadly, she probably spent many hours on that bench.

Once back on the train I watched three giddy twenty-year-olds without masks, the first non-compliant riders I had encountered, all scrunched together on two seats when the train was only half full. This mob scrunch gave them better access to each others' posts—a TikTok frenzy.

There appeared to be no need to have a ticket on the Light Rail until two Metro employees boarded the train in Phoenix and checked all passengers. All passengers I observed displayed the proper pass, but if apprehended the two-dollar ticket became a $50 fine. Forty minutes earlier I had witnessed the benevolence of the bus driver toward the riders unable to pay.

During my Light Rail ride back to Mesa I chatted with a 60-year-old man next to me who seemed in a sharing mood, especially after the lady he unloaded on departed. I quickly picked up the conversation about Indiana and rehab. He lived at the Hope House, a facility for those who have completed drug rehab. Before coming to Arizona, he drank five-fifths of high-end Vodka a day, about $150 outlay. This was the top amount of a progressive slide to hell. My later research suggested he may have taken liberty with the facts; five-fifths daily is a lot of booze.

He was about 5'8", bowlegged and appeared older than his stated age. He claimed his children, five boys, were 6'3" to 6'11". He had no other tall relatives. I thought he might want to check his sons' DNA, maybe the mailman was involved. I offered him encouragement as he stumbled from the train, near where I had my call center fun.

When I arrived back in Mesa it started to rain and sleet. What happened to the nice sunny day? I stood outside waiting for my last bus connection when I noticed the open roof of the bus shelter. It didn't matter, the rain and then hail flew in sideways. My wife thankfully volunteered to pick me up. As I ran to our car a passing truck hit a large puddle launching an unexpected dousing. A fitting way to end my Day Trip. At no point in the trip did I feel threatened.

A-Maize-Zing

Maize or corn, not to be confused with corn maze is gluten-free. In Europe the word corn was once referred to wheat and oats as well as corn, but in Germany, referred to just rye. In the US and Canada corn means maize or corn, not other grains.

This relatively useless information introduces the current upheaval in the world's food supply. Presently, 10% of the world's population goes to bed hungry, and many more remain undernourished. Currently we are dealing with a multitude of factors further complicating the international flow of food.

Putin and the Russian war with Ukraine get credit for some of this mess. Consider Ukraine produces and exports large quantities of wheat and corn. They also manufacture a wheel critical to the circular irrigation sprinklers you see been flying over Kansas and other states with large farming operations.

Sanctions on Russia—the source of nickel, copper, iron, palladium, platinum, and and neon—will affect microchip production and significantly impact cell phone production. Without cell phones, how will we order takeout?

Ukraine and Russia export large quantities of fertilizer but the US can tolerate this fertilizer loss except for the increased cost factor. After all we still have livestock that specialize in nitrogen products. Fertilizer, the modern version of manure is a critical part of grain production; consequently, a shortage affects the cost of a loaf of bread. Most farm animals consume grain; therefore, a ham and cheese or a Big Mac carries a higher price tag.

Sunflower oil production has been severely impacted by the Ukraine war. Consequently, sunflower product costs have escalated. Spitting costs related to eating sunflower seeds have remained stable. Rapeseed has been pressed into duty to fill the void left by diminished sunflower production. Other substitute oils such as palm, olive, and soy, have been challenged with poor crops putting further stress on the vegetable oil market. These oils are important to the making of margarine, mayonnaise, and bread. The cost of sunflower seeds is up but spitting costs remain stable.

Vodka production has risen slightly with only a moderate price increase since the start of the war.

The diminished Ukrainian wheat exports primarily affect the sub-Saharan countries, those that are least able to tolerate a diminished food chain.

In the US bird flu has dented the egg market. Approximately 12,000,000 chickens have been put to rest because they knew someone who had a virus. Chickens are treated more pragmatically than Covid patients. The bird flu makes us shell out more for the double-yolkers. One Iowa poultry operation euthanized 5 million sick chicks; that's a problem of having all your eggs in one basket.

Products like honey should be fine, or will they? With gas prices increasing the transportation costs, anything not grown in your garden will be affected. And as the bee population diminishes, honey production may be a sticky issue.

Curiously, transportation costs may lower the price of almonds. China customarily imports nuts from California, but with elevated transportation costs, China decreased their orders and now California has too many nuts. I guess we knew that a long time ago, but it is true now more than ever. So with excess almonds, supply and demand suggest cheaper nuts than before, and unlike grain crops that can pivot, it is hard to grow apples on an almond tree.

· · ·

There may be an opportunity to move the American diet toward insects. Bugs may not be on your diet, but over 2 billion people eat insects daily. Insect consumption is on the rise, not because of the war in Ukraine. The green wave to combat climate change will increase insect consumption in the Western world, as has already been demonstrated by rising sales of edible insects.

Insect-eating (entomophagy) has never taken off in Europe and North America but is wildly popular in warmer climates. Indeed Hindus, Buddhists, and even a few other religions, including a rare Christian, remain morally opposed to bug killing, but the insect lobby remains relatively silent regarding this trend. Just like the animal rights folks, I'm sure a PETA-like organization will rise in defense of crickets and such, considering they have a soul and feelings. The bugs eat us when we die so turnabout strikes me as an acceptable consideration.

This drift away from traditional protein providers will require a cultural shift for many. Insects are dirty and associated with the disease. Cook a critter and the threat of disease should be eliminated. African consumers snarf down bugs au natural. African natives in rural areas pound drums and eat termites evacuating their mounds. The termites think it is raining and come out to see, only to be gathered up for a noon luncheon. A forerunner of the dinner bell. These termites are consumed without cooking or condiments.

The selection of edibles blows the imagination. Chocolate-covered scorpions seem disingenuous. If you cover the insect with sweets, just skip the scorpion and go straight to the M&Ms. The Japanese enjoy large hornets, some up to two inches long. Their larvae are eaten raw, but lightly simmered after being soaked in ginger, or deep-fried. Grubs and larvae of multiple insects provide quick pick-me-uppers throughout the world from Thailand to Ghana. Crickets and grasshoppers lead the way in US consumption of insects, but the field is expanding.

Americans already ingest around two pounds of insects yearly without knowing it. Peanut butter is responsible for the majority of this hidden taste treat.

We also consume some disgusting food: Bologna, hot-dogs, and raw oysters rank high on my list. Lobsters are technically insects, and at one time were considered too dirty to eat. That concept left the station many years ago. As we shed the negative biases towards insects and the price per bug decreases, so will the bugs.

The Bible speaks of eating insects. Leviticus is clear. "Every swarming thing that swarms on the ground is detestable. It shall not be eaten—Detest certain insects that have wings and walk on four feet. You may eat those that have legs with joints above their feet so they can jump. You may eat: all kinds of locusts, crickets, and grasshoppers. But all other insects that have wings and four feet you must hate." John the Baptist survived on locusts in the desert, but not as a dessert.

I will have a hard time eating a scorpion or cock-roach anytime in the near future even with a thick coat of chocolate. A strong dose of bird flu or a virus sweeping through the cattle industry could force us into a bug-gier diet sooner than anticipated. Between war, climate change, drought, and a cultural shift, insects may be the center of every meal. Worms, grubs, larva beetles, spiders, crickets, and ants will push bread, beets, and bananas off the plate.

A-maize-Zing but likely. By the way, Popmaize is very hard to find.

Life's Challenges: Clubfeet, Fistulas, and Fish Bones

The first thing you saw when the doctor held up your newborn son was his mangled-appearing feet. Your heart sank. The suspected clubfeet viewed on ultrasound, unfortunately confirmed. The forty percent false positive reading didn't work in your favor. This story plays out 150,000 times a year worldwide, usually without the ultrasound warning.

The clubfeet story has taken a positive turn in the last twenty-five years. The treatment for clubfeet has expanded, however the ratio of club feet remains approximately one per thousand. Third-world countries now have the tools to treat clubfeet problems before the babies become adults and require surgery.

As a medical student in 1961, I serendipitously started working in the orthopedic department at the University of Iowa doing research for Dr. Ignacio Ponseti. I had no idea he would become an icon in orthopedic circles for his work with clubfeet. He had other interests such as scoliosis, where my small research project was focused, but his legacy stemmed from his insightful pursuit of the non-operative management of the clubfoot. I learned his technique of casting and bracing the babies and thought, as a medical student, that this was an old and universally accepted treatment method. However, as an orthopedic resident I was reintroduced to the technique six years after my first exposure as if were a new concept. The Ponseti method was not widely taught in orthopedic training programs at that time.

The foreign medical world remained relatively uninformed about the non-operative treatment of clubfeet until almost 2000 when some foreign doctors, such as in Kampala, Uganda, opened clinics and became proponents of the non-operative method of treating clubfeet. The internet was likely the reason the Ponseti procedure became well known.

On my two-week medical mission trips in the 70s and 80s to Brazil, Peru, and Ecuador I did clubfoot surgery, usually on older kids and adults, I realized the need for local education on the non-operative approach to clubfeet. I introduced the concept, but my stays in South America were not long enough to know whether the locals understood the procedure. I hoped the next orthopedic team could provide additional training.

My teams were very busy with surgeries and teaching the local providers the Ponseti Method. Because I did no clubfoot surgery in my Arizona orthopedic practice, the stress of performing a technically challenging operation in a mission setting consumed my attention—as did other operations we performed with less than the optimum equipment.

Clubfoot is a genetic condition resulting in a deformity of the lower extremity. Fifty percent of the cases are bilateral as opposed to one foot, with boys affected twice as often as girls. The foot is twisted inward, so as a patient with a clubfoot grows, the untreated foot remains turned, forcing the victim to walk on the lateral side of the affected foot. The person involved has an awkward gait and is often shunned by society. Ten percent of babies born with a clubfoot have other congenital deformities such as spina bifida. Chromosome 17q23 is affected either by duplication or deletion. No known drug or event has been found to be associated with the condition.

The Ponseti Method is now widely recognized throughout the world, and if carefully followed, results in a 95 percent or better cure rate. The results depend on the experience of the medical providers in any given country and the patient's age. The younger the patient, the shorter the course of casting. The feet are gradually repositioned by a series of casts to achieve a normal appearance. Unlike the old Chinese foot wrapping to deform the feet of some girls, the Ponseti Method restores normal anatomy. In addition to casting, 60 percent of the patients have a subcutaneous heel cord release done under local anesthetic in the clinic. Following the casting, a brace is worn initially 23 hours a day, then only at night for up to five years of age. This lengthy commitment is necessary to achieve a good outcome.

Resistant feet—casting failures—can still be helped by surgically moving tendons and bone to the appropriate location.

When I cast the children, I always enlisted a parent to help keep me dry. The naked baby was guaranteed to urinate either on me or the new cast. The parent was the designated preventor of this event. For cast removal, I usually had the parents soak the cast before coming to the office making it easier to peel the plaster off. Soaking eliminated the risk of cutting the baby when using a cast saw. With the advent of fiberglass casting material, there was parental enthusiasm for fiberglass as the preferred material. Most studies suggested the lower cost, safer removal, and better correction favored traditional plaster, but the lighter weight and cosmetics of fiberglass were preferred by parents even if treatment was moderately compromised. I much preferred old-fashioned plaster.

Serial casting is labor-intensive and time-consuming. The cast has to be molded and held in the proper position until the plaster hardens. Removing the plaster, even if soaked, is a slow process and if the cast saw is used one has to be careful not to cut the child. There is a tendency to shortcut the correction by applying excessive pressure or not following the proper cast sequence. The results of the Ponseti Method are rewarding but require a cooperative family invested in the process.

• • •

Dr. Ponseti, born in 1914, received his medical degree from the University of Barcelona in 1936, the day before the start of the Spanish Civil War. He enlisted in the Spanish Republican Army and treated hundreds of wounded soldiers. The Fascists (Nationalists) won even though the Republic received support from the U.S., albeit minimal, and Ponseti fled to France when he lost his citizenship. He immigrated to Mexico, which offered citizenship to Spanish refugees, and practiced family medicine for two years in rural Mexico. Because of his interest in orthopedics, he visited the orthopedic department at the University of Mexico in Mexico City where he met Juan Faril, the department head. Dr. Faril was severely handicapped with bilateral clubfeet, which just happened to be the orthopedic problem that later would consume Dr. Ponseti. Somehow, likely with Dr. Faril's help, Dr. P received a Guggenheim Fellowship.

Those fellowships funded by Mexico were started in 1930 just 11 years before Dr. Ponseti received his. The fellowship allowed him to go to the University of Iowa, a choice suggested by the doctor with severe clubfeet. There is no information this fellowship had any clubfoot connection.

Dr. Ponseti started at Iowa as a grad student and eventually a surgical resident. His interest in research and growth deformities led to studies of scoliosis and the effects of diet. I was involved with the rat component of his research, feeding rats special diets that produced abnormalities in their ligaments and resulted in scoliosis in the now crooked little rats.

In addition to his work in scoliosis he developed an interest in clubfeet, a problem that had no easy solution at the time. He was aware that non-operative treatments were unsuccessful, and the complications of the surgical correction left a tall challenge. His clubfoot project started in 1950, but no papers were published until 1963, the year I left his research project. I had yet to learn the Ponseti Method was primarily an Iowa City program or how his work would eventually influence orthopedic training worldwide.

Hats off to my mentor, Dr. Ignacio Ponseti, still working at age 95; he died in 2009, four days after having a stroke. His method has impacted millions and decreased the need for clubfoot surgery throughout the world.

Have you heard of a vesicle vagina fistula? Probably not. Although an obstetrical problem, most obstetricians in America have never encountered the condition. The vesicle, better known as the bladder, is usually not at risk during pregnancy or during delivery but occasionally gets in the way during a C-section, mainly when the urgency of the situation dictates that a bladder injury may be incidental to saving a baby.

. . .

In Bangladesh, and likely in other underserved countries where trained medical providers are at a premium, most women have home deliveries without a doctor's presence.

This lack of professional care frequently results in situations that threaten the baby and mother. One of the complications of protracted labor is prolonged pressure on the bladder and uterine wall, leading to inadequate circulation to both. Delivery may restore circulation, but the bladder can still suffer irreversible damage. A hole in the walls of the bladder and vagina results in subsequent incontinence of urine and sometimes feces—a severe price to pay for being pregnant.

Bangladesh society is brutal to these afflicted women. They are ostracized and can never be accepted members of society. No men will touch them and they never have any more children. Just having to deal with a continual urine flow is bad enough without the social stigma. At least a person with a clubfoot is dry and able to assume a place in the cultural hierarchy above an incontinent woman.

The fistulas are usually of the bladder but may involve the rectum, causing an even more odiferous discharge. The patients are often young teenagers, poor, and malnourished. They often die prematurely from infection, nutritional issues, or suicide because they are severely shunned. In Bangladesh about 1000 new fistula cases occur each year, and only 300 have surgical correction. The U.S. Agency for International Development (USAID) has spent $100 million annually since 2004 to address the problem. Some of the money goes to other countries but Bangladesh is still the primary location for the fistula tragedies. Annually, these pregnancy-related fistulas involve as many as three million women globally.

Until poverty is reduced and women are given more respect, which should improve educational and medical opportunities, the fistula problem will continue. Multiple agencies have thrown millions of dollars at the problem, but the solution is still far off.

• • •

Another of life's challenges comes from China and other fish-eating countries—fishbones stuck in the throat. For some reason the Chinese have a tendency to swallow fish bones, which become lodged beyond the reach of a finger. This unintended event is not associated with gender, age, or any known denominator other than eating fish. The tradition of a large celebratory group gathered around a rotisserie table featuring a large whole fish, including the eyes and tail, is a frequent antecedent to trouble. A Chinese New Year celebration would be a perfect opportunity to mis-swallow a few random fishbones.

These bones are not amenable to a Heimlich maneuver because they don't block the airway. They are also not life-threatening unless they enter the lungs or descend into the intestine and have an opportunity to perforate the gut wall. The frequent occurrence of incarcerated fishbones is high enough to warrant a special clinic in high-risk towns. The clinics have extraction equipment specially designed to remove the bony problem.

Like any self-respecting society, the Chinese have a variety of home remedies to solve this frequently dangerous situation. Sugar water and black vinegar will supposedly dissolve the bones. They also use a particular bottled water containing a Taoist spell. In Japan, swallowing unchewed rice is standard treatment. Bananas are preferred in the Philippines. Really, any food that pushes the bone into the esophagus is potentially dangerous. Maybe not as dangerous as having a baby in Bangladesh.

The special fishbone clinics, especially in China, see as many as 100 patients a year making me think eating fish needs to be in the curriculum of their public schools right along with sex education and carp lives matter. Would that be considered woke? At least the countries that are faced with this bony problem have adjusted their medical resources to compensate for the swallowing deficiencies of their "bone-efide" patients.

I am sure I will choke on a fishbone the next time I dig into a whole, tasty Chinese fish.

May your day be free of clubfeet, nasty fistulas, and fishbones.

Answers

There should be a law against responding to a question with the answer to a different question. When my patients give me a political response to an interview query, the diagnostic process can be severely impeded. Maybe my patients watch too much CNN or listen to too many interviews of our congresspersons. The majority of patients remain focused and respond to my questions with thoughtful and appropriate answers. Bernie is one who didn't.

A politician's reply to "Where do you hurt?" would be "Arky, my wife, insisted I make an appointment because I moan at night. I think she's the one who should see you."

"Have you seen anyone else about your condition?"

"You bring up a good point, I think I told my dentist about...well I'm not sure. We talk about a lot of things. I used to have a rash on my 'you know,' balls but that's gone away. I don't mean my balls have gone away, ha, the rash."

"Bernard, do you hurt any place right now?"

"Arky tells me I moan, but I'm tough, and I don't take any pain pills, except for migraines. Just sitting here, I feel great but when I go to the bathroom at night, I sometimes hit my toes on the mat. Now that can get your attention. I have to take water pills to get rid of water, but I take other pills so I don't have to get up as often. The water pills are winning because I get up four or five times. I moved into the other bedroom to keep from waking up my wife, my second wife. My first wife died when she fell out of the car. That was my fault. She thought I was stopping and she opened the door. I saw a better parking place and started up just as she tumbled out. Her fancy Easter hat didn't help cushion her landing enough, and she had a bad concussion. I felt real bad because she had never worn the hat before. She didn't make it but she lived until The Fourth of July. Her two dogs really miss her."

"I met Arky at a funeral. Arky's husband died about the time I started going to funerals to meet people after my wife died. Arky, of course, was at her husband's funeral, and that's how we met. We have been together three years. You know we aren't married because the kids don't approve, mostly her kids, but we still live together. Does that answer your question?"

"Well, I probably could help you more if you had a localized complaint," I interjected.

"Arky is a little nervous about medical stuff. Her husband had a very sad experience. He had diabetes and his feet turned black, a little at a time. I think he had six amputations, like a toe followed by a foot, followed by a leg or two. She felt she deserved a discount on the casket because she had to pay for a full-length box. It was too long for him. She wants me to go to the doctor for every minor issue, like shopping for one head of lettuce. She thought I might need a shot."

"Is there anything you are concerned about?"

"Well, I can't ride a horse anymore."

"Why?"

"I can't get my legs apart. I have trouble getting out of a car and getting off the toilet. I tried to ride on a merry-go-round with my grandkids, and I couldn't get on the zebra. I had to ride in a chair that didn't go up and down. I can't get my pants on without help and if I drop my keys, I can't pick them up. Nothing hurts but I am a little stiff. Last week I tried jumping over my granddaughter's stuffed animal and I fell on my face. My steps are very short. I guess at 74 I am getting a little stiff."

"Have you had any X-rays?"

"X-rays of what?"

"It sounds like you have arthritis in your hips."

"I don't think so... they don't hurt."

While waiting for the X-rays, I asked a few more questions. "Have you had any injuries to your hips?"

"Not really. I did rodeo in high school but never got hurt. I learned that bull-riding can be dangerous. My brother broke his back riding bulls. He's okay but he quit riding. He should have done calf roping; it is a lot safer. I played college football for two years but got beat up too bad. They carried me off a few times but nothing serious. Really liked football, but at 160, I wasn't going anyplace in that sport."

I examined Bernard and it was apparent he had almost no hip motion. He couldn't straddle a potato.

The X-rays clearly showed Bernard had advanced arthritis in both hips. Most people would have complained about the pain and limitations, but Bernard was a no-pain guy. His night moaning was unrelated to his bigger problem. If he had been a golfer or a little more active, he would likely have complained, but not Bernard in his current lifestyle.

"Mr. Berne, is your real name Bernard Berne?"

"Yes, but my friends just call me Bernie. My father's father was a Bernie, so that's where my Bernie comes from. Technically I should be the second or junior or something, but we could never figure it out."

"You have advanced arthritis of your hips. You have several options: you can take pain pills if you hurt; you can spend a year in therapy, but your hips are so tight you still couldn't ride a six-pound mongoose; or you can have a hip operation—actually two hip operations, but you have emphysema making you a surgical risk."

"What are you saying Doc? Should I quit smoking? I only smoke half a pack a day. Arky is the smoker in my house. Technically it is her house. It is fully handicapped because of her first husband. It's got ramps and bars and one of those showers that you sit in. I kinda like that deal. Arky not so much, but she's a little heavy. She really likes the Golden Corral. We go every Wednesday for the Senior Early Bird special. She has one of those purses with the plastic liner so for 8.99, she comes home with at least two meals. We sit in the back, and so far, nobody has said anything."

"Bernie, do you have any questions about your medical condition?"

"You mean about my peein' or breathin', or what?"

"I am mainly interested in your hip problem."

"You know, Arky is mostly worried about my moaning. We don't get it on much anymore so that's not a big deal. It's Arky, that's a big deal. I'm trying to get her to lose weight but it ain't working. I probably don't help much. I do like my Bud."

"Bernie, tell her not to worry about your moaning; you are dreaming about her. It's a good moan. Nothing serious.

"I'll be glad to answer any questions. Come back if your hips start to hurt or if you would enjoy a little more motion. It's been nice getting to know you."

The Unacceptable Line

As I pulled into a filling station to purchase gas, I noticed a car about to enter the site had stopped in a busy street waiting for me to make my move out of her way. I held my place allowing her to pass. Instead, she quickly turned in front of me to occupy the vacant gas pump space where I intended to park. *Why didn't I just pull in rather than be nice and help her avoid a possible accident? She could see I intended to occupy the pump she took, how rude.* I drove out of the waiting area and into a space adjacent to the impolite princess who remained in her car. From this close vantage I watched as she tossed out her cigarette, yelled at her kid, and continued a lengthy chat on her phone. I mistakenly thought she might say a pleasant, "I'm sorry." Not happening. *Maybe I should buy her gas to demonstrate an act of kindness, which she could apply next time she felt a rude streak coming on.* I filled up and left before she got out of her car.

Obviously, the world would not have been a better place had I confronted her for lack of consideration.

What does it take for each of us to act on what we perceive as unacceptable events? Most of the drawer handles in my kitchen are crooked. Not a lot, but as a discerning drawer handle observer, it bugs me. This malalignment doesn't cause me to lose sleep because it is such a tiny concern. We all know of obsessive-compulsive (OCD) folks who would not tolerate such an aberration. Correcting the problem requires seven new drawers—or $1500 of carpentry. I will wait for the fire.

How do you react when you see a shirt tag flipped up on the neck of an elevator passenger standing in front of you? Or what is your response to encountering a stranger with half a roll of toilet paper parading behind them, presumably following a recent restroom visit? I will tuck the tag with a sleight of hand if the mistagged victim is a friend. Even at times with strangers, I feel some responsibility to make the adjustment, whether I'm detected or not. However, the toilet paper I need to evaluate more thoroughly and consider the repercussions of reveal, removal, or retreat. Most likely a discrete comment trumps, "Hey lady, your Charmin is showing."

Children at some point will push you as a parent to respond; respond to bullying, respond to who is picked for a team, or respond to a teacher punishing your poor child. At what point do you fire into action knowing you have to let many, below the radar, events pass?

Dealing with bullying is the worst. "Fight back" may work for some, but often is out of the question. "Avoidance" advice has a limited success rate. And confronting angry parents, reporting abuse to the school, and calling the police all have repercussions. You can't conveniently produce a big-strong brother for your bullied child. Ignoring the facts and hoping the problem will dissolve may occasionally work, but is generally a bonehead approach.

What about a spill on aisle three? Do you go out of your way to inform management of a Paul Newman's salad dressing spill? You could do so or simply fall in the puddle and call your personal injury lawyer from the landing zone to report your tragic fall. I might stand guard until a stocker appears just so someone's slip and fall doesn't take legal advantage of the pond. Should I get a set of cones to carry in my cart so I don't have to wait for the stockers who, for some reason, avoid aisle three especially during puddle season?

We all have friends—I hope— friends who could be run over by a snow plow, to use a northern example, and not complain in the slightest. Then there are the hang-nail folks who are flummoxed by the slightest malady. We have hoarders and mini-hoarders who collect thimbles, shoes, or belt buckles. We have friends who are trans, gay, black, white, tall, short, Republicans, Democrats, Independents, Catholics, Baptists, vegans, obese, skinny, rich, poor, educated, and not. Jumbling the various options together creates infinite combinations of choices and responses. To further the complexity of responses, we view the world with internal bias based on our depression, mania, success, failure, responsibility, maturity, and a hundred other variables. No wonder there are so many responses to the same facts.

If somebody cuts you off in traffic and gives you the bird, I'm betting you are not angry enough to respond with your own middle finger. You might if you have good life insurance and wish to give your family an early gift, but not likely. I often justify the sign language by thinking the driver was late to his anger management appointment.

The harder call, you are following a car that shoots off the road and lands in the canal. You are a poor swimmer and have on a new blue suit, plus you are late for dinner. You left your cell phone at home and took the rope and poles out of your car last week. The car you were following has Mexican plates and you don't speak Spanish. But wait, maybe the guy in the canal is the Mexican Ambassador and could get you tickets to the World Cup or a trip to Mexico. You consider driving into the canal to make your heroic save easier, or not. You could start a Go-Fund-Me page when you get home to help with his expenses or funeral. You might at least turn around, now that you are two blocks away and go back and see what you can do.

A few years ago I was hiking with a friend and his grandchildren. As I was trudging along, I stepped on an ant crossing the trail. The young hiker with me saw this ecological faux pax and called it to my and his grandfather's attention. I readily admitted to the unintended offense, although it is true, I had made no effort to avoid the creature. A profuse apology was in order when I realized how egregious my behavior was in the eyes of this budding ecologist. His opinion produced a visceral reaction akin to the "Stop the Steal" and "I don't want a vaccination" crowd. It is fair to support whatever position you have. I crossed his line and he quickly pointed out the error of my behavior.

As an intern I watched an unpaid seventy-year-old man walk the hospital grounds several hours daily picking up scat. I labeled him scat-ter-brained, but he had OCD with a particular bias against dog feces. Maybe he had a garden or a fecal art collection, but he was certainly dedicated to his job. The homeless population may have contributed to filling his poop bag. He was very focused, and. not at all interested in my attempts to engage him in conversation. His response to a fecal landscape demonstrated his amazing enthusiasm to realign the world order. Me, I will stick to realigning shirt tags.

Sporting events offer a great opportunity to observe over-the-line activity if you think getting doused with Budweiser qualifies. Correcting this form of sports enthusiasm carries a risk similar to the bird vs. angry driver issue. No team allegiance seems worth a broken face.

When faced with somebody's social injustice such as Amazon's polluting or Chick-fil-A's opposition to LGBTQ, do we take action? Initially Chick-fil-A was boycotted by gay people after claims of prejudice, but then the company reversed course and refused to donate to organizations opposed to LTGBQ. While Chick-fil-A was being boycotted it grew to be the third-largest fast-food company in the US. Their initial antigay position didn't seem to hurt them nor did their reversal of that position. Maybe the good food helped.

In 1880 Charles Boycott, an agent for landowners and a rent collector, was ostracized and his landowners were boycotted because of high rent. I wonder how he felt about his name becoming a verb; probably better than Thomas Crapper. Mr. Crapper sold toilets and had toilet related inventions. The word crap came from old English and had no connection to Thomas and his plumbing occupation, although he might have been better off working in some other field. Mr. Boycott crossed the line whereas Mr. Crapper stepped into the wrong line (of work).

If you disagree with the practices of a company on labor issues, coal burning, gender positions, or anything else you find offensive, you have the right not to buy their product. You can also write a letter to the editor, pee in a bottle, or read the sports page, all of which are likely to generate the same results, but at least you have given a finger to the world by establishing your position.

We have opportunities to judge and possibly take action on a multitude of "over-the-line behaviors" daily, from misspelling on a menu to witnessing a Circle K robbery. Where do you fall regarding your threshold to respond? Hats off to those among you who wish to raise awareness of the egregious behavior of your fellow man. Just be careful you don't step on the tail of a cobra.

We all know people who are very vocal about cross-ing-the-line situations and spend their waking hours complaining, often a combination of self-pity, negativity and useless bitching. One of those is the city council's worst nightmare—someone who attends every meeting and frequently speaks of the city's shortcomings, poor decision-making, and lack of manhood.

Fortunately, most citizens are like the readers of this piece: levelheaded, nonjudgmental, and able to select the truly important issues before becoming unhinged.

Whatever Works

For the sake of today's discussion, let's say you have pain someplace—like your right shoulder. You could have a slight case of terminal cancer or a mild tweak of said shoulder. After the appropriate amount of self-diagnosis and using whatever worked the last time you had the same pain, you try your neighbor's favorite remedy. It doesn't work, and now you try Icy Hot, Aspercreme, Bag Balm, Bengay, or one of his friends, and your shoulder still hurts. Blue Emu, a catchy name for a popular Australian product, and Arnica are in vogue these days. The cannabinoids are the latest and greatest topical for achy anything. Or you may seek advice from someone on your insurance list. This may include homeopaths, osteopaths, allopaths, naturopaths, or psychopaths. You could also choose a shaman/medicine man, chiropractor, MD, DO, massage therapist, or palm reader.

The treatment you receive will depend, of course, on the diagnosis which will be determined by the bias of the practitioner. After all, you could have tendonitis, bursitis, myositis, radiculitis, or cholelithiasis—gall stones—which occasionally cause shoulder pain. Cancer needs to be ruled out before meaningful treatment makes sense. Regrettably, you may be selecting your diagnosis by your choice of doctors. The shaman may feel you have demons, the chiropractor alleges you have an alignment problem, and the infectious disease doctor is sure you have an abscess. I know of at least one family doctor who would treat you with trigger point injections regardless of the diagnosis.

You may choose a diagnostic obsessionist who will order a full blood panel, MRIs of all moving and non-moving parts, and an EMG to test your electrical issues, although they will likely be normal. If you are lucky, the doctor may take a history and find out you were clocked by a heavy cuckoo-clock that fell off the wall during the earthquake and struck you before time expired. If it had hit your head, you might be the cuckoo one. You might choose a therapeutic nihilist who thinks you are a head case and deserve no treatment.

Say you are drawn to mainstream medical care and a diagnosis is made. The condition suggested by the clock event is a simple contusion resulting in a dreadful, not terminal, discoloration of said shoulder. If you are perceived to be a patient who requires treatment, more than an explanation and dismissal, you will be treated. Aside from "wait and see", you will be given medication to ease the inflammation, and possibly a series of physical therapy sessions anywhere from two to eight weeks.

The medication has a 15 to 70 percent chance to make you feel better just based on the placebo effect. The placebo effect is enhanced by the enthusiasm of the provider and with a contusion, whether a shot or pill is given, the problem is likely 100 percent resolvable. The placebo effect is relatively useless against infections, tumors, and diabetes, but has a much better efficacy with pain-related problems.

The various inflammatory conditions such as arthritis, bursitis, and tendonitis are problems for which treatment options abound. The more placebo-ish the treatment, the more likely it is to be promoted in the news media. The copper bracelet or better yet the magnetic copper bracelet or back brace are very popular with the arthritis crowd. The medical literature has put these treatments in the "no valid support for statistical benefit" category. These items are still widely used.

A knee sleeve that provides no support is hard to prescribe based on science but may benefit the patient by creating skin pressure and "counter-current distraction" thereby decreasing knee pain. I put sleeves in the placebo-plus category based partly on the many avid older athletes who are adamant about their use.

Laser Therapy has daily advertisements in the newspaper regarding the predictable resolution of radiculopathy, arthritis, neuritis, and the subgroup—shoulder, knee, back, and anyplace else pain. A laser light beam focuses on the area of concern. Patients likely will require multiple treatments for the problem to be resolved, which might have occurred if the insurance had not terminated the coverage. Unfortunately, the results mirror an expensive placebo.

You may have been unable to make your own diagnosis; in that case, take your sweaty palm to a local palm reader. The modern version of this art allows the electrical energy in your hands to be analyzed by a special machine which has truly incredible insight. By simply placing your hand on the AI-charged gadget, a plausible explanation of what ails you will appear, including the determination of the underlying (root cause) responsible for your unfortunate condition. For example, you might be deficient in valerian or rosebud, maybe down a little in magnesium or molybdenum, or worse yet, a preterminal case of low selenium. Once your deficiency is identified, you can simply fork out $72.48 from the array of products conveniently available right there in the house of healing.

In the unlikely situation that your body doesn't respond as predicted by you, or the electronic palm reader, you can be retested. As far as I know these devices fall into the snake oil category and if this approach fails, which is possible if you happen to be a Scorpio, you can go next door to the acupuncture lady. In reality your zodiac sign will not impact your response to an electronic palm reader.

The scientific world relies on the validity of a treatment to pass the double-blind test. This means one person administers an unknown product—either real or fake. A second person evaluates the results of the treatment but doesn't know what product has been given. This creates an unbiased assessment because the evaluator is simply judging the results without his prejudice being involved. In many studies and treatments, the sponsor or company is both giving and judging the results creating an obvious bias.

Some treatments are hard to double-blind. My favorite is the high colonic enema. If you have had this enlightening event, it would be hard to convince you that it was a high colonic rather than a peanut butter sandwich or eye wash you had just experienced. High colonics are a method of keeping your toxins in check. I have generally left that job to my kidneys and colon, but some folks who eat dirt or worse may drift into the toxic range. There is no toxin meter, and I would not want to deny a person who perceives themselves to have chronic high toxins the delight of a good colonic, which may have some placebo value as well.

It is also difficult to do a double-blind test in the treatment for leg length differences. This malady is often considered a cause of back pain. Most patients realize the legs do not change length once you are fully grown. The benefit of "adjusting the leg length" would therefore fall into a placebo effect because the legs do not magically change length. But there is an up to 70 percent chance you will feel relief from your "whatever problem" following the adjustment. I know of many patients who have regular treatments and are completely satisfied and devoted to that approach. I am highly supportive of any treatment that "works," be it adjustments or vitamins.

No one knows for sure why the placebo effect works. It could be endorphins are released and the body provides pain relief from within. That is what happens with exercise.

Science be damned. If you feel better on vitamins, having a laser treatment, enjoying a high colonic, or getting your back cracked, go for it; it's only money, and you deserve a little hedonistic gratification. Besides, it is a good way to meet people, especially if the treatment is covered by insurance.

Whatever works.

Within These Halls

Dr. Diptish Morgan, an orthopedic friend, willingly shared his favorite life events with me; how he ran over his dog or fell into the swimming pool wearing his Sunday suit. The office tales seemed particularly worthy of elaboration. Jim, one of his assistants, whom I saw often, related his version of office mayhem, collaborated on these stories. Having heard two sides of the events made them more valid, but still sometimes hard to swallow.

Diptish called his office the House of Love, his way of attempting to guarantee a peaceful atmosphere in the workplace. That is akin to telling a friend your gentle pit bull doesn't bite, just before the dog rips your friend's face off.

Dan, a new hire, supposedly a well-trained office assistant, had just moved from the Midwest. Charming, blessed with 20/20 vision, and perceptive of the medical needs of Dr. Morgan, recognized that Millie, also a new hire receptionist, usually didn't wear a bra. Diptish, the primary interviewer, claimed he was unaware of this fact when he hired her. Diptish, a bit near-sighted, missed the jaunty breast activity entirely, and there were no tit-related questions on her application to tip him off. Regardless, she joined the practice.

According to Dan, who brought the situation to light, Millie's implants made her feel external support and embellishment unnecessary. A few weeks after the bra information came to light through back office and lunchroom chatter, I learned Dan had insider information. Not-so-subtle Dan boasted he slept with Millie. That confession gave credence to his unique insight into Millie's whole chest thing.

Dr. Morgan encouraged a friendly atmosphere that included socializing among his staff, but intercourse was not addressed in the office manual, nor had he dealt with the issue before. After many administrative aerobics, he decided it wasn't fair to have a vivacious receptionist pleasuring a rookie employee. A four-to-one vote canned the stud. Dan's release eliminated the potential for making the House of Love too realistic. Diptish kept the receptionist a few more weeks to convince him that Millie dressed inappropriately and performed below job standard—lousy. The patients didn't object and the boys in the back eagerly went to the front office to bring back the next patient. However, the receptionist had to do more than just put out a welcome sign. She received a pink slip, maybe the only underwear she owned. Diptish determined she was clueless, as well as braless.

An even less permanent employee, Royal, joined the practice as a two-week summer replacement X-ray technician. Royal was his mother's child, a kind man with a big heart but relatively little grey matter. Unfortunately, he lacked familiarity with Dr. Morgan's X-ray equipment and quickly demonstrated an inability to learn. A sincere, open kind of guy, the type who shares everything. By the end of his second day, he had revealed several chapters of his made-for-TV life. Following a bad car accident, he discovered his parents had not paid his auto insurance. He first married at age 45, but his wife died a week after the wedding from a G.I. bleed. He had no insurance when his house burned down a few months later. He blamed that on the confusion related to getting married and not paying attention to minor details.

His sad stories produced a Salvation Army response from Dr. Morgan's staff. Fundraising and emotional support created a dilemma for Dr. Morgan. On his second day of work, Royal approached Dr. Morgan and extended his hand holding a twenty-dollar bill. He explained the money covered the cost of the x-ray film wasted when he left the door open to the developing room and exposed the film. Being eager to succeed he took at least two

X-ray exposures rather than one for each position. He then selected the best of the two, hoping to satisfy Dr. Morgan. This approach wasted time and resources, but Royal's obvious truckload of insecurities drove the bus.

He served as a target for pigeons, a pothole magnet, and the guy more likely to incur hail damage than his neighbor. It's certain had Royal purchased a winning lottery ticket he would have left it in the jeans he gave to Goodwill. He lasted two weeks mainly on the strength of his unfortunate life. He owned a built-in pernicious insecurity that engendered the sympathy of most he touched—maybe not Dr. Morgan entirely. A permanent GoFundMe page would be Royal's best friend.

Other players made the office "odd" list. Marla, Dr. Morgan's insurance girl, had a visitor literally drop into her kitchen during Royal's two-week employment. Seems a vagrant routinely slept in her attic, accessed by a crawl space in her carport. He missed the stable footing only to step onto the unsupported kitchen ceiling. He parachuted into her kitchen as Marla prepared dinner. When questioned about the intruder, she blandly responded, "He lives elsewhere now."

Perfect employees are hard to find but Diptish hired several. Petula, better known as Pet, single, reliable, heavy, and Catholic, had been with him for 16 years and seemed as honest as a money-handling person could be. One day a call came from the bank to the office manager that the daily deposit had been made, but just checks, no cash. The bank teller, a long-time employee, recognized the unusual nature of this transaction. It happened again a few days later, and the manager received another call. An after-hours' review of the office transactions revealed no documentation of incoming cash. Further investigation confirmed the suspicion. For those two days, cash payers were written off as "no charge" and the payment never showed up. A review of the prior week's transactions showed no such issues.

Confronting the perfect employee produced a tearful confession. The explanation being her brother had come on "hard times" and Pet did what any supportive sister would do, she planned to borrow a little and pay it back when her brother was back on his feet and off the sauce. Her loyalty and longevity could have easily produced a loan or personal assistance program, but she chose to steal rather than deal. The amount of money she "real-located" was small, therefore a relatively palatable loss to Dr. Morgan, but enough for him to reluctantly relieve the bookkeeper of her job. She disappointed him by not talking about her situation rather than sully her name.

A few months later Pet found a job with the accounting department of a large department store. Doctor Morgan never received a call inquiring about her 16 years of employment in his office.

Diptish related one story he compared to locking yourself out of the house when you slip out to pick up the morning paper in your underwear. He hired Sue, a new assistant office manager, mainly to help with a transition to another office location. Mature, experienced, and theoretically savvy, she appeared a perfect fit for the job. He wanted to purge all old records but save any charts containing surgical reports, as well as charts less than ten years old, and charts of children. The instructions seemed straightforward. Sue made progress reviewing over 80,000 charts during the purging process. Near the later stages of the project, Dr. Morgan requested a chart of a former patient. The chart, which included the operative reports, could not be located. Upon questioning Sue where the chart might be, he discovered she had thrown away the charts he wished to keep and saved the others. The horse had left the barn. No way to go back and un-shred two months of worthless, destructive 'work'. No way to get back in the house without embarrassment. Sue became the next thing to be purged.

These strange gyrations demonstrated by Dr. Morgan's employees represent a microcosm of the working world. The flight of human behavior might be missing an aileron, but at no time did Dr. Morgan consider hemlock.

Holland

The concept of reclaimed land from the sea is hard to fathom. Polder is the official name for reclaimed land, which includes 27 percent of Holland that is below sea level. The reclamation project that began in the 8th century spawned windmills, which became the geographic icons of the country. In the 19th century there were 1,700 windmills in Holland, many initially built in the 16th century. Less than 1,000 remain in 2023. Paddling the water out of the low-lying areas made windmills essential to keep the land from flooding.

However, excessive water removal can result in unsaturated soil, further settling the land and increasing the threat of more severe flooding. Currently the majority of water control is accomplished by efficient, programable, electric turbines, and Archimedes augers pushing water from the canals into the rivers, which flow to the sea.

Windmills require much daily care and adjustments; therefore, they all had a family occupant. A thick cloth covered the wind blades and had to be rolled up or manually released depending on the wind speed. The large blades also needed frequent realignment to take advantage of the wind direction with 360 degrees of options. Windmill living was physical but also demanded mental acuity on a 24/7 basis. Crowding ten kids into one building was common. Family size was a function of boredom and their religion, which opposed birth control. In the past, the absence of electricity may also have affected family numbers. Agile retirees now staff the facilities for reduced rent, but they must take a three-year class to learn how to operate the mills.

Our enthusiastic 30-year-old tour guide, provided by Viking and the Rhine River Cruise Line, grew up in a nearby windmill. He showed us a spot on the canal trail where he and his brother fished.

Because of candles, kids, and friction from the windmill, fire proved to be a constant concern. Bigger threats to me were the low beams hitting my head or the risk of falling down the steep narrow stairs. Fortunately, our group survived the windmill visit and returned to our Rhine River cruise ship.

Amsterdam, our last cruise stop, provided us with a fun-packed day, barely long enough to accommodate our schedule. When we left the boat after arriving in Amsterdam a van picked up our luggage. One bag didn't get off the van when we unloaded at the hotel; hopefully, it was still on the dock. The Austrian driver gave me his phone number and said to call him in an hour. I called as directed but a message indicated an invalid number. On my second call I changed the G to 9, hoping I misread his note but still convinced I would never see my suitcase again.

"Voilà," the driver answered. "I am in the hotel lobby with your bag." My Swiss chocolates were not lost and my faith restored that the local drivers were honest.

The NH hotel perfectly located, allowed us to take a 15-minute walk to the famous but somber Anne Frank Museum. The museum is located at the site where the Frank family hid for two years during the Nazi occupation of Amsterdam. They lived in a secret residence behind Otto Frank's business, which was the location where Anne penned her famous diary—later made into a documentary film. The sad story of her life in a concentration camp in Germany ended tragically a few days before the conclusion of World War II. Miraculously her diary remained in the house when she and her family were transported to the camp on a freight train. The only family member to survive the internment was her father. This museum should be visited by those who don't believe in the Holocaust.

Following the depressing museum tour, we had time for a sandwich at a hole-in-the-wall spot close to the anticipated Damn Boat and Guys Tour. The restaurant, like others I saw, had multiple levels. The restroom was up three steep steps and guarded by a fat, green, cloth-covered chair. Once I squeezed by the chair and entered the narrow toilet, I encountered a mop bucket, a stack of unused toilet tissue, and a sign confirming the use of the facility would cost me one euro. A delicious and giant club sandwich made this random restaurant worth the price.

A short walk around the corner brought us to the departure location for the Damn Boat Ride. Our eight-passenger vessel was cozy but uncomfortable with U-shaped seating, no roof, and no one facing forward. The weather, information, and family bonding experience made up for any negatives. Mike, our guide/driver, an Irish lad with five years of canal experience, provided us with the latest statistics: nine people drown in the canal yearly, many cars and bicycles accidentally park in the canal, and the easily visible public urinal users seldom wash their hands after doing their business. There are no fences or restraints along the canal edges or even on the café decks that hang over the canal, making a minor misstep, drunk or not, an effortless opportunity for a bath of sorts. Mike spewed his disdain for the easily identifiable rental boat drivers for their frequently demonstrated unsafe driving. They apparently don't yield at the canal intersections or at the narrow passages under bridge openings and often don't know how hard it is to stop a moving boat. Mike waved at many of his driver friends but took greater pleasure in pointing out the bonehead driving habits of the rental boat drivers.

I found it odd that large houseboats, some with cement foundations, occupied the edges of the canals. One entrepreneur had caged chickens on the bow of his boat and was selling eggs. You could conceivably buy an egg while boating, motor a few yards to a café, and order an omelet to go. The boat with the chickens had a dental office on the other end, fortunately away from the chickens. Many half-sunken ships remained visible long after they died in the canals. These ships are in the wider canals but still narrow the channel. They were left in place to preserve the owners' valuable docking rights.

The many canals give the city a Venice-like quality, but Amsterdam's hallmark is the number of bicycles parked everywhere, which far outnumber the riders or street capacity. The narrow streets may be one-way for cars, but motorcycles and bikes flow in any direction. This threatens the unaware tourists walking with their heads down, watching the uneven cobblestone footing, or looking at a map. The riders' speed reflected a flagrant lack of concern for the gawking, naïve tourists.

The buildings lining the canals date back to the 15th century. They have common walls yet some are tilting front or back as the foundations settle unevenly. Because most buildings have no elevators, furniture is often winched to the upper floors assisted by the front roof overhang designed to protrude for this purpose; a house tilting backward diminishes this ability. Gradually sinking landscape puts Amsterdam on an uneasy timetable with the eventual loss of its buildings.

Global warming and rising seas are not welcome in this country where so much land is already below sea level. The polders dealing with the sinking land already experienced one devastating flood in 1953 when heavy rains and high tide combined to breach the dikes, causing the loss of 2,551 humans and 47,000 animals. Nine percent of Holland flooded. Borrowing land from the sea, as has been done for centuries, doesn't affect the population. Holland remains one of the most densely populated countries in the world, with a size similar to Massachusetts and Connecticut combined.

Mike also revealed that marijuana is illegal. Holland's Opium Act of 1976 distinguished between hard and soft drugs. Drugs such as marijuana are considered soft or less dangerous, yet are still unlawful. The authorities have decided not to enforce the laws relating to soft drugs, which is no secret among the users.

LAUGHING IS LEGAL!

At the conclusion of our trip, we off-loaded with minimal difficulty although my wife's purse nearly took a bath. We had 45 minutes to reach the next venue, the Van Gogh Museum. The distance was doable, although bikes and rough sidewalks elongated any time estimate, but walk we did. We arrived at 3:30 for our 3:30 ticket time.

The modern, high-tech museum was comfortable, roomy, and not overly crowded due to the ticketing-controlled inflow. Audio devices provided detailed information about the paintings and the story of Van Gogh's short life, which ended at age 37. The description of a painting was similar to a wine connoisseur describing wine by its aroma: flower, stone, or acidity, which is far beyond my perception. A droopy dried-up sunflower didn't leave me in awe, as I am sure Van Gogh would have wanted. I was intrigued that because he was poor, he often painted on both sides of the canvas, not always in the same orientation of the canvas. His mental illness may have played a role. I think I prefer the blur of Monet or the gravitas of a Ruben. Maybe those semi-nudes were not dignified, but they provided blimpy eye candy, more succulent than a vase filled with wilting flowers.

As I started to exit a four-person elevator in the museum, a young lady shoved me aside and burst out the opening with no verbal excuse. I presumed her water had broken and she was on her way for an urgent delivery, but she didn't appear pregnant and quickly immersed herself in the crowd. If I had been a bit frailer, I am sure I would have fallen, which I considered doing just to embellish her disrespect. Her disruptive activity, often a cover for pickpockets, apparently was not, and I lost nothing other than my balance.

Typical of museums, this one provided a handful of benches. All were popular and they became involved in an artsy version of musical chairs. Tired, like-minded pre-sitters would circle the benches hoping to, with subtle stealth, commandeer a seat without hurting any of the other players/art enthusiasts.

For anyone truly interested in art, the Van Gogh Museum is located in a mall close to several other renowned museums. There may be other attractions for me to see before I indulge in another museum.

Our last event before leaving this intriguing country: have a nice sushi dinner. Multiple languages resonated throughout the crowded restaurant, all some variation of foreign. We saw no California rolls on the menus. The Dutch version of sushi rewarded our palates.

Our busy day ended with a four-hour nap. We departed for the U.S. before sunrise the next morning with all of our bags, passports, and memories. Goodbye to the Rhine River and Holland.

The coveted Swiss chocolate, which we consumed a month later, still had Swiss charm and unique flavor.

Mosquitoes

It is hard for me to understand how Rohingyas, Uyghurs, Jews, or any minority group, including Blacks, can be considered targets for discrimination. Discrimination is wrong. Maybe this mental approach from the same mediocre emotional thinking engenders our fear of insects. How can an upside-down cockroach evoke emotions comparable to a home invasion by a hooded, knife-wielding midnight visitor? Rarely do these compromised insects convert from a supine position to attack mode and strangle the homeowner. Let me be clear: non-discriminatory folks can still be afraid of insects.

A laser pointer provides a focus for the somnolent students to perceive the important element of a lecture, if they are awake enough to see the cueing light. Even with a focus on the facts, even if exposed to correct information, some of us allow prejudice to fog our judgment creating phobias and fear of certain insects.

Mosquitoes make me uncomfortable. I'm not talking about itching but the legitimate fear of catching one of the eleven diseases these critters are known to spread. Chikungunya virus, one of those diseases carried by mosquitoes, can be painful and long-lasting. However, you must go to Southeast Asia if you're interested in acquiring it. Over a million people a year still die from mosquito-borne diseases, primarily malaria. Zika, La Cross Encephalitis, Jamestown Canyon virus, Yellow Fever, and dengue are all transmitted by this pest, but staying in the States is your safety net to avoid these viral diseases. These illnesses cast mosquitoes in a justifiably negative light. Although malaria has been reported in the States, it too is hard to contract in the U.S. unless you meet someone who brought back a mosquito from Africa and loaned it to you for a bit.

West Nile is the virus I worry about. When one of the pests wakes me by buzzing in my ear, I immediately think Nile, which is easier than thinking Chikungunya. West Nile was discovered in the U.S. in 1999 and has taken over 2000 lives since. Approximately 4% of those infected die and likely many more from diminished resistance after acquiring it. All this from one little mosquito bite.

The 3,500 species of mosquitoes don't seem so large. Cockroaches have 4,500 species and flies 110,000. If God went to the trouble to create 3,500 species, they can't all be pests. It is no secret that the male mosquitoes never bite humans; they live off pollen, as do the females. In addition, the females require blood as a source of protein needed for egg laying. Not all species are human biters.

Mosquitoes weigh 2.5 milligrams and each live only ten days, so you can't stay mad at one of them very long. However, if one is detected in my home, the life span is measured in minutes. I may be flattening a male or two, but it is tough to determine their sex, so I treat them all with the same courtesy.

Our concern and dislike for mosquitoes are justified, but they have redeeming qualities, which we tend to ignore while scratching a recent bite. They can detect CO_2 exhalation and body odors from 50 meters away, as you might guess when surrounded by mosquitoes after a short time outdoors. They are equally persistent at finding you under the sheets at night.

I need to step back and give newfound respect to these little vectors. They have real benefits. Pollination is an important function of mosquitoes, but they trail far behind butterflies and bees as pollinators. However, in the Arctic there is a large mosquito population and they are the primary pollinators of the region.

Once I was lucky enough to fly to a remote fishing lodge in Canada. My main memory of that trip was not the fish but the clouds of voracious mosquitoes. They say that only the females bite, which means a lot of hungry women attacked me. They bit through thick layers of clothing and enjoyed my repellent, which to them must have seemed a pheromone-laden cologne. My body was dripping with repellent to no avail. Facial nets helped, but these ladies were more aggressive than a Macy's blowout sale crowd. I am sure there were no blood banks in the area because potential donors would have been anemic.

Mosquitoes provide a source of food for many insects and birds. Bats and lizards feast on mosquitoes. Mosquitoes are not part of the human food chain, being too small to chocolate coat.

The female produces about 100 eggs at a time and can accomplish it thrice with one mating. If humans could kick out 300 eggs after intercourse, women would become more selective in mate choices. Who counts mosquito eggs: do mosquitos have obstetricians?

The Mosquitofish (Gambusia affinis) loves mosquito larvae and was introduced throughout the world to control mosquitoes. Like many good ideas this turned out badly. The Gambusia were aggressive and killed other fish, many of which also ate larvae. They also consumed algae-eating zooplankton, which increased algae and decreased water quality. Therefore this "beneficial fish" has been outlawed in Australia and the mosquito population has increased because of bad "conservation" measures.

Mosquito larvae eat detritus—yep, detritus, the dead organic material found in water. The by-product, frass (insect poop)/nitrogen, provides benefits for plant life. That ability may not sound like much, but at least there is no itching involved.

This story of the benefits of mosquitoes doesn't sit well with some folks at the Center for Disease Control and Prevention. In 1939 Paul Hermann Muller discovered the insecticide potential of DDT. It was used in World War II primarily to kill mosquitoes and defend against malaria. He received the Nobel Prize in medicine for his work. In 1962, Rachel Carson's book *Silent Spring* spoke to the agricultural impact and how DDT almost eliminated eagles and peregrine falcons. DDT was eventually banned for agricultural use in 1972. In 2004 a worldwide agricultural ban was formalized. Give credit to the mosquito for all environmental machination and Nobel activities.

The spin-off of having the world filled with irritating insects like mosquitoes stimulates a pesticide industry. DDT declined, but many new and better insecticides have replaced it. Insecticides haven't completely negated the negative financial impact of mosquitoes.

On the other hand, the study of mosquitoes has helped engineers develop drones that incorporate the insect's mechanics.

An odd but real benefit of mosquitoes is the protection of native forest land. The density of mosquitoes keeps certain tropical areas free of humans. Also, they prompt caribous to change migration patterns to avoid these insects, therefore allowing overgrazed land to recover.

As the study of mosquitoes' blood thinning saliva evolves, the anticoagulation characteristics may give scientists a better blood thinner. Milking an insect this size for saliva must be a challenge most scientists are ill-prepared to do.

Mosquitoes are a mixed bag of good and bad. I think Earth would be better without them, but they have millions of years of longevity, as proven by fossil evidence, and they do have a few redeeming qualities.

It seems like every time humans attempt to solve some environmental problem, we make it worse. The best solution still seems to keep slapping mosquitoes, even if on your friend's neck.

Illusions

In the days before the internet when there were only four doctors in my orthopedic practice, I assumed the role in hiring a new office manager after our previous manager, Barbara, suddenly departed by edict when I discovered she had been writing narcotic prescriptions for personal use. As a nurse she frequently called in prescriptions under my direction, but in this case, she became the subscriber/patient, contrary to the nursing code of conduct. I might have accepted her using the medication, but she didn't have me or any doctor in the loop. That behavior put me in professional jeopardy, and despite my urge to keep her because of her excellent managerial ability, I had no choice but to terminate her employment. The trust factor had disappeared.

I started my full-court press to hire someone as quickly as possible because we had no backup. The day after her termination, I placed an ad in the newspaper for a manager, and within a week, five people responded. The résumés I reviewed pointed to two reasonable candidates whom I interviewed briefly by phone. Both applicants sounded outstanding but Nancy—my first choice—had more experience.

Nancy, age 50, said she had worked for a three-man group of doctors. She provided me with four references. I ignored the fact that none of the references were doctors. Her home in north Phoenix posed a threat. How long could she tolerate the 20-mile drive to my office; definitely a threat to long-term job satisfaction.

I was sold on Nancy after a long in-person interview. She had worked at the same office for eight years and became available only when the doctors retired. I almost offered her a job at the conclusion of the interview but felt compelled to follow up with a few calls to the references. As a novice headhunter, caution, or at least thoroughness, made sense.

I failed to notice that Nancy's resume contained no information about nonprofessional activities: church, volunteerism, or hobbies. I also should have recognized that after her office management job she had had two short-term stints with no explanation regarding termination. I was impressed (blinded) by her computer and financial skills, skills I valued because an office computer conversion seemed imminent. Her experience and pleasant appearance worked in her favor. It didn't cross my mind she was looking for a job out of her normal territory, possibly because no one would hire her.

I made up for what I lacked in hiring skills and secretarial assistance, by my dogged pursuit of all the facts.

Trying to call her references proved challenging because I saw patients in the office or spent time in the operating room and could never sit down at a desk and complete the process. I needed a cell phone, but they were several years away, and even a cell phone could not diminish the time on hold.

I could not reach either of the first two references and when I called Nancy, she implied she would get more current numbers. That didn't happen. Finally, I contacted the third reference, who told me he did the accounting for the doctors' office but worked for a private firm. He was very positive about Nancy: great work ethic, prompt, fun, and energetic. She sounded perfect. He was a little vague about her longevity with the doctors and could not give me an exact address for the doctors' office. He said he thought they had moved. He had no idea where the doctors went after she stopped working for them or why they retired. Nancy was still a winner, even though a few questions remained unanswered.

I called Nancy again to confirm the information the accountant had given me and to request her help in reaching the other references and her former employers—the doctors. I called the accountant back to fact-check his answers against Nancy's comments. He may have inadvertently revealed he was Nancy's nephew. I was sort of okay with that, but she had never said anything about him being a relative or an accountant. When I asked her for the doctors' names and contact information, she said it had been two years since she worked there and had no information about them. She changed jobs because, "They all retired or went someplace."

I looked up the office address she gave me and the doctors' names. Remember, I was still high on Nancy, so I didn't want to call her again to ask what kind of doctors they were: G.P.s, osteopaths, chiropractors, maybe veterinarians. I tried to reach each of the doctors. None were listed in the phone book. Next, I called the closest hospital to their office to see if these doctors had been on the staff. I was still trying to do this detective work between patients, so being on hold for 15 minutes was painful. My call was particularly irritating because I was transferred all over the hospital. I probably explained my request to six different new hires—or at least slow-thinking folks who could not help me. I might as well have called the Kremlin. In reality, G.P.s don't usually practice at hospitals, so I was grasping at straws or strawmen.

If the doctors had retired only two years earlier, they should still be listed in the Arizona Medical Society database. No sign of them. The osteopathic database. No. The chiropractor database. No. By then I felt like Magnum P.I. or a dog with a bone. I would not let go nor call Nancy back because she wasn't helpful. How could three doctors and their practice be expunged? How could Nancy provide such a useless dearth of information and a blitzkrieg of fabrication?

So here I was, my first choice unable to provide me with a reference other than her nephew. Three apparition-like references remained just that, invisible, unreachable and ....

I had spent easily 40 hours trying to convince myself the lady was a good choice for the manager. No one would fabricate a complex, convoluted story like she seemed to have accomplished. What was the real story? Where had she worked, if at all? The deeper I dug the more lies that surfaced. The only "fact" that fit was her home address. Hiring a private detective crossed my mind, mainly to satisfy my curiosity as to who this imposter really was. I fleetingly considered hiring her to give me a chance to learn the truth.

Naturally, I finally had to accept the facts; she was a total fraud. Ultimately, I told her I could not hire her. A few months later I called her on the premise I reconsidered and wanted to know if she still needed work. She said she worked for another doctor's office but would not tell who. I wanted so badly to talk with her employer and learn what they might know. Because she didn't tell me the name of the lucky people she worked for, she saved me a phone call, which likely would have given her an opportunity to find another job.

Once Nancy left my list of managerial choices, I returned to my short list of one. I hired my second choice after talking to her references and a brief interview. Paula turned out to be a gem.

When this experience concluded, I felt like I had been rescued after spending many hours holding onto a piece of driftwood in the cold and choppy Pacific Ocean. I endured, spent but delighted with a happy ending to an intense three weeks.

Pregnancy

Two fossilized placoderms were caught copulating in a Scottish Lake 365 million years ago by an astute paleontologist, John Long, who has the fossil to prove it. Skipping ahead a few million years, it has been reasonably clear in most cases when a male deposits sperm into a female who has at least one egg to accept the visiting sperm, voilà, pregnancy can result. Evolution has progressed to allow homo sapiens to inseminate other homo sapiens, but not chimpanzees, who have 99.8% similar DNA. Human-faced goats worshiped in India are definitely not the result of a human-goat relationship.

Men can produce viable sperm into their seventies and women can still have viable eggs post-menopausal. Xinju Tian, at age 67, delivered a girl shortly before China instituted a one-baby policy. Maybe that's why she didn't wait longer to have her child. A 56-year-old mother is the oldest natural pregnancy to give birth in the U.S.. A 73-year-old lady conceived but there is no mention whether she delivered a viable infant.

With the advent of in vitro fertilization (IVF) fecundity has increased for those challenged with reproductive issues. A 57-year-old was artificially inseminated and delivered twins on behalf of her sterile daughter using the daughter's husband as the sperm source, thereby making her both mother and grandmother. A few women in their 60's have become pregnant with IVF. With a little hormone therapy and a few wigglies, you too can be enceinte.

IVF has assisted families unable to conceive but introduced the multiple birth issue, and maybe even worse, increased fetal morbidity. Multiple births are often associated with premature deliveries, which result

Be tuned in to the term "chest milk" replacing breast milk, which has a negative connotation for non-binary advocates. I am happy to accommodate this change but the milk still comes from the breast. Milk probably has a female connotation and likely will soon be degenderized into malk or he/she white juice.

Some pregnancies become completely unpredictable. If the fetus develops outside the uterus, many bad things can happen. The embryo will not survive and the mother's life remains in jeopardy until an appropriate treatment resolves the problem. The fetus cannot grow properly in a tubal location and basically dries up and calcifies or ruptures the tube and even passes out of the gut. More commonly, tubal pregnancy becomes painful and produces bleeding. Surgery to stop the bleeding remains the best treatment.

Pregnancy is potentially dangerous. In the U.S. 17 out of 100,000 patients die due to issues associated with childbirth. This is higher than in any other first-world country. Why? The answer is not clear: Maybe too many C-sections? Drug use? Domestic violence? Race, poverty, and access to care are critical factors.

The availability of appropriate obstetrical care is severely limited in many rural areas. Driving over an hour to a hospital that offers delivery services is common, and small rural hospitals have no obstetricians. Therefore, they simply, don't accept patients for delivery. Imagine thinking you might be in labor and trying to decide whether to go to the hospital, knowing the last three times you did so it turned out to be nothing more than a false-labor driving exercise.

My wife was pregnant with our third child, and she chose an obstetrician recommended by my new partner because we had just moved to town a few weeks earlier and didn't know the medical community. According to several of my doctor friends he had a respectable rating, but not in our book. The doctor checked all the boxes for a low rating, including inadequate privacy, no assistant in the exam room, disrespectful comments, and unsterile technique, so much for recommendations. He

cemented his low rating with us by an excessive episi-
otomy and leaving a sponge in the wound, which he discovered a few days later to be the source of significant
pain and infection.

The delivery was not the reason our daughter began
having seizures immediately after birth. A condition that
further clouded our pregnancy experience. The cause of
the seizures, initially difficult to discern, resulted in air
evacuation to Stanford Medical Center from Phoenix,
where, after a week of diagnostics, a partial pancre-
atectomy saved her life. The pregnancy had turned sour
but ultimately ended well.

As a surgical resident I rotated through OB. While on
that service I experienced the saddest medical event of
my medical career, the loss of a mother after delivery.
Paula had no prenatal care. She entered the hospital in
active labor, but I couldn't detect any fetal heart sounds.
I delivered a dead fetus within an hour after her arrival.
The baby was an anencephalic—meaning literally, no
head. Within a few minutes after the delivery the mother
started to bleed uncontrollably and nothing we gave
her slowed the bleeding. I made frantic calls to attending staff, other residents, and read textbooks while she
continued to bleed. Her entire body turned purple, secondary to disseminated intravascular coagulopathy
(DIC). Clotting factors, fibrinogen, and large amounts of
blood could not keep her out of shock. She died within
two hours. DIC is a rare condition in which the patient
bleeds as if she had received large amounts of antico-
agulants. There is no good solution to the problem once
it develops.

If she had been evaluated when the baby stopped
moving, which occurred several weeks before she came
to the hospital, she likely would have survived by induc-
ing a delivery.

Unfortunately, medical care is compromised by
Paula-like patients who, for whatever reason, do not
have prenatal care. They may deliver at home with no
one to assist them. Crazier yet, the U.S. cost for obstetrical care is over two times the world average.

Despite the cost, I recommend that if pregnant, you attach your wagon to a reputable obstetrician in the U.S.. I believe statistics regarding maternal deaths are misleading because women who don't receive prenatal care for whatever reason are counted along with those who have access to care. More importantly, fetal survival is improved by an appropriate C-section on those occasions where fetal distress is present.

Many doctors told me under the circumstances Paula would have died even if under ideal care. She had DIC. I still wish I could have done more. That episode made me respect pregnancy and how quickly life can change.

Pregnancy has its rewards but is often a challenging adventure. Hats off to those women who have made the trip.

Medical Jay Walking

Jay Leno periodically had a segment on his show called Jay Walking, which involved asking straight-forward questions on the street that most people would be able to answer correctly. For obvious reasons only the responses that generated laughter were aired. On many occasions I have asked questions that seemed to me critical to the evaluation of the patient but were answered with a response that should merit TV time for their unexpected and amusing character.

Other, non-orthopedic providers—my network of humor-grubbing resources such as nurses and doctors—have shared patient responses and medical records reflecting odd information with me. I should give credit for this essay to the doctors who often dictate with dangling participles and floating facts creating, a less-than-truthful picture of reality. With careful statistical assessment, it is clear the boneheaded doctors' reports outweighed the loony-humorous TV-worthy patient's quotes.

The number of misspeak opportunities is further elevated with the wearing of muffling masks. The patient may answer an unasked question from the doctor" and the doctor may hear a response not given. The mask effect also adds to the frustration of all parties and makes both try to abbreviate the interview by assuming they listened to the question and answered correctly.

Poor-fitting, underpowered, wax-compromised hearing aids worn by either patient or doctor further add to the communication scramble. All a good thing if you are seeking a funny conversation, but the purpose of a doctor's visit is generally aimed at problem resolution, not airtime on the tube.

Here are a few of my favorite office notes: "A fourteen-week uterus was found in the office." "The patient was advised not to have intercourse until she sees me in two weeks." "Patient had a spontaneous vaginal hysterectomy."

"Patient is a white Caucasian male." "The patient is stated to be a wine-drinking lover predominately during the weekends."

"The patient was nursing the fetus without difficulty." It is hard to nurse if the kid is still in the womb.

"History revealed that 59 years ago he was diagnosed as having TB and an appendectomy was done." TB is handled differently now, but it must have been effective because he has neither.

"Review of systems revealed this 50-year-old-unmarried female complained of heavy breathing in her ear at night." There may be more to the story. A different patient was reported to have bilateral cataracts in each eye.

"The patient had a stillborn sister with no known etiology." "She had a chronically running nose." It is uncommon for 80-year-olds to have anything running, so be happy even if it is just your nose that is running.

"The patient recently moved here from Texas to be near her younger sister who is an only child." Some clarification would be appropriate, but who cares?

Or a comment made regarding social activities: "The patient smokes herself." Sometimes the comments leave too much to the imagination: "She did not eat too well and has rectal pressure with the left foot falling asleep when she starts walking." But equally perplexing is the note stating, "She was bottle feeding and plans on a vasectomy." There may be an unidentified third party in this story.

"This seventy-year-old lady is childless although she tried several years ago." "Patient lives alone with her husband." He is the invisible man.

"The patient did fairly poorly while in the hospital, he became comatose and passed."

"He had never been sick or visited a doctor. He had an appendectomy 30 years ago." The appendectomy must have been performed by a vet in a moonlit field.

"She had known metastatic disease at the time of the original surgery and had a cervical node removed and replaced with cancer."

"The patient desires sterilization and epilepsy." That's a rare comment to make in a pre-op note.

"The patient smoked two pack of cigarettes for 40 years." This would suggest he was a very slow smoker

One record states: "He evidently had a circumcision in some other area." There are few body parts where circumcision works. Having your foreskin removed from your forehead would not be a good look.

"The patient was discharged as dead." I guess I understand, but usually when you die, you die, and no formal discharge is performed. That works for the military too.

The term bursitis rarely gets abused, but I have heard it referred to as burritis, burlitis, and burolitis. The patient knows what they have because their neighbor has the same thing and had to have a shot of cortalone or something. A bursitis patient had a slightly unusual presentation. With a choir director's enthusiasm, she waved her arms and more than adequately described the height of her cat rack, an elaborate floor-to-ceiling arrangement of semi-cages for over 40 adopted cats. Her arms flailed wildly overhead as she described this indoor zoo. When it came time to assess her shoulder problem, the shoulder, like magic, morphed into an excruciatingly painful joint. Her animated telling of her tale provided a morphine-like advantage for her shoulder pain, which dissipated then disappeared when her cat story time concluded.

These stories are a tiny percent of those that occur daily. The one that wins the prize by being slightly out of the norm is related to Orin, a patient I treated several years ago. He was new to me and he wanted to make sure I had a complete picture of his symptoms. When I give talks to retirement communities about how to be a good patient, I encourage them to bring a list of concerns to their appointment. I was not dismissive when Orin handed me his list. He must have heard my talk; he brought in four typed pages of problems, most of which were non-orthopedic. The pages were numbered and I found few spelling errors. This amazing document was a Who's Who or What's What of nearly everything that can be jangled in the human body. "Severe itching, burning and rash in the crotch area, violent reaction to sunlight, very frequent tension, sinus, migraine, and other headaches." Each complaint seemed worthy of several hours of discussion: "constantly reinfected moles, repeated very large boils on my scrotum, ass and lower stomach, insomnia." He had a case of diabolical intestinal confusion: "Some type of anal blockage, constant and continuous diarrhea when I pass gas it is the only way I can have a bowel movement and now I squirt or spray either feces, blood, or both." These complaints were certainly not in my sphere of knowledge or considered believable at least for earth creatures. He complained of short-term memory loss, thank goodness, or the list might have been even longer, as if 85 items were not enough.

I filtered out a few cogent orthopedic complaints I felt I could address in less than four or five hours and dove in. This man was truly living his dream, to be the sickest most tortured man on earth. He was the winner. Molière could not have concocted a more extensive inventory of problems. Orin, a modern-day "Imaginary Invalid," was more like an Orion—a giant constellation of out-of-this-world experiences.

Jay Walking in the medical world is sometimes more exciting than walking across a busy intersection and being challenged by ox, carts, buses, and motorcycles. "Good Luck" trying to sort it all out.

Pica

"For dessert, you ate what"?

"Dog feces."

"Have you considered rutabaga or parsnips?"

Dr. Morgan talked with Randy for the first time regarding his dietary muddle. It didn't take long to make a diagnosis of pica, a perverted appetite for items not normally considered food. Such things as buttons, paste, and chalk qualify.

As a child I remember chewing newspaper and making a mushy ball in my mouth, but I am sure I did not swallow it. This strange appetite lasted several years, probably during 4th and 5th grades. I never chewed much gum and don't think I had an ink deficiency or even an affinity for the want ads or whatever section I was chewing. The amount of print consumed or paper chewed must have been minimal because it was never discussed with parents or teachers. And honestly, newspapers were just a convenient taste treat; notepaper and napkins were also chewables. I was not mentally off more than any other elementary student and never took up dirt or rocks on my way to being a full-blown pica dropout.

Spit wads were a natural by-product of chewing paper, possibly the primary reason I started salivating over the morning paper. It is possible a few of these spit wads made their way across the school room, but that behavior has been completely erased from my memory. I was not partial to the Wall Street Journal or New York Times, they all tasted like my local paper. The need for ammunition shaped my spit-ball fetish/stockpile.

Ambrose Pare, in the 1500s, allegedly coined the term pica as it relates to those who eat non-food on a regular basis. It came from the Latin for Magpie, a bird who demonstrates a non-discretionary appetite. Authorities claim 18% of children are affected, and eat anything. People like me may even be included in that percentage. The bigger question is, what are the numbers related to mental illness? With a rise in mental illness there will likely be an increase in pica patients. Obsessive-compulsive disorders and schizophrenia are the major psychological conditions connected to pica. Besides those with untreated issues and children with unusual tastes, pregnant women are the most often affected.

Dr. Morgan was dealing with a real-live pica patient. He wasn't eating nails because of iron deficiency or to promote nail sales for a friend in the hardware store business. Randy had emotional issues yet to be diagnosed and treated.

Randy had passed the benign consumption of ice and ice cream and drifted into more toxic non-food choices like dirt and now even feces. So far most of his diet was real food, but dirt soon replaced cornflakes, and mulch became his new filet mignon. I don't care what color poker chip one eats; the payoff is, you will feel like crap, not like the winner at a blackjack table. That creates an odd visual of a man pulling chips out of his butt at the poker table when his stack is shrinking.

Randy had relationship problems. After not connecting with an internet contact for a few months, Dr. Morgan learned Randy tried to be more transparent with his internet dating. Randy indicated online he was experiencing an eating disorder and was currently having soil for lunch. That internet approach also produced a deluge of silence. He retreated to his list of hobbies as a come-on. But apparently, most females don't play dominoes or collect zebras.

Binge-watching a TV series or cutting your wrist can satisfy some mental issues, but eating toys and rubber balls takes more imagination. There is little value in knowing the transit time for an unwrapped suppository is quicker than a small salt shaker, something only an avid pica person would have the opportunity to observe.

Dr. Morgan pursued other causes of Randy's pica. Mental retardation and mental illness were high on his list. Because Randy was not a pregnant woman and not eating clay like an Australian Aborigine to increase his fertility, those considerations were off the table. Dr. Morgan ordered blood work to rule out magnesium and iron deficiency.

Lots of bad things can develop from eating non-nutritional items, lead poisoning being one. A handful of dirt gives some lonely parasites a chance at adventure with a nice host. Bezoars are unwelcome obstructions of the gut and can effectively block the passage of real food. These are made of undigestible material typically forming in the stomach and act like a cork. Kind of a poor man's weight loss plug.

To me, pica is an acting out, a physical manifestation of a mental disorder in most cases. True, a dietary deficiency could precipitate pica, and babies do what is natural, but just like cutting your wrist, pica is the event, not the cause. If a person dies from a screwdriver in their intestine because of the goblins in their head, it is just as sad as suicide from a drug overdose.

Pica brings genetics into play. Do you think humans will evolve to be able to digest rocks and dirt eventually? Will clever restaurants ever cater to pica folks like they do for vegetarians? Will Frys have chocolate-covered dung bars or rock candy that is real rock candy? How long before you see "Slide it Thru," a super lubricant to assist in passing those big and abrasive items a serious pica person eats? There may be padded toilets, chip-proof for the metal consumer who has diarrhea. At pica birthday parties, the treats will be bags of dirt or rabbit droppings. Soon the English will have paperclips and tea instead of crumpets.

Guinness will have records for the longest pencil-eraser first—that was able to finish the alimentary trip.

Pica is an unfortunate condition to have land in your lap. If you are looking for a way to cope with the way life has treated you, I would suggest: paint by numbers, composting, or going for a ride with Elon Musk, but don't use pica as a solution to anything.

Randy eventually controlled his passion for a pica-driven diet and became a dietician.

Mushrooms

If you are a character from a Dickens novel, on hearing the word mushroom, your mind naturally goes to a dining room to eat porridge on a cold winter day and a small voice asking plaintively, "Sir, I may have some more?" If you are from Alaska you are dreaming of a training facility for teaching dogsledding with eight Huskies, "mush" being the "go" command. As a WWll historian, your thoughts may slide to a visual of the dynamic mushroom cloud produced by an atomic bomb over Hiroshima. Sorry, but now we are entering the exciting fungi world, which ranges from the microscopic to the sliced, sautéed variety accompanying your filet mignon. Technically a mushroom is a part of a fungus, the fleshy, spore-bearing body (sporophore). For this action-packed story, I will consider them the same. We will explore some ubiquitous, sometimes delicious, sometimes mind-altering life forms. Toadstools is a term generally reserved for inedible or poisonous sporophores.

What are mushrooms? They have been classified with vegetables for a long time but are now their own group: fungi. Mushrooms have no chlorophyll, therefore depend on a host to provide the essentials of life. Mushrooms have mycelium, small thread-like roots that break through the soil to form the mushroom or fruit, the edible part of the plant. They fall into two categories: Asian and European/American, in all, containing 140,000 species.

Fossil evidence of fungi has been identified in rock 750 million years old in the Democratic Republic of the Congo. I won't trifle with truffle details, but the literature has mentioned mushrooms since Hippocrates in 450 BCE. The French cultivated mushrooms around

1650 ADE and developed cave-centered techniques, successful because of the darkness, high humidity, and constant temperature.

Although fungi have a bad name—they play a significant role in several medical diseases, whether it be toe fungus or valley fever. However, the literature regarding mushrooms is very positive. They contain compounds that lower blood pressure, prevent inflammation, and even decrease cognitive decline. I'm not talking about the fungus between your toes, but mushrooms found in the grocery store that have no side effect other than causing a rare allergy. They are also low in calories and contain a moderate amount of fiber. Maybe the most beneficial aspect of mushrooms is the anticancer effects afforded by one of the ingredients called ergo-thioneine. Umami, one of the five basic tastes, is present in mushrooms and adds a flavor to many foods.

Psilocybin is a hallucinogenic chemical in six varieties of "magic" mushrooms. The benefit or risk of consuming a hallucinogenic mushroom is an altered mental status. The appropriate mushroom is a cheap way to gain an advantage over reality. If the psychedelic fungi are eaten by mistake, and the patient's motor and mental function is compromised, they could injure or embarrass themselves, just as if they were compromised by alcohol, narcotics, or LSD. Those drugs kill thousands a year; mushrooms kill only 100.

Beyond the hallucinogenic effects is the more significant damage to the liver and kidneys caused by the "death cap" mushrooms. An antidote is available but has not been released by the FDA and is only proven to be effective in mice. A few mice have been given death caps—a poisonous mushroom—and treated successfully with the new drug. I think the average mouse eats very few mushrooms, making them unlikely to benefit from all this research, but I am glad they consented to participate in this experience. Given the relatively small number of mushroom users and the many test subjects needed to meet the FDA requirements, it may be many years before the antidote is released.

Throughout history, Egyptians, Greeks, the Aztecs, and others have relied on mushrooms for their hallucinogenic effects and have embedded mushrooms in their religious culture. In America, we have skipped the religious connection and gone straight to the hallucinogenic "benefits."

Magic mushrooms were popular in the 50s with tourism to Mexico to visit Maria Sabina and her religious ceremony using hallucinogenics. Bob Dylan, John Lennon, and others visited the site. Maria was eventually shut down for degrading a sacred religious event. These mushrooms became illegal in the U.S. in 1969.

Some magic mushrooms amplify the fight-over-flight response of self-preservation. The Vikings were feared-bloodthirsty warriors known as the Berserkers. Their bravery and "mad as hound" behavior were attributed to a mushroom known as Liberty Cap. This "no-holds-barred" behavior smacks of the "enhanced" performance seen in professional sports attributed to cocaine, pot, and steroids.

What would attract an average human to be enthusiastic about mushrooms? Are these the same people who collect thimbles and spools of thread? Not really. These wild and crazy adventuresome folks will band together like birders and travel into the dark recesses of the wild to collect the not-so-obvious fungi. Unfortunately, they are not assisted by a mating call or fluttering flight.

The searchers can train a fungus-identifying dog (truffle hound) to lead the hunt. Chanterelles and morels are popular types of mushrooms that dogs can detect. Some dogs are eaters of stuff, like grass, feces, and mushrooms. If a dog shows an eclectic diet tendency, it should be excluded from mushroom training because some types of mushrooms are lethal. This results in a handler's depression, something not appreciated during a mushroom hunt. A dead dog and a pissed trainer dampen the spirits of a happy, half-tanked, fungi crowd.

Before dogs were trained for hunting, pigs served that purpose, but they ate too many truffles and man's best friend replaced them.

Searching for mushrooms is similar to bird watching in the challenge to identify as many species as possible. Calling In a mushroom with a recording of mating calls is not an option. Identifying mushroom scat, equally ineffective. Dogs can help but training for multiple fungi breeds requires a special dog not commonly found outside of Fungigovia.

Your best bet to assist in your search is the trusted *Foragers Guide to Wild Plants*. There are other guidebooks, also costing over $100, but the Forager guide gives you big pictures of mushrooms and the geographic distribution of 400 wild and edible plants. Plus, the book features a section on poisonous-look-a-like plants. This is no ordinary book; you get recipes and harvest times. There is even a section on the medicinal properties of these wild plants. The novel's protagonist might be the mushroom, but the evil sidekick, the poison toadstool, makes one searching for the elusive fungi pause before becoming too crazy with mushroom enthusiasm.

One of my patients related her recent mushroom adventure. She, her husband, and a friend experienced a flat tire on a desolate, dirt road in the pines. The driver had no clue where her jack or spare tire were hidden, plus being in a GPS dead spot added stress. My patient, driver, and husband were concerned by the setting sun and they also had no clue where they were. No one had considered that searching for elusive fungi on a desolate forest road should require a modicum of preparation.

The uplifting discovery of the spare tire's location was minimized by the low, almost nonexistent air pressure in the spare tire. That fact remained unclear until the spare was substituted for the really flat tire. The forest service vehicle that arrived at a critical juncture helped extricate the fragile, ineffectual, inexperienced fungi crowd, a godsend. The tire was changed but demonstrated an air pressure likely in the low teens. It mattered not; they went with it, thirty miles to the nearest air supply.

The fungi party, forty-plus, had by then dispersed and were of no help. Before the flat, they had identified several often difficult-to-find fungi, which were easier to spot than the spare tire, and they were happy to conclude the hunt prior to the tire exchange.

The best things my patient experienced from this exciting venture: she identified a horny toad, better known as a horny lizard, and she returned home safely.

A sign in a French cemetery reads, "All mushrooms are edible, some only once." If you join a mushroom society and decide to hunt for mushrooms, let your friends do the tasting.

Slow Learners

Sporadic articles about the effects of diet on health first appeared in literature in the 1700s. Even earlier, in 400 B.C., Hippocrates referred to coarse flour as being better than fine flour as a laxative.

Gradually, a few doctors became interested in the possibility of dietary causation for medical conditions such as constipation and malaise. In 1880, Dr. T.S. Allinson blamed white bread for many health problems, from constipation to varicose veins. He didn't pull in AIDS, schizophrenia, or dengue fever, but he threw white bread under the early bus. He subsequently caught the wrath of the industrial millers—white bread makers—for suggesting their money-making white bread represented an unhealthy product and paled compared to the time-honored virtues of whole grain bread.

Sir Arbuthnot Lane (1856-1943) also needs to be included in this conversation. Lane was a remarkable general surgeon. He developed surgical procedures for cleft lip, rib removal for lung abscesses, and internal fixation for long bone fractures. He became most infamous for removing the colon in cases of constipation, suggesting intestinal obstruction as the cause. The operation was not widely accepted and consequently abandoned. He switched to "roughage" as a more appropriate treatment for constipation. Dr. Lane practiced in the early 1900s making him an early enthusiast for fiber, as was Dr. Allinson a few decades earlier. Fiber was still not accepted as a valid bowel-management solution.

Dr. C.H. Kellogg, a Seventh-day Adventist and a friend of Dr Lane, pushed the antitoxin benefits of bran, a message later supported by Dr. Dennis Burkitt. The way to better bowel function moved forward.

Dr. Peter Cleave, from Great Britain, became interested in the stark differences between Western-type diseases and those seen in rural Africa. He focused on the harmful effects of consuming refined sugars and white flour. During World War II he became famous as the "bran man" for his insistence that his sailors consume large amounts of bran, which prevented them from becoming constipated while on board his battleship for long periods.

In 1952 Dr. Burkitt, an Irish doctor/Ugandan missionary, and his brother, Dr. Robin Burkitt who practiced medicine in England, co-wrote a paper about the cultural differences in diseases, specifically Africa versus England.

By the 1960s, missionary doctors in Africa became aware of how many diseases and conditions were geographically dependent. Western cultures are associated with conditions like colon cancer, which is rare in rural, less affluent societies. These differences are only evident if, like missionaries, one has experienced both cultures. Myocardial infarctions (heart attacks), hemorrhoids, appendicitis, and diabetes are also uncommon in rural Africa. A person from a Western culture would find moving to the Congo is not enough to evaporate their hemorrhoids. However, they could throw away their ties and make new friends, in addition to changing diets and reaping the appropriate health benefits.

Dr. Denis Burkitt's main claim to fame is related to his understanding of a tumor, a fast-growing lymphoma commonly seen in Africa. This tumor, referred to as Burkitt's tumor, was named for his landmark work on its discovery and treatment. Burkitt's lymphomas were present in other third-world countries such as Sri Lanka and Sumatra. Even though Dr. Burkitt was well-known for his tumor, he also researched African diseases and their relationship to diet. His observations of the European diseases that were absent in Africa and his ability to coordinate the experiences of other missionaries made him the centerpiece of this dietary story.

LAUGHING IS LEGAL!

Three men, the Burkitt brothers, and Dr. Cleave sparked a search for answers to the underlying causes of geographically distinct problems.

A justifiable medical race heated up to solve the incongruence of diseases, much to the benefit of the patient and the scientific community. Prizes were offered, although big rewards were not likely the motivation for valid research. Doctors were investigating the dietary causes of real and serious diseases which affected a huge population. How many people die from coronary heart disease or lymphomas in Western cultures? And why is appendicitis rarely seen in rural Africa? Pie à la mode and bacon cheeseburgers are as common to Africans as hard green bananas are to Chicagoans. Uber Eats has not reached Rwanda or Eritrea, so what produced the disease differences? Could the diet differences be the key?

Like many discoveries in medicine and technology, competition is a great motivator. Would the cause of constipation and colon cancer be related to sugar consumption, as Cleave believed, or the lack of fiber, as espoused by Dr. Burkitt?

Burkitt studied the transit time for food to pass from mouth to anus, trying to define the role of fiber in the poop passage program. He sent questionnaires to 150 African Mission hospitals. The responses revealed that many Western diseases, such as hemorrhoids, were never seen in those facilities. This naturally led to his next research step: measuring the transit times of food through the alimentary tract. The subjects swallowed 24 barium markers. The stools were X-rayed and weighed to determine the transit times. He did this study on both local Africans and English subjects in England. Despite of the limitations of the mail and before the internet, he completed an amazingly successful data collection project.

Dr. Alec Walker, a biochemist and a very smart Alec from South Africa, focused his research on the disease differences by comparing African and Western stools. The African stools were larger, softer, and quicker to pass. He concluded this resulted in no appendicitis, minimal diabetes, and no colon cancer in the Africans. The opposite results applied to the Europeans. Dr. Walker brought fiber into the discussion as a significant dietary difference.

Dr. Cleave attributed the now obvious disease distribution to refined sugar consumption, therefore making the race to the truth more meaningful.

Dr. Burkitt continued evaluating stools for weight, hardness, and transit times. Three to five days was routine time for a Western diet to cross the line. African stool times average 30 hours with stool size over twice the Western stool. Metamucil doesn't sell well in rural third-world countries.

Despite the research of several doctors, the American Cancer Society still believed colon cancer was related to fat, not a fiber deficiency. Constipation and appendicitis were not addressed by the Society before 1970.

Dr. Burkitt received a boost from Dr. Hugh Trowel, a missionary doctor who worked in Uganda. His book, *Non-infectious Diseases in Africa,* focused on nutrition and the benefits of fiber. Dr. Trowel had demonstrated that inadequate fiber was a key element in diseases related to the colon. Still he was concerned that high-fat consumption was likely behind other Western diseases—coronary artery blockage/heart attacks. Dr. Cleave still held out for blaming refined sugar as the major player in heart disease, but he considered fat and fiber to have a role.

Later studies done on Seventh-day Adventist vegetarians revealed a marked reduction in cancer, heart disease, and diabetic deaths associated with the typical African diet versus the typical European diet.

In the early 1970s consuming fiber became popular. In England, fiber's importance remained in question. The researchers were using African morbidity statistics to help resolve Western-type death rates and fiber moved into a leading position as a significant ingredient in the prevention of heart disease, diabetes, hemorrhoids, and colon cancer, among others.

Wheat bread contains far more fiber than white bread. The millers' resistance to producing high-fiber bread conflicted with the recommendations of Dr. Burkitt and others who researched the subject extensively. It appeared the millers' position was more psychological than financial. The millers had spent years reducing fiber and now were being challenged to restore fiber to bread by adding whole wheat.

Dr. Burkitt lectured and received awards worldwide as he promoted the benefits of fiber. While he visited all corners of the world, he continued to perform research such as his high potato diet, which produced shorter transit times and large soft stools in the willing participants. If you are interested in weighing stool and measuring the poop pace factor, you too, could start your own research. Artichokes are high in fiber but you hear very little about artichokes as a stool softener or constipation buster.

The tide turned further in 1975 and the benefits of fiber gained acceptance worldwide. That is not to say everyone had soft and bulky stools, but people realized the value of fiber. White bread, which has more sugar than whole wheat, is still popular. The incidence of Western diseases such as colon cancer has declined, but more screening is also performed so fiber doesn't get the credit on this one. The decline in colon cancers is in older people, but the numbers are up in those under 50 years old.

Recommended minimum daily consumption of fiber is now printed on food containers suggests fiber has achieved a position of medical importance—25 grams in women and 38 grams in men. With a diet including fresh fruits and vegetables more people will get their fiber fix. If you are addicted to white bread, chips, and ice cream you may not consume the necessary amount of fiber.

Fiber is a complex carbohydrate that contains almost no calories and is not absorbed. If you are thinking of eating paper to fulfill your fiber needs, think again. Paper treated with sulfuric acid is not a recognized supplement, and toilet paper is recycled from who knows what. Paper could provide you with fiber but is currently not recommended. If you need a fiber booster. you could still swallow a few cartoons and an obituary or two.

To me, the public health component of medicine is the holy grail of modern medicine. Polio vaccinations are a great example of prevention versus treatment on the backside. Having done medical mission work in several third-world arenas, I share Dr. Burkitt's philosophy regarding the benefit of surgery or medical intervention on an individual basis. While I often felt satisfaction from my work in Africa, I reflected on the need for—the big picture—safer drinking water and better birth control education. The rewards resulting from using seatbelts far outweigh the surgery on a single-broken femur. Surgery is a good thing but determining the cause of a tumor or slowing the development of diabetes could bring enormous benefits compared to the treatment of the disease after the fact.

People need to catch on to the benefits of fiber and accept known information. Why invite constipation, hemorrhoids, appendicitis, and colon cancer? All you need is a bowl of Grape-Nuts and a few sweet potato fries every day to keep you busy making number two your number one priority.

Thank you, Dr. Denis Burkitt.

Blankie

Do you still have your blankie? Does the inseparable attachment to the magnetic blankie follow a predictable pattern into adulthood? I find no study that connects blankies to future drug use, wealth, or cannibalism. Supposedly a third of adults maintain a close tie to a childhood supportive item. That doesn't imply they take a smelly, torn towel or even a stuffed toy to work, but statistically, they have a more than casual connection to a childhood item.

The adult attraction to inanimate objects is a common experience that may grow stronger with aging. An art project produced by a child may hang on the parent's wall as a vital treasure and strong memory of their child's youth. The ultimate form of "holding on" is your neighborhood hoarder who has a house stuffed with newspapers and trash, giving the appearance the house is about to explode with one more retained item. The fully committed hoarder may need help negotiating through their narrowing halls inundated with objects encroaching on the shrinking space. To locate their original blankie would be a challenge.

How does this process begin?

Nipples and pacifiers, both blankie precursors, enter a child's life at an early age.

Croatia and Rwanda lead the world in breastfeeding with 85% participation. I'll go out on a limb or breast and reflect that the accuracy of these numbers is suspect. Most literature doesn't indicate if one time versus one year of breastfeeding counts the same. One survey stated 44% of U.S. mothers were breastfeeding three-year-old children, while other studies indicated only 20% made it to 6 months. Conclusion: breastfeeding is still popular for some including the Chicago girl who was on the breast past her ninth birthday. The girl occasionally sneaked into her mother's room at night to have a nightcap. I've treated patients who were breastfeeding their four-year-old, but never a nine-year-old. Clearly there are no universal standards for weaning.

The same is true for the pacifier. Pediatricians are not all on the same page, but age three is, a generally accepted time to stop using them. When you have some anti-vaxxers giving medical advice, you can be sure there are pacifier opponents who will drive the bell curve in some unpredictable direction.

The blankie may morph into a stuffed animal or a herd of stuffed objects, all having a cherished position. These silent companions might, when misplaced, elicit an emotional outpouring akin to losing a close relative. Sleeplessness and short-breath sobbing take an emotional toll on even a strong parent. To wean away from these cherished possessions is oft-times a long and challenging process. To discard seems impossible. Long live the blankie and its stuffy friends.

Other forms of gratification gradually replace the blankie. As children move into elementary school the rewards and life-giving excitement come from farting, burping, and comparable sounds made by a hand in the axilla. I could whistle but never accomplished the cherished arm burp. A casual comment about any stool-related subject was funnier than an hour with *I Love Lucy or Seinfeld*. *Winnie the Pooh* became Winnie the poop. A night in a cabin of Indian Guides became a giggle fest as each of the six campers produced his own original fart sound, sleep therefore delayed well past the curfew of ten o'clock. The "knock it off" recommendation repeated by the offended campers was followed by another fart sound. One oddball kid who wanted to sleep had said his prayers and didn't participate in the fart-arama. He even tried to read under the covers with his penlight, thereby setting himself up to be the butt of jokes in the morning. I'm sure girls never behaved that way on their outings.

Junior High brought for me more of the same with a slight shift toward the recognition there were girls. Some of them well developed, some wore makeup, and supportive garments, which made them worthy of chatter. In the old days it was real chatter now; social media has become the entertainment method of choice. A choice that also extends deep into the night or early morning, producing a hungover, grumpy teenager, especially when awakened at 11 a.m. The stuffed giraffe or Disneyland elephant, the replacement for the blankie had by then generally moved to the back-burner, although for some, were still objects of comfort. The junior high period was known for cliques/gangs—a source of belonging that helped to replace the stuffed animals.

In high school the blankie replacement continued with greater polarization: the good guys, bad guys, cheerleaders, and drug users, which might be one and the same, the car guys, FFA, Boy Scouts, church attendees, motorcycle boys, the jocks, the thespians, band, orchestra, and a whole lot of none of the above. Each group generated its rewards or blankies substitutes. A drag race didn't trump a trombone solo or a lead in the class play unless, of course, you liked to drag race.

The students had all grown up and sort of able to make the best choices, occasionally. For some it was work, some play, for others "I can't wait to get out of here." Whatever it was, game on, find a best friend and enjoy.

Once out of high school, probably no blankies and new groups are created. But wait, over 50% of young adults continue to live with their parents after finishing high school. There's your blankie. If you go off to college or the military, the programming warps your path and changes your "blankie." Do you like marine biology, accounting, archeology, or girls? There are always video games and social media, but since college costs parents more than their first house, maybe you should study. Maybe you drop your strong religious ties or ramp them up. Like your roommate, you may need to taste every beer available at the local pub. Maybe you find a favorite instructor who takes you under his wing, and off you go in a new direction, like earth science, and become consumed by the teacher's interest in you and in the subject.

You keep looking for your blankie. You might be among the 30% of students who drop out after the first year of college. Even in the military over 10% drop out after one year. Marriages fail too, 10% in the first two years. There are no guarantees in life, but hopefully, you find a blankie that doesn't stink.

The next level of life is the compete-for-survival phase. You have kids, responsibilities, family leadership challenges, and three credit cards to pay off, not counting your free-spending wife's plastic purchases and plastic surgery. You're on a terrible bowling team, your favorite baseball team is in last place and the ice maker in your refrigerator needs to be fixed again. A new organization just bought your company and the boss's friend said this could be the end of us. It isn't all bad; your daughter was student of the month, not shabby for a fifth-grader. You have to be proud. That position was not available when you went to school, but you would not have received it anyway.

Your current support prop is the wife, hopefully yours. She knows your weakness and is okay with the monthly poker group and the lid-up problem. She modifies her spending after the car repairs ate into your savings. And she doesn't leave you after she reads your text to an unknown lass. Somewhere in there is your blankie. Life is good.

You could always go home and work for your relatives or go to work in the prison to be near relatives. You get a little blankie effect either way. The idea is to connect to a plan that gives you pleasure, not money. Pleasure.

What about the "finishing" years, the retirement plus? You have a dog or at least an animal in the house. The dog provides a subject for daily conversation. He sheds, vomits, pees, and poops in geographically inappropriate locations at inappropriate times. He has scratched furniture, eaten shoes, and bitten the kid next door. You gotta love a conversation maker like Bo, soon to be Boo. But he is your blankie.

You could take up beading, model airplanes, or just suck up a little more TV. The neighbor is into land-scaping, a bone of contention because Jill, your wife, has fallen in love with azaleas. Why can't she just like *Gunsmoke* or *Magnum P. I.* reruns? The future is trending more and more around Bo. Too bad because Bo is a savings-sucking magnet. The veterinarian sends Bo birthday cards, not a positive sign, but better than the neighbor sending flower seeds. The nursing home is just around the corner.

If you haven't picked out your favorite retirement facility, make sure it has indoor plumbing. Actually, that isn't so important as it once was thanks to Depends, a truly wonderful invention. The progression from your own home to heaven/hell is independent living, assisted living, incarceration, and fetal position in a terminal care unit. At the assisted living stage, you connect to a new blankie, a velvet pillow, or maybe a vodka tonic if you connected to regular alcohol at an earlier stage. This is also a good time to reestablish your religiosity, collect turtles, or enjoy fireworks.

What is your Blankie?

Born Again

Reincarnation, the rebirth of the soul, is a philosophy supported primarily by several Indian religions: Hinduism, Jainism, Buddhism, and Sikhism. The concept exists in many indigenous cultures and is also embraced by the Unity Church and isolated believers in mainstream Western religions.

Like most things based on faith, the science to fully support the idea one's soul came from another living "animal" is not strong. Skeptics, however, must not ignore the stories of young children describing past events related to deceased persons. The children would not have been exposed to these past facts often occurring before they were born, yet the stories they tell related to previous lives are often true. The gender of the child may change from that in the previous life, but many young folks can recall details suggesting they had experienced an earlier life that is verifiable. Childhood imagination aside, the veracity of the details of a former life has been confirmed often enough to give support to rebirth. The soul feature of reincarnation seems especially important as espoused by Buddhists and Hindus.

Other supporting stories from non-Hindus come from the regression or hypnotism of adults who reveal, in remarkable detail, information about a previous life that proved to be accurate. The most publicized example relates to a pilot who was shot down in the Second World War and whose reborn person forty-years later with no connections to the pilot, recalled specific details of the battle with intimate accuracy.

Bridey Murphy is a good example of a famous reincarnation story from 1959 about a lady in Colorado who, under hypnosis, recalled details of her prior self in Ireland

100 years earlier. Much of the story was discredited, but some revelations seemed true including her Irish accent spoken when in a trance. The hypnosis revealed just enough information to make it hard to completely disregard reincarnation.

Frank Baranowski, a former professor at Glendale Community College, had a two-hour talk show and did regressive therapy for people having a variety of mental disorders. I heard him speak about one of his patients who had related, under hypnosis, details of his experience in the war, especially the day he died in his previous life while on duty during the Pearl Harbor attack. Most of the story was extracted under a trance, information below his normal consciousness.

These modern-day reincarnations were, from Frank's experiences, a piece of his regression pie. During his therapy sessions he uncovered the connections of his patients to medieval personalities: King James, Joan of Arc, Charlemagne, and others. Not all of his patients had a connection to elite historical figures. In a previous life one might have been a fisherman or a shepherd. He usually connected his patients to a past person and I never heard him make reference to an animal.

Reincarnation comes in two forms. In the first, the people are faith-based and have no understanding of what life they may have come from or even what planet. They cannot trace where they were in their last life and leave it up to faith where they will be after death. I cannot find literature that suggests that the faith-based souls have used regression therapy. The second form—unrelated to religion—is composed of those people who connect with a deceased person, usually through hypnosis.

The more traditional reincarnation stories emanate from religion and karma. This is where reincarnation becomes complicated. Karma will influence who we become in the next life. If you are loaded with bad karma, does that mean you were reincarnated from a "bad" person? And going forward, is the person who receives your soul in for guaranteed jail time or will they be able to flip the switch and obtain sainthood? It appears that if you are a "bad" person you could be an animal or even a plant in the next cycle. Like many religious questions, there is no clear answer. A happy, generous, loving person produces good karma—where did it come from, and where are you going in your next life?

An unanswered question related to religious reincarnation is who decides where our souls will go? What critical elements come into play regarding whether your soul is worthy of landing in another human or, if judged harshly, you might end up as a rodent? Even a bush is a possible next stop. I may be missing something, but the ground rules are a little fuzzy.

I am not being judgmental; all religions lack the definite lines we usually see in sports, where if you step on the out-of-bounds line, you are clearly penalized. Religions lean more toward the often-arbitrary rules such as charging in basketball and interference in football—both subject to human judgment. In the reincarnation arena, religious-style, the referee/God knows the rules, but the players are not as certain. If a little white lie (maybe not politically correct, or a lie of uncertain hue) should it be told? Is that lie equivalent to a gang rape? And can you neutralize a significant abhorrent behavior by penance or grant yourself absolution? Does donating $50 to a homeless person get you a better reincarnation body? Where is the line in the sand for a visit to hell or a rat for your next living body form? And if you are sin-free, will heaven or moksha be waiting?

Religions that support reincarnation contain many areas of disagreement regarding the guidelines about karma and what it takes to get a passing grade. The good news is that religions, in general, support a kinder, more considerate way of relating to man/womankind. Oh, I forgot about religious wars, persecution, and occasional deviant behavior. Nobody is perfect.

Christians say "Go to Hell" when putting their friend in their proper place. So, Hindus may say "Go to Goat" when blasphemy has been heard, or a lack of enthusiasm for another's opinion demands a response. I would not remonstrate if told I may not make it to heaven, no more than I would protest if told I would likely relocate to the body of a politician. Would we be better, more knowledgeable people if, when hypnotized, we found that in a past life, we were Fijian therefore explaining why we don't tolerate cold weather, or an artillery officer in World War II resulting in a hearing loss?

I hope for those of you who will be reincarnated, you will have a step-up in pay grade, a beautiful spouse, and a happy, litigation-free life.

Unique

If asked to describe yourself, chances are you would promote a characteristic that gives you "Uniqueness." Maybe you have the biggest something, a mole or a ball of string. As a college student I found a huge potato chip in a standard potato chip bag. It retained its shape and wholeness despite of the spud's enormity and its vulnerable environment. I kept it on a bookshelf, hoping to frame it someday. Finally, it was shattered by a jealous, inebriated fraternity brother. I survived the emotionally depleting incident but unfriended my fraternity brother for the rest of the year. Who should be allowed to irreverently smash a chip, especially a unique, one-of-a-kind specimen?

That silly chip became part of my identity, the guy with the big chip, not a car, muscles, or IQ, just a chip.

Daily I hear unique, proudly chronicled stories from my patients with little prompting. Often the proud event, accomplishment, object, or characteristic is random and unrelated to the reason for their visit.

I didn't work hard to discover the chip. Lottery winners are lucky, but they don't have to do much to win other than keep wasting money until their fortunes turn.

"I lost three brothers to heart attacks, and I am older than anybody in my family." "I saw Evil Knievel jump 19 cars in Barstow." That's enough uniqueness to last a lifetime.

• • •

"Margaret, it looks like you have had a few operations."

"Doctor, I have had 39 surgeries."

I thought she must have included haircuts and man-icures. But she indeed survived legitimate operations, most of which were big-time, full anesthetic, often life-saving stuff. The surgeries included well-known body parts such as the heart, lungs, kidneys, and bladder. Skin cancers were numerous but vein and artery surgeries were close behind. Unlike Hollywood folks, none of her work was related to cosmetics. According to my nurse, that was too bad. You would have thought they could just as well have done a two-for-one and sneaked in a little plastic surgery with all the times she was asleep. As a freebie I often trimmed patient's toenails, espe-cially the thick ones, after a knee replacement.

Margaret started to describe each operation in chronological order starting with her tonsils and appen-dectomy. I let her expound until the hysterectomy, the telling of which became a novella.

• • •

Another patient, Walter, followed a similar high-volume surgical pattern but with his own twist. Every major surgery had a complication, usually an infection. His total knee replacement started draining a few weeks after surgery, as did his hip replacement. An infection became a ticket for two more surgeries. His eight-hour back surgery failed to relieve his pain but lightened his bank account. His identity revolved around his failed surgeries. He was spending so much time in the OR that he didn't have time to be good at anything else.

• • •

Arnold and Alice told of their recent unique event. While traveling on the freeway a large sledgehammer fell from the back of the truck in front of them and shattered their front window, whizzed between their heads, and ended in the backseat. Even so, they pursued the truck. A mile later they were able to pull the driver over and confront him about the event. The place where the truck stopped happened to be adjacent to a policeman chatting with another driver regarding an unrelated incident. The police became involved in the discussion when they saw the shattered window. The truck driver denied having any hammers in the bed of his truck, but the hammer recovered from the back seat revealed the name on the handle—Harlem Construction—matched the name on the side of the truck. The arrest and unique event made Arnold and Alice proud, maybe their finest moment—forget about the five grandchildren and student of the month stuff. They had been hammered and survived.

. . .

Speaking of items being in the wrong place, the same day I heard the flying hammer tale, Millie, in her eighties, related her chest pain story. She had been concerned by the persistent chest pain, unrelated to activities. I lifted her blouse to inspect for a skin rash that might reveal shingles. She had no rash. But her bra was positioned across her chest above both of her breasts. I didn't interview the breasts to hear their point of view but did notice a red line across the area where bra contact took place. Not completely confident about elder fashion, I cautiously advanced the idea the bra might be of better service if worn slightly lower, which also may decrease her chest pain. Millie was grateful for my suggestion but likely will continue to include botched bra wear in her arsenal of uniqueness.

. . .

Tom, a recent patient, visited because of a self-inflicted gunshot wound. When I asked for details of the accident, he showed a video on his phone documenting the unique event. He discharged an AK-47. The bullet ricocheted off the target and returned to sender, striking him in the arm and lodging near the ulnar nerve. This nerve is critical for a normally functioning hand and fingers. He was anxious to have the bullet removed immediately, thinking removal would restore the nerve function. I assured him a scheduled removal and nerve exploration would provide a better treatment plan. Removing the missile was less important than repairing the nerve or at least evaluating it for repairability. Surgical exploration the next day revealed a bruised but intact nerve; therefore, recovery was highly likely. I gave him the bullet to further establish his uniqueness.

• • •

You are what you say you are. A friend of mine had lost both hands in Vietnam. When registering at a hotel, the clerk asked about his line of work. He calmly replied, "Brain surgeon." The clerk mechanically recorded the information on the intake form. His disability promotes him to uniqueness among brain surgeons.

• • •

I played in a recent tennis tournament against Monty. I had heard tales about Monty from others, but you had to see him in action to believe his uniqueness. He retrieved only the balls against the fence. If a ball stopped at his feet, he kicked it to the back fence rather than bend over to pick it up. When serving, he tossed up two balls. Nobody in the world does that. He brushed the extra ball aside after striking the primary ball and continued with the point. Prior to serving he hiked his shorts up with two jerks, not counting himself. His left knee brace routinely slipped down to his calf. Usually, about four games into the match, after several attempts to secure it, he would undo the strap and fling it against the fence, claiming he didn't need it anyway.

Throughout the game, he carried on a self-analysis of every point loud enough for all to hear. "Nice shot," followed by, "You shmuck, don't over-hit it, you can beat this guy." His line calls were fair to a fault; often he was overly generous with the calls and yelled the location of close shots even when in and returned. I was convinced the day we played he forgot to take his medication, but others told me I witnessed his customary behavior, unique Monty. A full bizarre Monty, if you will.

• • •

Dotty seemed like a regular patient. I examined her arthritic hand including touching it and manipulating the joints. Later when I brought out a wrist brace Dotty became unglued as I removed it from the box. She expressed, in a high-pitched panicky voice, her concern about germs and that I touched her brace. I repentantly replaced the brace in the box, and presented her with a new unopened box. She took the box from me, satisfied that the brace remained germ-free as long as she opened the box. This after I had fawned over her hand for several minutes without the slightest apparent concern about germs. At no time during our encounter did I see even one germ. I put her in the unique intermittent phobia category.

• • •

Slick gained his unique status by demonstrating bullet-proof survivability when he lost control of his motorcycle traveling at 70 mph on the freeway. He flew forward and skidded to a stop. Not one bone was broken, but Slick left several square feet of skin on the pavement. No helmet, no leathers, no way he survived, but he did. You can't teach luck. Some good and some bad. He can be proud of his unique freeway slide.

• • •

Bobby stood out for his amazing lust for life, totally blind yet an avid skier. I saw him for a minor ankle sprain unrelated to skiing. Somehow, he maneuvered around my office as if he could see. His cane and sonar receivers gave him flawless navigation ability. I felt guilty holding his arm to aid his orientation to the chair or exam table. He talked to the walls and detected obstacles with ease. Yes, he skied, including challenging terrain, much of which I had also experienced. I appreciated the difficulty negotiating those runs even when sighted. He won the prize for the most unique patient that week.

You have heard my experiences with unique patients and why they are such. I am sure you are unique or have had a noteworthy experience. If you want to be called unique, here are 30 ways to spell your new name.

Uneeke, Unike, Lunike, Eunique, Unik, U N'q, UNeek, YouNeek, Younique, Uneke, Youneek, Uneke, Youneke, Ukneek, Uneq, Uneeq, Youneq, Yuneke, Yuneek, Yooneek, Yun'k, Un'k, U'Nique, U'Neeque, UNeek, U'Neik, U'Kneeke, Unyik, Uoonique.

Being Unique is Unique.

Shiver In The River

A **Colorado River trip should be on everyone's bucket** list.

The Colorado River has been around for millions of years as suggested by the depth of the Grand Canyon. Several other canyons are rated as deeper (located in Tibet and Peru) but are in mountainous terrain and measured by a different yardstick.

The Colorado River is vitally important to the water needs of California, Arizona, Nevada, and Mexico. The river changed character in 1966 following the construction of the Glenn Canyon Dam. Environmentalists and politicians battled its development and are still battling how to manage the river. Some feel the dam should be removed; others feel several more dams should be built on the river. The 710-feet-high dam forms Lake Powell, a reservoir with a capacity of 27 million acre-feet, slightly less than Lake Mead. The dam is also a source of hydroelectric energy, providing four billion kilowatt hours per year. The recreational benefits of Lake Powell—boating, fishing, and water skiing—give additional value to the dam. One of the concerns about a large lake is the loss of water by evaporation. The good news, the lake provides a stable water source in times of drought. The dam is still there and likely will remain for many years.

The flow from the dam into the Colorado River varies from day to day depending on the electrical and water needs. The usual flow is 8,000 to 25,000 cubic feet per second. The average flow could fill 10,000 backyard pools in a second. Variations of the release amount change the dynamics of the river downstream and make river running even more of an adventure.

In 1978 I joined a group of friends for the adventure of floating the Colorado River on large motorized pontoon rafts. Before running the river with a guide, I had no idea of the challenges the boatman faced as the river flow fluctuated.

Two rafts traveled together. My raft hosted 14 passengers: five long-time couple friends, Ken, my golfing partner, me, and the two guides. By chance, one of our guides (Ann), happened to be my next-door neighbor, a seasoned veteran of the river who traveled the water without her soon-to-be ex-husband. She reminded me of Jerry Garcia's girlfriend, whom I did not know. The passengers in the other pontoon boat, strangers to us, consisted of a pair of female librarians, a writer for *Arizona Highways* who was making his sixth trip, and two twenty-plus-year-old German photographers. The other passengers were friendly random folks looking to have fun.

The fun of a river run depends on your enthusiasm for danger. Some float trips on quiet rivers are just that, float trips. The passengers enjoy a leisurely, safe venture, listening to guide stories and enjoying the deep blue sky and spectacular canyon scenery. A Colorado River float trip was a little more exciting and dangerous. River rafting trips produce many injuries and "I almost drowned" stories. I have enjoyed rafting trips on the Snake River in Idaho, the Uwharrie River in Denali National Park, and the Tena River in southern Ecuador; each had its own character. The Colorado River was more than a float trip; it was an eight-day outing with 11 friends—a bonding experience.

We started the trip at the end. Driving to a parking lot near the exit point of the journey made sense. From the assembly point we were airlifted to Page, Arizona, where we had our orientation meeting and stayed overnight for an early morning departure from Lee's Ferry. All float trips depart from the same general area, with many outfitters competing for space on the relatively small, available beach area.

Our motorized crafts were the largest of the boats allowed on the river. Everything from one-man kayaks, canoes, four-man row boats, and others were part of the river armada. We had chosen what was supposed to be the safest, most informative, and highest-rated gourmet float trip. The luggage list was small: a swimsuit, a change of clothes, a hat, toiletries, a flashlight, sunscreen, bug repellent, a camera, a towel, hiking boots, and a book. Our group tolerated the August weather—the hottest time of the year—but even in the summer the water stayed cold.

We were schooled in proper etiquette, environmental considerations like not leaving our dead bodies on the shore, and waste disposal. There was no porta-potty onboard. Wearing a life jacket was required attire. We were given a book with a river map to help us anticipate the next rapids, calm water, stopping points, and potential hiking trails. It revealed the location of a warm spring and plan for a bathing day.

The boarding process was chaotic. The novice riders scrambling onto the bobbing slippery raft, all trying to analyze the most desirable seat, made an entertaining spectacle. The seats being similar, none looked particularly luxurious or safer than another, except for the horn seats. These positions were on the front prominence of the boat and required holding onto a rope, especially when encountering the rapids. The horn seats were clearly the place to be if you wanted to go overboard, or at least they increased that option. It was not the place to be if reading was your activity.

The American Whitewater Association rated the rapids by a somewhat arbitrary system based on the usual river flow. As the amount of water released from the dam changed, the rating for a given rapids changed. A lower or higher flow rate could increase the danger level of a given rapid because either could significantly change the pattern of the current.

Within 20 minutes after starting down the river we reached a relatively low-rated rapids. That gave us a clue about the accuracy of the rating system. As we rounded a corner, anticipating seeing our first rapids, we encountered an overturned raft the same size and capacity as the one we were occupying. There were 12 passengers swimming to shore, food sacks scattered about, and a guitar in the middle of the river detached from its owner. There was little evidence of any rapids capable of turning them over. Most of the critical supplies were tied to the raft, but cameras, glasses, and personal items were on the bottom of the river—on the first day of their eight-day trip. If an almost nonexistent rapids could flip the biggest boat, we were definitely in for trouble. At least the stage was set for an anxious ride. The overturned event flummoxed our guides. We helped as much as possible, righting the boat and extending sympathy before drifting away. I can still see the guitar owner shaking his freshly baptized instrument as water poured out.

None of the passengers realized how dangerous the Grand Canyon could be. Twelve people die every year visiting the Canyon. Tourists die by suicide, natural causes, falls, and drowning, which might be the most likely way my group would go. But even those on the river trip participate in challenging hikes and risk-taking, which could be fatal. The thought of dying pops up, especially as you go over the first big rapids, or bounce over any large white-water challenge.

• • •

The Native Americans who lived in the Canyon were first visited in 1540 by the Spanish explorers, and after that, no recorded visitor came to the area for 200 years. Even in 1848 when the United States acquired the Grand Canyon territory from Mexico after the Mexican-American War, there was little to document any non-native visitor coming to the Canyon. During the 1850s, several surveyors and Mormons sought a crossing site over the river. In 1857 the U.S. War Department sent John Ives to the area to investigate for the presence of natural resources. He declared the land valueless and suggested no whites visit the area again. An assistant who traveled with Ives was much more enthusiastic about the

Canyon than Ives. The assistant convinced John Wesley Powell to explore it a few years later.

Powell was an amazing Civil War vet who, along with five other men out of the nine who started, finished the first known river run in 1869. He had only one arm but still managed to lead four boats down the Green River into the Colorado, completing the trip in 96 days.

In 2016 three boaters traveled the Colorado portion in record time, only to be beaten three days later by a 34-hour and two-minute pace, this time by a single kayaker. These records seem a little arbitrary; I never saw a marker indicating the end of the Canyon.

Powell was not an ordinary man; he had walked across Wisconsin at age 21 and at age 24 rowed down the Illinois River and eventually to Central Iowa via the Mississippi and Des Moines Rivers. His 68 years of leading a restless life were packed with adventure, geological pursuits, and anthropologic research.

Powell's stories filled our raft for eight days. He had no idea whether he would encounter large waterfalls or if the Native Americans would allow him passage when he started his Colorado trip. Powell's first expedition needed better funding and a photographer. Two years later Powell returned with better equipment and a photographer. He cataloged animals, plants, and geological and archaeological sites. He then presented that information on a lecture tour.

In 1908, Theodore Roosevelt named the Grand Canyon a National Monument, and in 1919, under Woodrow Wilson, it became Grand Canyon National Park.

Hearing the Powell stories made me grateful for having a motor, cook, and guide, but also cheated by not having the challenges of Powell's venture.

Options for entertainment while floating the Colorado are limited. But Bill, the writer/photographer, provided much geological information in addition to his tales from previous trips, as did the guides and boatman. We learned a lot about each other. Fishing became a worthwhile venture because we caught enough to have fresh fish nearly every day. We looked forward to shore stops with bathroom breaks, hiking, lunch, or evening dinners. The dining experience turned into a pleasant surprise, considering we had no electricity or refrigeration, and yet we were treated to amazing gourmet food. Our euphoric attitudes and glutenous appetites may have elevated the epicurean ratings.

On our second day out we reached Sockdolager Rapids, the biggest we had seen. Mike, one of my passenger friends, confirmed the seven-rating appropriate as he was quickly tossed out of the boat. He remained underwater for half a minute or more and I was convinced he was gone. Mike resurfaced on the opposite side of the raft from the location where he was sitting when he went over. We pulled him on board once we reached calmer water. The danger of being under the boat is being struck by the motor, which the boatman immediately cut once Mike went over. Even with a life jacket on you could hit your head. Mike was the only one who unintentionally left the boat.

Following the evening meals we played cards, tossed horseshoes, and enjoyed frisbee, sometimes compromised by errant river throws. After dark the Germans were getting under the covers of the librarians and not book covers. At night we occasionally saw a ringtail cat. The stars were the stars for me. Being outdoors, away from the city light and observing the millions of stars, added to the serenity of the trip.

We learned from our guides the unique window the Grand Canyon provides to show the development of North America. The Canyon exposes the Vishnu Schist at the bottom of the gorge, which dates back two billion years. The volcanic rocks near the top of the Canyon likely appeared less than three million years ago. Several layers of sandstone indicating there were sand dunes and marine activities present in the area at one time. The geological window and the presence of five of seven life zones in the layers of the Canyon are unparalleled in this country.

The river drops seven feet a mile from Lee's Ferry to Lake Mead. The water flow speed is deceptive. One evening while playing catch with a tennis ball and awaiting dinner, the ball flew into the wide, slow-moving river. As I swam to retrieve the ball, I realized I had drifted much further downstream than anticipated. Also, the Canyon walls were looming up steeply. Without a life jacket and not a good swimmer, I panicked when I realized I had no sand beach to climb on if I went into the deep canyon. I have never swum faster or with more focus and conviction than I did for the next five minutes. The current was moving with renewed enthusiasm as the river narrowed. I barely made shore before reaching the high walls ahead. No one in my group sensed the urgency with which I was trying to save my ....

I rested on the rocks about half a mile from my starting place, and then slowly walked back to a relaxing supper. My heart rate was in the thousands but I still held the tennis ball.

Each day brought new rapids, new hikes, and more Grand Canyon facts. We survived sunburns, mosquito bites, abrasions, and lack of news. A civil war could have raged and we would not have known. We were out of touch with the world, living for the moment, devouring bacon and eggs, and taking in more stars.

Lava Falls, the primo rapids, was conveniently positioned at the end of the trip. There were no more falls of any consequence farther downriver. We stopped the float just before reaching Lava Falls so the guides could survey the flow pattern and we, the nervous passengers, could anticipate what might be. As we observed the scenery, we were momentarily distracted by five young, topless travelers. I was told my furtive camera wandered from the cataract to the rock formations supporting these damsels. I reminded my friends we had sufficient photos of rapids and I had been camping with a guy for eight days.

Lava Falls was as advertised. A wild and unpredictable ride that left us all drenched but still on board. A fitting ending to a bucket list trip.

House of Learning

Starting a job in a new town where I knew no one and barely knew the names of my partners was an exciting experience. On my first visit to the O.R. of my new hospital in Mesa, Arizona, I learned that I did not know the names of many of the surgical instruments. Most instruments were at one time named after the inventor. Regional difference in names, like dialects, confused the identification process. When I requested instruments by the names I used in Tennessee, even the common tools, and frequently drew a blank stare or "I have no idea what you want." I resorted to pointing at the desired instrument and asking what was its Arizona name. "That retractor is called a what?" My request for a Kocher clamp was greeted with silence.

After the first few weeks of learning the new names, I decided an opportunity existed for renaming the instruments to personalize them. Many of the nurses were young and not entirely certain what the correct names of the instruments were anyway. I started by naming instruments that had no names. A long retractor used in hip joint surgery became a "marfans"–named for a genetic disorder, resulting in a thin frame with long arms–therefore an appropriate name for a long, narrow piece of stainless steel. That caught on, so I continued naming and renaming common surgical tools. An army-navy retractor became a "flat brush," pickups with teeth became "teeth," and pickups without teeth became "toothless." Some names like the Kocher clamps were reinforced. The whole naming thing was more of a game for me because I was a grabber. Rather than ask for an instrument it was simpler to snatch the desired instrument from the tray rather than ask for it. That prevented being stabbed by a sharp instrument and eliminated the need for new nurses to worry about knowing the names of the tools, especially when I had my personal thesaurus of names. My flying elbows kept assistants at a distance, therefore not impeding my speed or performance.

I brought instruments from home including the "Polish toothpick." My grandfather, a railroad engineer, had given me a 12-inch-long probe with a sharp pointed hook at one end and a straight point at the other end. He used it on the train for some unknown task. I realized there was no similar surgical instrument, and it worked well in arthroscopy. This became a "Polish toothpick."

I modified several standard surgical tools. To create a tool for moving soft tissue from tendons I filed the tip down to an abrasive end. This standard hemostat, a small clamp to grasp blood vessels, now had a dual purpose. Naturally I called it a Wilson Stat. The problem with that instrument, it looked like a regular hemostat and would get lost and placed with the other hemostats. So, I would "steal" another stat and grind it down, hoping it could be put in a special place for my use. It proved to be a logistical challenge to keep it separate. These new names crept into the vocabulary of the surgical personnel, although I may have been the only surgeon using that nomenclature.

The trigger finger retractor I designed worked great for me but apparently, maybe an ego thing, other local surgeons were not using it. That was also true of a measuring device I made to use in knee replacements. I should have named it by a more neutral name rather than the Wilson Trigger Finger Retractor and Wilson Jig. My double-bladed tendon cutter was used locally but my name was never attached to that instrument. Trade meeting sales were modest and not encumbered by the threatening name.

One of my favorite personalized instruments was a retractor called a Hohmann. I added a large blob of ceramic cement used in joint replacements to the handle. This addition of an ergonomic handle made it much more comfortable to hold for long periods. For ease of identification from other Hohmanns, I added my name. These unique instruments were kept in a special place, a drawer with my name on it so the new personnel could easily find them. Often, I pulled them out before my surgery when I knew they might be used. Visiting surgeons not familiar with my operating room were amused by the strange names of the instruments and the unique tools available.

These instrument additions and modifications were performed before new illogical hospital rules were established. Now, any device not purchased by the hospital would be "illegal" and not allowed in the O.R. Worse yet, I had for years collected and frozen the femoral head from patients who had broken hips. The bone was removed and replaced by a metal ball. That, of course, made the bone no longer of value to the broken, but now fixed patient. I requested the femoral head be saved and frozen for future use as a bone graft. We could always buy bone graft from the bone bank, but that was expensive, plus it required planning—so impractical in an emergency. A change in hospital policy eliminated my local bone bank, part of their backward-progress program.

Despite of my grumbling about new policies, the hospitals have been very responsive to doctors' requests to purchase necessary surgical equipment. We were rarely short of the latest and greatest, including robots.

About the only activity I performed outside my usual orthopedic area was administering an occasional spinal anesthetic when the anesthesiologist was having a problem accomplishing the job. They would let me try my hand. Although not a hundred percent successful, my tricks to enter the spinal canal were highly effective and could therefore avoid having to give the patient a general anesthetic.

Other hospital protocols have changed; it is no longer acceptable for me to scrub the O.R. floor or bring the next patient into the surgical suite. I need to stay in my lane. Sometimes the efficiency of the system is akin to a guided tour where the slowest participant determines the pace of the trip.

On medical mission trips, I didn't worry about the rules because there were none. We could operate as fast as we could go. That was not entirely true, because most third-world countries have a third-world pace—slow.

• • •

The O.R. was a serious venue, but the mood had to be kept light as well as professional. To make sure things were not too staid, we could count on an orderly named Billy Smiley, a self-deprecating Afro-American who regaled the staff with the most racist jokes you can envision with no filter for using the N word. The white staff was generally shocked by the content and his late-night Las Vegas humor.

The following was a rare "clean" story related by Billy in his most Afro flavor. "Jacob, a new prisoner, entered the federal penitentiary and sat in the dining hall consuming his first meal. After the meal had concluded, a convict stood at the end of the table, commanding everyone's attention and shouting out "57." There was a vigorous response and everyone roared their approval. After the noise settled, another prisoner at the next table stood and yelled, "78." Again, there was a lengthy response including hardy laughing and clapping. Jacob was perplexed by the events, and that evening asked his cellmate what had just gone down. His new roommate explained that the prison had a joke book and each joke was numbered. "The convicts were telling the number of one of their favorite jokes, which everyone knew because they had memorized the joke book." Jacob pondered this explanation and decided to participate by telling his joke the next evening. Seemed simple enough, just call out a number. An easy way to become an accepted member by the boys.

The next night Jacob screwed up his courage to stand and "tell his joke" after another chap had already warmed the crowd with a number. Jacob confidently stood and called out a number. Complete silence followed. Jacob quickly sank to his bench, disappointed and confused by the response. Back in the cell he asked his roommate what just happened. "Jacob, some people just can't tell a story." Billy's story added another element to the O.R. learning experience.

The house of learning (OR) should also be a house of doing, doing what works to the patient's advantage.

Alimentary Watson

If you ever experienced **Shigella or Salmonella as I** have, you know how your intestines try to rid you of the problem. They speed up to bullet train mode. You are given little time to interpret the warning signs that a toilet needs to be located—taking precedence over any other planned activity. Such unpleasant memories surfaced as I began having abdominal cramps while preparing for a colonoscopy.

For many years I have avoided the colonoscope. I treated two orthopedic patients in one week who experienced serious complications following a routine colonoscopy. These complications came to light during my standard questioning, and I didn't treat the patients for these problems. Both were hospitalized following perforations related to the procedure. Granted, the incidence of perforations is small, but it does happen, and I made no effort to have something stuck up my virginal rectum without a very compelling reason. The advice routinely given to me, "You should have it done on general principles." But I had no symptoms and "Let a sleeping dog lie" made perfect sense.

There was a time when routine chest X-rays were popular. That is no longer the case. Like old rules of preventative medicine, many are no longer accepted because newer methods have replaced the antiquated ones. In addition, the cost-versus-benefit ratio has changed the indications for many procedures. In reality, the opposite applies in some offices where profit (income) is a more significant motivator.

The risk of complications from a colonoscopy is 1.6% compared to the risk of getting colon cancer at 4.6%, but the incidence of complications, including perforation, is

60% higher in 80-plus-year-olds. A little bleeding I can handle, but a perforation such as occurred with my two patients, not so much.

I acquiesced to the procedure when a stool sample detected blood. A stool sample was obtained when a short digit tried desperately to reach my reluctant prostate. I could hear my hemorrhoids protesting during the process and giving up a little blood seemed more than accommodating. Said blood was my auburn ticket to meet a new friend, the driver of the soon-to-be investigational tool entering my private domain. My new friend—my Sherlock Holmes of the colon industry—would sniff out (bad choice) the source of heme, for him no problem.

My meeting with a new provider—a youngster born the same week as my oldest granddaughter—gave me a few details about the procedure and his low complication rate. He had experienced none of the serious problems that have been reported. I thought the fact he had been in practice for 14 days had something to do with his track record. Turns out it was 14 years not days. His medical training sounded above average and gave me no pause that his paws could do the deed. Naturally I am suspicious of anyone who chooses a job looking up where he has to look up every day and smell what he has to smell to make a living. Dinner talk at his house must be exhausting, if you get my drift.

I asked the usual question, "How far can you see with one of those scopes?"

"When I see your tonsils, I have gone too far."

It was nice he knew his limits. I left the encounter feeling positive about the banality of this anality invasion. Because of my fear of heights, at least the colonoscopy would be done on land and not while skydiving. Plus, an anesthesiologist would be present to watch over me and give me peace, or fentanyl or propofol, (Michael Jackson's go-to drug.) It was time I stopped anal-yzing my concerns.

The day before the big show was the really big show where I, as well as millions before me, clean our colons.

In Mesa there used to be several very busy chiropractors who sold the world on the benefits of a high colonic. Why go to a shop like that when I can, for the low price of $60, clean my own colon? Having never done this before I was schooled to do it right. About 12% of colonoscopies are a waste of time because of poor visibility. Not anxious to do this twice, I adhered to the direction on the doctor's to-do list.

Down went the first of the 12 pills and a pint of water. Each pill had sufficient girth to make swallowing it a challenge. Approximately 61 minutes and nine seconds later I experienced a giant abdominal cramp, I am sure similar to labor pains, which was followed in approximately 27 seconds by a tsunami-like event. When the cramp warned me of a potential upcoming episode, fortunately I wasted no time planting myself in the bathroom. I had no more control over the activities of the next two hours than I do over the urge to sneeze. If my body wishes to sneeze it does so. The same with the explosive events that followed. After the initial burst, I checked to see if my intestines or maybe a kidney, were in the toilet. My intestinal mobility had to be 90 mph, so I remained fixed to my Kohler wishing I had a seatbelt. Each time I experienced an intestinal ejaculation I thought it might be the last—I was wrong. Any attempt to sneak out to watch Judge Judy yoyoed me back to the throne for more afternoon drama.

The second pint of water went down 30 minutes after the first and then a third in another half an hour. The flood assisted by the 12 magic pills reached the end of my tired colon in record time. After several hours of occupying my bathroom for fear of redecorating my home, I regained the confidence to roam again, but by then Judge Judy was long gone.

The instructions stated I should repeat this scenario six hours after starting the exercise. Despite of drinking a quart and a half of water I was thirsty. The nasty pills were dehydrating me. The tablets were no smaller the second round and the results equally confining. It was as if someone had pushed my Niagara Falls button, and all hell broke loose.

My diet for the entire pre-scope day was one non-red power drink (a glass of apple juice) and water.

At 6.30 a.m. the next morning my colon, my wife, and I departed for the hospital for the paperwork signing marathon. I signed multiple sheets of tiny print information, none of which I read, and only hoped I didn't sell my house or annul my marriage.

Nurse Tom deftly inserted the I.V. on his first try and within 30 minutes after "going back" I woke up with no recollection of anything other than, "Roll on your left side." Although I remained a little unsteady the rest of the day and passed a metric ton of gas after going home—life was good. No C was discovered and the biopsy came back negative on the polyp I had created to make the procedure more meaningful.

Would I do it again? Hell no. It wasted two days of my life and two rolls of toilet paper. I was delighted to have escaped any complications, but my alimentary tract will remain closed to future visitors, even Watson, whoever he is.

Cryonics or Crying Out Loud

Newton, Einstein, Franklin, and Gates: all thinkers who generated ideas that unveiled previously unknown truths. There are others on our planet who hear ideas but lack profound thinking and become fervent followers of fuzzy "facts." I believe in the power of positive thinking. I don't comprehend electricity, gravity, or the ability to hold enormous amounts of information on a tiny chip, but I remain convinced these phenomena exist. Cryonics, particularly the ability to freeze a human body, especially a dead one, and expect it to be melted and functional many years later is currently not a road I can follow.

Cryopreservation of humans and animals has been an art form for 50 years, including Arizona's own Alcor, a cryopreservation company. If you are a member, you are in line to be frozen, either your whole body or your head. The idea is that in the future when science has reached into its bag of tricks, and right after we land a spaceship on the sun, your body/head will be restarted in a "you have risen" fashion. I can't see that happening, but I made a hole-in-one once, Dewey lost to Franklin Roosevelt in 1944, and women were given the right to vote in 1920. All once seemed improbable.

Throughout history, accepted "facts" have been proven false. In 240 BCE. Eratosthenes, a Greek mathematician, correctly calculated that the earth is not flat. Although many don't care, a few folks continue believing in the flat earth concept.

Christian Science has chosen to ignore accepted best practices in medicine creating problems for children needing life-saving measures. Two of President Nixon's cabinet were Christian Scientists who facilitated the passage of a law forcing states to protect parents from legal action when they refused to give their children accepted medical care. The law even allowed a child to die when parents persisted in their religious beliefs. It took nine years for Congress to reverse this decision that initially allowed states to make laws that endangered children. The law prevented some federal funds from flowing to the states if the states didn't support the Christian Science doctrine. Thirty-eight states still have residuals of that legislation protecting parents, not children. In Arizona a legislative attempt was made to shield the Christian Science parents from legal action if they didn't allow appropriate medical care for their children. The bill failed, meaning valid care needs to be offered. Missouri, however, allows the parents to make medical decisions, including never having any accepted treatment. Flat-earth thinking still hangs over these vulnerable children.

Historically, many ideas and supposed "facts" have surfaced, some of which turned out to be completely false. In 600 BCE the earth was considered the center of the universe. In 1543 CE Nicolas Copernicus gathered sufficient data to put the universe in its proper perspective.

The miasmatic theory of disease persisted until the late 1880s when Antony van Leeuwenhoek discovered that bacteria caused illness. Bad air still plays a role in disease but not the way it was judged years ago.

Luminiferous aether had scientific support as a medium that allowed light to propagate. This concept was disproven in 1887. Not a big deal, but still, the idea was supported by science of the time.

For years, ulcers were thought to be caused by stress. That premise flipped when an Australian investigator proved the bacterium H. pylori was the culprit, not stress.

In 1912, continental shifting was conceptualized. Prior theories asserted that continents didn't move, but evidence of tectonic shifting shifted our thinking.

Phrenology, one of my favorites, a close second to tarot cards, was a popular "scientific theory" that contended the shape of your head determined your personality characteristics. I guess if your head is an inch wide your personality might be contracted, or two feet wide from hydrocephalus, you will have diminished thinking. The phrenology theory of predicting a personality is no longer credible.

During Hippocrates's life the human body was thought to be composed of four humors: black bile, yellow bile, phlegm, and blood. At least we kept the blood part with a bit of black bile. Can't you see Hippocrates now looking through an electron microscope or reading a DNA report and exclaiming, "Wow, what happened to yellow bile?" Science does have surprises in store; could cryopreservation be successful?

Perry, one of the recently interviewed members of the Alcor Life Extension Foundation, a cryopreservative organization, presented his enthusiastic perspective. He cited Ted Williams as a cool member and his predecessor to freezer occupancy. Ted's whole person is preserved, although the head and body have been separated. If just the head is frozen there is a price break.

Perry seemed an odd candidate to be considering a return visit to life. As a child he had some issues with sexual identity, if I can read between the lines. In his early teens he had the balls, or lack thereof, to castrate himself using a razor blade. Truly a eunuch situation. Although self-castration is a relatively rare event there are several explanations motivating this irreversible procedure. You will not find a caption in the high school yearbook explaining the event or reason for same, more of a cloak and dagger activity. This gentleman or ex-man, unconvinced the orchiectomy was sufficient to guarantee success, then "cut" the nerves to his penis. This organ has been known to be quite vascular and the vessels tend to hang around the nerves. Even an experienced urologist must be careful if attempting to neutralize the nerves with a razor. Perry somehow survived and was satisfied he had altered God's penile plan.

He chose to preserve only his head, which actually makes sense since his poor, bent, fragile, 120-pound body might be replaced with a more robust specimen.

Another member of the group indicated she was looking forward to a new, or in fact, several new bodies. Nothing in the contract speaks to the type or number of bodies to which you might have access. I'm sure she would be disappointed if she was matched with Perry's— no balls, no boobs, and the sex drive of a petrified forest. I struggle with the possibility of joining another body on the return trip

If you were frozen quickly after dying, your body might serve as a delayed organ donor. Who knows whether that option might exist in 40 years, but it would require you to pay the high fee for whole body preservation. Would your budget preclude such a generous consideration?

The preservation scheme is rich with unknowns. What if there is a power failure and you melt? What if your ex-wife joins the club? Would she go in the same vault? And would she have any say on whose parts you connect with on the awakening? Do you get a discount on the rate if you are missing parts besides the testicles, uterus, gall bladder, appendix, and legs, or pay extra for artificial parts, such as hips, heart valves, or breast implants?

If you were concerned about finishing your novel, in the middle of completing a world record, or even trying to convert your person to a new and improved life, you might want a few more years to finish the job. But for me, I like the sun, and 40-plus years on ice seems counterintuitive.

The Scottsdale address where I would be held, even if next to Ted Williams, is insufficient incentive for me to commit to this pie-in-the-frozen-sky folly. I'm not paying $220,000 plus the monthly pre-freeze dues. No way I'll come back, especially if it might be 140° in the shade.

To be fair, Alcor theoretically does not focus on members returning to "life" later as much as performing medical research. Hats off to the organization if freezing fresh specimens lends itself to medical progress. And hats off to the members if they are willing to pay significant dollars to assist in this research.

Social Injustice

Most newspapers have an advice column like "Dear Abby" to respond to social injustices. The spectrum is enormous: incest; burglary; murder; and yes, dogs pooping in neighbors' yards. The victims' questions range from "pathetic" to "How do I get into such a mess?"

Shelton, a usually happy arthritic patient, unloaded his recent dog dumping tale on me while receiving a knee injection. I listened and responded with a silent but engaged, sympathetic head nodding.

I'm thinking a small poop deposited in your yard by the neighbor's dog could easily be tolerated and dismissed with little anger, especially if it were a small dog who happens to find your yard convenient on a spurious visit. But if you have OCD, as Shelton apparently had, and the depositing dog is a St. Bernard with a fetish for daily dumping in your yard, there could be a reaction. If the next-door neighbor and giant dog owner is deaf to your complaints about his animal's regular trips to his favorite rest stop, "Look out for Shelton."

Do you start with a friendly call to "educate" the neighbor about his animal's pattern of elimination? Now elimination is the exact thing you would like to do to the St. Bernard.

To put things in perspective, if you live in Uganda or many African countries, the concept of a yard with grass is a foreign idea. The village dogs, of unknown breeds, have no allegiance to a person, yard, or village's aesthetics. For the natives, obtaining food is a priority. Gathering water and firewood takes precedence over dog droppings. In developed societies, poop droppings are elevated to a more significant and occasionally contentious position. Would you believe in the U.S. these dog misdemeanors have the potential to produce physical confrontation and even involve the court system? Not so in rural Africa because they lack manicured lawns and attorneys. Africans accept laissez-faire dog actions.

So now Shelton has a dilemma: how to resolve the doggerhead. The dog owner is of the redneck mentality; the first amendment outweighs any domestic peacemaking or logical coexistence policy. Shelton, neighbor A with the green spotty lawn, makes the call to Brock, Neighbor B. Neighbor B's response is: "He can shit wherever he wants to."

The options run the gamut. Neighbor A, thinks: "I'll let it go; I don't want to cause trouble." He also knows Neighbor B leans toward mean, capable of pulling something worse like the generous display of beer cans found scattered on his lawn one Sunday morning. He is not the person you ask to watch your house when on vacation for fear of returning to an empty house. So, the initial action taken is inaction. Shelton considers collecting the daily deposits and delivering them by Fed Ex, or better yet, the unwrapped version straight to the front porch on a copy of the church bulletin. Finally, with the encouragement of other neighbors he decides to follow standard deterrents. First, a sign indicating that no dogs are, allowed on the property. Second, send a bag of plastic gloves designed for poop pick up to the neighbor. Next, he could purchase animal deterrents such as *I Must Garden Dog and Cat Repellent*. If these defenses fail there are motion-sensor sound machines that are irritating to dogs. If Sheldon goes to war, he prefers to spend as little money and time fighting the battle as possible, but victory is the end game.

Where to from here? He could do an electric fence, a full-blown security camera, a letter from his attorney, or my suggestion: an invitation to come over for dinner. If he considers doing the dinner invitation, timing is important. It should precede the electric fence and even the plastic gloves. I would consider the invitation before any other communication. Couple it with a request for other neighbors, at least one, to join as well. It is more subtle and gives you an independent party to defuse any potential hostile activity. This approach could miraculously resolve the problem without the anticipated drama.

If you like confrontation, then skip the dinner invitation. Use that massive pile of poo to launch your whacky, volatile personality on a legal, vindictive path.

To put things in OCD perspective, I once treated another patient with serious fecal OCD. He lived near the hospital and I saw him daily with his bag and gloves cleaning the hospital grounds of any visible animal deposits. I don't know how big his OCD territory was, but he was extremely thorough in purging the hospital of unhospitable feces.

I'll mention Jack—a third patient—who relishes confrontation of the dog pooping variety. He will sue and sue and sue again whenever suing is a remote option. He has bonded with a lawyer who has a similar enthusiasm for the frivolous complaints. No confrontation should be allowed to be settled by the Golden Rule. His golden rule is "Sue for the Gold." I have talked with Jack about the direction of his life and how odd I find his fixation with the legal community. He must have had a hearing aid battery failure because he did not respond.

Jack definitely would have taken Brock to court. He would not have called him, offered gloves, or thrown the poop back into Brock's yard. He would pick up the phone, probably after discovering the first dump, and start legal action. Jack's attitude would not work in an African society. The attorney population was way too sparse in Africa for Jack.

Shelton, however, was spared by a stroke of divine providence. Brock's dog suddenly died. He allegedly choked on a Lhasa Apso. I am not at liberty to refute that story. Maybe poison was involved. I know the dumping stopped before the curtain opened on what was billed as the best neighborhood brouhaha in years.

Reacting to social injustice, such as described, produces a bellicose bell-shaped curve of responses. Are you a drive-by shooter or a turn-the-other-cheek person? Would you send your Shih Tzu to attack the Giant Shitter next door or play the Golden Rule one more time in your head?

I Want to Be Known For

My brand of medicine lends itself to "off the rail" discussions. When I give an injection, apprehensions can be high, especially with the first injection. I am talking about joint injections: shoulders, knees, fingers, hips, and ankles. If it is called a joint, I have probably injected it. I use a very tiny needle (30 gauge) to numb the skin, and frequently the patient is not aware they have had a shot, but this is where the distraction/conversation comes in.

It is true that 20 percent of people cannot be hypnotized. Approximately that same percentage holds when trying to convince patients an injection will not hurt. That core group of apprehensive patients has helped me create a list of distractors—questions—which will cloud their brains with the latest foggery I can spew. Trypanophobia—fear of needles— can be debilitating for the patients and annoying to providers. These relatively few folks may be the same folks who will walk up 50 flights of stairs rather than take an elevator or cross the street to avoid a clown. They perspire profusely, hyperventilate, perform various acts of withdrawal, cry, or produce an industrial-size grimace when facing an injection. They require a "little" extra time to get on board the injection express. Even if I demonstrate an injection on myself or tell a story of how I occasionally give myself a knee injection, they may still be unconvinced, but we always work through it.

The "average" apprehensive patient is more amenable to my "Have you heard the one about?" stories. These injection monologues have to be tempered with an assessment of the patient's need for or lack of concern about how serious their doctor should be. Some patients thrive on light banter and others discharge me if I try to elicit a smile. This evaluation usually takes place before "shot time." I strive for an injection discussion that will engage the patient's cognitive activity while minimizing their focus on the dreaded needle. Once they understand the necessity of the shot and learn I have performed such an event upwards of 40,000 times, I proceed.

The injection talks are similar but shorter than TED Talks (Technology, Entertainment and Design). In my case the D stands for distraction. The talks surrounding the first shot in a series will relate to questions about family or state of origin. Occupational queries will be introduced. I may even venture into why did you get divorced, how long have you been off or on drugs, and how many of your relatives are incarcerated now or ever? The older patients get relatable questions such as, "Does your husband know who you are?" or "How long have your daughter and her family, including married grandchildren, lived with you?"

Policemen get the usual "How many criminals have you shot?" and "How many times have you been shot?" Number answers are not as thought-provoking/distracting as the "Why did you shoot the last person you shot, and what were you thinking at the time?"

Random questions requiring a moment of reflection include, "What was the luckiest thing that ever happened to you?" Answers include having a winning pig at the state fair, marrying their first wife, getting rid of their first wife, and selling their boat. Occasionally, some patients are still focused on the injection and will interrupt my quizzing with, "What is this stuff supposed to do?" and "Why are you injecting on the outside when the pain is on the inside?" Naturally I will field those questions as they arise, hopefully after learning why their stepmother left Bulgaria before the War started.

Despite the fairly personal and potentially invasive nature of the questions, no one has acted like they were offended. Many times the response allows for a cathartic reply regarding issues with a demented spouse or domestic circumstances that go beyond anticipated information. The offloaded stories can be happy recollections of childhood or deeply painful. The injection questions provide a dual benefit: decreased focus on the shot and an opportunity to share "stuff" barely hidden below the surface.

Several years ago when I saw more Jewish women patients from Germany who experienced the Nazi wrath, I would have lengthy discussions with them about their horrible experiences. They described seeing neighbors disappear, frequent trips to the air raid shelters, and losing everything they owned. These talks were not injection-related but gripping tales spinning off the medical interview. It was hard to stay on task when the patients had riveting stories to tell with little prompting.

One of my favorite tactics is to use my unpredictable ESP, searching for a thread to the patient's past. "You grew up around goats"? or "Who do you know in Massachusetts?" My batting average is at least 70 percent positive connection, including narrow questions that resonate with the patient. My questions are not "You had a mother, didn't you" type, but "Isn't your daughter a teacher?" The really odd aspect of these random questions is when I'm spot on, like, "Didn't your family raise peanuts?" Rarely does anyone say, "How did you know that?" The conversation continues as if I had inquired about their favorite restaurant or hair salon. This backdoor connectivity is, in part, a test of my ESP, which can be completely miswired or a direct hit, "Were your knuckles ever hit with a ruler for being left-handed?" Subtle clues, like the location of their watch, the slanted handwriting, the hand used for pointing, and the word Catholic on the intake form, provide clues to amplify ESP. This may seem an odd approach, but I believe the closer I can connect to the patient, the more I know about them, the more the trust factor goes up, giving me more information to work with in solving their medical problems.

Recently I began asking the question, usually related to the third injection of a three-shot series: "What do you want to be known for?" Depending on the response, a corollary question might be whether their friends would agree with their assessment. Most patients will take a minute to respond, but many seem prepared to answer quickly as if they were on Jeopardy: kind, helpful, resilient, lucky, and outgoing. As a good grandpa, husband, and mother, are typical quick responses. Like a job self-assessment report, the employee/patient usually rates themselves higher than the supervisor. I am in no way judgmental. But I learn much about my patients' finances, altruism, confidence, motivators, and burdens.

Responses are sometimes humbling, for example learning what my patients do for others with little means. Stories of grandparents taking care of dysfunctional families. People surviving cancer, accidents, death threats, homelessness. The more measured responses may last several minutes and several paragraphs, while patients justify their answers. My one-sentence query, sometimes invites a sermon or political statement about what others should be.

No one has stated that they are weak, indecisive, and not too bright. Nor have they commented on personal appearance, skin color, or sexual orientation. The follow-up question about how others see them is usually deflected with, "I don't know, uh," or "I never thought about it."

My "What Do You Want to be Known For" question, although used exclusively in the injection connection, is proving to be a popular and beneficial inquiry that may have a place in the general medical interview. Stay tuned.

Standup

Recently a patient asked me if I was still doing Standup. Surprised, I responded, "How do you know I did Standup?" She then recalled a joke I told 15 years ago when I performed at Scottsdale Community College as a student in the Standup Comedy Class.

"I was at the event where you performed."

"Why so?"

"Two of my coworkers took the same class as you."

Although not a patient of mine at that time, she had been treated in my office by another physician for a broken tibia. She knew of me and parked the joke story in the back of her head for 15 years. No other patient ever mentioned my performance. The audience at the event consisted of relatives and a few friends of the 14 students. None of my patients had been invited.

Naturally my respect for this woman's taste in comedy and her superb intellect went through the roof. She indicated she laughed out loud but was careful to avoid mentioning which performers moved her humor needle.

The Standup class, worth three hours of credit, caught my attention when I perused the college catalog looking for a change of pace. I have always enjoyed making people laugh but considered myself too introverted to consider a public appearance doing comedy. I thought the class might allow me to expand my ability to coax a laugh out of a few folks.

I had previously attended several international humor festivals, but performing was a minor part of those events. I felt confident my lengthy history of medical experiences would give me a wealth of material for Standup class assignments. The night class fit my schedule and back to college I went surrounded by students slightly younger by 40 or 50 years.

I should give credit to my father who was a superb amateur standup comedian performing into his late 90's at his retirement park. Prior to that gig, he did weekly entertainment for his Lions Club for 35 years. He specialized in interpreting the news much in the format of late-night television, Jack Paar style. I occasionally attended his club meetings and marveled at his timing and natural comedic ability.

Having been exposed to Norman Cousins and the medical benefits of humor/laughter from involvement with the Humor Institute, I eagerly signed up for the class. My commitment to humor would provide another element to better medical outcomes. I had no idea that I had become a chortleist. I had no designs on being the next Rodney Dangerfield or Don Rickles. The more I learned about Patch Adams, the more I appreciated his approach to medicine. The TED talk Gesundheit Institute: Patch Adams at TEDxUtrechtUniversity is worth watching.

Patch Adams was the Mother Teresa of modern medicine and a worthy role model. Dr. Bill Farmer fits the mold but doesn't focus on humor like Patch Adams.

Orthopedics falls on the more mechanical end of medicine. Orthopedic patients are just as lonely, depressed, and anxious as the rest of society. Once they become incapacitated, the psychological issues often increase. Sleeping in a recliner, wearing a cast, or adding a walker to your routine seldom elevates one's spirits.

Prior to taking the class I made an effort to engage my patient's facial muscles in a smile by decorating the office walls with humorous posters. I may quote a bumper sticker: "I'm not as think as you drunk, I am," or, "No radio—already stolen." I tried to customize the comments. For cat lovers "I love cats, they taste like chicken." That worked well if I tried to get rid of a few obnoxious animal-loving patients. It was best to avoid a joke with hearing impaired patients. If the joke was not germane to the medical conversation the hearing-challenged patient didn't always understand the transition and repeating the story led to further confusion. A handshake worked better as an icebreaker.

During class we worked on various types of improv type presentations. I didn't do well with a rubber chicken, balloon, or a harmonica. Give me a femur, a hammer, or a drill and I rocked. Turn a bunch of 20-year-olds loose with a rubber chicken and they played the chicken dance on the harmonica and mutilated the poor chicken like miscreants performing Colonel Sanders's mayhem. My group used the chicken as a scarf, ignored the balloon, and played "Mary Had a Little Lamb," and the doctor fainted.

Each week we read about various forms of humor and comedians' styles. Vulgarity was not encouraged but we honored the Second Amendment. We spent part of the class time rehearsing for the final presentation. Creating a ten-minute standup piece was stressful for most of us and impossible for some.

I had intended to use a growing old theme for my entire shtick. "You sit down in a rocking chair and you can't get it started. Your little black book has only names ending in M.D. You're worn out dialing long distance. Your pacemaker opens the garage door when you see a sexy girl go by. A dripping faucet causes an uncontrollable bladder urge. The best part of the day is over when the alarm goes off."

Instead, I switched to how I became a doctor with a Saturday Night flavor. "I didn't know I was going to college but my mother signed me up for night school. She took all the tests because I was working as a bag boy. She did pretty well because I was accepted to medical school." Here is the joke my patient remembered: "I thought I was on a Fulbright Scholarship but it turned out my mother's grades were only good enough for a half-bright Scholarship." Original, lame, and self-deprecating, but my patient remembered it.

"I intended to go into obstetrics, but my mom put OR, not OB, on the application. It worked out okay because most babies are born at night and I need my sleep.

"Things got a little rough when I had to take the tests

in medical school, rather than my mother. She helped a little with the reviews but I mostly had to sit near my buddy Randy to whom I paid a fair amount for the answers. I didn't feel bad because Randy needed the money.

"Medical school was dangerous. My lab partner was the epileptic son of one of the instructors. We were to draw blood from each other, but he seemed to be in pre-seizure mode when he sized up my trembling arm. He never came close to entering my elusive veins. The only way we could complete the draw was for him to hold the syringe steady while I moved into the needle. Although unconventional, that worked. This one-time event lasted about 20 minutes longer than anyone else in the class that was drawing blood. Fortunately, he didn't participate on my cadaver dissection team.

"One of my jobs in medical school was to clean the cages and feed twenty rats. The rats were to be sacrificed after 20 weeks to measure the strength of their ligaments, but during the last week I discovered the rats had eaten off their markings, making me unsure which rats had been on one of the four special diets. The 20 fat rats never knew their gnawing saved their bacon but put my lab job in jeopardy. I blamed the whole rat fiasco on my mother, she gave me literally no rat training and only a tiny exposure to mice.

"Poor medical school education was responsible for my inability to communicate with real patients. I asked patients to walk on their toes and they would step on the toes of the opposite foot. Technically that was an option, but really. One hearing-impaired gentleman tried to step on my toe following my request. I would hold a patient's leg out straight and ask them to bend their knee. Their response was "Which way?" Where do you go from straight? When I asked a patient to relax, I was promptly kicked in the groin. Maybe due to a dead hearing aid battery or subtle revenge?

"I am glad my mother slipped me into medical school. Otherwise I would never have had this chance to share my zany experiences with you. Come back next week and I'll show you how to do an easy-peasy rectal exam."